THE TAHOE CITY GIRLS

A NOVEL

STARLA DEKRUYF

The TAHOE CITY GIRLS

a novel

STARLA DEKRUYF

THE TAHOE CITY GIRLS: A NOVEL

STARLA DEKRUYF

Print Edition ISBN: 9798992133820

Digital ISBN: 9798992133837

For friendship. New and old. Long-term and short. The friendships that began quickly and the ones that needed time to grow.

CONTENT/TRIGGER WARNINGS

This book is intended for readers who are 17+. Please note that there may be content in this book that may be triggering for some readers. This list is not exclusive, so please proceed with caution. Your mental health is important to me.

- Closed door—fade-to-black
- Mild explicit language/cursing (no f-bombs)
- Talk of death, drowning, cancer (in the past/off page)
- Alcohol consumption
- Talk of cheating
- Chronic illness/disease
- Panic attacks
- Physical assault
- Grief

CHAPTER ONE

NOW

Rounding the corner onto Oak Street, her feet pounding against the asphalt, Jolene's heart raced as flashes of red tore through her memory. A red car, a red sweater, a red pool of blood. She sprinted past towering pine trees and hefty juniper bushes, not stopping until she reached her ranch-style home.

Standing on the weather damaged porch, hands on her hips and bent over at the waist, she fought to catch her breath. At the same time, she struggled to not throw up. She'd pushed herself hard, maybe too hard. But when the memories from that dreadful day taunted her, running was the only thing that pushed them away.

Closing her eyes, she inhaled the dry Central Oregon air as she straightened her stiff body. Opening the front door, she glanced down at her Apple Watch. The time displayed on the screen mocked her. *Thirty-two minutes and forty-nine seconds.* After completing her usual three-mile route through the neighborhood, she had averaged almost eleven-minute miles.

Pathetic.

Thirty-two minutes and forty-nine seconds had been her worst time all week and it enraged her. She envisioned ripping the blue band off her wrist and chucking it against the wall. But that wasn't her. She wasn't compulsive. Being a sensible person, Jolene contemplated each action before performing it, each word before allowing it to escape her mouth.

So instead, she tossed her keys onto the kitchen counter, the clattering sound upon contact unsatisfying to her anger. She supposed there was a bit of fear etching behind the anger. Her average run time for the three-mile route used to be twenty-seven minutes but had recently jumped to thirty. And now this. If her running time was increasing, her window of being able to even run at all was closing. Her doctor had told her to run for as long as her body would allow. But how long would that be?

Filling a glass with water from the fridge, she gulped down nearly the entire thing in one session. Then she dragged herself down the long hallway to her office. She may not have made good time on her run, but she'd at least worked up a nice sweat, drenching her sports bra. That counted for something, didn't it?

In her home office, sprinkled with contrasting shades of grays and yellows, she eased herself into the unsupportive chair and opened her laptop. She'd attempted to work earlier in the day, if the definition of work meant drinking numerous cups of coffee while scrolling through hair care products and DIY home projects on Pinterest. But unfortunately, fatigue set in earlier than normal and as much as she tried to rally her focus, it seemed impervious.

Owning a brewery hadn't been her dream job, but she'd put her longtime hopes of being a novelist on hold to support her husband, Travis's dream of opening a craft brewery. Travis had heard about the boom of craft breweries in Central Oregon and after some serious convincing, he got her on board. They had packed their belongings, and with two small children in tow, moved from Reno, Nevada to Sisters, Oregon.

Jolene had been nothing but loving and supportive of Travis's dream. And in the end, that was what bit her in the ass. Eleven months ago, Travis decided not only did he not want to be married any longer, but he also didn't want to run the brewery either. The brewery was their livelihood. And as much as she didn't want to admit it to Travis, after all these years working on the books, schmoozing distributors, and creating alongside him in the brew pit, she'd grown to love it.

Learning about the brewing process, using the correct amount of hops in which batch, and the intoxicating fruity aroma during the fermentation process—she loved everything about it. She couldn't see herself simply giving it all up. And when Travis left her and pulled himself further and further away from the brewery, it was the one thing she had left to cling to. Besides the kids, it was the one thing that was considered *hers*.

After seventeen years of marriage when her husband had told her he was leaving, she'd tried to put up a fight. Because her marriage was something worth fighting for. But in the end, it hadn't made a difference, he'd left anyway.

Travis's words from that horrific day still played through her mind often. *"I'm sorry, Jo. I've tried. And I just can't anymore. I didn't sign up for this. I'm done."*

Shaking her head, she attempted to rid the painful memories from her mind. If she dwelled on them too long, she'd begin blaming herself for how everything unraveled between them. And deep down, she knew the separation wasn't her fault. She knew the real reason why Travis left her.

Her phone's ringtone startled her—the jingle reverberating and growing louder with each ring.

Jolene glanced at the screen, her shoulders tightening, and she hesitated before answering.

"Hello?"

"Hey, Jo. I've got news. Do you have a minute?" Kendra Kingsley, her successful childhood friend, blurted into the phone.

"Of course. Everything okay?"

"Things are good. Just busy, as usual."

And there it was, the reminder of how busy and important her friend's life was, living it up in Los Angeles, running a prominent monthly women's magazine. While Jolene lived in the small town of Sisters, Oregon working sometimes grueling hours at the brewery and taxiing around two teenagers. It was no wonder the two women hadn't remained a close friendship over the years. They lived completely different lives.

It had been almost a year since she received a phone call from Kendra, her friend since the seventh grade. Before now, they'd been staying in touch through texting. In the last few years their phone conversations had dwindled and become practically non-existent.

Her stomach pinched and sadness filled her while thinking about the massive distance between them. The lack of contact left a void in her life. Especially lately. Without a doubt, she'd needed Kendra this past year.

"One would think living so close to the beach, I'd actually get there on occasion." Kendra exhaled a mirthless laugh. It came out sounding forced and shaky. "But there's just so many things that need to get done to ensure this magazine runs smoothly."

The row of women's magazines lining a shelf in her office caught her attention. Kendra's magazine—POSE. It had been in circulation for almost a full year now. She had bought and saved every issue. But she'd never told Kendra that. How could she? Kendra's life was picking up momentum at the same time as Jolene's was crumbling—fast and furious.

"I can't imagine," she muttered.

"And what about you? How are you? How's the brewery?" Kendra asked.

At the mention of the brewery, Jolene's stomach did a flip flop causing anxiety filled nausea to creep up her throat. "Um... good, staying busy too. And the brewery is going great, busy all the time." She silently prayed Kendra wouldn't ask about Travis. She wasn't ready to tell her fabulously successful childhood friend that her husband had left her.

"I'm so glad, Jo. Really."

She swallowed. "So what's going on? What's your news?"

"Right. So, listen, there really isn't an easy way to say this so I'm just gonna come out with it." A deep exhaled sigh came through the phone. "I got a call from Cristina Gray this morning."

Cristina. Just the mention of her name sent a shiver running through her—and with it, the memories flooding back. Ones filled with adventures and many gut-aching laugh sessions. But also, pain and heartache. Jolene pulled herself to standing and made her way back into the kitchen. The toe of her right foot dragged slightly, and she braced herself with a palm pressed against the cool wall.

"Early this morning," Kendra continued. "I almost fell out of bed when I heard her voice on the other end of the phone."

She pictured Kendra, probably tangled up in her eight thousand thread count sheets and hungover from Ambien. She shook her head, some things never changed.

"Of course, she greeted me with her usual, '*what up biatch?*' I mean, really? Is she ever going to grow out of that?"

A rueful smile tugged at her lips. "It's Cristina, so my guess is—no."

"It's been nine or ten years since I've spoken to her. And that conversation ended in an all-out yelling match," Kendra said.

Jolene remembered how often Kendra and Cristina got into petty arguments when they were growing up. Sometimes they'd go several days without speaking. On more than one occasion, their arguments put a damper on their weekend plans to spend them in Lake Tahoe. She hated confrontation and it gave her so much anxiety.

Her anxiety worked overtime now, pumping through her veins. She pressed her back against the counter, the edge of the hard granite digging into her spine. "So, what's going on? What's the news?"

Kendra exhaled a deep sigh into the phone. "It's Becca," Kendra's voice softened. "She's gone, Jo. Passed away two days ago."

Kendra's words hung in the air between them, and the phone nearly slipped from her grasp. A bad taste formed in her mouth, a mixture of metal and bile swirling together. Becca Gibbs—*was dead?*

"Jo? You there?" Kendra called.

Tears pricked at the corners of Jolene's eyes, and she cleared the gravel from her throat. "I'm here," her voice sounded hoarse.

"She drowned."

She felt like she'd just been sucker-punched in the stomach. "Wh-what? No. That's not possible."

Becca had always been a strong swimmer. She was the captain on their high school swim team. She practically lived and breathed water. She might as well have been a fish.

"She'd been sick. She was weak. She went swimming alone at night near the cottage. They said she likely got too tired and couldn't make it back to shore."

"Sick?" She shook her head and swiped at the betrayal of tears rolling down her cheeks. "I didn't know."

"It was ovarian cancer. They discovered it much too late, and it progressed too quickly."

"That's awful." Jolene squeezed her eyes shut, pushing back the memories from that day—from the accident.

"Jolene," Kendra paused, her typical nasally voice now coated in syrup. "I'm sorry, but you know what this means, right?"

Her stomach tightened. "Yeah, I know," she said on an exhaled breath. "But you don't honestly think she expected us to keep up the pact? We haven't been friends in almost twenty years."

"She did. She told Cristina...before." Kendra paused before continuing. "Cristina thought it would be best if I talked to you since you two haven't spoken in a while."

She glanced down, crossed her feet at the ankles, and sucked in a breath. She thought about Cristina. Strong, badass, and always crass Cristina. When she'd remained friends with Becca after the accident, it had felt like a betrayal to Jolene.

It had been difficult for her to forgive Becca and not blame her for the accident and the death of her brother. And once she finally had, far too many years had passed to pick up the friendship with Cristina again.

But there was a time during their friendship, the four of them had promised to be there for one another—for all the big things life threw at them.

Kendra sighed heavily. "The three of us need to go. Cristina has already made plans for us to stay at the Gibbs's cottage. Mr. Gibbs will bring Becca's ashes to us so we can spread them in the waters of Lake Tahoe."

Jolene spun around and pressed her free hand to the counter's edge, gripping it for support. She gazed out the window at the landscape of scattered pine trees with pinecones spotting the ground below. She studied her neglected garden congregating behind the concrete patio. Her vision shifted down to the windowsill where a multitude of prescription and vitamin bottles gathered.

"Put aside everything that happened with the accident and your brother and please tell me you're coming?"

All the anger, hurt, guilt, and sadness she'd been clinging to for nearly twenty years arose in her and she broke. Her unsturdy leg gave out on her, and she slid her back against the cupboard door, landing on the hardwood floor with a thud.

She swallowed back the tears. "Of course I'll be there."

"Good. You know you're not going to be alone. Cristina and I got you."

"I know." She wiped at her damp eyes.

"After we do this, you'll never have to go back there again."

But she had already planned on never returning to Tahoe City. And she wasn't sure how she'd muster up the strength to return now. The thought caused her stomach to clench—a metal vice gripping and twisting. How could she go back there? It had been nineteen years since she stepped on Lake Tahoe sand. Nineteen years since the accident. Nineteen years since she said goodbye to her brother, to her favorite place, and to Bo Dean.

"So, I'll see you next Friday?"

If the plans had been made, if Kendra, of all people, could get away from her busy life, then she supposed she could as well. Jolene wouldn't be the one standing in the way of their pact being broken.

"I'll be there."

CHAPTER TWO

Jolene tossed a clean pair of clothes into a bag and dashed out the front door of her ranch style home, silently cursing her legs for not moving as fast as she'd like. She climbed inside her black Chevy Tahoe, glancing at the clock on the dash. She was heading to the brewery later than she'd planned, Kendra's phone call and the terrible news digging up old emotions at fault.

As if out of habit, her urge to run kicked in. And also out of habit, she urged to run to Travis. For as long as she could remember, he had been her rock. Her place of refuge. The one person who made her feel safe and secure.

Travis had been her older brother, Jacob's roommate in college. Both boys had attended California State University in Sacramento on basketball scholarships. Jacob brought Travis home to Reno, Nevada over their first Thanksgiving break from school.

When she laid eyes on him, she thought he was the hottest guy she'd ever seen. Dressed in a Sacramento Kings basketball jersey, it was hard to miss the muscle definition in his arms. He was tall and lanky with a head full of adorable brown curls. When he'd introduced himself and winked at her with those big chestnut brown eyes, she could've sworn her knees buckled. She thought he'd have to scrape her off the floor, because surely, she was about to faint.

The age difference between them seemed to bother Travis at first, but less than two years later, they began dating. Jolene was a senior in high school by then. They visited one another every chance they could. Which was easy considering Jolene's brother Jacob was dating her best friend Becca.

Before Travis, she'd been the third wheel. Always tagging along with Becca and Jacob. She'd have to climb in the back of Becca's red Honda CRX which didn't even have a backseat. She crammed her body next to the giant subwoofer with the bass booming in her chest and her fingers shoved in her ears.

After Travis, she was no longer the third wheel. The four of them were constantly together, spending weekends in Sacramento or Reno. And sometimes they'd visit Tahoe City and stay at the Gibbs's family cottage. They loved to take the canoes out on the lake and make s'mores in the fire pit.

But the main thing that kept Jolene and Travis's long-distance relationship working, was her plans to join him in Sacramento at California State University once she graduated high school. Though her plans were never fulfilled. After the accident and losing Jacob, Jolene didn't even bother with college that Fall. Travis left CalState and moved to Reno to be near her since she'd decided to continue living with her parents. Just the thought of leaving them had felt impossible.

Her heart tugged at the memory. It seemed a small miracle she and Travis were married just two short years later. But having one another filled that missing void Jacob had left in each of them. Losing a best friend couldn't compare to the loss of a brother, but the shared grief had deepened their bond.

Each with a broken heart, together their heart somehow became a whole again.

She knew they were stronger together—she hadn't forgotten. But why had he?

High Desert Brewery was about a twenty-minute drive into town where she was sole Brewmaster since Travis had decided to have his little mid-life crisis was apparently done with the brewery. She drove past the open land where deer grazed and farms with moving tractors turning up their fields. The landscape out the passenger window flaunted mountains still capped with snow that stretched all the way across the horizon.

The negative thoughts consuming her mind pounded like jackhammers trying to work their way out. They occurred more often now and sometimes threw her into a complete and full fledge panic attack. The annoying negative thoughts constantly reminded her that she and her husband, Travis had been separated the past year. He could no longer be her safe place anymore.

He didn't *want* to be her safe place anymore.

When she reached the brewery, she scanned the parking lot. Spotting the red Ford F-250, she suddenly wished she'd taken a shower before rushing out of her house and heading straight for the brewery. At the very least, she wished she would've changed out of the running clothes saturated with sweat.

Sighing, she hushed the negative thoughts and made her way to the back entrance of the old brick building. She passed by the rows of trellises of hops growing and admired them. They looked healthy and were thriving. Deciding to grow his own hops for their beer had been a good idea of Travis's. She shook her head, if only he had spent as much time on the growth of their relationship.

The aging brick building they leased years ago for the

brewery stood at nearly fifty feet tall. It had once been a part of the old timber mill that began operating in 1916 and was surrounded by other old buildings including three towering smokestacks. Jolene and Travis saw the potential of the building and had taken it over after the last business failed to complete the renovations during the Country's financial crisis. Which meant they were able to lease the building at a steal of a price. It was risky starting a business in the middle of a nation-wide financial crisis, but they had both been determined to make this dream of Travis's a reality.

Swinging open the heavy metal door, she let out another deep breath and stepped in. She spotted Carrie, the brewery's part-time manager on the phone at her desk in the corner of the large industrial space. Jolene gave the blonde, tanned skin, and toned legged woman a quick wave. Carrie had been the brewery's manager for the last year and a half. She was one of the sweetest women in town and she'd been a lifesaver when it came to managing the books when they'd become too busy for Jolene to do both the brewing and the books.

Scanning the brewery, she searched for Travis. She reveled in the appearance of the renovated building—all of it still beautiful in her eyes. The place hadn't yet been tainted by their separation. The stainless-steel counters lining the middle of the brewery caused her body to warm. Her children, Cole and Julia had spent many evenings sitting atop the tall metal stools finishing their homework while she and Travis worked. She'd fill orders, set up meetings with vendors, and update the High Desert Brewery's Facebook page and website.

Jolene spotted Travis in the brew pit, standing on the high metal platform. She narrowed her eyes and crossed her arms while she watched him open the door of the large kettle, hot steam instantly rising in a large puff of vapor. When the steam evaporated, she attempted not to admire Travis with the sweat dampened curls sticking out from underneath his baseball hat, but she failed miserably.

His muscles tensed beneath the rolled-up sleeves of his flannel shirt as he lifted the buckets of hops, and one by one, he poured them quickly into the boiling brew. She waited, albeit not patiently. It was crucial to get the hops into the kettle in a hurry or it would alter the taste of the beer.

The process of beer making was all too familiar for her. When Travis first began brewing beer, he did it in the garage of their home. Early on, his passion was obvious each time he produced a new distinctive beer. He'd rush into the house elated, a wide toothed grin and eyes animated, with a pint glass in his hand possessing his latest brew. He'd urge her to try it. His eyes locked on her, awaiting her approval. In those early brewing days when her approval actually mattered. When it truly meant something to him.

A gruff clearing of a throat sounded, stealing Jolene's fixation from Travis. Joy Williams approached, eyeing her while she was so obviously checking out her husband's physique.

"Don't let the sweat fool ya, he's been here maybe five minutes. Ten tops," Joy said, featuring a permanent frown line between her grey-blue eyes.

"And I see he just couldn't help himself to the brew pit."

"You know it." Joy glanced in Travis's direction again. "That's about all he's good for these days," she muttered.

Jolene's chest tightened as Travis made his way down the ladder, the empty buckets in tow. "What's he want?"

Joy opened her mouth to speak but thought better of it and clamped it shut, gesturing with a wave of her hand for Jolene to meet Travis halfway. She hesitated but forced herself to proceed, inhaling a long breath.

Travis gave her a pleasant smile. He had a mouthful of beautiful, straight white teeth causing his smile to sparkle.

Placing the buckets down onto the concrete floor with a clatter, he wrapped her up in a sweaty, tight hug and her body went limp. The awkwardness radiated between them.

"Just the woman I was hoping to bump into," he said.

She finally had enough sense to shrug off his hug and took a step back. "Makes sense considering I pretty much run this place," she muttered.

"Ouch. But alright. I guess I deserve that." He scratched the scruff on his chin, peering down at his hiking boots.

His appearance caused her heart rate to speed up, heat coursing through her body like a perimenopausal heat flash and she needed to regain her composure and focus. "I'm actually glad you're here." She brushed past him and talked over her shoulder. "I need to talk to you about something."

"Yeah? Cause I need to talk to you about something too." He shuffled his feet faster to catch up to her.

She bit the inside of her cheek. *Well this should be good.* She entered the brewery office. It still featured the building's original concrete floors and brick walls with a large window that overlooked the brewery. A wood desk sat in the middle of the narrow room and pushed toward the back wall.

She set her bag with her laptop and the fresh change of clothes in it onto the desk. "Remember my friend Becca Gibbs?"

"Oh, you're going first. Okay." He slumped into a chair across from the desk appearing irritated. "Of course I remember her. Why? What's up?"

Hearing the words had been tough enough but saying them aloud felt impossible. "She passed away. Cancer. Well, she drowned, but ultimately it was cancer."

"Wow." He took off the ball cap and pushed back his sweaty hair before returning it to his head. "That's awful. I'm sorry."

Anguish clawed up her throat causing it to feel raw. But she needed to push through. "The girls are all meeting in Tahoe City next week and I really need to be there." She busied herself, fiddling with a stack of papers strewn across the top of the desk.

"Seriously?" he asked.

She glanced out the office window that overlooked into the brewery, stilling her fingers. "Look," she said, returning her attention on him. "We made this pact when we were kids. That we'd always go back to the lake together when anything big happened. This is big. And you should understand more than anyone why I need to go."

"I mean, it sucks, but I just don't see why you gotta go. You haven't gone back before now."

She sighed, resisting the urge to glare at him. "That's because nothing big like this has happened before."

He leaned forward, resting his elbows on his knees. "So, getting married, having babies, starting a business, those aren't big things?"

She clenched her jaw. "Not big enough to convince me to go back there." She pulled her laptop from her bag. "Could you please just keep the kids for the week?"

He steepled his fingers. "Actually, that's why I'm here. I'm going out of town next week and won't be able to have the kids come for the weekend."

"You're kidding?" she asked, incredulous.

"Sorry." He shrugged, looking anything but sorry.

Travis didn't let the kids down often, so he had to have a good reason. Okay, she'd give him the benefit of the doubt. "Where are you going?"

"Just a quick trip to Palm Springs. Five days."

She narrowed her eyes. "For what?"

"Oh, c'mon, Jolene. You know my folks are there."

"Yeah, and you haven't been over there to see them for at least five years. Why now? Who's going with you?"

The smallest hint of guilt passed over his expression. She'd been married to him for seventeen years. She could decipher all his expressions.

He pushed back in the seat, straightening. "You don't get to ask me that anymore."

"The hell I do, we're still married."

"Hardly. Besides, I think the biggest problem we should be discussing is what we're gonna do with the kids. Can you take them with you? They've been dying to go to Lake Tahoe, see where you spent your summers growing up."

"Well maybe they've been dying to go to Palm Springs to see their grandparents. You even ask them?"

A knock sounded on the open office door. "Knock, knock." Joy stood in the doorway, glaring at Travis before returning her focus on Jolene. "We got us a situation out here. Gonna need you to come and go over the spreadsheet with Tim before his shift is over."

Jolene held a finger up to Joy. "I'll be right there." She rounded the desk swiftly, stopping in front of Travis. "As you can see, I'm a bit busy, as usual. Unless you'd like to help, I'd really appreciate you helping out with the kids next week."

"C'mon, Jo. I can't be two places at once."

"And neither can I," she snapped.

Travis stood, clearly keeping the corner of his eyes set on Joy with her tall, and burly physique. "Can't you push back your trip?"

Tears pricked her eyes, but she was too tired to fight them back this time. "She's dead, Travis. What don't you get about that? We have to go spread her ashes. You can't just push that back."

"You're right, you're right," he mumbled, lifting his hat off his head again and swiping a hand across his sweaty brow.

Joy cleared her throat. "If you need someone to keep the kiddos, I can help?"

Both Jolene and Travis glanced at Joy, her heart aching inside her chest. "No, we couldn't ask you to do that," she said.

"We'll figure something out," Travis mumbled.

"C'mon, it's obvious you're in a pickle. I don't mind. Those kids know me better than they know their own grandparents." She shuffled into the office, hands pressed to her hips.

"I don't know." Jolene chewed her bottom lip, considering.

"You know that if it was *him* asking, I wouldn't offer. But it sounds like you need to go. Besides, it's been forever since you took time off."

"I'm fine with Joy keeping the kids for the week, if you are?"

Heat flashed across her cheeks, and she tried to form words to bite back at him, but Joy positioned herself between the two of them and waved a hand at him as if dismissing him.

"Oh, pipe down, Mr. I-didn't-sign-up-for-this. No one's trying to save your sorry behind." She whirled around to speak to Jolene. "Jo, you need to go. Your doc said you need to make sure you're resting and not taking on too much stress. And since Travis left," she paused, shooting him an unmistakable glare over her shoulder, "you've been here every day. Tim and I will hold down the fort here, make sure production keeps moving."

"I don't know. Carrie's out all next week on vacation."

"You know her, she's efficient and we can trust her. She'll have all her ducks in a row before she leaves."

Biting on her thumbnail, her heartrate pulsed quickly. She made the mistake of glancing at Travis who appeared antsy, shuffling his feet, and raising his brows at her. "Are you sure about this? Because the kids can be a handful these days."

"Positive. And don't you worry about me or those kids. They give me any problems and I'll have them cleaning out the mash." She nodded her chin mischievously.

Travis hunched his shoulders and made his way toward the open door. "Looks like it's settled then. Thanks, Joy. I really appreciate this." He called over his shoulder, "We'll discuss the details by phone next week?"

She clenched her jaw and simply nodded. Because if she opened her mouth to speak actual words to him, they'd definitely be words she'd regret later.

Joy shook her head. "Good Lord almighty, that man," she muttered before composing herself. "So your friend who passed, this is the one who was responsible for the accident that killed your brother?"

Jolene rounded the desk again. "That's the one." She dropped into the chair.

"Sweetie, you're a much bigger person than I." Joy backed up a few feet. "I'll give you a minute before I send Tim in." She stepped lightly out of the office.

Jolene glanced out the window at the stainless-steel counters and the taps. She didn't feel like the bigger person. Maybe the bigger person would've forgiven Becca years ago. Or maybe the bigger person would have given up on this brewery when Travis had. But she was no coward. She'd return to Tahoe City and somehow try to make things right—even if Becca was already dead.

TELLING her children she was leaving without them wouldn't be easy. Both Cole and Julia had bugged her and Travis for years to take them to Tahoe City. She carried a soda in each hand, her stomach a mess of worry. She set the glasses down on the stainless-steel counter where Cole sat drawing, his earbuds in his ears, and Julia worked on her homework. Joy followed behind her, sliding plates of burgers and fries in front of the kids.

"So listen you two, there's something we need to talk about." She took a seat on a tall stool and Joy hovered behind her causing her nerves to flutter even more so.

Julia set her pencil down, ready to engage but Cole hadn't noticed her or the food's arrival. She waved a hand in front of his sketchbook.

He yanked the earbuds out. "What's up?" He pulled the plate closer and picked up a fry, stuffing it into his mouth.

"Your dad is taking a trip next week—"

"Where's he going?" Julia asked, combing her fingers through her long, straight brown hair.

Joy huffed loudly, letting out an exaggerated sigh.

"Palm Springs."

"To see Grandma and Grandpa?" Cole asked.

"Um, I think he's going for business."

Julia's brows furrowed. "Can we go with him?"

Jolene snagged a fry off Julia's plate, attempting to make this difficult conversation easier. "Not this time."

"So we'll just stay home with you?"

She glanced back and forth between her kids and Joy. She hated to disappoint them—more than anything.

"Actually, I have to go out of town too. So the two of you are going to stay with Joy."

"Where are you going?"

She bit on her lip, hesitating. "Tahoe City."

Cole perked up. "What for?"

"An old friend of mine died. You've heard me talk about Becca? I made a promise a long time ago and I need to fulfill that promise."

"Wait. The one from the car accident?"

Jolene's stomach pinched, and she could only bring herself to nod.

"Can we come?"

She swallowed the growing lump in her throat. "Sorry, buddy. Not this time. It's an all-girls trip."

"We won't bother you. Julia and I will do our own thing."

"I need you two to stay here and hold the fort down. Since your dad's not here, I'll need your help around the brewery."

Cole shoved his plate across the counter and stood abruptly, forcing his stool to scrape backward against the concrete floor loudly. "This sucks!"

She sucked in a breath. "Hey, watch yourself there."

"Don't be mean, Cole. Mom's friend is dead."

"So what? Maybe we're dying here. Dad's gone, you're leaving. And we're gonna be stuck here the first week of summer? You and Dad always said you would take us to Lake Tahoe but you never have. And it's pretty damn obvious, you never will!" He snatched his phone and earbuds from the counter and stomped toward the back door.

"Nobody should be talking to their mama like that. Otherwise you and me are gonna have a long week," Joy called after him.

Cole didn't turn around, he swung open the heavy metal door and stormed out. She rested her elbows on the counter and buried her face in her palms. The guilt balled up in her stomach. Cole was right. She always had talked about taking her kids to Lake Tahoe. But she hadn't been able to build up the courage to go back there. Now she had no choice. Didn't Cole understand that? That she had to do this? Not for Becca, but for herself. And for Jacob. Because she owed her brother that at least.

"Don't you worry about him. Just hormones is all. I'll have

him in ship shape when you get home." Joy gave her a rough pat on her back. "We'll have fun, Julia. The three of us. Just you wait. I'll even consider paying you two for helping me out around here."

Jolene lifted her head, resting her chin on her fist.

Joy winked at Julia and squeezed Jolene's shoulder. "I'm gonna load a few six packs of our finest into your SUV for your trip," she called as she backed away.

She mouthed, *thank you.*

"Mom?" Julia said quietly.

She wiped her wet cheeks and sniffed. "Yes, baby?"

"I'm sorry about your friend."

Jolene forced a smile through her sorrow.

"Do you think Becca went to heaven?"

The question felt like a fly ball into left field. She frowned. "Why are you asking?"

"You know, because of the accident? She was the one driving the car when Uncle Jacob died."

Sighing, her shoulders eased slowly. She took her daughter's hand into hers and caressed it. At least she was doing something right with one of her children. Julia was a sweet girl, always putting others before herself. She was a lot like Jacob, always helping others. She peered into her eyes that were sea blue just like her own. "Just as you said, Uncle Jacob died as the result of an accident. I'd like to believe we aren't held responsible for accidents."

Jolene's kids knew all about Jacob. She'd remind Cole to look out for Julia just as Jacob had done with her. Sometimes the way her daughter smiled reminded her of Jacob and she'd say, "You have your Uncle Jacob's smile." And of course there was her son's hook shot, sinking the basketball into the net with a perfect swoosh as if Jacob himself had taught him the move.

Her heart ached, wishing Jacob was still alive so he could

have a relationship with his niece and nephew. So she didn't have to go back to Tahoe City alone. She'd give anything for the chance to play a game of one-on-one basketball in the old, cracked driveway of their childhood home in Reno. Each time after she lost—because she always lost—Jacob would take her by the shoulders, bend down and peer directly into her eyes. He'd say, "Jolene, I'll always have your back. But I will never go easy on you. You know why?" She'd shake her head and he'd reply, "Because no one else will go easy on you in this life." And he wasn't wrong. Nothing seemed easy these days.

CHAPTER THREE

W ith her purse over her head and stretched across her chest, a gray bag on one shoulder, and a few hats in her grasp, Jolene stepped out the front door of her house. The cool air of the early summer morning rushed at her body. It hit her hard, the realization the beginning of summer in Central Oregon was upon them. This brought chilly mornings that prepared you for hot scorching sunny days followed by slightly cooler evenings. The tan-colored exterior paint on the house exposed signs of the Central Oregon weather taking its toll. Signs of the long winters, high desert winds, and sizzling summers distressed the paint.

The faded color distracted her, and her eyebrows drew together. She could feel the two hard creases form on her forehead right where they always did, starting in between her eyes and running skyward. The lines appeared more regularly these days. And they might as well. The years were piling up, but that didn't mean she hated the aging signs any less.

Jolene pushed the thoughts of the distressed paint out of her mind. There was no sense in worrying about it. Having the home repainted was on Travis's to-do list. He'd promised to still take care of the exterior of the home, and she had no other choice but to trust he would follow through.

Cole and Julia followed behind her, each pulling along a blue rolling suitcase for her and a bag of their own. They loaded the luggage into the back of her black Chevy Tahoe. She tossed her gray bag, purse, and a sweater onto the floor of the passenger side and they all climbed in.

When they reached the brewery, Jolene made sure everything in the office was tidy, the order sheets had been emailed to not only Travis and herself, but to Tim and Joy as well, the schedule was posted on the dry erase board near Carrie's desk, and all supplies had been accounted for.

But who was she kidding? Certainly not herself. She was stalling.

She didn't know which was more difficult, leaving the brewery or her children for an entire week? In a way, the brewery had become like a third child, or an extra appendage. Most days she loved the brewery and tried not to think of it as just one more responsibility Travis had abandoned her with. But she knew she was leaving her kids and the brewery in good hands.

Joy entered the office, took Jolene by the shoulders and shoved her toward the back door of the brewery. "Stop worrying. I promise, this place will be in better than standing shape when you return."

"Are you sure about this?" She attempted to plant her feet into the concrete floor with no avail.

Tim stood near Carrie's empty desk, clipboard in hand. "We can handle it. Now go," he insisted. "We love ya."

Her persistence sagged and she smiled. "I'll call and check up on you," she called to Tim over her shoulder.

He pinched the bridge of his nose. "Please don't," he muttered.

Cole and Julia followed Jolene and Joy outside. They crossed the hot asphalt in the parking lot toward her SUV. The morning sun already beat down on the top of her head, though the breeze was chilly. She chewed on her bottom lip, nerves zinging through her.

Julia wrapped her arms around Jolene's waist. "Have fun, Mom. I'm gonna miss you."

Jolene pressed a kiss to the top of Julia's head, inhaling the scent of green apple wafting from her hair. "I'll miss you too. I love you."

She pulled a resistant Cole in for a hug. "Please be a big help for Joy and Tim. Please, behave?"

"Yeah, yeah, we know the drill." He pulled away and she tousled his shaggy brown hair.

"And hey, it sounds like if you two do a good job, you may even get paid."

Out of her two children, she worried about Cole the most. He had seemed to lose all former interest in his favorite things since Travis moved out. She had to bribe him with a new phone just to get him to agree to join the basketball team this year. He used to love playing. Sometimes, she could see so much of her brother Jacob in Cole. The way he moved on the basketball court was magic. When she'd play one on one with him in their driveway, she could anticipate his next move just as she used to be able to do with Jacob.

When Jacob got irritated with her for knowing his next move, Jolene responded with, "Well stop being so predictable then."

Now Cole spent most of his time at home, making sure she was taken care of. It was a big responsibility for a teenage boy, too big. Just because his dad left didn't mean he had to step up and be the man of the house. But he had. And it simultaneously made Jolene love her son more as well as cause her heart to crack down the middle at the unfairness.

"Alright, enough of this. Your mama needs to get on the road." Joy hugged her tightly before pushing her toward the driver's side of the SUV. "Now go. You've got a long drive ahead of you. And if you get tired, you pull yourself over and take a rest, you hear me?"

She fought back an eye roll. "I will. Okay, love you all. See you next Sunday." She climbed in behind the wheel, took one last glance at her children, Joy, and the High Desert Brewery sign hanging on the brick building, and shut the door.

She picked up the fedora hat and Jacob's old Sacramento Kings hat from the floor and tossed them onto the passenger seat. Dressed in denim shorts, a t-shirt and beach style flip-flops, she thanked God it wasn't quite warm enough for the backs of her bare legs to stick to the leather interior. The stretch of the drive through the Nevada desert would be sweltering. Although, once she arrived in Tahoe City that evening, it would be much cooler.

Tahoe didn't reach very high temperatures in June. However, she'd read on the weather channel website Tahoe City was experiencing record high temperatures for this time of the year.

By the time she put the key into the ignition, Jolene found it difficult to catch her breath. She could easily run two miles before feeling this winded. But she knew it wasn't physical exertion making it hard to breathe, instead it was most likely anxiety about her trip. She worried a panic attack might come on, so she closed her eyes and inhaled a deep breath. Her best guy friend growing up used to refer to her panic attacks as having a *case of the crazies*.

Bo Dean.

He'd been her first best friend. The only kid in school to accept her for herself. She had been a bit of a tomboy then. She loved playing basketball and wearing her brother Jacob's Sacramento Kings hat. Spud Webb had been her favorite player on the team. He'd played the position of point guard and she admired him because he was the shortest player on the team. She smiled at the memory.

In the sixth grade, Bo taught Jolene how to throw the perfect lay-up. In seventh grade, he taught her how to sink a three pointer with ease. And by eighth grade, not only had he helped her be a more suitable component for her brother, but he had also given her the nickname Ollie. When all the guys in school who played sports were referring to each other by their last name, Bo thought Jolene should be included. Oliver was already taken by her brother Jacob, so Bo had come up with Ollie.

Until they were about fifteen, Bo treated her like one of the guys. She had liked it at the time. But once she quit playing basketball and finally accumulated more girl friends than guy friends, she didn't want to be looked at as just one of the guys. But the nickname he'd given her stuck and to this day, he was the only person to ever call her Ollie.

More thoughts of Bo continued to flicker through Jolene's mind as she fastened her seatbelt and backed out of the brewery. She couldn't remember the last time she thought about him before now. And she couldn't even pinpoint when the last time was that she'd seen him. Maybe her wedding? She tried to look him up on Facebook a few years back using the brewery's business page but had come up empty handed. There were several Bo Deans that popped up but none of them confirmed to be *her* Bo Dean.

With the flip of her signal, she made a left onto US-20 and pushed the button to unroll her window. The warm air gushed inside the SUV, whirling around and causing her hair to whip every which way. The air smelled like dry dirt and pine trees and she embraced it.

Jolene thought about the childhood friends she would see before the days end. Cristina had moved to Reno Nevada their sophomore year in high school after her dad's job transferred them there. Jolene and her friends welcomed Cristina into their group easily. Having a friend who was tough and looked out for them came in handy on more than one occasion. When kids picked on her for being short, Cristina had her back. She'd be the first one to point out the other kids faults or even threaten them.

Jolene and Kendra had been friends the longest. They'd met in the seventh grade while Jolene was still a tomboy. Kendra was her first close female friend. They were quite the pair, Kendra was tall with long, dark brown hair and wore designer clothing while she was short with shoulder-length blonde hair and dressed in baggy jeans, jerseys, and hats.

She thought about Becca next. Images flashed through her mind, one after the other. They played like an old home movie on an 8mm movie projector. All the images were old, while Becca was young and dressed in her favorite color red and while the two were the closest of friends. Even though the four girls had been pretty much inseparable back then, Becca and Jolene had the closest bond.

The two met the first day of school in ninth grade. Becca was cool and confident and a bit bossy. Her personality meshed well with Jolene's people pleasing, pushover personality. Becca dressed in red constantly. It complimented her porcelain skin and chocolate brown hair and eyes. Becca had been an exceptional swimmer and by tenth grade had worked her way into the position of captain on the high school girls swim team. When Becca swam, she wasn't the bossy girl Jolene had come to know, instead she was graceful. Jolene attended all of Becca's swim meets and watched proudly from the bleachers.

She shook away the distracting memories and focused on the road stretching before her.

The best thing about going to Tahoe City—no one there knew about her failed marriage—her husband who decided life would be easier without her, without the children, and the business they started together. No one knew about the debilitating disease that threatened to take control over her body more and more with each passing day.

CHAPTER FOUR

THEN

Dressed in a one-piece red swimsuit, a red swim cap and goggles, Becca takes her position on the blocks. Her friends watch with anticipation. Cristina is cool and relaxed. Kendra bites her nails down to the quick beside her, and Jacob is perched on the edge of the metal bench. Jolene's heart races furiously inside her chest.

From the bleachers, Jacob cups his hands around his mouth and hollers, "You got this, babe!"

She elbows him in the ribs. "Shhh." But it doesn't faze him, he's too focused on Becca up on the blocks. She turns to face him, puckers her lips, and blows him a quick kiss. Jacob grins the widest smile, revealing one dimple in his cheek.

Smiling, she shakes her head. "I don't know how you aren't a distraction for her out there."

"A distraction? No way. I'm more like a good luck charm. Just call me her lucky rabbit foot." He waggles his blonde brows.

Jolene rolls her eyes. Her brother and her best friend's relationship is sickening but also, it's the best kind of comfort too.

"Did she rub you for good luck?" Cristina snickers beside me.

I gasp and bury my face in my palms. "Gross," I mutter.

But Jacob doesn't answer, *thank God*, he's concentrating on Becca.

She has one foot stretched out in front of the other, her toes wrapped around the edge of the block. Bent over, her fingers gripping the block, her focus is on her knees. She doesn't have to wait long before the beep sounds and she springs forward, throwing her hands into a streamline.

"She's got this," Kendra whispers.

Once Becca's head breaks the surface of the water, she's already in first place. Her movements are quick and controlled. She's determined, like she always is. She remains her momentum the entirety of the race. Not once hesitating a stroke or second guessing a breath. Until it's over—and she's won. First place in the girls 200-meter Freestyle.

From the bleachers, they all cheer, jumping up and down and pumping their fists in the air. They run down to meet Becca by the side of the pool. Dripping wet, Becca tears off her swim cap and goggles and flings herself into Jacob's arms.

"I did it," Becca says breathlessly.

Jacob kisses her wet cheek. "You were awesome, babe."

Becca hugs Jolene next.

"I'm so proud of you, girlie," she whispers into her friend's ear.

Becca pulls back, a wide smile across her face, beads of water on her porcelain skin. They all join in one big group hug.

"Let's celebrate. A weekend at the cottage? Swimming? S'mores and beer around the fire?"

"You had me at beer." Cristina smiles.

"I don't know." Jolene bites at her thumbnail. "I've got a crap ton of homework."

"Jo, please? I can't handle another weekend with the parentals and their nonstop arguing." Her eyes are pleading.

"Well, you know I'm in." Jacob drapes a towel over Becca's shoulders.

"Fine, you're right. It sounds perfect," Jolene agrees, squeezing her friend again.

Graduation Night Turns Deadly for One Local Teen

A crash on Saturday evening leaves one dead and one person with serious injuries. Per a Placer County Sheriff release cited by KDVR, the accident took place around 6:00 p.m. PCS reports that the 17-year-old female driver was heading northbound on Manson Blvd in Tahoe City. Witnesses said the car entered the s-curve too quickly, causing the driver to veer into the opposite lane facing oncoming traffic. The front driver's side tire hit the curb causing the vehicle to ricochet and flip before coming to rest on the shoulder of the road. No other cars were involved. Speed and inexperienced driving appear to be the cause. Drugs and alcohol are not a factor at this time. One passenger in vehicle, located in passenger seat; Jacob R. Oliver, 19. Pronounced dead on the scene. Driver, Becca N. Gibbs, 17; taken by Airlife to Barton Memorial Hospital, is stated to be in serious but stable condition.

CHAPTER FIVE

NOW

Jolene and Becca's tightknit friendship had ended in one final catastrophe on that dreadful day nearly two decades ago. But Jolene couldn't think of the accident now. That wasn't what this trip was about. This trip was about paying tribute to Becca and be a support system to her friends. Jolene had gone nineteen years without Becca and yet, being without her this past week after hearing of her death, had been agonizing. The feelings of guilt flooded back, of not being there for her. Her stomach pinched, and her throat burned.

She continued down highway OR-31, which would take her on the long and uneventful route past Red Rock and Summer Lake that had long since dried up. Several hours remained, several hours of regrets and anticipate the reunion between childhood friends.

Kendra was flying into the Reno-Tahoe International Airport later that night. Cristina planned on picking her up and together they would make the one-hour drive to the Gibbs's cottage in Tahoe City. Then the three of them would be together again.

It felt surreal to think about seeing Cristina and Kendra after all these years. What would they talk about? What would they do to pass the time? How strange would it be, having all of them together? Except they wouldn't all be together.

An image of Becca, now older, flashed into her mind. Her frail body, weak, lying in bed. Alone, scared and in pain. The image of Jacob appeared next. A helpless and crumpled unmoving heap of a body. Jolene's stomach twisted in knots, and she felt nauseous.

AS JOLENE'S car crept down Manson Blvd, inching closer to the section of the road where the horrifying accident occurred, her heart beat fast and loud. Her breathing altered in accelerated breaths, her chest tightening around her lungs. Feelings of suffocation overcame her. "Breathe, breathe," she chanted under her breath, as if she needed the reminder to complete such a natural task. Beads of sweat formed and raced down her spine.

Was she strong enough to do this? Hadn't she grown stronger the past year? Taking on more responsibilities at the brewery and taking charge of her disease head-on. Her friend Joy referred to Jolene as brave, strong, and determined. Although she'd begun to believe those things, at this moment they didn't ring true for her.

The last thing she felt was brave. Right now, she felt as if she resembled something minuscule and weak, insufficient to complete what's been asked of her. How could she if she couldn't even drive the route that would ultimately lead her to her destination?

The negative voices in her head commenced, taking over her legitimate thoughts. *You can't do this. You're not strong enough, you're not brave enough.* The taunting rang in her ears. Her throat went dry, and she shook her head, blinking back the tears burning at the corners of her eyes. The negative voices were relentless, showing no mercy this time and they devoured her. She had no choice but to give into her weakness, letting the tears spill and wrenching her car to the shoulder of the road.

She silently cursed herself for thinking she could do this. She peered out the windshield and through glassy eyes, spotted a restaurant up ahead. The sign read *Anders Bar and Grill.* She wiped the wetness from her cheeks with the heels of her palms. Her jaw dropped at the recollection of the restaurant still there, still open after all these years. It was a place the four girls would frequent every time they were in town.

Jolene had many memories of her, Cristina, Becca, and Kendra sitting in their favorite booth in the restaurant sharing plates of fries—back when they were young and none of them cared about calories. They'd talk about their crushes and their dreams. How Kendra was going to be a famous model and travel all over the world. And how Cristina was going to join a band as a back-up singer. Of course, Travis and Jolene would get married, and Jacob and Becca would get married, and they'd buy houses next to one another right on the lake.

Not many of those dreams were fulfilled. Kendra had become a model but there hadn't been much worldly travel. And Cristina was now an elementary school teacher, not a back-up singer but she did sing in her church's choir. Jolene and Travis did get married, but now it was over. And then there was Jacob and Becca. Both gone too early, neither of them having a fair chance at even attempting their dreams.

Her stomach growled, bringing her out of her memories. In her attempt to reach the cottage before nightfall, she hadn't stopped for lunch, and now she was starving. So, she eased her car back onto the main road and pulled into the lot for Anders Bar and Grill. Anders had always been a favorite spot of the locals making it a busy hangout. It was also the beginning of summer, so the only open parking spot was near the back of the building.

Jolene reached for her cardigan sitting on the passenger seat and slipped it on without buttoning it up. She flipped the visor down and checked herself out in the mini mirror.

Eesh. Her eyes were swollen and red rimmed. Brushing her fingertips under her eyes, she attempted to wipe away the traces of smeared mascara. She gave an unconvincing half smile to her reflection. *It is what it is.* She stepped out of her SUV and slung her purse over her head.

Once inside the restaurant, Jolene was a bit taken a back with the appearance. It had obviously been remodeled since she'd been there last. All the varieties of lighting drew her in, creating a luminous atmosphere.

In the lobby of the restaurant hung a burnt orange chandelier. Above the bar, several globe lights dangled at varying lengths and can lighting shone on the bottles of alcohol lined up on the glass shelves. Wood planks lined the walls as well as the ceiling with smaller lights speckling the walls at varying heights. Barn wood tables had been arranged with coordinating chairs throughout the main section of the restaurant. Its design had a welcoming effect, helping to ease her nerves.

Spotting an empty stool at the bar, she set her sights on it and walked at a slow pace as to not draw attention to her stagger. She held her head high—her attempt to give off the impression she was a confident woman.

She probably wasn't fooling anyone.

Taking her seat at the bar, she placed her purse underneath the stool by her feet and picked up one of the folded laminated menus off the wood counter. She peered over it, checking if the bartender had noticed her yet. His wide back remained turned to her and was adorned in a wrinkled black collared shirt. Her OCD screamed at the sight, wanting to iron the man's shirt for him.

Didn't this guy own an iron?

As the bartender reached for a bottle of alcohol from the glass shelves, a black widow spider tattoo on his forearm peeked out underneath his rolled-up sleeve. There had to be a story behind a tattoo like that. His shaggy black hair could use a good comb through along with the ironing of his shirt, although this wasn't a fancy restaurant. The crowd was laid back, eating burgers and Reuben sandwiches, and drinking wine and beer. Conversations and laughter hummed around her while R&B music whirled through the speakers overhead.

Still waiting for the bartender's attention, Jolene scanned the entire restaurant searching for all exits and the restroom. Being aware of her surroundings had always helped her remain calm in case she needed to leave in a hurry. In case her urge to run kicked in.

Drinking alcohol wasn't ideal for her condition, but tonight, she didn't care. She wanted to relax her nerves. And eventually, she'd have to make it to her destination which meant driving through that familiar section of the road. She needed liquid courage.

The bartender turned and finally noticed her. He beamed a wide, yellow-toothed smile at her. His dark brown eyes twinkled when the lights hit them. The shade of brown was so incredibly dark, they took on a near black hue as if they were two black onyx stones. He ran both hands of spread fingers through his disheveled hair, raking it back.

"Evening, ma'am, what are you having?" he asked gruffly.

She gave him a small smile. "What do you have on tap?"

"Let's see, we currently have Ponderosa IPA, Stonehill Stout, Rainer Pale Ale, Boston Lager, and Ponderosa Porter."

She straightened, blinking back her disbelief. "You've got to be kidding me," she muttered, rolling her eyes.

"Excuse me?"

"I'm sorry." She shook her head. "Nothing. I'll take a Ponderosa Porter."

"Great choice. Ponderosa Porter coming up." He grinned, his lips near hidden under his dark overgrown mustache attached to a matching beard. He grabbed a pint-sized glass and filled it from the tap, not once taking his eyes off Jolene.

First, she couldn't get the guy to notice her and now he wouldn't stop staring. She bent her head and studied her hands in her lap, fingers interlocked and thumbs fidgeting. She was shocked to hear the restaurant had beer from High Desert Brewery on tap. She was even more shocked Travis hadn't told her. She'd only taken over as brewmaster last year, but she wasn't in charge of distribution. Travis had been slowly handing over that responsibility to Tim.

Her stomach pinched. This was something she would have known if her and Travis were still together—if her opinion mattered. On one hand, she was extremely proud of Travis for expanding the business and landing a deal to distribute in California. On the other, she wasn't sure how she felt about him doing business in a town that held so many hurtful memories for her and not even tell her.

The bartender set the glass down on the cardboard coaster in front of her interrupting her thoughts. She lifted her head and met his gaze; those two black stones stared at her and gave her the creeps. She forced a smile.

"Thank you."

"No problem. Anything else? You want to order some food?"

"Ah, yes. I'll try the French dip sandwich with fries please. Oh, and on a gluten free bun. If you have it. Thanks."

"You got it." The bartender nodded, his shaggy hair falling into a mess and framing his round face. "You're not from around here."

It wasn't a question.

"Guilty." Heat licked the back of her neck, and she placed her hand there in answer.

"Where you from?"

"Oregon."

"Oregon, hmm?" he said it like he was trying to place her, and she didn't like that.

"I'm just here visiting a friend for a few days," she partially lied.

Someone called to him, and his attention finally tore from her. "Well, enjoy your time in Tahoe City. And by the way, I'm Owen. Just holler if you need anything else." He turned on his heel and began pulling drink orders from the computer.

She studied the beer in the glass sitting in front of her—admiring the half inch of foam on top, known as head. This was a good sign. Foam was essential in delivering the true flavor of the beer. It enabled the beer to taste how it was intended when it was brewed—how *she* had intended. The thick, creamy foam also told her the beer dispensing system was in balance and the carbonation being brewed into the beer was being managed to her requirements.

Picking up the glass and holding it underneath her nose, she paused, inhaling the aroma before taking a drink. The liquid was cool and smooth as it ran down her throat. She examined the glass. The bubbles clung to the sides, creating a lacing effect around the inside of the glass. Another good sign, meaning the glass had been cleaned correctly.

She scolded herself for paying such close attention to the

details. Why couldn't she just simply enjoy drinking a beer? But when she took another drink from her glass and tasted the smooth chocolate flavor, delight bloomed in her chest. She was proud to have High Desert Brewery's beer in Tahoe City and she was proud of herself for learning how to brew this fantastic tasting concoction.

When Jolene's food arrived, Owen shot her another yellow-toothed smile and gestured to her glass. "You need another?"

"Yes please, thank you."

If she was being honest, *need* wasn't the correct word. *Want* would be more accurate. Though she did need that liquid courage to get her down Manson Blvd. Otherwise she'd never be leaving this place. And the thought of being stuck here with Owen, the burly, yellow-toothed, black-eyed bartender gave her chills. Okay, maybe only one more beer, then she'd get out of here.

Owen placed a fresh cold beer in front of her on the cardboard coaster, damp from the condensation of the first beer. Her eyes shifted from the full glass to his dark eyes, and they bore into her. He grinned and winked before returning to his computer screen. A shiver ran through her as she fought back the urge to bolt.

The guy had to be at least ten years younger than her. Sure, it was nice for the ego she supposed. Especially since she was feeling less than glamorous these days. Even still, she debated whether to stay or ditch her food and retreat.

But the sandwich and greasy fries sitting before her smelled heavenly and her mouth watered. Her stomach ached from extreme hunger which made her decision an easy one.

Picking up a fry and examining it, she took a small bite at first and then devoured the rest. It left an oily residue on the roof of her mouth and although this wasn't an ideal feeling, the savory taste caused a longing for more. The fries tasted exactly how she remembered they did when she and her friends used to come to the restaurant. They might have given the inside of this place a facelift in the last two decades, but the food remained the same.

"Well would you look at what the cat drug in," a husky voice said in singsong.

Jolene turned her head in the direction of the familiar voice. With her eyes a bit blurry, she attempted to blink her vision into focus.

As the unknown person approached, she felt uneasy and got up from the barstool placing her hand on the back of it, bracing herself. Her heart thumped hard against her chest. Closer, closer—her stomach clenched. She clutched the back of the barstool turning her knuckles white.

When her vision cleared, recognition finally settled in, and she couldn't hold back the wide smile tugging at her lips. She went weak in the knees and *oh, thank you, Lord,* was she thankful to be holding the back of the barstool. Even though she hadn't seen him for several years, Bo Dean still had the same eyes. But his face now had straight lines and a cut jawline covered in just the right amount of stubble.

"Bo Dean," she said.

"Jolene Oliver."

With both muscular arms wrapped around her body, Bo picked her up off her feet. Leaving her legs dangling, she had no other choice but to wrap her arms around him and hold on for dear life. Not that she was complaining. His arms were firm, and the toned muscle continued up his shoulders, and stretched around to his back. She couldn't help from inhaling his beach scent, still familiar after all these years.

After releasing her from the bear hug, he placed her back onto her feet. She grasped for the barstool and stumbled a bit, unable to catch her footing. Heat filled her cheeks and she hoped he hadn't noticed her shin smack into the leg of the barstool.

Jolene tugged at her shirt that had climbed up during their greeting. His height towered over her, and she had to crank her neck to look at him. He had to be well over six feet, exceeding her height by at least a foot. That hadn't changed, he'd always been tall. But the muscles were something new, and she welcomed the view.

Bo's wide body made it obvious he spent several hours a week lifting weights at the gym. And his white Henley t-shirt stretched taut against his broad chest and solid biceps. He had on a pair of shorts and leather flip flops. The look suited him.

"It's actually Jolene McCabe now," she corrected him, peeking through long eyelashes and trying not to wince from the burning pain shooting from her shin.

"Oh, that's right. I forgot. Some flannel wearing lumberjack stole you away from all of this." He opened his palms, lifting them at his sides. Then he flashed her a bright white smile and waggled his eyebrows.

She blushed, her face feeling flushed. Those green eyes of his still held power in them.

"If I remember correctly, you were already taken. What was her name again? Some Miss Teen USA contestant, wasn't it?" She smirked and nudged his arm with her elbow.

"Right...Jessica. Yeah, that didn't last long."

"She was your girlfriend after high school, wasn't she?"

"I think she was. I'm surprised you remember." He grinned, raking a hand through his dark blonde hair. "Mind if I sit?" He gestured to the open barstool next to hers.

"No, please. I'd love to hear what you've been up to. How've you been?" Jolene sat and Bo took the seat next to hers.

Holding up a finger, he signaled Owen the bartender who nodded in acknowledgement. Owen filled a pint glass of beer from one of the selections on tap. When he placed it down on the cardboard coaster in front of Bo, foam spilled over the edge and ran down the sides of the glass creating a pool of liquid on the coaster.

She watched them curiously.

Bo picked up his beer, and placed the glass to his lips, taking a long swig.

"Come here often?" she asked.

He licked his lips, and she felt an instant swoop low in her belly.

"What makes you assume that?" He smirked, looking at her out of the corner of his eye before taking another sip of his beer and causing goosebumps to race down her arms.

"Oh, I don't know, maybe the fact that the bartender knows what kind of beer you like."

"Coincidence?" His eyes flickered with mischief.

Her mouth curved into a smile, and she rolled her eyes.

"Fridays. I come here every Friday after work," he relented. "And if I'm not working, I still stop in here for dinner. Sometimes I meet the guys from work or friends, or I come by myself." He took another long drink.

From the corner of her eye, Jolene watched his Adam's apple rise and fall with each gulp, the action sending a thrumming in her depths.

"Besides," he continued, placing his glass down. "They've got the best beer in town."

"Oh yeah? What are you drinking?"

"Ponderosa Porter. Looks to be the same one you're drinking." His eyes gestured toward her beer.

"Yep, it is."

"It's my favorite right now. It takes me a long time to find one I like. And just when I do, the bastards go and switch it out on me. I hate that."

Wrapping her hands around her glass, she wiped at the condensation. She debated if she should tell Bo that his favorite beer was brewed by herself and the flannel wearing lumberjack at the brewery they owned together. But was it really important?

Owen interrupted her thoughts when he slid a plate of food in front of Bo. A burger with all the fixings and a side of fries. The aroma of oil, salt, and grease reminded her of her own food sitting in front of her, most likely growing cold.

"So, are you just getting into town?" Bo asked after taking a bite of his burger.

"Yep. I'll be here for the week."

"Yeah, I heard that."

She quirked a questioning brow at him while wiping her mouth with a napkin.

"Word gets around." He shrugged. "And I bumped into Cristina. You know? At the funeral."

"Oh, right." How had she forgotten about Becca's funeral?

"No Kendra yet?"

"No, I'm meeting them both at the Gibbs's cottage tonight. Cristina is picking Kendra up from the airport and they'll text me when they're on their way." Jolene's voice sounded hoarse. She cleared her throat with no avail and attempted to change the subject. "So, what's new with you?"

"Not much. Still living in my family's vacation cabin. Except it's mine now. I bought it from my parents about six years ago. I transferred from the City of Reno's Police Department over to the Placer County Sheriff's Department."

"So, you're still a cop?"

"Yep, still a cop. I'm a patrol deputy." He answered her question with pride in his tone. "So, you and I would've never worked out I suppose." He threw a smirk over his shoulder.

"What was that thing you used to say in high school? That you would never marry a cop?"

She gasped, incredulous. "Hey, now that's not fair. That was a long time ago." She shoved her shoulder into him. He felt firm, all hard muscle against her arm, and she pulled back quickly, sitting upright on the barstool. Warmth filled her cheeks, and her entire body went hot.

Peeling her sweater off, she hung it on the back of the barstool and then reached for her beer. When she picked it up and brought it to her lips, her hand shook a bit. What if he noticed?

"How are your parents doing?" Bo asked.

"They're good. They've retired and moved from Reno to Arizona."

"I heard that." He took a sip of his beer. "And how about you? What have you been up to? Because the word on the street is, you've been hiding out in Oregon with Mr. Lumberjack."

Her mind snagged on *Mr. Lumberjack,* and she tried to force the negative thoughts away. "It's true. We moved about eight years ago, to Sisters, Oregon. We have two kids. Fifteen and thirteen."

"No way?"

"And Travis and I own a brewery."

"Seriously?"

"High Desert Brewery." There, she'd said it, like ripping off a Band-Aid. Jolene shyly peered up at him, awaiting his reaction.

Removing his beer from his lips, he held it out to her, brows raised. "Are you trying to tell me that this—my favorite beer—is made by you?"

She nodded, biting her lower lip.

"Unreal." He gave a slight shake of his head before

finishing the rest of his beer and raising a finger to Owen, signaling him for another. "You have some secrets, Miss Jolene." He looked at her then with intent and mischief. "And my goal is to somehow sweet talk you into spilling each and every one to me tonight."

Her skin burned underneath his gaze. *Oh, she had plenty of secrets that was for sure.*

While he continued to look at her like he wanted to peel back all her layers and maybe, quite possibly her clothing as well, her mind deviated and sifted through memories of the two of them. Ones that felt ancient and unreachable. Ones from the two summers they spent working at the Tahoe City Sweet Shop together.

Those lengthy blistering days were spent scooping ice cream into cones and listening to kids beg their parents for more. It didn't faze Bo and Jolene. They never really thought of it as work. It was more like social hour for them. They spent their working hours conjuring up pranks to play on one another, telling jokes, and bantering. Recalling the way his face used to turn pink and blotchy when she flirted with him, sent a swoop of desire low in her belly.

CHAPTER SIX

As Bo and Jolene clean the smoothie machine, they talk about their relationships. Bo confesses to her that he's tired of his clingy girlfriend. Jolene's boyfriend is irritating her, and she's been contemplating breaking up with him. With Bo's relationship on the rocks, she allows herself to imagine now could finally be the right time for the two of them to date. Her mind conjures a plan—the two of them ditching the party altogether.

"Hey, Bo?" She bites her lower lip, her stomach uneasy.

"Hmm?" he asks, distractedly from atop a ladder.

"How do you think they'd react if we didn't even show up at the party tonight?" Will she have to come out and say it? Tell him she wants to be with him?

"They would freak for sure," Bo answers, his arm deep inside the smoothie machine.

Jolene continues washing the outside of the machine with a

dishrag and considers his response. Okay, she probably *was* going to have to just come out and say it. He was quiet and so she tried again.

"What if you and I just get out of here, together? And we skip the party?" She cranks her neck to peer up at him.

He stops scrubbing the machine and his eyes widen, meeting her gaze. She quirks an eyebrow, mischief shining on her face. He blushes a deep shade of red, a color she's never seen on his face before.

"What do you mean?"

She presses her lips together. Was her best guy friend seriously this clueless?

"Let's go to the south side of the lake, to the marina. Just the two of us. We can sneak out on one of the boats, lay out, look at the stars. You can't see a sky full of stars in the city like you can out here. C'mon, what do you say?" She sounds pathetic, she's nearly begging him.

Leaning back atop the ladder, he rubs his shaved head. "Ollie, we can't. What will they say? What will that look like?"

"Who cares. Why do you care what they think? What *she* thinks? You don't even like her anyway," Jolene bites out.

"Hey, c'mon, that's not fair." He climbs down from the ladder, adjusting the space between them. "We've never talked about the two of us before, uh...you know, as a couple."

"And you know why, Bo." She looks into his eyes with intensity. "Whenever you don't have a girlfriend, I have a boyfriend. And when I don't have a boyfriend, you have a girlfriend. The timing is never right." She drops her head and studies her sticky tennis shoes where drips of melted ice cream have landed.

Bo places his hand on her shoulder. "Maybe that's a sign. A sign we aren't meant to be together. C'mon," he says, giving her shoulder a shake. "You're one of my best friends. Do we really want to ruin that?"

Jolene looks at him, biting the inside of her cheek and mulling over his words. There's a tugging in the depth of her belly, a craving for something more between them. She senses he feels it as well. But at the young age of sixteen, how do you differentiate the feeling in the pit of your stomach as love or lust?

She sighs, reluctantly agreeing. "I guess not. I mean, you're not really my type anyway." She gives a dismissive wave and returns to cleaning the smoothie machine, her heart aching deep in her chest.

NOW

"So, when were you diagnosed?"

Bo's question startled her, bringing her back to the present. "Excuse me?"

"I asked, when were you diagnosed?" Bo held his glass to his lips, facing forward but his vision pointed down, fixated on his beer. When she didn't answer right away, he took a long swig before turning toward her. "My Aunt. She has MS. She was diagnosed about fifteen years ago."

Her body went rigid, and tears burned at the corners of her eyes. It was as if her deepest darkest secret had just been revealed—announced through the stereo speakers, written on the cardboard coasters. It all felt unreal as if she stood on the outside of her body and looked on as a spectator. She cleared her throat and parted her lips, but words failed her.

This wasn't the plan. He—of all people in Tahoe City—wasn't supposed to find out her secrets. Especially this one.

"Ollie, I'm sorry...I didn't mean—"

Raising a palm, she interrupted him. "A year ago, last spring."

Hearing him say her nickname caused shivers to course through her entire body. It had been almost twenty years since she'd heard it, and it was surprising the effect it still had on her. A single tear slipped out of her eye, and she let it roll down her cheek, then her neck, not bothering to wipe it away.

"Although my doctors suspected it for a couple of years," she continued. "It was a long road to a diagnosis."

She glanced at the near empty glass in front of her, picked it up and swiveled it, causing the last of the foam to swirl around at the bottom.

"I'm sorry," Bo said, tenderness in his voice yet sympathy in his eyes.

"It was that obvious, huh? What gave it away? My lack of grace?" She exhaled a forced, bitter laugh.

"Let's just say, I've been familiarized with the symptoms for a while now. And by the way, how's your leg?" His chin gestured at her shin where she'd smacked it into the bottom of the barstool earlier.

Jolene winced, from both the pain and the fact he'd noticed. Nope, she couldn't hide anything from this guy. She ran a hand over her throbbing shin before glancing at it and noticing the beginning of a bruise forming. It already had a bluish-green hue. By the next day it would transpose to a bluish-purple shade with magenta veins running through it.

Just lovely.

"You should put some ice on that," Bo said.

"Nah, it's fine."

"Otherwise, it's gonna feel worse in the morning."

"I'll be fine. Thanks," she said flatly.

There was a vibration near her feet. She reached down into her purse, retrieving her phone. A text from Kendra flashed across the screen.

KENDRA

Hey girl! Just got picked up. We're on our way. See you soon!

She placed her phone on top of the bar next to her plate before excusing herself to use the restroom.

When Jolene returned, she found a newly filled pint of beer at her place. She raised a quizzical brow at Bo, and he simply shrugged, offering her a smile.

"I thought you might need another."

"Two is usually my limit. Especially since..." her voice trailed off.

"I know alcohol doesn't mix well with the symptoms. But I thought you could use another before heading to the cottage." He faced her, the corners of his mouth turned down and his eyes resembling a darker shade of green. "There's only one route there."

She was well aware of that fact and didn't appreciate the reminder. "I shouldn't. I only have about forty-five more minutes before I need to head to the cottage." She glanced at the time on her phone.

"Don't worry about it. I was already planning on giving you a ride. I don't think you're in any condition to be driving tonight."

"That's really sweet, but I can manage on my own."

"C'mon, I'm not gonna take no for an answer. Besides, even if you left in forty-five minutes, your blood alcohol count would most likely be above the legal limit. Remember, you're in the presence of a cop." He playfully elbowed her. "I'll tell you what, I'll pick you up in the morning at the cottage and we'll swing by and get your car. I'm off work tomorrow so I can come anytime you need me."

Although still hesitant, she gave in. "Okay, fine."

For the past year, she'd been taking care of herself. She found it difficult to accept an offer of help. But she did have to admit, the thought of not having to drive that route tonight, and by herself, took a huge burden off her shoulders.

After downing a few gulps of her third beer, Jolene's head felt light and fuzzy. She was completely relaxed, which was a foreign feeling for her. She eased back in the barstool, releasing an elongated breath.

"Are you worried your husband will be upset that I'm giving you a ride?" Bo asked.

She had her glass up to her mouth, midway of a drink and coughed. The shock of the question caused her to choke on her beer. *Right, like Travis would be upset or jealous.* She picked up a napkin and wiped her mouth, coughing a few more times.

"You alright?"

"Uh, no. Not worried about that at all," she finally managed to say. Then cleared her throat and took another sip.

"So, Mr. Lumberjack isn't the jealous type huh?"

"I guess you could say that."

"Well, he should be." Bo raked a hand through his hair, not making eye contact with her. "You look great, Jolene. He's a lucky guy."

In that moment, her imagination had her swooning and smashing her lips against his.

"Um...thanks." She drummed her fingers on top of the bar. "You've sure come a long way from that shy teenage boy."

"I guess I grew up. That was a long time ago."

"It was," she agreed.

"But I guess not *that* long ago. It feels like yesterday you and I were cruising around this town getting into trouble." He chuckled.

The sound of his laugh caused a quiver to course through her. "Performing pranks at the ice cream shop," she said.

"Going to tailgate parties at the lake."

"Our jamming sessions on all those drives back and forth between Reno and here," she added.

"We had some fun times," he said, quirking a brow at her.

"We did. In fact, about half of my good memories from school include you."

"Same."

"I suppose the other half include Becca, Cristina, and Kendra." She gazed at her near empty glass of beer, caught in the memories. If Becca were here now, she'd be making kissy faces behind her hand. She'd always thought Bo and Jolene would make a cute couple. She'd always say, "If it's true about blondes having more fun, imagine how much fun two blondes would have together."

Owen, the bartender appeared, interrupting them once more. He placed a black case on the bar in front of Bo who pulled a credit card out of his wallet and slid it into the case before handing it back to Owen.

She watched the exchange and frowned. "Uh...excuse me. I still haven't received my bill."

Owen and Bo shared a look, then he gave Jolene a wide smile. "Your bill has already been taken care of, ma'am."

"How?" She scanned Owen's face. Then realization set in. "Ahh...I see. You?" She gestured in Bo's direction.

"Guilty." Bo raised his palms.

She picked up her purse from underneath the bar stool, retrieving her wallet. "That's not necessary. I can pay for my own." But Owen had already walked away. "Fine, let me pay you back then."

Bo shook his head. "Nope, I'm not taking it. Your money's no good to me."

"C'mon, please just take it." She pushed the money in his direction.

"I'm not taking it. How about we consider it a thank you."

"A thank you? A thank you for what?" she asked.

"To you and your husband, for brewing the best beer."

"Oh, fine." It was obvious she would not win this battle. "Maybe we can meet up later in the week, my treat."

"I'd like that."

As Jolene finished her beer, she wished she could sit on the barstool and converse with Bo all night. Her head felt light and fuzzy. Warmth worked its way throughout her body, beginning at her toes and making its way up her legs extending to her torso, and ending in her fingertips.

"It's probably about time we get out of here. It will still take us at least ten minutes to reach the cottage." Bo stood.

"Sounds good," she said, using her go-to phrase. She picked up her phone and stuffed it into her purse. Then, she slipped her sweater back on and slung her purse over her head and across her chest.

When she trailed behind, Bo paused a beat waiting for her to catch up. He hooked his elbow and offered it to her. She hesitated at first, then gave into his invitation, slipping her arm into his. It fit there perfectly.

"Is this okay?" he asked.

She peered up at him, noticing the tenderness in his gaze and feeling a swoop low in her belly. She smiled. "It's okay."

They made their way through the dark parking lot. The air oddly damp with humidity and carrying a stale musty scent, signaling rain was approaching. It felt familiar and she hadn't realized how much she'd missed it until that moment. Bo led her to the passenger side of a blue Chevy pickup. Opening the door, he cleared the seat from books before gesturing for her to climb in.

"Books, huh? Funny, I never took you for much of a reader." Jolene climbed in and picked up a book from the stack. "Fourth Wing?" She raised her brows at him. She was familiar with the title, even read it herself, but most would argue it was a young adult novel.

Bo shrugged and took the book, returning it to the stack he'd moved to the floor.

She smiled and wanted to tease him, he was so fun to tease, but her head felt funny, and she couldn't complete her thoughts. She'd need to tuck that away for another time.

"Why don't you give me your car keys and I'll grab your suitcase so you'll have what you need tonight." Bo held out his hand.

"Good thinking." She searched through her purse, trying to locate her keys. "Here they are. I'm the black one right there." She pointed to her SUV a few spaces over.

Bo loaded her luggage into his pickup and handed back her keys. He held his hand out for her phone next. "Phone."

She didn't argue or question, simply dropped her phone into his palm.

He programmed his name and number into her contact list so she could get a hold of him in the morning. Then he pulled out of the parking lot of Anders Bar and Grill.

Unfortunately, the alcohol hadn't granted Jolene the courage she'd hoped for. As Bo drove down Manson Blvd, her body stiffened. It was as if a weight sat on top of her chest, pinning her down. Her throat tightened as nausea stirred in her stomach.

Images of the aftermath from the accident flashed in her mind. Becca's red Honda CRX laying on its roof next to a giant sugar pine tree. The dark red blood. Jacob's folded body.

Jolene, Kendra, Cristina, and Travis had arrived on the scene mere seconds after the crash. The four of them had been in a separate car, following Becca after she'd sped out of the parking lot of Mel's Grocers with tears streaming down her face and rage in her eyes.

THEN

When Jolene reaches the horrific scene, she finds Becca's red car flipped, the metal of the roof smashed in and resting on the ground. She runs straight toward the havoc, reaching Becca on the driver's side of the car first. Finding Becca's body upside down, Jolene's stomach does its own flip flop. Becca is held in by the seatbelt and wedged in between the seat and the steering wheel. Blood gushes out from the side of her head. When she sees Becca blink, she knows she's alive. That's all Jolene needs to know before she can leave her and run to her brother's aid.

Rushing to the passenger side of the car, Jolene is instantly aware it's taken the brunt of the accident. The roof is caved in, causing the metal to crush Jacob's body, smashing it into the dashboard. "No, no, no," she says. "Jacob! Jacob! No, no, no." Jacob's body is crumpled in an unnatural position. Bile claws its way up her throat, burning it. Jacob isn't moving. And the blood—there is so much blood. Jolene has just enough time to turn and bend at the waist before the vomit releases.

But the puking doesn't faze her. Frantically, she curls both hands around the door handle and pulls with all her strength. "C'mon. C'mon, c'mon!" she says, each time the repeated word growing louder. But the door won't budge. The glass from the window is completely shattered. She reaches inside to touch her brother, her hands gliding across the broken and jagged glass. She winces at the pain while she attempts to pull the door open from the inside.

"C'mon, open dammit." But it's no use, the door is still stuck. Her hands shake and her heart is beating too loud and too fast. "Jacob! Jacob! Jacob!" she screams his name, desperate to make him hear her over the thumping of her heart. In a last effort, she reaches both arms through the open window and tries slipping them under Jacob's arms to pull on him. But the angle is all wrong and his body too awkward. "C'mon, Jacob."

Jolene isn't exactly sure when Travis arrives next to her, maybe he's been there the entire time. He wraps his arms around her and pulls her away from the wreckage, away from Jacob. She protests, "No, no, no!" a growl in her voice.

Travis wraps his t-shirt around her bloodied hands as he looks directly into her eyes. "Jo, leave him. He's gone."

She shakes her head and shoves Travis in the chest. "No, no!" her words coming out in between broken sobs. She hears ear-piercing screams and there is more blood. Her head feels discombobulated and her body trembles uncontrollably. In Jolene's daze, it takes her several minutes to realize it's her own screams she hears and her own blood she sees.

NOW

It was as if the accident had happened yesterday. The images of red so vivid and raw. A car, a sweater, a pool of blood. Jolene's breathing was too fast, and her head reeled. She glanced down at her hands that still portrayed the white scars from the twenty-four stitches she'd received after the broken window glass cut them that day.

"Hey, you okay?" Bo asked.

"I...I, I don't know."

"Ollie," he whispered. "I'm sorry. I'll try to get past here as fast as I can."

"I...I...I," she stammered in a strangled voice. "I think I'm going to be sick."

Bo jerked the truck over to the shoulder of the road and all at once, Jolene unbuckled her seatbelt, flung the car door open, and jumped out, throwing up on the side of the road. Bo jogged around to the passenger side of the pickup to her aid where she was bent over with her hands on her thighs. Bo grabbed her hair in one fist and patted her back gently with his other hand.

"You okay?"

Jolene cleared her throat. "I'm okay." Her words came out hoarse and almost in a whisper.

"I've got some wipes in the truck. Hold on a sec."

He returned with a package of antibacterial hand wipes.

She kept her chin tucked to her chest, her cheeks burning and unable to look at him. "Thanks." She wiped her mouth and hands. "I'm so embarrassed."

"Don't be. Guess I should've listened to you about your two-drink limit." He chuckled half-heartedly.

"Not funny."

"Sorry, too early for jokes. Maybe tomorrow." He smirked.

"Can you just take me to the cottage. I'm pretty tired and my head is pounding." Jolene pressed her fingers to her temples.

"Sure thing." Bo guided her back to the passenger side of the truck, and she climbed in.

Jolene fastened her seatbelt, leaned her head against the head-rest and closed her eyes. The relaxing feeling had vanished and now all she'd been left with was a disgusting taste in her mouth and a gigantic headache. Not to mention a bit of a bruised ego.

How humiliating. She'd just puked in front of Bo. And if she remembered correctly, it hadn't been the first time. There had been a tailgate party in high school where she'd gotten so sick and he'd witnessed the entire thing.

When they arrived at the cottage, she sat forward quickly. Too quickly. "Ugh," she groaned, rubbing her fingertips at her temples while her head pounded like a jackhammer.

What had she been thinking? Since when did liquid courage help anyone?

Bo flung open the passenger door and reached out a hand to assist Jolene to her feet. She placed her hand into his, using it to brace her weight as she slid out of the truck. Gripping it tightly, she pulled him in closer to her, breathing in his intoxicating scent once more.

"I don't want them to see me like this," she whispered, tears pricking her eyes.

"They've seen you drunk before."

"I'm not drunk."

Bo's eyes scanned hers.

"Wait. They...they don't know?" Bo asked, his expression scrunched and concerned. "About the MS?"

She shook her head. Tears pooled in her eyes.

"You gotta tell them, Jo. They're gonna figure it out. Or at least figure out something's off with you."

"I know. I'll tell them." She dipped her head. "Just not tonight, okay?"

Bo brushed his thumbs under her eyes, sweeping away her tears. He gave her an uneasy smile and her heart heaved. "Okay, fine. Your secret is safe with me. But you're gonna need to tell them." Pleading shone in his eyes.

She nodded.

He sighed and made his arm into a hook once more,

offering it to her. She accepted, giving him an appreciative smile.

"Thank you," Jolene whispered.

"Anything for you, Ollie." He leaned over and pressed a kiss to her temple. The gesture was sweet and caring, and it caused warmth to travel through her entire body.

After tapping on the front door, it swung open, and they were greeted by Cristina.

"Jolene," she said in delight, her face bright.

She managed a smile. "Hey."

Cristina embraced her in a tight hug and Jolene found herself clinging to her old friend with a heady nostalgic melancholy. Cristina took notice of Bo and pulled back. She scrutinized the two of them, looking back and forth.

"Jolene, you look like crap. What happened to you?" But she didn't wait for an answer. "Hey, Bo. What are you doing here?"

He cleared his throat. "I bumped into this pretty gal at Anders Bar and Grill. I guess I bought her one too many drinks." He chuckled and braced Jolene again, leading her inside. "Thought it best I drive her, be sure she gets here safely."

"That was sure sweet, Bo." Cristina patted his arm. "Real gentleman like." She raised her dark brows at him. "And real suspicious too."

"What?" his voice went up. "Just looking out for her is all."

"Hmmm...yeah sure. Trying to take advantage of a drunk married woman is more like it. I see how you are." Cristina smacked Bo's backside as he passed her.

He shook his head, exhaling a mirthless laugh. "Same old Cristina. It's good to know you haven't changed a bit," he retorted over his shoulder.

"Don't you know it. And hey, if you're into hitting on married women..." she winked.

"Oh my goodness, Jolene," Kendra said, entering the main room in a flourish. "You okay?" She embraced her.

Jolene bit her lower lip.

Yep, I look like crap and you look as beautiful as always.

"I'm okay. Just tired from my drive, I guess. And I think I had too much to drink. Thanks to this guy." She hiked a thumb at Bo, thankful he agreed to play along with her.

"Guilty," he admitted. "I think it's best we get this gal to bed. I'm sure she'll feel more like socializing in the morning. Which way to her room?"

"She can take the room on the first floor, just past the bathroom. Good thing too, probably not a bad idea to have her close to a toilet." Cristina snickered.

"Ha ha, very funny, Cristina." Kendra rolled her eyes. "She looks terrible. I sure hope she doesn't get sick."

Too late for that.

Bo guided Jolene down the hallway, the murmurs from the two women drifted from the other room. It hurt her to keep this secret, but now wasn't the right time to tell them.

Bo led her into a cozy room with pale, sea foam green walls and a white shiplap headboard. The bed sat centered in between two windows with mismatched farmhouse style nightstands on either side. A white comforter stretched across the bed with an arrangement of white, navy blue, and coral throw pillows resting on it.

With the room spinning, she had to lean further onto Bo for support. The hardwood floor buckled under her feet—all the variations of colors in the room jumbled together, dancing before her eyes. The room smelled musty, the scent causing a queasiness to stir in her belly.

"All right, let's get you into bed," Bo said.

"Thanks, but I think I can manage from here." She pulled her arm out from his and took a step. Her leg gave out and Bo reached for her, grabbing her arm, and yanking her back up to her feet.

"Whoa. Okay, Miss Stubborn. I don't think you *can* manage on your own. I'll get the girls, and they can help you change into something more comfortable and get you in bed."

"No," Jolene protested. "I'm just going to get in bed. I'm beyond exhausted." She raked a hand through her messy hair.

"Okay, here we go." Bo brought her over to the bed and with his free hand pulled the comforter back. He eased her down to a sitting position, her feet dangling off the edge. He tossed the extra throw pillows to the other side of the bed. Jolene slipped her feet out of her sandals and then slid her arms out of her cardigan.

She tilted her head and their eyes locked for a moment before her vision blurred and his image shook. "Thanks," it came out in a hoarse whisper, sounding seductive.

Pink tinted Bo's cheeks and one corner of his lip turned up, giving her a half smile. "Anytime, Ollie."

The sound of her nickname made her body heat up in all the right places. She had to fight the urge from asking him to stay. The feeling of not wanting to be alone tugged at her. It wouldn't be the first time she'd told him she didn't want to be alone and asked him to stay.

On the night of the accident, she'd shown up at the Dean family cabin devastated, exhausted, and angry—devastated over losing her brother, exhausted from the hours spent crying, and angry Bo hadn't been there.

Her cheeks burned at the memory. She dismissed the urge to ask him to stay. Technically she was still a married woman.

Wasn't she?

She sighed, pulling her legs into the bed, and resting her

head on the pillow while Bo covered her up. The walls convulsed as her blinks lengthened. The pounding in her head declined and the possibility of sleep teased her.

"Bo?" she whispered. "Do you really believe Becca drowned?"

Bo bent down, swept her hair off her face, and pressed his lips on her temple. "We'll talk tomorrow. Get some sleep."

CHAPTER SEVEN

The early morning sun rays beamed through the white curtains of the cottage's cozy room. The brightness ricocheted off the white accents and caused Jolene's eyes to flutter open. The plush comforter ended up at the foot of the bed and only the sheet remained tucked around her body. She stretched her arms above her head and yawned.

Reaching toward the nightstand, she fumbled for her cell. When she located it, she held it in front of her and waited for the screen to light up and reveal the time, but it remained black. She tapped at the screen. Still nothing.

Then it hit her like a punch to the gut. She hadn't charged her phone last night. Ugh. This trip was off to a great start.

Sitting up, she scanned the room. The night before she hadn't noticed the two oversized baskets holding extra blankets and pillows at the foot of the bed. Or the navy-blue coastal style area rug and the tall antique dresser along the wall. And there were her blue suitcases, both sitting upright next to the tall dresser. But she didn't see her gray bag. Bo must've forgotten to grab it off the passenger seat of her SUV the night before. No gray bag meant no phone charger.

On the nightstand she spotted an antique silver clock revealing it was 5:46 a.m., along with a glass of water and two Tylenol.

"Oh, thank you, Bo," she said aloud in a hoarse whisper. She popped both pills into her mouth, chasing them with several gulps of water.

Jolene picked up her cardigan from the opposite side of the bed and put it on. She slipped her feet into her sandals and padded out of the room and across the hall to use the bathroom.

The reflection in the mirror distracted her from her urgency to pee. Black mascara and eyeliner smeared around her eyes gave her the raccoon eye effect. Her hair was disheveled, and her teeth had a film on them. A shower sounded heavenly. A toothbrush sounded even better. But all she really wanted was an enormous cup of coffee. Scratch that; several cups of coffee.

Tip toeing into the kitchen, she blinked trying to bring her vision into focus. She caught sight of a note attached to the fridge by a magnet with the phrase, *What happens at the lake, stays at the lake.* Jolene smirked, shaking her head. Then she read the note.

Hi girls, I've stocked the fridge and cupboards with some basic items just to get you started. There are fresh towels in the linen closet and extra laundry soap in the laundry room. Firewood for the pit is around the side of the porch. Wifi password is: GIBBSFAMILY#1. If you need anything else, give me a ring. Thank you for doing this! XOXO Ms. Gibbs

Jolene glanced around the kitchen, taking notice of the

renovations done on the cottage since she'd been there last. Almost the entire place appeared remodeled. Probably on Mr. Gibbs's dime. How Ms. Gibbs ended up with the cottage in the divorce was beyond her.

Jolene found herself thinking about Becca spending time here while she was sick. Reflecting on her life, swimming, relaxing, dying. She shuddered after the last thought. It was difficult to picture Becca here in the remodeled cottage. All of her memories of Becca at the lake had been in the way the cottage used to look. When it was all white wicker furniture and yellow accents. All but Becca's room, which had been painted red. Ms. Gibbs hated the red walls. But Becca loved red—it was her color.

The remodeled kitchen featured stainless steel appliances, white cabinets, and an enormous island that also included a large farmhouse style sink. Pendant lights hung in a row above the island and the counters were a smooth, light grey Quartz. Hardwood floors ran throughout the kitchen stretching into the dining room and living room.

A beautiful trestle table took up most of the dining room with six wooden chairs tucked in around it. In the living room, two aqua colored sofas arranged in an L shape with two patterned gray chairs positioned in front of the windows.

The wall running the length of the back of the cottage featured tall, oversized windows that showcased the stunning view of the lake. The morning sun filtered in through the windows where the white curtains remained drawn open. The wood burning fireplace appeared to be the only original element of the cottage. And although it all looked alluring, the changes made her melancholy.

Jolene searched the cupboards for coffee and filters. She prepped the machine with water and coffee grounds. She couldn't remember the last time she'd made coffee in a regular machine. A few years ago, Travis had bought her a Keurig machine which poured a cup of coffee in a matter of seconds with the push of a single button. She didn't have patience to wait on a regular coffee machine today.

After she pushed the brew button, Jolene wandered into the living room and inspected the details of the cottage and took notice of the lack of personal touches. Jolene assumed Ms. Gibbs must've hired someone to do the decorating. Her heart tightened in her chest at the sight of pictures of the Gibbs family lined across the mantle of the fireplace as well as hung on some of the walls.

A picture of a blonde woman with a salt and pepper haired man and three blonde haired little boys was displayed in the largest frame on the mantle. Jolene stepped closer to get a better look. When she did, she recognized the blonde woman as Becca's older sister, Trisha. It surprised her to see Trisha this way—aged with wrinkles etching around her eyes. She always remembered her as petite, and baby faced. The picture portrayed Trisha with a wide happy smile, causing Jolene to smile as well.

Trisha had been three years older than Becca and always acted like Miss Perfect. She could do no wrong in their parent's eyes. Which meant any little "wrong" Becca did evolved into a huge deal. She seemed to be grounded constantly. But it had never stopped them from hanging out.

Mr. Gibbs would still allow Jolene to come over, even when Becca was grounded. That could be added to the list of the things Becca's parents argued about. On those nights, they'd eat popcorn and turn a movie up loud, drowning out the fighting while Becca planned her next free weekend out to a T. She'd say, "When I can finally bust out of this place," then proceed with her plans. Most of the time they involved piling into her red CRX and heading to Tahoe City to Ander's Bar and Grill for plates of fries. Or, after Jacob was away at college, her plans involved a trip to Sacramento to visit him.

Seeing the picture on the mantle reminded her of the last time she saw Trisha—at Jacob's funeral. It had been considerate of her to attend. Becca hadn't even bothered to show. Ms. Gibbs tried making excuses for her, talking about complications with her broken collarbone. Mr. Gibbs on the other hand, chose to be honest. He explained how difficult the accident had been on Becca and she'd been experiencing immense guilt and depression.

Like the situation hadn't been difficult on Jolene? But she didn't have the option to not show. It was her brother's funeral. And after being Jacob's girlfriend for three years, she should've been there too.

While Becca had still been in the hospital after the accident, she tried to visit her, but Becca hadn't wanted to see her. She'd simply pulled herself out of Jolene's life completely, allowing the guilt to consume her and leaving Jolene to deal with the loss of both her brother and her best friend.

Her gaze drifted to the next picture. This one was of Becca and a blonde-haired little girl with striking green eyes. She tried to inhale but the breath caught in her throat. Her heart sank and she placed her trembling hand on her chest.

This was the first time she remembered Becca had a daughter. How old was she? At least a teenager. Possibly older than Cole? She remembered hearing Becca had a baby. She also remembered how shocked she'd been Becca had moved on so quickly after Jacob's death. It had made forgiving her even harder. Hadn't Jacob meant more to her? How had she gotten over him so quickly?

Kendra had said Becca was a single mother and Jolene wondered who was taking care of Becca's daughter now. Her eyes glistened and she exhaled a heavy breath. She pinched the bridge of her nose—it was too early in the day for tears. Scanning the remaining pictures across the mantle, most of them were of Ms. Gibbs's grandkids—Trisha's three boys and Becca's daughter.

When whe turned her gaze from the mantle, a picture hanging on the wall caught her eye. Fresh tears burned once more and this time she couldn't fight them. Staring back at her was her younger self along with Becca, Kendra, and Cristina.

Ms. Gibbs took the picture of the four girls when they had come and stayed at the cottage over spring break their junior year of high school. The picture reflected them sitting out on the dock on the lake, arms linked, heads turned into one another, smiles stretched wide. It was a picture-perfect day.

When the four of them returned to the cottage over Labor Day weekend, they found the picture of them hung on the wall. Ms. Gibbs had it printed and framed because she said it reflected the exact essence of why they had purchased the cottage. They had hoped it could be a place for family and friends to find happiness, refuge, and relaxation. And that's exactly what it had done for Jolene.

It was then the four girls made the pact. They agreed to meet at the cottage anytime something big came up in their lives. No matter how busy they were, they would make their friendship a priority. Jolene carefully took the picture off the wall, studying it. She brushed her thumb across Becca's face, her chocolate brown eyes hidden by small oval framed sunglasses. Turning the frame over, her eyes swam with tears. The words written so many years ago remained on the back of the frame. Tears slid down her cheeks and she wiped them away as she read the words.

We, Becca Gibbs, Cristina Torres, Kendra Kingsley,
and Jolene Oliver solemnly swear that we will gather in

Tahoe City at the Gibbs's cottage each time something big occurs in our lives.

And below that, each of the girls' signatures.

Jolene's heart ached unforgivingly as the realization of the meaning of those words set in. Besides a few trips back to the cottage, nothing would become of the pact they made all those years ago. Soon after they signed their names on the back of that picture, the accident occurred. She sniffed and wiped her wet cheeks with the sleeves of her sweater. What had she been thinking, reading the words written on the back of that old picture?

THEN

With their beach towels laying on the dock, the four girls stretch out on top of them. Jolene shivers while she waits for the sun to dry her wet body and swimsuit. She presses her stomach against the towel, feeling the warmth on her body as it travels from the sun-kissed dock and penetrates her skin.

They'd just gone for a swim in the lake even though it's spring and the temperatures are still cool. Becca had insisted and none of them wanted to argue with her. As frigid as the water was, and as cold as the air is, Jolene doesn't regret it. Every single moment spent at the lake, at the Gibbs's cottage, in Tahoe City, is magical.

So even though Becca had pressured them to jump into the lake today on this chilly spring afternoon, Jolene would've done it willingly. She knew real life was knocking on their doors—adulthood looming and waiting for them in less than a year.

They needed to take advantage of these moments they had left together, to swim, and to laugh.

Mrs. Gibbs pads down the dock, her bedazzled flip-flops slapping against the worn wood. "Oh, girls," she calls, her voice shrill against the peaceful, spring day.

Jolene sits up, leaning back on her elbows and squinting behind her sunglasses.

"Girls, don't you look adorable out here in your bikinis soaking up the sun." She shakes her camera in the air. "Scooch together, will you? I wanna take a picture. I need to capture this moment."

Becca groans, pulling herself up.

Mrs. Gibbs shoves a balled fist onto a jutted hip. "C'mon, Becks, humor your mother, will you?"

"Fiiiiiine," Becca drawls out. "One picture."

The four girls scoot close together, throwing their arms around one another's shoulders and sitting cross-legged.

After Mrs. Gibbs gets her one picture that turns into three, Jolene relaxes back on her towel once again. She closes her eyes, reveling in the moment while the sun dries the beads of water off her skin. Kendra and Cristina are already deep into an argument over which band's latest album is better—Green Day or Snow Patrol. Jolene couldn't care less.

"Jo?" Kendra sits up, resting on her palms. "What do you think?"

She fought back an eye roll before prying them open. "Which cover looks better?"

Kendra sniffs. "Who cares. I'm asking which one has the best songs? The best lyrics?"

"The sexiest voice?" Cristina adds, waggling her brows.

Jolene sits up and exhales a sigh. Kendra and Cristina will not let this go until someone else weighs in. "I've barely paid attention to the lyrics. But I will say that I don't think another guy can quite pull off eyeliner the way Billie Joe Armstrong does."

"And we have a winner, folks." Cristina does a small fist pump.

"Fine. I don't think that's grounds for determining a good band, but whatever." Kendra lays back down, her stiffened shoulders noticeable.

Becca sits cross legged, peering out at the canoes rocking in the trembling water. The sun slips behind a crowd of puffy white clouds and the wind picks up, sweeping over Jolene's still damp swimsuit and causing goosebumps to pebble down her arms and legs. In an instant it feels ten degrees cooler, and she pushes herself up, hugging herself.

"It's getting cold. Should we go inside?"

"Not yet," Becca mutters, mindlessly. "Can we just sit here a few minutes longer?"

There's something like sadness conveyed in Becca's eyes and it sends an ache in her chest. She nods solemnly, glancing over her shoulder at Kendra and Cristina who are still bickering back and forth.

Jolene swallows the hesitation creeping up her throat. "Is it your parents again?"

Becca finally tears her attention away from the lake that seems to be mimicking her mood, dark blue peaks building. "They're arguing more often than not these days," her voice sounds small, and masked.

"What are they arguing about now?"

"Anything and everything. Or nothing at all."

Jolene bites the inside of her cheek, weighing her words.

"It's getting bad, Jo." Becca tucks her long legs in, and she hugs herself. "They're better when we're here...at the cottage. But even still, they're not good. They argue long after I've asked them to stop and even longer after I go to bed."

"I'm sorry," her apology sounds dull.

Becca was tough, she didn't let much get to her. But this thing with her parents, was eating at her and maybe even interfering with her swimming. She's got college scouts coming out next week. If she isn't performing like her reputation has promised, it will be bye-bye full ride scholarship to Cal State next year.

"I don't know why they can't just get their crap together. I'm not asking for much. Just one more year. Then they can do whatever the hell they want."

"When they split, can I have the cottage in the divorce?" Cristina gives Becca's leg a light push with her fist.

"Ha, ha." Becca mocks a laugh and sniffs.

"Do you really think they'll get divorced?" Jolene rubs warmth into her arms.

Becca shrugs. "I mean, I hope not. What would happen to me? And the cottage?"

"Remember when my parents got divorced two years ago? It's not so bad." Cristina pulls her dark hair into a high ponytail.

"Not helpful," Jolene mutters.

"I just don't get it, though." Kendra moves in closer to Becca, plopping down next to her on her towel. "If they're both so unhappy, why stay together?"

"Duh?" Cristina deadpans. "Why do most parents stay together when they're unhappy? The kids."

"But your mom, she's been having an affair, right? Or was it your dad?" Kendra bites her lower lip when Becca shoots her a glare.

"Your guess is as good as mine. And theirs. That's one of the many things they argue about. *Is it an affair if it's only emotional or does there have to be sex involved?* It's a question they ponder constantly." Becca pulls a red sweatshirt over her head.

"I think—yes. That's definitely an affair." Kendra moves behind Becca and fingers her damp hair, parting it and beginning to braid it.

"And grounds for divorce?" Cristina quirks a dark, thin brow at Kendra.

"I mean, if it were me, yeah. No question."

"I don't think it's that easy," Jolene says.

"I agree with, Jo. Divorce isn't cut and dry. It effects a lot of people. Nobody gets out unharmed."

Becca bunches her fists inside her sweatshirt, wiping her nose with the sleeve.

"Except for you," Jolene says, smirking at Cristina and silently hoping she'll lighten this heavy mood.

Cristina holds up a finger. "Truth. I mean, I got two bedrooms, two Christmas mornings. It is a pretty sweet deal."

Becca looks at her, a forced hopeful gleam in her brown eyes.

"Oh, I forgot the best part. No. More. Yelling."

"I wouldn't mind that." Becca exhales a sigh.

Seeing the hard exterior of Becca threaten to crumble is unsettling. While Cristina is definitely the tenacious one in their group, Becca is the adventurous one—doesn't back down from a challenge. It sends an aching pang in her chest seeing her friend's weakness. And since Jolene is the peacekeeper in their group, she feels the strong desire to help in some way. More than saying the sometimes unhelpful and empty words— *I'm sorry.*

"You know what the best remedy is to clear your head?" Jolene asks.

"Tailgating in the Sweet Shop's parking lot while getting smashed?" Cristina snorts a laugh.

"Swimming. It's your therapy."

"It's getting dark. And cold," Kendra warns.

"We can come back out tomorrow?"

Becca glances at the lake before landing her focus on Jolene. She grins wide, her porcelain skin pale against the darkened sky. "Jo is right. Swimming is my therapy. Looks like we're night swimming, girlies."

NOW

The coffee machine beeped, signaling the brewing had finished and brought Jolene back to the present. Her breathing was accelerated, and her palms were clammy with sweat. She focused on taking deep breaths and exhaling, worried a panic attack might come on suddenly. The idea of Becca drowning still didn't make sense. But she did like to take risks.

Dragging herself into the kitchen, she poured a cup of coffee. Bringing it up to her nose, she inhaled and closed her eyes, smelling the robust aroma of the Arabica coffee.

Mug in hand, she padded outside onto the deck. She found it too difficult to stay inside the cottage with all the pictures and memories of Becca floating around. The air was crisp, and it bit at her bare legs. The sun sat low just above the horizon, and it carried the promise of a warm day. Jolene traveled down the steps and sat on one of the Adirondack chairs around the fire pit that faced the lake.

The view looked more spectacular than she remembered, with clear aqua water at the shoreline and dark blue at the horizon where it was the deepest. Tall sugar pines surrounded the lakes edge. The modest beach area stretching in front of the homes on Lakeshore Drive appeared vacant. Just down a few hundred feet she spotted a man playing ball with his golden retriever. And even further, two women jogging on the rocky sand along the water's edge.

Her heart gave a tug. She should be out there running. That had always been one of her favorite things to do at the cottage. Her and Kendra had the perfect route mapped out here.

Jolene crossed her leg, an attempt to create some warmth and wrapped her hands around the mug. The heat radiated through her fingers. She raised the mug to her lips and took small sips of the steaming coffee.

Being at the Gibbs's cottage, sitting around the fire pit, gazing at the old dock stretching out over the water of Lake Tahoe, her mind sifted through the memories. Even though the temperature was cold, if Jacob were here, he'd be doing cannon balls off the end of the dock. It wouldn't matter what time of the day it was. And no doubt, Becca would be right at his side, toes curled over the edge of the dock, streamlining into the lake.

If Jolene and Travis hadn't wanted to swim, Becca would convince them, making them all stand together on the edge of the dock holding hands and counting down so they could jump in together. Jacob would say to her, "Babe, c'mon it's freezing. Is this countdown thing really necessary?" And she'd reply, "Absolutely."

When a memory of Bo from the night before came to her mind, she thought about how Jacob had felt about him. Jacob got along with everyone but when it came to her and Bo's relationship, she sensed jealousy. As if he felt Bo had been trying to take over his role in taking care of her. Jacob hadn't liked it when Bo had helped her perfect her lay-up. Plus, Jacob was more of a fan of Travis. She found herself wondering what Jacob would think of Travis now after the way he'd treated her, leaving her and the kids.

Jolene should've told Bo about her and Travis being separated. When they were kids, she told Bo everything. She could've easily mentioned it when the topic of Travis came up the night before. But the truth was, she felt like a failure. She didn't want Bo thinking less of her. He already knew about the dark cloud of Multiple Sclerosis looming over her.

And it wasn't as if the news of her separation would mean anything to him. It wasn't as if after all these years they could finally have a relationship. He hadn't mentioned anyone the night before, but she assumed there had to be a significant other in his life.

Even if Bo was single, and she doubted he was, someone that perfect was never single. But even if he was, he wouldn't want her anyway. Jolene heard how he talked about his own aunt who struggled with the very same disease. And the way he looked at her the night before, with pity. Those gorgeous green eyes pitied her.

Besides, they had already been down that road before. And she'd made a complete fool of herself in the process. Bo had made it clear he didn't have feelings for her in that way and didn't want to ruin their friendship. She gave a bitter laugh out loud. What friendship? They hadn't even had a friendship for almost twenty years. Besides, she would be gone in a week. Back home, with her kids, and the brewery, and her chaotic life.

"Hey, Jo?" someone called.

Jolene turned and watched as Kendra jogged toward her, her brown hair pulled up in a high ponytail and her bangs laying straight across her forehead. Beads of sweat gathered on her face and caused her smooth skin to glisten. The rising sun flickered against her brown eyes giving them a glassy effect.

Dressed in running clothes that showed off her perfect body, Jolene couldn't help but gawk at her friend. Kendra somehow looked even better now than she did two decades ago. The woman was drop dead gorgeous.

"You're up earlier than I expected." Kendra gave her a quick hug.

"Coffee was calling my name." Jolene shrugged. "But I wish you would've woken me. You know I would've loved to have joined you for a run."

"I figured you'd rather sleep." Kendra planted her butt on the arm of Jolene's Adirondack chair, reaching for her hand. She pulled it into both of hers and scanned her face. "How are you doing, Jo?"

The intimacy of their physical contact caused nervousness to thrum through Jolene and she had to fight the urge to recoil. Not only was she not a touchy-feely person, but it had been a long time since they'd been together.

"I'm ok. How about you? How are you holding up?" Jolene asked.

Kendra pouted, pondering the question. "I'm," she paused, hesitating, "I'm okay. Just okay, I guess. It was tough to get away. Work is crazy busy right now. There's a million deadlines and I have to review each picture, each article, and each ad, and then sign off on them."

"I can't imagine," Jolene said, turning her attention from Kendra and gazing out at the slow movement of the trivial waves.

"I've missed you." Kendra squeezed her hand.

Kendra's words resonated in her ears, and they were exactly what she wanted to hear, what she *needed* to hear. "I've missed you too." Jolene smiled, finding it unforced.

Satisfied, Kendra let go of her hand and stood to her feet. "That coffee smells wonderful. Any left?"

"Of course. I made a full pot. But I wasn't sure if you drank coffee anymore," Jolene answered.

A rush of sadness hit her after the words left her mouth. She didn't even know if her childhood friend drank coffee anymore. How could they have let so much time pass between their conversations or visits? Now she didn't even know Kendra's likes, dislikes, habits or interests?

"Absolutely. I could never give up my coffee. I justify that it's healthy for me by adding a few scoops of protein powder in it." Kendra gave her a mischievous smile. "Be right back," she called over her shoulder and jogged up the steps, slipping into the back door of the cottage.

Jolene took a gulp of her coffee and grimaced—it was luke-warm now. The rising sun reflected against the lake, causing it to shine. She sat in silence anticipating Kendra's return. It felt unnatural and a bit awkward to be here with her, especially without Becca.

If Becca were here, she'd be out in the water already. The weather or temperature of the water couldn't keep her out of it. Her and Jacob were alike in that way. Becca was an exceptional swimmer. She'd tell Jolene, "You enjoy your run, I'm going for a swim."

A few minutes later, Kendra returned with a coffee mug in one hand and a protein bar in the other. She sat in the Adiron-dack chair next to Jolene, resting the mug on the arm and opening the bar's wrapper with her teeth. The sweat had vanished from her face but a trace of it still trickled down her chest and dampening her sports bra.

She couldn't help but admire Kendra's body, who wouldn't? She had a round backside, large breasts, subtly defined abs, and tan skin that Jolene could only assume was the result of a spray on tan. Kendra was too worried about wrinkles and skin cancer to get a tan the natural way or to use an indoor tanning salon.

After Kendra's son, Quinn was born, she'd been worried

she wouldn't be able to lose the baby weight. But there was no sign she'd even had a baby. She was just blessed that way. As well as hated by mothers of newborns. And don't even get her started on those long legs of hers. Jolene had always been envious of Kendra's legs that went on forever while hers were short.

"This coffee is amazing." Kendra took a few sips, closing her eyes.

"Well, we have Ms. Gibbs to thank, I guess. I found it in the cupboard. Hey, did you see the note on the fridge?"

"I did. What a silly lady, huh?"

"That's a bit of an understatement."

"Was she always this eccentric or did we just not notice?" Kendra tore a big bite off her protein bar with her straight white teeth.

"I think we just didn't care."

Jolene laughed. And Kendra laughed too. It felt good to laugh with her.

"What do you think of the remodel?" Kendra asked with a full mouth of protein bar, gesturing her chin in the direction of the cottage.

"It looks great. The color scheme is perfect for a cottage at the lake. But, I will have to admit, I was a little shocked and sad." Jolene tipped back her mug and drank the last of her coffee. "Now my memories of this place seem tainted or something. I can't quite explain it." Tears pricked her eyes.

"No, I get it."

"When I saw that picture of us, near the front entryway, I lost it."

"Me too. Cristina and I noticed it almost immediately when we stepped inside the cottage last night." Kendra's vision shifted out to the lake for a moment before resting back on Jolene. "Did you read the back of it?"

She nodded. "I did."

"Yeah, us too," Kendra admitted. "Pretty wild to see it still there after all these years, huh?" But she didn't wait for an answer. "I mean, it's weird Ms. Gibbs kept it up there, even after the remodel. Or maybe she put it back up after Becca got sick. Who knows?"

Jolene wasn't ready to talk about Becca's time while she was sick. She stood. "I'm going to get a refill, you ready for more?"

Kendra glanced at her mug. "Sure, that'd be great, thanks."

When she returned with the refilled mugs of coffee, Cristina followed her out the door a few steps behind. She had an afghan draped over her shoulders and a mug of steaming coffee in her hand. Trudging down the steps in her bare feet, she slumped onto one of the Adirondack chairs.

"What up, hoochie-mamas?" Cristina greeted the other women in her all too familiar crassness and rawness.

Jolene laughed. One might be offended or appalled by the way Cristina spoke, especially at a time like this. But it comforted her, being in the presence of Cristina and knowing she hadn't changed. She still seemed as vulgar and loud mouthed as she used to be, not caring what anyone thought of her, and Jolene loved it.

"*Cristina*," Kendra shrieked, giving her arm a slight push.

"What?"

"You're so crass."

"Thank you."

"That was not a compliment," Kendra said flatly.

"Could've fooled me. Besides, I've cleaned up my vocabulary just for you two straight-laced hussies."

This bantering caused her body to warm and her heart to swell, it promised to be the perfect distraction for her. She listened to the two women continue, and sipped her coffee, unable to keep from smiling. Maybe this was what Becca wanted. The three of them here, together, talking and laughing. Just like old times.

Except not like old times—because Becca was missing.

CHAPTER EIGHT

"I t's too early," Cristina whined. "Why are we up so early?"

"Early?" Kendra asked, incredulous. "I've already gone on a three-mile run."

"Well pin a freaking rose on your little nose."

Kendra rolled her eyes. "And Jolene and I are already on our second cup of coffee."

"Explains the relentless chattering," Cristina snorted, then sipped her coffee. "Who made the coffee anyway?"

"I did," Jolene answered. "Why? Do you not like it?"

"It's okay, at least it doesn't taste like cat piss."

Spoken like a true compliment out of the mouth of Cristina.

"Ya know, Cris," Kendra began, "it wouldn't kill you to join me on a run this week."

Cristina narrowed her eyes at Kendra. "Yeah? Well, it wouldn't kill *you* to skip a run this week."

"I'm just saying, exercise is good for not only your body, but for your soul as well."

"And who says I don't exercise? And who says I don't have a good soul?"

"I'm sorry, just forget it." Kendra shook her head and relaxed into the chair.

"Running isn't the only exercise ya know? Remember what Becca used to say? Swimming is good for the soul."

The reminder of Becca's words was comforting and eerie at the same time.

"I remember. And she was right. Swimming is good for the soul. And great exercise."

Cristina, still narrowing her eyes at Kendra and obviously debating if she should let this go or if it was worth the fight, kept her lips pressed together. She exhaled a deep sigh. Then took a sip of her coffee.

"Alright, I'm up this early, better make it worth it. Jolene? Spill it." Cristina gestured her mug in Jolene's direction.

She felt as if someone ripped the air straight from her lungs. *Spill what?* Had she found out about her disease? Or somehow heard from someone, maybe her parents, about the separation. Jolene shifted in her seat, and she had to grip her mug to keep her hand from shaking.

"Spill what?"

"Everything."

"Everything?" Jolene tensed, her shoulders tightening.

"Don't play innocent with us. C'mon we want to hear all the juicy details about last night. What were you and Bo Dean *really* doing together?" Cristina narrowed her eyes.

Relief flooded her. Jolene knew she had to tell them, and she'd planned on telling them—everything. She didn't want them hearing through the Reno or mom grapevine. But she wasn't quite ready to see their looks of pity and hear all their questions.

"Oh, that."

"Yes, that," Cristina answered, incredulous.

"It was no big deal. I got into town early and I hadn't eaten all day, so I stopped for dinner and a beer at Anders Bar and Grill. Bo showed up and we ate and caught up." Jolene tucked a strand of hair behind her ear before staring into her empty coffee mug.

"That's it? What got you to the point of him driving you back here? You two looked pretty cozy when you strolled on in." Cristina waggled her eyebrows, her lips curved up at the corners.

"I couldn't drive. I had too much to drink. Normally my limit is two, but..." she hesitated. "But I needed an extra push to get me down Manson Blvd."

"Man, Bo Dean." Cristina shook her head. "He sure grew up and filled out in all the right places. What I wouldn't give to get him alone," she said, wistfully.

"Cristina," Kendra shrieked. "You're a married woman for goodness' sake."

"Yeah, I'm married. I'm not dead." Cristina chuckled. "How some woman hasn't snatched him up yet is beyond me."

Jolene's mouth fell open in shock. "He never got married?" How could God's gift to women not be married?

"Nope. Says he's married to the job. Lame excuse if you ask me. I think he just enjoys playing the field. He probably gets laid more than all three of us married women put together." Cristina tipped her mug back and gulped down the rest of her coffee.

"Oh, Cristina, c'mon. Do we really have to talk about Bo Dean's love life?" Kendra asked.

"Why not? Would you rather talk about your sex life?"

"Just stop," Kendra muttered and flicked her gaze away.

"What happened to you? You used to be so much fun. That L.A. or model lifestyle turned you into a boring prude."

"I'm not a model, not anymore. And I'm not a prude. I guess I just don't have an interest in this conversation."

Kendra placed her mug of coffee onto the edge of the stone fire pit. Then she scooted her butt into the crevice of the chair, resting her head back and closing her eyes. Kendra looked like she might cry. Not being a model anymore was a touchy subject for her. That had been the topic of one of the last conversations the two of them had on the phone.

Kendra felt old and washed up. *The industry wants young and perky models. What will they want with me? All I'm going to be good for now is ads for hemorrhoid cream and Depends,* she'd said. Jolene found this to be absurd. Kendra had only been thirty-six at the time.

Although, at that point in Jolene's life, she had felt old as well. She'd just been diagnosed with MS and been abandoned by her husband. The things she didn't want to bother Kendra with when she was obviously dealing with her own problems.

Sensing the tension, Cristina shrugged her shoulders and muttered, "Whatever."

"So, how is Philip? It's been what, eight years of marriage now? And the girls, how are they?" She attempted to change the subject, not wanting to witness one of Cristina and Kendra's heated discussions that got to the point of them saying hurtful things to one another.

"Yep, eight years. And the girls are great. Montana is fifteen and Dakota is seven already." She leaned her head back against the chair. "Man, we're pretty lucky to have Phillip. I still say, he's the best thing to ever happen to me. How the two of us ended up together after all those years being friends and working at the same school still baffles me." She gave a slight shake of her head. "And how is he in bed, you ask?" Cristina raised her dark brows and shot Kendra a sly look—obviously an attempt to get a rise out of her. "Well, he's extraordinary and attentive. And not afraid to go downtown, if you know what I mean?"

Kendra rolled her eyes but couldn't resist snorting a laugh. "We didn't ask."

"Oh, c'mon, you know you love me, Kendra." Standing with her blanket, Cristina embraced Kendra, wrapping herself and the blanket around her. Then she plopped herself on top of Kendra's lap.

"Geez, Cristina," Kendra wailed and tensed her body as she endured the weight of her friend. "You're crushing me!"

"You missed me, admit it. Your life has been dull without me," Cristina said in singsong. She pressed her body against Kendra and grinned. "I missed you too."

Cristina rose to her feet and sauntered back over to her chair. At an average height, she had a small middle, wider hips, an ample chest, and a round backside. Her long, thick dark brown hair with burgundy streaks running through it was pulled into a messy bun a top her head. Cristina's round face with olive skin featured a small straight nose and green eyes that were edged with a thin line of brown around them.

"Of course I've missed you," Kendra finally admitted. "But you know what I haven't missed? How you're still habitually late." She turned, directing her attention to Jolene. "Do you know that she was twenty minutes late picking me up from the airport last night?"

Cristina rolled her eyes. "I said I was sorry. And ya know, miss-high-and-mighty, you're not the only person who is busy and has responsibilities. We all had to adjust our schedules to be here this week."

"I never implied that you weren't busy, Cris. Don't be so dramatic." She waved her off.

"Dramatic? Ha." She exhaled a mirthless laugh. "Who's the one making a big deal about twenty measly minutes?" Cristina glanced at her coffee mug in hand. "And you say I haven't changed? It's comforting to know you haven't changed either."

Gazing out at the slow-moving water of the lake, the three girls sat in silence. Jolene hoped the entire week wouldn't be full of tense and awkward moments. If Becca were here, she'd tell them both to get over themselves. She was bossy enough, they usually listened to her.

"So," Cristina said, breaking through the silence. "What's on everyone's agenda for the day?"

"I need to head into town to pick up a few copies of POSE. July's issue went into print today. I've looked at it online but I'm anxious to get a physical copy of it in my hands," Kendra said.

"Me too," Jolene agreed. "I never miss an issue. I have every single one."

"Aww thanks, Jo, that's so supportive of you." Kendra smiled.

"Well, I'm just so proud of you." Because in all honesty, she was. The magazine wasn't number one priority for her, but it was for Kendra. And that meant it was important to her too.

"I did a small photo shoot and an interview in this issue." Kendra raked her fingers through her straight bangs. "This one's extra special, it marks one year since my first issue. My editor thought it would be a good idea to feature a story about me and my family."

"Whoa, it's been a year already? That went fast. Congratulations," Jolene said.

"That's really great. Proud of you." Cristina gave her an assuring nod.

"Thanks, girls. We're so pleased with what we've accomplished in such a short time. But we have a long way to go."

"Well, I have no doubt that you'll get there. You're a determined and successful woman, always have been," Jolene said. She'd always admired her friend's determination.

"Now I guess I better go buy one just to see how sexy you look. And what about Devin? Did he take the photos? Are there any of you two together? Because I gotta see that. Damn, your hubby is one hot piece of ass," Cristina said.

To her surprise, Kendra laughed. "Yes of course he took the photos. He's only the best photographer on the west coast. And yes, there happens to be one photo of the three of us. Me, Devin, and Quinn."

"That settles it, I'm definitely buying one." Cristina winked. "What about you Jolene? Anything planned for today?"

Jolene bit her lower lip. She needed to get her car but that meant texting Bo and seeing him again today, and she wasn't positive she wanted to. But she didn't have much of a choice.

"Well, since Bo had to drive me here last night, my car is still sitting in the parking lot at Anders Bar and Grill. He told me to text him when I was ready and he would take me to pick up my car," She paused. She was surprised she didn't hear a peep out of Cristina. "Then I'd like to check out Buffy's Book Cafe before stopping at Mel's Grocers. I thought I'd get some things to make us dinner tonight. Is that okay with everyone?"

"Buffy's Book Café?" Kendra asked, shifting in the chair.

She frowned. "Yeah, why?"

Cristina shrugged. "Sounds fine to me. And if I don't have to cook, then I won't. To be honest, I was looking forward to getting a break from cooking for those ungrateful kids. Dakota won't eat any rice or beans anymore and Montana has suddenly gone vegan. Do you know how hard it is to cook for those two when they change their likes and dislikes as often as I change my underwear?"

"Kids." Jolene shook her head. She could relate, her two had always been picky eaters.

"Well that sounds wonderful, Jo. But I do have a few diet restrictions if you don't mind," Kendra said.

"Don't you worry. I was thinking, gluten free pasta in a pesto sauce, a strawberry spinach vinaigrette salad and sautéed asparagus. Sound good?"

"Sounds Perfect."

"Yep, sounds good to me too. I'll replenish my missed calories from your healthy meal with a couple beers." Cristina smirked.

Kendra rolled her eyes. "Cristina."

With the plan to meet up at Buffy's Book Café later, Jolene borrowed a phone charger from Cristina and hurried to get herself ready for the day. She dressed in a pair of shorts, a tank top, and a long-sleeved denim button down shirt. The buttons gave her fingers difficulty, and she silently cursed them, ultimately deciding to leave them undone. She hated that the simplest of tasks took so much time and energy now.

Fatigue set in and all she wanted to do was lay down. Her arms and legs felt heavy, as if she was dragging around bricks. If she rested for a bit, she hoped she'd be as good as new. She laid down on the sofa, propped her head on one of the throw pillows and closed her eyes.

THE SOUND of a phone ringing sent Jolene jolting upright. She hurried to her phone being charged on the kitchen counter. Her legs didn't move as fast as she would've liked, but there wasn't anything new with that. When she reached it, she didn't have time to read the contact info before answering.

"Hello?"

"Jolene? Oh, thank God. I've tried calling you half a dozen times. Are you okay?" Travis sounded frantic.

"Huh? Yeah, I'm fine." She rubbed her eyes and cleared her throat. "I was only going to rest my eyes for just a minute. I must've fallen asleep. Sorry."

"The kids have been worried. You told Julia you would text her when you made it there last night. Joy said she fell asleep with her phone in her hand."

"Poor girl." The mom guilt caused her muscles to tense across her shoulders in tight knots. "By the time I made it to the cottage my phone was dead, and I couldn't find my charger. I borrowed one from Cristina." It felt as if she was in a fog. She rubbed at her eyes trying to bring herself out of it. "I'm sorry she interrupted your trip."

"It's fine. Just call her, please."

"I will right now." She disconnected and as she pulled up her daughter's contact info, wondered why Joy hadn't called her.

"Mom?" Julia answered.

"Hey, baby."

"Mom? You said you would text last night. I was worried. Are you okay?"

"I'm okay. And I'm so sorry I worried you. My phone died and I was so tired by the time I arrived at the cottage last night, I crashed. I'm here though, safe and sound." She attempted to assure her daughter by making her voice light.

"I'm sorry I told Dad."

"What do you mean?"

"I'm sorry I got him involved. I know you guys don't really want to talk anymore. But I was worried when I didn't hear from you."

"Oh, baby, don't be sorry. It's okay. I'm glad you told him. If something had been wrong, he's the first person who would come to my rescue," Jolene said, trying to convince herself this was true. "And remember, you can always tell Joy. She'd be second in line."

"Right, I know. Okay, I'm glad you're okay. I'll let you get back to your friends now," Julia said.

"Thanks, Jules. And thanks for worrying about your mom. You're such a sweet girl, how did I get so lucky?"

"Please don't do that again. Please make sure your phone is charged. Next time I might make Dad come home early from his trip and drive us all the way there just to make sure you're okay."

"I promise, my phone will remain charged at all times." She put up a palm as if she were pledging. "I love you. And tell your brother I love him too. I'll see you in a week."

"Okay, bye, Mom. Love you too," Julia said before disconnecting.

Jolene pressed her phone to her chest and shook her head, thinking about what her daughter said about making Travis come there. He sounded annoyed, his voice grated and clipped just by having to call her. As if he would end his mysterious trip to Palm Springs early and come all the way there to check on her, his estranged wife and by the sharp tone of his voice, the last person he wanted to speak to.

CHAPTER NINE

When Bo's truck pulled in front of the cottage, Jolene stepped out onto the porch and held up a finger, insisting he stay put. It wasn't as if this was a date and he needed to pick her up at the door, that would be weird. Wouldn't it? She locked the door behind her with one of the extra keys provided by Ms. Gibbs. before gripping the wood railing for support and descending the stone steps.

When she climbed inside the passenger side of the blue Chevy pick-up, she glanced at Bo and smiled. Her heart beat double time. She reminded herself there was nothing to be anxious about—this was Bo, she had known him practically forever. But then why did she feel so nervous? Sweat formed on her temples and she swept it away with her fingertips.

"Morning." Bo smiled wide, flashing his pearly whites.

And oh, that smile, those eyes. She was clearly in trouble. "Morning."

Jolene peered up at the cottage as Bo pulled away. It looked even prettier in the daylight. Arched white wood framed the windows with turquoise painted shutters and grey shingles. A white wooden balcony ran across the second floor with huge, squared columns. The flagstone steps led up to a wooden porch and a turquoise painted door.

"So, are you in a hurry to get back to the girls?" Bo asked.

"Not really." She shrugged. "They're off doing other things. We're going to try to meet up for coffee later at Buffy's Book Café. I just need to get some groceries. I promised I'd make the girls dinner tonight."

"Buffy's Book Café?"

She glanced in his direction. "You know it?"

"Uh...yeah. Of course." He scratched at his chin. "Great little place."

"Why? What did you have in mind?"

"I had an idea. I thought we could go to the Tahoe City Sweet Shop and grab some ice cream. For old times-sake?" Bo hunched a shoulder.

"It's not even eleven in the morning. And you're ready for ice cream?"

"I could eat ice cream any time of the day."

"Okay, now there are quite a few ways you've changed since we were kids, but that is apparently not one of them. You still can eat ice cream any time of the day." Jolene laughed.

"So, I'll take that as a yes?" He raised a brow.

"Sure, why not?" *Ms. People Pleaser at your service.*

Bo proceeded down Lakeshore Drive. He was dressed in khaki cargo shorts and a polo short-sleeve shirt. Jolene noticed the tightness at the bottom of his sleeves caused by the bulges of his biceps. She swiped her palm across the back of her neck. Cristina was right, his body filled out in all the right places.

"How are you feeling today?" Bo fiddled with the radio buttons.

"Huh? Uh...ah, okay." She darted her vision back out the

windshield. "I had a headache earlier. But the Tylenol helped, thanks."

"You're welcome. Thought it might. And the girls, how are they?"

"They're fine. Kendra is about the same and well, you know Cristina." She exhaled a mirthless laugh. "She never changes."

Bo laughed too. "Yep, sounds about right."

"You said you ran into Cristina at the funeral?" She looked over at him, but his eyes stayed on the road. He had one hand on the steering wheel, the other rested in his lap with his elbow on the console. He turned the truck onto Manson Blvd.

"I did."

"And...how did she seem?"

"She seemed as you would expect her to. I suppose not her, but how anyone would be at a funeral. She wasn't her normal self. She was more reserved. Didn't cause a scene or anything. Why?"

"I was just curious." She pushed her fingers through her hair. "I felt awful I couldn't make it to the funeral. I would've liked to at least pay my respects to Becca's parents and Trisha. And Becca's daughter. But I just couldn't swing it. Not with having to come this week."

Bo cleared his throat. "I'm sure they understood."

"I suppose."

Jolene glanced out the window. The landmarks coming into view meant the dreadful S-curve in the road was drawing near. Her body went rigid. Jolene couldn't have a breakdown like she'd had the night before when she rode this route. She couldn't do that every time. She'd be making this drive nearly fifty times over the course of the week.

Closing her eyes, she tried to think of the breathing technique she'd learned in yoga class. After her diagnosis, her neurologist, Dr. Whalen recommended she start taking yoga.

Jolene had to admit, she did benefit from the classes. Not only did it make her body feel better, but the breathing exercises helped with her anxieties as well.

She'd also made a few connections at the yoga studio as well. It felt good to have acquaintances that were outside the circle of her and Travis's married friends. She found it difficult to maintain a relationship with those friends anymore. They were too connected with Travis and she didn't expect them to choose sides.

She also made some new acquaintances in the Multiple Sclerosis support group she had joined, again, after much persuasion by Dr. Whalen. There were eight people in total. The leader of the group, Jim, suffered from MS himself.

The other six people in the support group ranged in age and symptoms. The youngest in the group was twenty-year-old Savannah. Her diagnosis was new and raw like Jolene's. But Savannah's symptoms started in her eyes, unlike Jolene's symptoms, which seemed to be all over the place. That had made it more difficult for the doctors to diagnose. Jolene had five MRI's on her brain and two on her spine. It wasn't until Dr. Whalen performed a spinal tap on her when he'd finally confirmed the diagnosis.

Once Bo's truck passed the dreadful S-curve in the road, she let herself relax. The air from the open window blew in causing her hair to whip around and while she dreaded having to rake through tangles later, she welcomed it. The dry air carried the scent of dirt and trees, reminding her of home.

They passed Mel's Grocers and she shuddered. She wasn't sure how she'd muster up the courage to go there today. But she didn't have a choice. She needed to pick up supplies for tonight's dinner and the only other grocery store was several miles away on the south side of the lake.

"Here we are." Bo pulled the truck into an open parking spot in front of the Tahoe City Sweet Shop.

Jolene gazed out the windshield, her jaw dropping at the sight of it. Seeing this place rattled her. It transported her to a time when she wore sneakers splattered with sticky ice cream and wore her bleach blonde hair high atop her head in a ponytail. A time before the accident—before everything changed, leaving a dark stain on all the good things in her life.

"Ready?" Bo asked.

"Sure." She bit her lower lip.

Bo rested his hand on the small of her back, ushering her inside. His touch sent a shiver coursing through her. Partly because it was Bo, touching her. The other part was, the familiarity of a man's hand on the small of her back reminded her of Travis.

Inside, the breath caught in her throat. The long-ago familiar scent of fresh waffle cones filled the air. Not only did it smell the same, but it looked exactly the same as it did twenty years ago. Not a single thing was out of place. Black and white checkered tile floor, pink walls scattered with old Coca-Cola signs, chrome chairs with red and turquoise vinyl cushions, chrome legged tables with Formica tops and an old ice cream case.

"What do you think?" Bo asked.

She tried to swallow the lump caught in her throat. *What did she think?* She wasn't sure. The familiarity was comforting but at the same time, maybe she'd clung to hope it had completely changed so she didn't have to face the old memories of their carefree days—where the innocence of adolescence still existed.

"I...uh..." she stuttered. "I'm a little surprised. Everything looks the same."

"I know. A little unreal isn't it?"

"Unreal," she echoed. Yes, that's the word she was thinking. *Unreal.*

She paced in front of the ice cream case running her fingers along the cool glass as she read the names and descriptions of the flavors in her head.

"What are you gonna get?" Bo asked.

She continued to pace and at the same time, attempted to shake the memories from her mind. "I'm not sure yet. Everything looks so good."

The chocolate fudge brownie, chocolate chip cookie dough, and rocky road all tempted her. Sometimes she hated being on a strict diet. She had to miss out on luxuries like ice cream. But if she indulged, she could end up causing an unwanted flare up. And she wasn't willing to take that risk. She came to Tahoe City for a reason, and she had every intention to see it through.

"Hi, Mr. Dean," a young girl called from behind the ice cream case. She eyed Jolene skeptically.

Bo cleared his throat. "Hello, Abbie."

The girl's pale face was sprinkled with freckles and her auburn hair was pulled into a ponytail. She wore a red polo shirt with a name tag attached. Her eyes shifted back and forth between Bo and Jolene as she smacked the gum in her mouth.

"My friend here hasn't had the Sweet Shop's chocolate chip cookie dough in almost twenty years, so you better make it a double." He grinned.

Jolene's ears snagged on the way he'd emphasized, *friend.*

"Actually," she paused. "I'll take a scoop of the raspberry sorbet in a dish please," Jolene said to the girl.

"Oh, c'mon. Seriously?" His brows arched.

"What?"

"One scoop? Of sorbet, in a dish? That's it?"

"That's it."

"What happened to the double scoop of chocolate chip cookie dough in a waffle cone?"

"What can I say? I'm in the mood for sorbet." Jolene shrugged at the young girl who just stood there smacking her gum and blowing bubbles.

"Okay, fine. *I'll* have the double scoop of chocolate chip cookie dough in a waffle cone please, Abbie," Bo said.

The gum smacking and bubble blowing routine continued while Abbie scooped their orders from behind the case. She handed them their treats and pushed her gum over to one side of her mouth. "That will be $9.50, Mr. Dean."

"Here, let me." Jolene pulled her wallet from her purse.

"No, no, I got it." Bo stepped in front of her, shoving her out of arms reach of the girl.

"No, *I* got it," Jolene said sternly. She pushed Bo with her elbow, stretching her arm and placing a ten-dollar bill on top of the case. "Remember, it's my turn to treat."

It was obvious Abbie was not amused by the no-let-me-pay game. She hesitated in picking up the cash, eyeing them both. She blew a large pink bubble, letting it pop on her nose before sucking it back in her mouth and beginning the routine all over again. After glancing from Bo to Jolene then down at the cash, Abbie reluctantly picked it up.

They found an empty table by a window. The sun shining in created warmth but thankfully the air conditioning roaring in the shop was assurance she wouldn't overheat which eased her anxieties. The last thing she needed was a flare up while in Tahoe City.

"Miss Abbie a friend of yours?" she teased.

They sat across from one another, both leaning on the Formica tabletop and hovering over their treats. Jolene scooped a big bite of raspberry sorbet. It felt cool in her mouth and tasted tangy on her tongue.

"You know Tahoe City? Small town and all." He licked his ice cream cone. "I really wish you would've let me pay."

"Well, I had to return the favor from last night. Even though ten bucks is nothing compared to how much last night's bill was. I still feel like I owe you."

"Please don't. I told you, that was my treat. It was no big deal. I was happy to do it."

"I can see you're not used to having a woman pay for you," she teased again.

"No, I suppose I'm not," Bo said, before taking a big bite of ice cream.

"Does that mean it's safe to say there's no Mrs. Dean who pays for things for you?" Cristina had already told her this, but she needed Bo to confirm it.

"No, no Mrs. Dean." Bo shifted in the vinyl seat.

"I have to say," Jolene began. "I'm surprised."

"You're surprised? Surprised I'm not married?" His light brows arched.

She nodded.

"Why?"

Because any woman would be thanking her lucky stars if she had the chance to marry this hottie, is what she wanted to say. But out loud, she only said, "I don't know, I guess I just assumed." Feeling her cheeks warm, she studied her sorbet, scooping it and causing it to ripple on the spoon. "You were always a good catch."

Bo coughed out a laugh. "Right, a good catch, huh? Except I wasn't ever good enough for you."

Jolene gasped in mock horror. "What are you talking about? If I remember correctly, it was *me* who wasn't good enough for *you*." She pointed at him with her plastic spoon. "Not the other way around."

"I don't think so. You must be mistaken." Bo lifted his

brows and their vision clicked. His green eyes darkened, and her body went hot in an instant—like a switch had been flipped.

She brushed her fingertips against the back of her neck. "No, I don't think I am. Have you forgotten about that night we closed the Sweet Shop late and the conversation we had?"

Bo lowered his head. "I remember."

"See, told you. I'm right and you're wrong."

He shook his head, his lips curving into a delicious smirk. "Man, you still love to be right."

"Me?" shock in her voice. "You were the one who always needed to be right."

"Okay, okay," Bo chuckled. "How about we agree we both liked to be right."

"Fine." She ate another bite of her sorbet. She was the people pleaser; how could she be the one who always needed to be right? And yet maybe she hadn't always been that way.

Bo cleared his throat, barely lifting his eyes from his ice cream. "You know, I never did forgive myself for turning down your offer that night. Three weeks later Bren and I had broken up and you had already got together with the lumberjack."

"Ahh, that's right." Her face heated.

Why was he telling her this? The past was the past. And she really didn't want to talk about Travis. She debated if she should tell Bo about the separation. But was it really relevant? What did it matter if she and Travis were separated? *There's no reason to tell him*, the negative thoughts began. *It's not like Bo is going to want you when he finds out you may be available. Travis didn't want you, why would Bo?* The thoughts sifted through her brain, the air-conditioner whirling, and she found it difficult to concentrate on their conversation.

A tall man with an aging face and a full head of graying

hair approached their table. "Hey, Bo," he said in a somber voice.

Bo jumped to his feet and extended his hand out to the man. "John, good to see you."

The man, John, seemed taken aback. He hesitated before shaking Bo's hand. "It's great to see you. How are you doing? You still off work?"

"I am. But I'll be back tomorrow." Bo adjusted the collar of his shirt. "John, this is Jolene McCabe, an old friend of mine." He presented an open hand toward her.

"Hi, nice to meet you."

"And you." John nodded, shaking her hand. He slid Bo an uneasy look that wasn't hard to miss. "Well, I saw you in the window and thought I'd come in and see how you're doing. And Mary," John paused and said to her, "My wife," then directed his attention back to Bo, "she feels just terrible. Please let us know if you need anything, will you?"

"Oh," Bo said. "Well, isn't that kind of Mary. Be sure to tell her thank you for me. Hey, John? Let me walk you out." Bo placed his hand on John's upper back. "I'll be right back, Jo."

"It was nice to meet you, Jolene. Hope you enjoy Tahoe City." John waved to her.

"I will, thank you." She watched as Bo hurriedly ushered John out of the Sweet Shop.

They stood out front and she watched their interaction. Bo fidgeted with his ice cream cone which appeared awkward in his hand for what came across as a serious conversation. The two men only exchanged a few sentences before shaking hands. John placed his other hand on Bo's forearm and gave it a squeeze before the two parted ways.

When Bo returned, her gaze darted to her sorbet. Watching the conversation between the two men had made her feel uncomfortable, like she'd just witnessed something extremely personal.

"Everything okay?" she asked.

"Yep, everything is fine."

"What was that all about?"

"Nothing."

"Didn't look like nothing." She paused for a beat. "Looked too serious to be nothing," she pressed.

Bo set his lips in a firm line and studied her before responding. "Okay, you're right. It wasn't nothing. But, it" police business and I'm not at liberty to discuss it."

Jolene had never heard that tone in his voice before and she was taken aback. Although she supposed she hadn't spoken to him for so many years maybe this was a "cop" tone he had picked up. Either way, she didn't care for it.

"Sorry," Bo apologized, his voice now back to his normal husky tone. "John is a retired policeman. I was fortunate enough to work under him for two years before he retired. He's a great guy, was an even better cop. He's always poking around at the station. Drives the rest of us guys crazy. But he has a big heart."

Bo's explanation seemed acceptable enough and she didn't feel right prying any further. Just because they were close when they were teenagers, didn't mean they were close now. She wiped her mouth with a napkin before crumpling it and placing it in her empty ice cream cup, pushing it aside.

Back inside Bo's truck, he asked, "So, where to next?"

"I guess my car. I think I'll skip the bookstore today. There's always tomorrow. I need to get groceries for tonight's dinner and get back to the cottage. And I don't really feel up for coffee anymore." She raked her fingers through her hair and her arm felt heavy.

"You okay?"

"I'm fine," she lied.

She wasn't fine. Part of her was annoyed Bo's tone and body language had shifted so drastically toward her, and part of her felt sad the two of them had allowed so much time and separation to ruin the close friendship they once had.

"Okay, to your car then, I guess." Bo gave her an unconvincing smile.

As he drove his truck down Manson Blvd, Jolene's vision moved over him, trying to be non-conspicuous as she studied him beneath her sunglasses. His demeanor had changed from when he first picked her up from the cottage. His lips now set in a hard line and his eyes glazed over. He watched the road and didn't glance in her direction, not even when she turned the volume up on the radio. They didn't speak the rest of the way to Anders Bar and Grill where her SUV waited for her.

When they arrived in the parking lot, Bo pulled into the empty spot next to her SUV.

"Looks like it's still in one piece," Bo said, finally breaking the silence.

"Yep, looks that way." She chewed on her bottom lip. "Well, thanks again for the ride. Both, to the cottage last night and again today."

"Don't mention it." Bo smiled his normal, melt-your-heart kind of a smile.

Her knees went weak like she was that lovestruck teenage girl again. "Okay, well maybe I'll see you around this week."

"I'd like that. And hey, I'm sorry about earlier. If I was acting strange. You know, sometimes this job gets in my head. It can be tough to not always be in cop mode."

Jolene nodded. She knew nothing about being a cop. All she knew was when she was younger, she'd gone around vowing she'd never marry anyone in uniform. Those were dangerous jobs. The thought of losing a spouse that way felt unfathomable.

She turned to leave, her hand hovering over the door handle while she debated telling Bo about her separation with Travis. It's not like she owed him anything. She wasn't obligated to tell him. And yet, being back in his presence once again caused all the comfort and familiarity to return.

"There's something I've been meaning to tell you," Jolene said, then bit her lower lip, twirling her hoop earring around her finger.

Bo raised a brow.

"Here's the thing." She turned her body toward him, propping a knee on the seat. "My husband, the flannel wearing lumberjack, and I...are separated."

"Really?" Now he arched both brows.

"Really. It's been a year. Well, just over a year now."

"Wow, a year. And I was such an ass last night." He scrubbed a hand over his face. "I'm so sorry, Ollie."

Zing, that bolt of lightning shot through her again at the sound of her nickname escaping his lips. His nickname for her. The only person to speak it.

"Since my diagnosis."

"What? Wait a minute. Since you're diagnosis?" He narrowed his eyes. "What happened?"

"I guess he couldn't deal with it, with me," her voice trailed off and she glanced away, gazing out the windshield.

"You're telling me, that he left you after you were diagnosed? *Because* of your diagnosis?" anger stirred in his voice.

Jolene's throat thickened and she nodded.

"Bastard!"

"It's okay," she said with a dismissive wave of her hand. "I mean, it's not okay but it will be. Or, I will be. I'm getting there," she stammered. "Travis is not a bad guy. I don't blame him."

"He left you instead of dealing with this thing together. Supporting you. And you're defending him?" He shook his head and stabbed his fingers through his hair.

"I don't need him," she bit out. "I don't need anyone to take care of me. I'm doing just fine taking care of myself."

Okay, so that wasn't entirely true. In the past year, she'd relied heavily on both Joy and her kids.

Resting his hand on her raised knee, he gave her a look of sympathy. If it wasn't for the distraction of the warmth traveling from his hand throughout her body, the look he was giving her would send her retreating from the truck. The sorrow in other's eyes and their comments of pity were tiresome and the last person she wanted to receive them from, was Bo.

"Look, I just thought I should tell you. That's it. Please, don't look at me like that."

"Like what?"

"Like that." She raised a palm gesturing at his face. "I don't need your pity."

"Jolene, c'mon. You know me better than that."

"Do I?"

"I don't pity you. You're one of the strongest people I know. But do I feel bad that you've been dealt a crapshoot hand? Yes, absolutely."

"But I don't need you feeling bad for me. I don't need your sympathy," she choked out the words, her throat growing tight with tears. She turned in one swift motion, opening the passenger door and climbing out of the truck.

"That's not fair." Bo jumped out of the driver's seat, coming around to meet her on the other side of the truck. He grabbed her by the wrist as she tried to walk away. "Fine, you win," he said, pulling her in front of him. "No pity, no sympathy."

Tears burned and threatened to spill. She searched his face. It revealed kindness and worry. To her surprise, she couldn't find pity in his eyes any longer.

"You got this. I've watched you overcome obstacles in your life before. Like when you lost Jacob. I have no doubt you'll do it again. You'll get through this."

The sun sat high in the sky now, the rays beaming down on her without forgiveness. She felt the heat of it and realized it was no longer being caused by her temper. Her breathing was quick and shallow. She swept her unruly bangs out of her face with her free hand.

"I don't need your pep talks either," she said incredulous. But deep down, she appreciated his words. They came across as genuine. The bond they formed years ago caused her to know when his words were sincere.

"Fine. I'll back off." He dropped his head in defeat and released her wrist.

She placed her hand on the wrist he'd been holding and rubbed it, even though he hadn't held it tight enough to cause any pain. Fighting back the tears, she bit her lower lip.

When he raised his head, their eyes met. The corners of his mouth curved into a smile and there was a glint in his eyes. The look confused her, and her brows drew together as she took a step back.

Bo adjusted the collar of his shirt. "Sooooooo," he dragged out the word, his voice sounding light and boyish now. "Ollie is a single woman." He waggled his brows at her.

She blinked at him, stunned. Tears slipped out of her eyes and she wiped them away. "What?" She exhaled a light laugh.

"You're single. And I'm single," he said, stretching out the words conspiratorially like. "Could it really be possible? You and I—single at the same time?" The corners of his lips curled up and the sun shimmered against his green eyes.

Jolene's smile matched his and the anxiety stirred in her belly. It nipped at the edges of her toes and the asphalt of the parking lot felt like quicksand beneath her feet.

CHAPTER TEN

The scent of garlic sautéing with olive oil in the pan rippled through the air in the kitchen. Cristina sat atop a barstool at the kitchen island drinking a glass of Sauvignon blanc. Jolene typically didn't care much for wine, but when Cristina and Kendra had come back to the cottage with the bottle insisting this was their contribution to dinner, she felt obligated to have a glass. She also caught sight of the receipt Kendra left on the counter and it had been expensive.

"We were bummed you weren't able to join us at Buffy's Book Cafe today," Cristina said to Jolene, after taking a sip of her wine.

Once the water began boiling, she carefully placed the gluten free noodles into the stainless-steel pot.

"Me too. I was really looking forward to going."

"You'll have to go," Kendra said as she entered the kitchen.

She was not surprised to discover Kendra was completely put together. She had on a bright yellow knee length dress, and even though Cristina and Jolene were barefoot in the cottage, Kendra had on a pair of nude pumps.

"Books everywhere. New, old, I mean ancient, Jo. Really up your alley. You'll love it. Though knowing you, you'll probably want to help organize the place. There are stacks of books everywhere." Kendra poured herself a glass of the Sauvignon blanc. "I still can't believe that place has a printer and a fax machine. This town may have that, 'lake charm,' she made air quotes with her fingers, "but c'mon, they need to get out of the dark ages. It seriously blows my mind."

After Kendra's rant, Jolene shot a look at Cristina. She raised her brows—a pause before the perverse joke about to take place. Cristina's head bent back, and she let out a cackle and murmured under her breath, "Blows."

Kendra smacked Cristina's shoulder.

Cristina let out a cough laugh, bringing her fist up to her mouth. She cleared her throat before saying, "Sorry." Followed by, "You guys really have no sense of humor anymore. I mean, I spent the majority of the day with this one over here," she gestured at Kendra. "And she walked around like she had a stick up her butt."

"I did not," Kendra's voice went up an octave.

"She's so serious. And I had to hear her complain about how unhappy she was with the magazine. All day long it was, *oh, can you believe the angle they used? It makes me look bloated. And, they didn't even airbrush my crows-feet in the picture with Quinn, now of course it looks like I'm old enough to be the mother of a sixteen-year-old. And, my teeth are showing, I specifically told them not to publish any with my teeth showing. I didn't sign off on that picture. Oh,* and my favorite one, *no one at that stupid magazine can do anything right.*" Her imitation of Kendra so spot on it was a little unnerving. "What's it gonna take to get you to ease up and relax?"

Kendra shook her head and rolled her eyes at Cristina before taking in a gulp of her wine.

"Well," Jolene said, picking up a magazine off the corner of the counter. "It just so happens I have my copy of POSE right here." She shook it in the air. "And I think you look fabulous. Just perfect. Not too wrinkled or bloated and way too young to be Quinn's mom, except your smile reveals too much pride to *not* be his mother."

Kendra beamed. Jolene knew every word she spoke played like beautiful music in Kendra's ears. Because that's what friends did for one another. They boosted their confidence and assured their insecurities.

She placed the asparagus in the pan with the sautéed garlic, sprinkling in some pepper and sea salt. She stirred the pasta before pulling out the ingredients for the salad.

"Need some help?" Kendra offered.

Jolene hesitated. She wanted to prepare the entire meal herself but slicing the tomatoes for the salad would be a challenge. Especially with an audience—an audience who didn't know about her debilitating disease.

"That would be great, thanks. Would you mind slicing the tomato and onion?" She placed a plump tomato and a red onion onto the cutting board.

"Well crud, guess I have to offer my help now too." Cristina pulled herself up off the stool. "What else do you need help with, Jo?"

"Nothing, Miss Cristina. You sit back down and relax."

"Are you sure?"

"Positive."

The kitchen timer began to ding signaling the pasta was done. She drained it into a colander sitting in the deep farmhouse sink. Steam swirled around her face the same way it did when she or Travis poured the hops into the kettle. The thought sent a chill through her, equal parts missing and longing for the moment she could be back in the brew pit as well as anxiety over informing her friends about her current position at the brewery. Gone were the days of scheduling, updating the Facebook page, ordering materials, and meeting with vendors. She was officially a Brewmaster.

"Since you didn't make it to Buffy's, then what did you do all day?" Cristina asked.

Her muscles tensed beneath her skin, her shoulders tightening. "Bo picked me up and took me to the Sweet Shop before dropping me off at my car."

"Oh really?" Cristina dropped her chin, raising her dark brows at Jolene.

"What?" Now her voice went up an octave.

"Twice in two days? What are you, dating the guy?" Cristina teased.

"I think it's sweet," Kendra said. "Him and Jolene were really close. It must be nice to see each other again."

"It is," she answered.

"Hey, if you want to cheat on your husband, that's your business." Cristina held her hands up in surrender. "Okay, but honestly, if you're gonna cheat on your husband with Bo Dean, we want to know every scandalous detail."

"Don't be silly, Jolene would never." Kendra tossed the ingredients for the salad in a large bowl. "But seriously, Jo, Cristina's right. If something's happening between you two— anything, you better tell us."

She stirred the pesto in with the gluten free pasta noodles in a bowl. Then she placed the asparagus onto a platter.

"Ladies, I can assure you, nothing's happening," Jolene emphasized her words. "We're just having fun catching up. That's it." Her fingers trembled as she refilled her wine glass, but she couldn't bring herself to look up to see if either of her friends had noticed. This would've been the perfect time to just tell them. *Travis and I are separated. And he left me to take care of the brewery. Oh, and I've also been diagnosed with a debilitating disease that fights against me every single freaking day.* But she couldn't bring herself to say the words aloud.

"C'mon, let's fill our plates. Dinner is ready."

"Everything smells wonderful, Jo," Kendra said.

"Yeah and surprisingly, it actually looks good too." Cristina dropped a heaping pile of pasta onto her plate.

"Well, let's just hope it tastes as good as it smells and looks," Jolene said.

After they filled their plates, they headed outside with them. A glass table with six metal chairs lined with cushions sat on the back deck. Two strands of party lights stretched overhead, and tiki torches lined the edge of the deck. Cristina flipped the lights on while Kendra lit the torches.

The three women talked about non-serious topics, rubbing the surface of what their lives were like now. Jobs, kids, and husbands. They talked about traveling and past vacations. All things she considered as safe topics.

"Don't take this the wrong way or anything," Kendra said, looking in Cristina's direction.

Oh no, here it comes. She braced herself in her chair, preparing for a fight between the two women. Wishing for the hundredth time Becca was here to play referee, to tell them both to get over themselves.

"But I'm still a little shocked that you're a teacher."

"I know, right?" Cristina said. "Sometimes it surprises me too." She laughed. "But I really do love it. I mean, don't get me wrong, it can get a little annoying being with thirty ten-year-olds all day. But by the end of the year I end up loving all thirty of those little bastards." She laughed again.

"Geez, Cris, I hope you don't say that to their mothers," Kendra scoffed.

"No, of course not. That's for your benefit. Haven't you noticed, I've cleaned up my vocabulary a lot?"

Kendra shrugged and glanced at Jolene. Cristina looked at her as well, as if to say, *c'mon, help me out here.* Because why wouldn't she—she'd always been the peacekeeper. Her eyes shifted from one woman to the other a few times.

"I've totally noticed, Cristina," Jolene finally said. "In high school, you cursed so much you would've been an R-rated movie. You said words I hadn't even ever heard of. Looking back, I think you made some of those up." She exhaled a laugh. "And you were so vulgar. You were the only person I knew who could turn any word or object into something sexual."

"Now that, is true," Kendra agreed.

"Why thank you," Cristina said in her best cutesy voice, adding a slight bow from her chair.

Kendra rolled her eyes and smiled. "And again, only you, Cristina, would take that as a compliment." She took a sip of her wine. "What about you, Jolene? How's work going? You still doing all the behind the scenes at the brewery?"

She pulled her lower lip in between her teeth, deciding the best way to answer this question. Technically, she was still doing some of the behind-the-scenes work. But since Travis left, she'd been handing more of those jobs to Joy and Carrie, their office manager and taken on sole Brewmaster responsibilities.

She attempted to skirt around the question. "It's good. Staying busy with inventory, meeting with vendors, scheduling. What about you Cristina? Did the school year finish for you yet?"

"No, this next week is the last week. I scheduled a substitute teacher to come and finish out the school year. It's just too bad, the last week is the best. The kids bring in all kinds of teacher gifts. I usually end up not having to purchase a drink from Starbucks all summer." Cristina grinned. "Some gifts started trickling in last week, you know all those butt kisser parents who have a younger child that could potentially end up in my class in the next few years."

"Well, it's worth it to miss I suppose, right?" Jolene asked.

"Oh, absolutely. I wouldn't have missed this."

"Yeah, me either. I'm glad I decided to come."

"I'm sure it wasn't easy," Kendra's tone sounded soft and soothing.

Her throat tightened. "It wasn't, but you know I forgave Becca a long time ago." Tears burned at the corners of her eyes. "Hey, Cristina? When you went to see Becca, you know, after she got sick, did she say anything about me?"

"Oh yeah, all the time."

This response surprised her. She supposed she had assumed all these years that Becca wouldn't want to think about her, much less talk about her.

"Really? Like what did she say?"

"We talked about all of us. We talked about everything. Like all the parties we went to at the lake. The times we spent here, at the cottage. Swimming of course. And you two with that running route you mapped out. We talked about that time we all drank so much we hardly found which house was hers and you puked in the neighbor's bushes." Cristina laughed.

Her eyes watered as she too laughed at the memory.

"And we talked about Jacob, too."

Jolene's stomach did a flip flop before it churned. The sound of Jacob's name—here at the cottage felt somehow wrong. Her own memories of her brother swished around in her mind like a cyclone.

He hadn't spent as much time in Tahoe City as Jolene had, not until he and Becca got together. Then you could hardly get Jacob away from the lake. He and Becca would race to see who could swim to the end of the dock the fastest. And when he'd lose, which he did every single time, he'd say, *babe, whatever. I let you win.* He'd smile and shake out his head of wet blonde hair, spraying her.

Becca had been the competitive one. Not Jacob. Even though he was an exceptional basketball player, he was a team player, not a ball hog. Being competitive wasn't in the Oliver genes.

Her eyes glazed over. She'd known they couldn't go the entire week without speaking about Jacob. And if she were being honest, she felt a strong desire of needing to know how Becca really felt about the accident. Did she feel remorse? Did she still think it was her fault, or had she forgiven herself?

"What did she say?"

"That she really loved Jacob. She said when she started having feelings for him, she was worried to act on them because she didn't want the friendship she had with you to change. But she said, how could she not act on them, when you practically worshiped your brother. And then when they started dating, your friendship hardly changed at all because you and Jacob got along so well." Cristina took a sip of her wine.

Jolene rubbed a hand at the back of her neck. She had looked up to her brother. Jacob was sweet and caring. He had been the perfect big brother. When they were young, Jacob always watched out for her. Either clasping her bike helmet for her, opening popsicle wrappers for her, and taking her hand when they'd cross the street.

When they were teenagers, her and Jacob played video games together. And when his friends came over to play basketball, he'd always let her join in. Jacob used to help Jolene with her math homework. Math had come easily for him whereas she struggled. He had plans to be an engineer when he grew up. He would've made an excellent engineer.

Cristina continued. "When she talked about them having a future, she'd break down. I left her in tears every time those last few visits."

"And was that here?" Jolene asked.

"No. I guess she asked her mom if she could stay here until the end but she told her this was a place for happy memories, and she wouldn't let her die here and have this place be remembered that way. Pretty harsh if you ask me."

"That sounds like Ms. Gibbs," Jolene admitted.

"Sure does," Kendra agreed.

But the irony was, she did end up dying here. Drowning right out in the waters in front of the cottage. If she knew Becca still, she probably did it on purpose. Just to stick it to her mother. One last, *screw you.*

"Mr. Gibbs had one wing of his house set up for her and her daughter so they wouldn't have to move her when it came time for her to be put into hospice."

"And Becca's daughter, is she still living with Mr. Gibbs?"

Cristina hesitated, taking a sip of her wine before answering with a shrug. "I guess."

Jolene nodded methodically. She couldn't imagine leaving Cole or Julia behind. Losing a mother at any age had to be horrendous, but as a teenager, it felt so much worse.

"When you visited Becca while she was sick, did she mention anything about wanting us to do this? To come here and spread her ashes?"

"No, nothing."

"Nothing?" Kendra leaned forward, propping her elbows on the tabletop.

"No. She talked about the cottage a lot. Once she did mention about how she'd been the one who ruined our pact. About us meeting here together each time something big happened in our lives. She said she ruined our friendships and if she could've changed anything, she'd want to have a do-over of that day." Cristina glanced at Jolene.

The alcohol in her stomach burned and she worried it might work its way up, along with the pasta and the asparagus. The thought of the green shade of puke was almost enough to force it out. Talking about Jacob was one thing—talking about the accident was something completely different. Especially hearing Becca wished she could've done things differently. Something she had never bothered to convey to Jolene.

"Hey," Kendra perked up. "Remember my eighteenth birthday? The three of you planned a party for the four of us at the Gibbs's house?"

"Oh yeah, I remember." Cristina sat back in her chair.

"How could I forget?" Jolene said. "That night I got so sick Becca had to clean up my puke."

"That was a fun night," Kendra said.

"Man, we all got so wasted. I don't know how we thought we could drink all of that alcohol." Cristina laughed.

"But we did. And that's why I got so sick." Jolene twisted her earring. "I can't believe how much I could drink back then. If I tried to drink like that now, I'd put myself into a coma."

The other women laughed and nodded in agreement.

"Speaking of alcohol," Kendra said in a melodious tone. She slipped through the French doors back inside the cottage, before emerging with another bottle of Sauvignon blanc. She waved it in the air. "I thought we may need two bottles. A nice way to kick off our week together."

Kendra opened the new bottle of wine with a corkscrew like a pro. And Jolene couldn't help but wonder how often Kendra did that. She refilled each of their glasses. Jolene didn't want to refuse and be rude, it was free wine after all. But she'd need to nurse this third glass and make it last the rest of the evening. She wanted to be in top notch shape for her run in the morning.

"I think we should toast." Kendra raised her glass.

"Ok, what should we toast to?" Cristina asked.

Kendra shrugged. They both glanced to Jolene. Kendra gave her a pleading look. Here we go again. Jolene to the rescue. She was the last one who wanted to come on this trip and here she was, given the responsibility of making the toast.

"You want to?" Kendra asked.

"Sounds good," she said, giving in and using her famous go to phrase. The three women raised their glasses. "How about, Becca's mantra, 'Never give up the fight'."

"Here, here."

The three women clinked glasses.

After the sun set, only the glow of the party lights and tiki torches reflected on each of their faces. It was just after nine o'clock and she already felt the weight of the day's emotions. She replayed the conversation between her and Bo from earlier in the day. He knew about the MS, and he still wanted to date her? Seeing his aunt suffer through this was one thing, dating somebody with this was completely another. Travis couldn't even deal with it. Her first flare up and Bo would run for the hills.

"You okay, Jo?" Kendra lifted her thick brows.

"Yeah, I'm fine."

"How's the brewery going?"

"It's actually going really well. Travis has turned that business into a success practically overnight it feels like," she said. "Did you know they have his beer on tap at Anders Bar and Grill?"

Or was it *her* beer now?

"I didn't," Cristina said. "But I've actually seen it at a few of the grocery stores in Reno."

"Really?"

"Yep. Every time I see it, I think, wow look at what my friend Jo has accomplished. It's pretty cool."

"Well, what Travis has accomplished. He's the Brewmaster." She swirled the wine in her glass, pushing back the emotions she felt over giving him the credit when she'd been the one sweating in the brew pit for the past year.

"What are you talking about? It's your business too. I'm sure you've had to sacrifice a lot. You can't brew beer that good without it taking up a lot of your time, am I right?" Cristina arched her brows.

"That's true," Jolene agreed. And they didn't even know the half of it. All the sacrifices she and the kids had made over the years were too many to count.

"I haven't seen it anywhere in L.A. yet, so I haven't been fortunate enough to try much of his beer."

Kendra had just told her that the brewery was every much hers as it was Travis's but then she'd gone and called it *his beer*. Her stomach tightened and she resisted the urge to spill her guts right there, right then.

"We'll have to go to Anders Bar and Grill this week so I can try some." Kendra gathered her long, straight hair and pulled it over one shoulder, showing off her perfect complexion in the glow of the dim lighting.

"That's a great idea." Cristina scooted to the edge of her seat. "My favorite is your IPA. I love the bite." She chomped her teeth together, revealing them after saying the word *bite*.

"Travis would love to hear you say that. He worked hard on that one. He grows his own hops, which he said was the key to finally getting the recipe right." Jolene glanced at the glass in front of her. She didn't think she'd be able to drink anymore. Her head hurt and she was a bit dizzy.

"That's really cool. I didn't know you guys grew your own hops," Cristina said.

"You should be really proud." Kendra smiled.

"I don't have anything to do with it." She wasn't sure why she continued to lie to her friends. She was proud of herself for taking over the Brewmaster responsibilities after Travis left instead of tucking into a ball and falling into a dark depression for the past year, like she'd felt like doing. But her friends seemed to always go way over the top with the compliments. Like her life was boring and like she wasn't doing enough with it.

"Don't sell yourself short. I hate hearing you cut yourself down."

"I'm not, I just don't like taking credit for something I have nothing to do with." Her voice grew louder.

"Can't you just take a compliment?" Cristina asked.

"No," Jolene barked.

"Whoa." Cristina raised her palms. "What crawled up your butt?"

"Look, I'm sorry." Her mind scrambled for words and her stomach flip flopped. She couldn't hold everything in anymore, it was all bottled up. She just needed to get it out—the secret and the alcohol. "Travis and I separated," she blurted. Luckily, the words came out on their own.

Kendra inhaled sharply, and she cupped a hand over her mouth.

"Well, shit. Seriously?" Cristina muttered. "Why did you wait so long to say something?" She stretched her arm across the table and rested her hand on top of Jolene's.

"It's been a year," she mumbled.

"A year?" shock sounded out in Kendra's voice. She shot to her feet and moved toward her, bending, and hugging her friend tightly.

Tears slipped out of Jolene's eyes and rolled down her face. Instead of feeling embarrassed or less than, the release of both the secret and the tears felt liberating. Kendra slid into one of the chairs next to her.

"Why didn't you tell me?" Kendra asked through a mess of their intertwined hair.

Jolene swiped at her wet cheeks. "I don't know. We just haven't talked much lately. I guess I didn't want to bother you with my problems. And things are going so well for you...I don't know..."

"You should've told me. I can't believe you've been dealing with this all on your own."

"It's okay. And I haven't been on my own. You know I have Joy? I've told you about her. And I have the other gals in my book club. And my church. They've been really supportive." She didn't dare mention her MS support group, all those people knowing before Kendra did.

"You told all of them? And not me? Not us?" Kendra looked hurt and it stirred a bit of remorse deep in her gut.

"I'm sorry. I told you, we haven't talked much lately. I didn't know how much you'd care."

"Of course I care," Kendra said, obviously offended.

Cristina reached for Jolene's hand again. "You shouldn't be the one who is sorry. I'm sorry, for not being there for you and that we didn't keep in touch all these years. I'm such a jerk."

The tears were streaming in a constant flow now and she felt silly for allowing them. "I'm sorry about that too. I wish we could go back and have all those years, all that time together."

"I wish I would've been a better friend to you," Kendra said.

"Me too." Jolene forced a pained smile.

"Well, we're here now." Cristina handed Jolene a napkin for her tears. "You wanna tell us what happened?"

She nodded her thanks and wiped it underneath her eyes. How could she tell them what happened without telling them about the MS? But she really didn't think she could let out another secret tonight. The pity already felt unbearable with the release of the first secret.

"I don't know. Everything started to change and unravel. It began a few years ago and I guess just spiraled downward until Travis decided he'd had enough. Last April he told me he was done, said he needed a break. And he left."

Cristina said a few choice words under her breath, before settling on, "bastard."

"He needed a break? A break from what? The most fabulous wife? I agree with Cristina, what a dirty dog." Kendra patted Jolene's hand.

"It's not entirely his fault. I'm not an easy person to live with." Sniffing and wiping her nose with her napkin, She thought about how, in all honesty, she should be the *easiest* person to live with. She went along with anything Travis wanted or suggested. She never argued or started fights.

"Ha, it's highly unlikely this is your fault," Cristina huffed. "Is there someone else? Did he meet someone else?"

"I don't know...I don't think so," she mumbled.

Slamming her fist into her palm, Cristina blurted, "I bet he's screwing someone else. It's the only logical explanation."

Jolene's mind raced with that thought and she let it go to places she didn't want it to. Travis, with another woman? But what other woman? If he'd stayed working at the brewery, she'd say Travis had no time for a woman. Practically all his hours used to be spent at the brewery. But now that he'd gone back to his job as a realtor, he was constantly meeting with people. She'd had suspicions. Especially when he announced his trip to Palm Springs and he'd been so secretive about it.

And then her mind shifted to Carrie, the High Desert

Brewery's manager. Beautiful, tone-legged, doppelganger to Carrie Underwood. She was on vacation all this week. Said she was visiting her parents in Colorado. But Joy had seen a poolside photo of her on Instagram.

Her head spun and acid burned her throat. She shook her head, trying to rid her mind of these thoughts. She'd always suspected Carrie was a girls-girl. But maybe not.

Cristina consoled her by rubbing soothing circles on her back. "Sorry," she muttered. "But what else could it be? You're perfect and he's a jackass."

Jolene sniffed and wiped her nose with a napkin. She glanced at Kendra and found her sitting rigid with her own cheeks wet from tears. It was a rarity to see Kendra cry and the sight sent a stirring in her stomach.

"Kendra, what is it?"

She scrunched her face before blurting, "Devin's cheating on me."

"What? Are you freaking kidding me?" Cristina threw her hands up. "Have your husbands both lost their damn minds?"

"Oh, no, Kendra. Are you sure?" Jolene set her wine glass on the table.

"Oh, I'm sure." Kendra sniffed. "I've caught him."

"Wait. Hold up." Cristina held up her palm, pumping the brakes. "What do you mean, you've *caught him*?"

"I've caught him lying about it, not in the actual act. I mean, could you imagine if I had? Or if Quinn had?" Her expression went stony. "Women have actually called the magazine, looking for me. Do you know how humiliating that is?"

"Oh my, women? As in plural?" Jolene lifted her brows.

"Yep. I don't even know how many women. It's been going on for at least the last five years."

"*Years?* Why in the hell are you still with him?" Cristina asked.

"That's a ridiculous question." She shot Cristina an incredulous look. "Because, do you know what that would do to my career? To his career? To the magazine? And to Quinn? I can't even imagine what it would do to Quinn if the media got a hold of this information." She paused, sucking in a deep breath, and then said softly, "And because I love him."

"Surely something would've leaked out in the media by now if it were true, right?" Jolene said, attempting to sound hopeful.

She glared. "You'd think, wouldn't you? But nope, because Devin makes them sign a release. He doesn't think I know, but c'mon I haven't been living under a rock. I know how these things work. Plus, I have people who keep me in the loop. I know everything that's going on."

"Oh, Kendra, I'm so sorry." It was Jolene's turn to comfort her now. She placed a consoling hand on her friend's back.

"When it first began, I thought it was harmless. I found some texts on his phone from a woman I didn't know. When I asked him about it, he said it was regarding a photo shoot he was trying to set up. I knew he'd been trying to land this gig for weeks, so I just let it go. It was over in Costa Rica, taking photos of a new resort that had just opened. But when the same woman kept texting after the gig was done, I knew something was up. I questioned him about it again. He made up some story about her needing him to do another gig. I believed him until one day I found her scarf in the glovebox of his Porsche and a text on his phone saying she couldn't wait to go for another *ride*."

"Disgusting," Cristina sneered. "What a pig."

"That was five years ago. It's been going on with different women ever since."

"Oh, Kendra," Jolene said. "And you never told us?"

"I guess we all have our own little secrets," Kendra admitted, shooting a look at Cristina that was hard for Jolene to miss and it sent shivers running down her spine.

CHAPTER ELEVEN

A steam of vapor spiraled in the air, heating Jolene's face. The fabric of her tank top and running shorts clung to her skin. Her breath quick and heavy and she panted hard. She pumped her legs harder and harder and yet the sand beneath her bare feet made it impossible to move at a rapid pace.

To the left of her, she could barely make out the moving water of the lake amongst the misty fog. The wind was humid and sticky. All the nerves in her body commanded to her to stop but the voice encouraged her to keep up momentum. She blocked out the pain in her head and pushed her body towards the sound of the voice.

When she met a metallic and sickly-sweet copper scent, the pit of her stomach churned, and bile burned in her throat. The voice grew louder, she was close.

In the distance, amongst the mist and steam, she found him. His body twisted in an unnatural position and covered in a pool of blood. She wrapped her arms around him and managed to choke out, "I'm here, Jacob." But when she looked down at his face, it wasn't Jacob, it was Bo.

Jolene jolted upright in bed covered in a cool, wet sweat, her breathing fast. She had to do some serious convincing to herself she'd only been having a dream. But it had felt so real. She blinked her eyes repeatedly. *Not real*, she told herself.

Her eyes darted around the room—same antique dresser, same rug. She was in the same room she had fallen asleep in. She resituated her tank top that had twisted around her torso, damp against her skin. Her breathing began to slow. She was a busy woman and had zero time for a flare up.

For the past year, the same reoccurring dream visited Jolene, but typically Jacob's face wasn't visible. Her intuition told her it was him. But now, she found herself wondering if it had been Bo in her dream all along. Every time she had this dream, her urge to run kicked in and lucky for her, she had the perfect route to fulfill the urge.

The clock on the nightstand read 4:36 a.m. She mustered up the strength to drag her sorry excuse for a runner out of bed. After dressing in her running clothes, she gathered her hair into a ponytail and shoved the old Sacramento Kings hat on her head. She laced up her running shoes and snatched her phone and earbuds off the dresser.

When she came out of the room, she took notice of the quiet and stillness in the cottage, wondering if Kendra had already left for a run. She'd hoped the two of them could run the familiar route together, but after she woke from that dream, she wanted to run alone. Finding a bottle of Tylenol in a cupboard in the kitchen, she took two, washing them down with a few gulps of lukewarm tap water.

Jolene snuck out of the French doors onto the back deck, the cool air biting at her bare skin. She descended the steps off the deck, landing on the rocky sand of the beach. The sky was clear and the water from the lake lapped on the shoreline, taking on a rhythmic sound. Gazing out at the lake, the swift movement captivated her thoughts. The memories came to her mind—the four of them as young girls. Swimming, sunbathing on the dock, riding their bikes to town, and geocaching.

A time when life was fun, easy, and magical.

THEN

The four girls peddle their bikes fast and hard, hair whipping behind them and the sun already slipping below the horizon. Jolene's forehead is slick with sweat, the excitement bubbling in her chest. The four girls have been at the treasure hunt for a week straight. Even with the coordinates and Mr. Gibbs's fancy, new Garmin GPS, the girls have left empty handed and frustrated each time the search for the geocache. Becca is determined but Jolene's hope is waning.

They reach the Tahoe City Sweet Shop and lock their bikes up out front. From there, they'll go on foot. Jolene is tempted to tell the girls to go on ahead without her. She wants to grab an ice cream cone and sit in the air-conditioned shop and flirt with Bo Dean all night.

"You sure you don't want to take a day off?" Jolene swipes the back of her hand over her forehead.

"I wouldn't mind. Ice cream sounds pretty damn good right now," Cristina says on a dramatic exhale.

"No. We're close. I can feel it." Wrapping the chain around her bike, Becca closes the padlock with a click.

Kendra juts out a hip and exhales an exasperated sigh. "You said that yesterday. And the day before."

"I mean it this time. We're close. We have the coordinates. We just aren't looking close enough."

The door of the Sweet Shop opens, and Bo Dean shuffles out, overflowing black trash bags in each hand.

"Hey, Bo," Cristina's voice purrs and she sidles up next to him. "Need a hand?"

"I got it. Thanks though." He passes them, calling over his shoulder on the way to the dumpster. "Where are you ladies off to?"

"We're going on a treasure hunt," Kendra says.

Bo quirks a light brow, tossing a bag into the dumpster.

"Kendra's being silly." Jolene waves her off. "We're geocaching."

He heaves the last bag inside the overflowing dumpster. "Oh, you mean you're on a Stash Hunt."

"No one calls it that anymore. It's called geocaching. And I've got my dad's cool GPS thingy." Becca cinches her backpack around her waist.

"What are you gonna leave when you find the stash?"

Jolene glances at Becca who looks at Kendra and then finally Cristina. They hadn't given that part much thought. Only about taking the stash of cash that was rumored to be hidden. But what would be worthy to leave when they would be getting money in return?

"C'mon, don't tell me you weren't gonna leave something? That's BS." He runs his hands down the front of his apron.

"I guess we sorta forgot."

Bo pouts his lips. "I got something for you. Hold on a sec." He rushes back inside the Sweet Shop.

"We don't have time for this," Becca groans. "It's gonna be dark in a few hours. And I have swim practice early."

Jolene digs the toe of her running shoe into the hot asphalt. "Bo's right, we have to leave something."

"If we even find it," Kendra says.

"We're gonna find it," Becca snaps.

The door swings back open and Bo saunters out, handing something to Jolene. "Here, when you find your stash—"

"Geocache," Cristina corrects.

Bo rolls his eyes at her. "When you find your stash, leave this in its place."

Jolene holds up the small rectangular paper, eyebrows furrowing. "A coupon for the Tahoe City Sweet Shop?"

"That's right." He nods triumphantly. "It's a BOGO. You know they don't just hand these out to anybody."

"Fine." Becca snatches the coupon from Jolene's hand. "Thank you," she mutters.

The girls take off toward the corner, waiting to cross the street. Jolene walks backward. "Thanks, Bo. I'll see you tomorrow?"

"Alright, my PIC," he teases, and her heart threatens to swell out of her chest. "Hey?" Bo hollers. "Ollie?" She turns and he says, "don't forget to sign the log with something epically unforgettable."

She waves at him, before jogging to catch up to her friends, her heart hammering in her chest.

NOW

A soft sprig of mist kissed Jolene's face reminding her of her mission—her urge to run. She did a few stretches, but it all seemed pointless, stretching before running. Her body ached before, during and after a run, regardless of the stretching.

The beach looked deserted. She glanced at her phone—4:54. Shoving her earbuds into her ears, she slipped her phone into the built-in pocket in the leg of her running pants. Typically, she opted to listen to country music, especially the older stuff like Johnny Cash, Merle Haggard, and Hank Williams. But when she ran—especially when she ran after having that dreadful, reoccurring dream, she liked to listen to anything with a fast beat to help her pace.

Well, here goes nothing. Her three-mile runs had been pretty pathetic lately. She took off in a slow pace at first, staying close enough to the shoreline to keep it in view but not close enough to get her running shoes wet. The adrenaline pumped through her veins and helped to push away the visions of her dream—of the flashes of red; a car, a sweater, a pool of blood. The image of the mangled body and the sickly-sweet metallic scent.

Jolene's stomach twisted until the lyrics of Justin Tiberlake's song *Rock Your Body* cleared the dream from her mind. J.T.'s voice had that effect on her, and every woman who had a pulse. Anything to help get her body moving.

The rocky sand beneath her feet made it difficult to maintain a fast pace. She pushed hard against the surface with each stride. Her legs and feet cooperated with her brain and she ran as if she had no debilitating disease at all. This encouraged her to move that much faster. If she ran to the point where the beach disappeared, there was a dock that stretched out from a house all the way into the water, it would be one and a half miles. That distance added to the one and a half miles back to the cottage equaled three miles.

Her and Kendra had clocked the distance once when they came to visit the cottage their junior year of high school. They were really into running back then. It shouldn't surprise her they were both still avid runners. Becca and Cristina didn't get the hype of it all. They opted to swim or lay out on the dock working on their summer tans. Only on some occasions would they join them on the run, and only once did they reach the end destination where the long dock formed a dead end.

She smiled at the memory from that day. Cristina and Becca thought they were going to die because of the strenuous run. They laid down on the dock in exhaustion and Jolene and Kendra thought they were going to have to carry them back to the cottage.

As she reached the end destination, the familiarity of the dock comforted her. As if no time had passed at all, as if the four women, and Jacob were all still alive and well. And as if her and Travis were still happily married and their family whole.

But the negative voices in her mind were quick to bring her back to reality. *You're a failure*, they hissed, like a snake whispering in her ear. *You've lost everything. Nothing is the same as it was. And nothing will ever be the same again.*

Tears burned at the corners of her eyes. Her throat went dry, and she wished she had brought water with her. Taking a break during her runs made her feel weak and so she would often push herself to the point of throwing up. But today, she had to stop and catch her breath.

Leaning with her palms flat against the dock, her legs trembled beneath her. Her breaths quick and her mood angry. She scolded herself, stealing the satisfaction from the negative voices. "You're acting like a pathetic loser. Catch your breath and get moving again. You are better than this," she mumbled in between her panted breaths.

When Jolene noticed the sun rising, she cringed, afraid to check the time. She wasn't making good time today and that angered her even more. But it was enough to get her butt moving again.

Pushing off the dock, she took off like a bull being let out of the pen. Sprinting fast and huffing out both her nose and mouth. The lyrics to Beyoncé's song, *Party* sounded through her earbuds, causing her to pump her legs vigorously. Her body would cry out and complain later, but at this moment, she didn't care.

As she continued powering her way back to the cottage, her breathing had accelerated to a heightened level. She pushed her body harder than she had in a long while. She had chosen a pace that matched the beat of the music. Although it had become difficult to hear the lyrics over the sound of her loud breathing.

An overwhelming sensation washed over her that someone was following her. If she looked back, her speed, and possibly her footing would falter. She was probably imagining it. But then there was weight of extra footsteps on the rocky sand behind her.

She was just about to pause her music and say *screw it* to her time, when a hand grasped her arm. She let out a shriek so loud it rang in her ears, reaching above the sound of Beyoncé's voice. Recoiling her arm, she spun around and stumbled backward, unable to catch her footing.

She was going down.

A flash of light from the sun shot in her eyes as she fell, her butt landing on the rocky sand. There wasn't enough cushion on her bony behind to handle the blunt force and she winced. She reached up, ripping the earbuds out of her ears.

Raising a hand to the bill of her hat, she pulled it down to shield the sun from her eyes, getting a better look at the stranger who stood over her. The image appeared in shadow. Then a large arm and rough hand reached out for her, the beginnings of a tattoo peeked out of the sleeve. Her first reaction was to pull back and scream again. But then his image finally came into view and she recognized him.

"You okay?" a gruff sounding voice asked. "I'm sorry I startled you."

Jolene slipped her hand into his and he helped her up. She stumbled before planting her feet firmly on the sand. Readjusting the hat on her head, she wiped sweat from her temples.

"Oh, Owen, right?" she said between panting breaths.

"Yeah, that's right. The bartender over at Anders Bar and Grill."

"Right," she managed to say.

"Hey, sorry about that. I didn't mean to scare you."

Owen was dressed in black running pants and a black sweatshirt with the hood over his head. He reached for his hood and pulled it off, revealing his pale pitted face and long messy black hair. His round dark eyes burned into her. He seemed larger than he'd appeared that first night at the bar. Tall and burly.

"No, no, it's okay." She waved dismissively before placing both hands on her thighs, bending over and trying to catch her breath.

"I was back a-ways," Owen began, hiking a thumb over his shoulder. "And I saw you pass by. It took a second to register where I knew you from. Anyway, I just thought I'd say hey. But you zoomed by in lightning speed, I wasn't even positive it was you." He let out a gravel sounding laugh as he raked both hands through his hair.

"Oh yeah, well, my music." She gestured to her earbuds that now hung around her neck. "It really gets me in the zone. Obviously." She exhaled a nervous laugh.

"You're not kidding, I had to really hustle to catch up to you. I guess I better train more. A tiny thing like you could run circles around a brute like me."

"I doubt that. You just caught me on a good day, that's all." She *could* run circles around him but hoped it wouldn't come to that. The guy seriously gave her the creeps.

"I haven't seen you around here before. You mentioned you're just visiting?" He pushed the hair out of his face again.

"Yeah, I'm just in town for the week. And it's Jolene," she offered.

"Ahh, Jolene. It's nice to finally have a name for the beautiful face."

She bit her lip.

"You here visiting Officer Dean?" He raised his brows inquisitively.

"Nope, just visiting a couple girlfriends. We're staying at a friend's family cottage on the lake."

"Oh yeah? Where at?"

"Just up ahead, a couple hundred feet. The grayish one with the fire pit out front." She squinted toward the cottage.

"I think I know that one. Has your friend owned the cottage long?"

"Since she was a kid."

"Bet it was nice to have a place for you and your friends to come in the summer, get out of the city for a bit?"

She swung her attention back to him, biting the inside of her cheek. Had she told him she lived in Reno as a kid? His black eyes held her gaze, sending a shiver shooting down her spine. He studied her intensely again, like he had that first night at the bar. She placed her hands on her hips and shifted her weight from one foot to the other.

"So? What are you up to?" she asked.

"Same as you, out to get some exercise and my daily dose of vitamin D." He gestured at the sun with his chin. "Although I guess it's obvious I don't run as often as you do."

It was obvious he didn't get much exercise. He wasn't necessarily overweight, but he wasn't fit either. That, along with being tall, he was right, he was a brute of a man. But rather than run circles around him, what she really wanted to do was run away from him.

"Sorry for interrupting your run," Owen said.

"Don't worry about it. I pushed myself pretty hard today, so I think I'll just walk the rest of the way back."

"You want some company?"

Did she want company? *Heck no.* But she didn't want to be rude, and she hated confrontation. Although this guy rubbed her the wrong way, she didn't see him as a threat. Maybe he just had a thing for older women, some fantasy to pursue.

She planted a fake smile on her face. "Sure, that would be fine."

They turned and walked in the direction of the cottage. There were a few colorful kayaks out on the lake now. The sight caused the twisting anxiety in her belly to ease slightly, because at least she wasn't alone.

"So, you're here until...when?" he asked.

"Sunday. My kids," she began, hoping the mention of having kids would send him running for the hills, "they'll be expecting me Sunday evening."

"You have kids, huh?" His face brightened and his voiced perked up. "How many?"

Oh joy, if it was possible, he seemed even more interested. What was this guy's deal?

"Yep, two. They're fifteen and thirteen."

"Wow. You don't look old enough to have kids that age."

She let out a forced nervous laugh, feeling herself blush and hoping he didn't mistake it as flattery. Creepy Dude was laying it on thick.

"No, really," he continued. "I mean, I knew you were older than me. But, not by that much."

"I'm sure I'm several years older than you."

"Nah, not that many. But unless you had your fifteen-year-old when you were ten, then I guess you're a few years older than me."

Jolene exhaled a mirthless laugh. "You're twenty-five?"

"Yep, guilty." He raised his palms.

"Wow, to be twenty-five again," she said in a whimsical

tone. And for a second, she forgot she was talking to Creepy Dude.

"C'mon, I told you. Now it's your turn."

"Fine." She sighed. "I'm thirty-seven."

"No, you can't be?"

"Yep, guilty," she repeated his words.

"Well, you look at least ten years younger. Why do you think I keep checking you out and fumbling around like an idiot when I'm around you? You're an attractive woman."

Glancing over at him, their eyes clicked and before she could look away, he winked at her. The same chill from earlier shot down her spine again.

"Well, we're just about there. I can manage the rest of the way. You should get back to your run," she insisted.

"Now I've made you feel uncomfortable. I'm so sorry about that. I'm an idiot." He studied his shoes, yet continued his stride, keeping up with her pace.

"No, it's fine. You've been really kind. But I should get going. My friends are probably wondering what's keeping me. Normally I make good time on my runs."

"I really am sorry, the last thing I wanted to do was make you feel uncomfortable." He wrapped a hand around her arm, pulling her to an abrupt stop.

She jolted back. "Please, don't worry about it."

"Okay, I'll get going. But just one quick thing." His fingers laced around her arm tightly. "I was wondering if you would want to get a drink sometime."

"Oh, I don't know if that's a good idea," she said, her voice sounding weak.

Didn't he see the wedding ring on her finger? Or did he just not care? The confrontation caused the anxiety to twist in her stomach.

"Just one drink. Beer? Coffee? You pick, whatever you

want," his gruff voice elevated with a pleading tone in it now. "I'd love to get to know you better."

"Owen...I...uh," she stammered, "I'm married."

Owen's eyes darted to her finger she now had waggling in the air. His grip became tighter, constricting her arm like a snake coiling around its prey. His eyes darkened, like two glossy, black onyx stones.

She wriggled a bit in his grip. "I'm sorry, if you assumed...I mean." She couldn't get out the right words. They were floating around in her head, and she tried grasping for them but only the wrong ones came out. "I'm married, but we're separated. And I haven't started dating again."

"So, you're not *really* married then. C'mon, just one date? We don't even have to call it a date. Just coffee," he begged. "You never know, we may just hit it off. We could talk about our experiences growing up at the lake. And hey, you know what they say, age is just a number."

Obviously, she knew about the familiar saying. She thought about saying yes, using her go-to phrase, *sounds good* just to get away from him—out of her personal space, away from those dark eyes. She wanted his hot breath off her face, and to be free from his grasp.

Out of the corner of her eye she spotted Kendra, bounding toward them like her savior. All she needed was the sight of her old friend to give her the boost of courage to jerk her arm out of his grip. "I said, I don't think it's a good idea."

"Hey, Jo," Kendra said in a bubbly tone as she approached them.

Owen took a step back in surprise, as if Kendra had broken him out of a trance.

Kendra gave him the once over, her thick brows furrowing. "Who's this?"

Owen stretched out his hand. "Hey, I'm Owen. I'm a bartender over at Anders Bar and Grill."

"Nice to meet you, I'm Kendra." She placed her hand into his and gave it a limp shake. "And you two know each other, how?" Her finger gestured back and forth between Owen and Jolene.

"I was fortunate to have met Jolene the other night at the bar," Owen said.

Kendra nodded. "I see."

"So you're one of the friends?"

"That's me." She smiled.

Jolene stood still, her back stiff and her words gone. She had her arms wrapped around her sweaty body.

"Well, I better get back to my run. It was nice meeting you, Kendra. And Jolene, I'll be seeing you later." He winked, and pulled the hood of his sweatshirt back over his head before taking off in a jog.

Was that a threat or a promise? Either way, it sent a chill shooting down her spine. And she didn't want to find out.

CHAPTER TWELVE

"What was that all about?" Kendra asked once Owen was out of earshot.

"Ugh, that guy gives me the creeps. He served me my drinks at the bar Friday night. He kept winking at me and flirting with me. I tried shrugging it off but then when I bumped into him just now, he asked me out. I tried explaining that I'm married, but he was relentless."

"Look at you, miss heartbreaker." Kendra chuckled, bumping a shoulder into her.

"It's not funny." Jolene rubbed her arm. "He grabbed me by the arm. Pretty hard."

"Really?"

"Yeah, it kinda scared me."

"Whoa, seriously?"

"And he asked about the cottage. Saying something about us coming here as kids and getting out of the city in the summers. But I don't think I told him I was from Reno." She turned on her toe, glancing in the direction Owen had run off.

"Okay, you're right. That is super creepy. I'm sorry, sweet-ie." Kendra wrapped her arm around Jolene's shoulders, giving her a light squeeze.

Jolene blinked back tears. "I'm so relieved you came when you did. Who knows what he might've done."

"No kidding, me too."

"Thanks." She bit her lip.

Kendra let go of her friend, stretching her legs out. "I'm just about to go for my run, I'd ask you to join but it looks like you've already gone."

"Yeah, I did."

"Guess I'm running solo today. You gonna be okay?" Kendra bent over at the waist, stretching her arms above her head.

"I'll be fine. Thanks. Hey, you be careful," she said.

"I will. Don't you worry about me." Kendra started jogging backward and waved. "See you back at the house in twenty-three minutes."

She rolled her eyes at the comment. She was aware Kendra could complete the three-mile route in only twenty-three minutes, but this was her way of reminding her. Jolene's average time was twenty-seven minutes.

For a while in her twenties, she could manage a three-mile run in twenty-five minutes. But that wasn't the case once she hit thirty. Now she was doing good if she finished in thirty minutes. But anything over that and she'd curse herself or wait and let the negative voices do it for her.

Heading up the back steps of the cottage, she felt defeated—for stopping halfway through her run, for falling, for allowing Owen to interrupt her. She showered and tried to push away the morning emotions, along with the worriment that the creepy bartender knew where she was staying.

Jolene dressed in a taupe-colored cotton maxi skirt, a white fitted tee, and a pair of strappy sandals. They were heading into South Lake Tahoe to take the boat tour on the M.S. Dixie II. With it being early June and heading out on the water, it would be cooler, so she dressed a bit warmer. After running some products through her damp hair, she grabbed her cardigan and headed into the main living area of the cottage.

Jolene found Cristina sitting at the island counter on a bar stool sipping a cup of coffee. Her dark locks were pulled up in a messy bun again and she was dressed in a light blue peplum top paired with white jeans. Her fully made-up face and several coats of black mascara made it look like she was heading to a club rather than a day outing with the girls.

"Morning, biatch," Cristina greeted in singsong.

Jolene's heart warmed at the terse endearment, and she smiled. "Morning."

"How'd you sleep last night?"

"Okay."

"All that wine get to you?" Cristina asked over the brim of her coffee mug.

"Nah, just don't sleep good these days I guess."

"You never did sleep much," Cristina said.

The comment surprised her. A reminder of their once tight-knit friendship. Those were the kind of things they used to know about one another. And apparently, still did.

"I guess some things don't change." Jolene shrugged. She grabbed a mug and poured herself some coffee before sitting on the stool next to Cristina.

"And I suppose it's harder to sleep when you're sleeping alone," Cristina said.

"It is."

"I remember."

"You remember?" Jolene cocked her head to the side.

"Yep. I know what it's like. One minute your married,

sleeping next to the same guy every night. Then, *bam*, next thing you know, you're not married anymore and you're alone, and you're sleeping in that giant bed all by yourself."

Cristina was referring to her first marriage, with Mason. Things had ended badly between them. He was an alcoholic. One night he got so drunk and became rough with their daughter, Montana. Turned her little eye black and blue. Cristina, being the strong woman that she was, didn't stick around after that. She took Montana and left, not once turning back.

Jolene's chest heaved, the guilt spiraling in her stomach. "I'm so sorry I wasn't there for you when all that went down."

"It was a long time ago." Cristina shoved a shoulder into her. "And you called, you checked on me."

"Yeah, but I should've done more. I should've been there."

"Seriously, Jo, stop. Don't worry about it. Philip and I are really happy. I'm grateful for everything that happened with Mason. Without that experience, I wouldn't have got together with Philip. And without Mason, I wouldn't have Montana."

Kendra entered the kitchen looking classy as always. Her hair hung down and straight along with matching bangs across her forehead. Her skin looked flawless.

Cristina let out a whistle and Kendra rolled her eyes but couldn't hide her grin.

"Oh, Jolene," Kendra crooned. "That skirt is adorable."

"Thanks," she said. "I really love your outfit."

"Oh thanks." Kendra shrugged off the compliment. For being a retired model, she was surprisingly modest. And she was almost always the first one to give out a compliment. That hadn't changed about her since they were young. She'd always been sweet and caring. "Jo, I have the most perfect necklace to match with your outfit. Hold on a sec, let me go get it." She hurried off down the hall and up the stairs.

Kendra and Cristina had claimed the two bedrooms on the

top floor that held queen beds, leaving Jolene alone on the first floor. She could've stayed in the remaining empty bedroom upstairs, so she didn't have to be alone, however that room held two sets of bunk beds. Having a queen bed sounded more appealing than a bunk bed. Plus, Becca's room had always been upstairs. And she couldn't bring herself to go up there and see if the walls were still painted red or if Ms. Gibbs had painted over them.

When Kendra returned, she dangled a silver chain with a key pendant hanging off it in front of Jolene's face. The gesture was sincere, but it had to be expensive. Far too expensive to be hanging around her neck and be entrusted to her. But she didn't want to be rude, and it would make Kendra happy if she were to accept.

"That's so pretty, thanks."

She held her hair up while Kendra clasped the necklace around her neck. Kendra stepped back as if she were an artist admiring her piece of work. A wide closed mouth smile stretched across her face. Jolene held the key pendant out and in small, engraved letters on top of the oval of the key, it read: TIFFANY & CO. Her stomach dropped. Definitely expensive.

Craaaap.

"It looks so great. Just perfect. I knew it would." Then, turning her attention to Cristina, her eyes lit up. "Cristina, what a cute top. So flattering on you."

"Thanks. I may or may not have read the article in POSE a few months ago titled, *Dressing for Your Body Type.*" Cristina smirked.

"Well, I'm glad it helped you," Kendra said nonchalantly, like she could care less either way if Cristina read her magazine or not. But she couldn't hide the satisfaction on her face. Kendra's phone chimed signaling an incoming text. After glancing at the screen, she ignored it and slipped it into her handbag. "You ladies ready to go?"

Jolene nodded before downing what was left of her coffee. The muffled sound of Kendra's phone chimed from inside her handbag every few seconds. It was surprising Kendra continued to ignore it.

The three women piled into Cristina's white Toyota 4Runner, each with an extra bag filled with books, magazines, and snacks. Their excursion planned for the day would be long and they'd need to fill in some time. Jolene volunteered to sit in the back seat, giving up the passenger seat for Kendra.

"You be in charge of the music," she said. "Don't let Cristina play any of that punk rock she likes so much." She laughed.

But maybe Cristina didn't even like punk rock anymore. That was the old Cristina. The one who didn't take crap from anyone. The one who would blast Green Day out the windows of her Ford Bronco while she drove double the speed limit through the school zone. The one who had once keyed another girl's BMW their sophomore year because she'd kissed Jolene's boyfriend at a party.

"What about classical, you ladies like classical?" Kendra asked, her eyes shifting back and forth between the women.

If looks could kill, Kendra would've been a goner. Cristina gave her a death stare combined with a dropped jaw.

"Whoa, okay guess not," Kendra said.

"Ok, maybe I should've ridden shotgun." Jolene laughed. "Why not check for a pop station. Or connect your phone."

"Fine." Kendra scanned through the radio stations before settling on one playing an older Taylor Swift song, *We Are Never Ever Getting Back Together*. Finally something they could agree on.

When Jolene glanced in the rear-view mirror, Cristina's

eyes, now taking on a hazel hue rather than the normal green with brown outline were staring back at her. She mouthed, *Thank you.*

Kendra pulled her cellphone out of her bag and began tapping frantically away at it again. Jolene's own phone chimed. When she retrieved it, she found a text from her daughter Julia. Her heart gave a tug.

JULIA

Hey Mom. Checking in. Send me a pic of you doing something fun today. Love you!

She sent her a response back letting her know she was fine. She told her about her run by the lake that morning and said she would send pics later. Then she told her to pass her love to Cole, unsure if he'd care. She was getting nowhere with that kid.

The dreadful stretch of Manson Blvd was quickly approaching, and she had no energy left to deal with it, so she closed her eyes. She scooted down in the seat, resting her head on the headrest. The morning sun seeping in through the car window blanketed her eyelids and her breathing became slow and steady.

When Jolene woke up, she heard the low hum of a conversation between Cristina and Kendra. She sat up and saw they were in a parking lot, surrounded by cars and people hustling about. She spotted the water and the large boat. And then she remembered. They were at Zephyr Cove, where they were set to board the M.S. Dixie II.

"Hey, sleepy head," Kendra called in singsong.

"Hey." Jolene felt groggy and ran a hand through her hair. She wiped at her eyes that had blurred up from sleep.

"We're here," Cristina announced. "We thought about just leaving you here to rest and we'd go ahead and board without you. But Kendra thought you'd die of suffocation from the heat if we left in the car all day, ya know, like dogs do."

"Oh, how nice." The comment took her by surprise. Maybe she really didn't know Cristina after all. Twenty years ago, Cristina probably would've taken a bullet for her. It was clear, that was no longer the case.

Jolene stepped out of the car, taken aback by the amount of people there. It was a good thing they got there early as the parking lot appeared almost full. The boat was massive, two stories with an upper deck—the ability to hold up to five hundred passengers.

The women made their way to the dock and boarded the M.S. Dixie II, the boat that would take them on a tour of the lake including a trip to Emerald Bay where they would have lunch. Once, when the girls were younger, they had taken a hike near Emerald Bay. Kendra had led the pack of them, and Cristina brought up the rear.

Becca, dressed in all red, had been extra cheerful that day. The lake was her happy place. And maybe losing out on the scholarship to Cal State hadn't been so terrible for her in the end. Jolene couldn't imagine Becca ever leaving the lake.

They went out on the upper deck as the M.S. Dixie II left the dock of Zephyr Cove and made its pursuit. The view was spectacular. The Sierra Nevada Mountain range was breathtaking, featuring the tops capped with snow. She'd grown accustomed to mountain ranges living in Central Oregon, yet each one had their differences and was unique in their own way.

The water sputtered behind the boat as it coursed up the lake. The air grew cooler the faster the boat traveled. Jolene snapped a picture of the lake with the Sierra Nevada's behind it with her phone and sent it in a text to Julia. It saddened her that her children were missing out on all this beauty. Saddened that she hadn't ever brought them to Lake Tahoe.

When she and Travis talked about having children, he couldn't wait to bring them here. He wanted them to fall in love with the luscious greenery, the water, the small town. Just like he had. But it was just too painful for Jolene to come back. All these places reminded her of Jacob. And now, Becca. Lake Tahoe used to be her favorite place in the whole world. She could've never imagined it would've turned out to be the place she dreaded most.

After a few more pictures on the outdoor deck, they moved inside and found some empty seats where they could relax and wait for lunch to be served. Cristina took the seat by the window and Jolene sat next to her with Kendra across from them. Cristina slipped off her ballet flats and tucked her feet under her body, resting her head against the window of the boat. Two kids behind them argued over who's turn it was to play on their mother's phone and a baby cried toward the back. Cristina rolled her eyes, then pushed her earbuds into her ears.

"Wake me up when we reach Emerald Bay," she mumbled before closing her eyes.

Jolene pulled out her laptop in hopes to get a little work done, even though she'd planned on taking the entire week off. If she kept her mind busy, she wouldn't be able to think about Jacob, and Becca, and the reason she was even in Tahoe City to begin with.

The phone Kendra had been ignoring began ringing from inside her bag. She pulled it out and glanced at the screen. "Ugh, I better answer this. You gonna be okay?"

"Oh yeah, of course."

Kendra stood, passing her an appreciative smile. She answered her phone as she walked toward the back of the boat. Then she proceeded outside to the deck.

When Jolene was in the middle of reviewing the brewery's supply Excel spreadsheet, her phone chimed in her purse. A new text message from Bo. Her cheeks burned. She glanced over both shoulders, feeling like a schoolgirl again—nervous and excited all at once. But she was getting herself all worked up over nothing. Sure, her and Bo were close, but that had been a long time ago.

A *very* long time ago.

> **BO**
>
> You up for an adventure tonight?

That was it. Only those six words. What did they mean? The teenaged Bo Dean could be referring to a prank. Back in their day, that wouldn't be unusual. But as adults, what could it mean? Surely he wouldn't be referring to anything illegal, after all he was a cop now.

> **JOLENE**
>
> What did you have in mind?

> **BO**
>
> The old Jolene wouldn't ask questions

She rolled her eyes. Then tapped at her phone.

> **JOLENE**
>
> The old Jolene didn't have kids and adult responsibilities.

> **BO**
>
> When have I ever steered you wrong?
>
> Trust me.

> **JOLENE**
>
> Fine. Let's do it.

> **BO**
>
> Now there's the girl I remember.

Pick you up at 8.

What exactly had she just agreed to? A date with Bo? No, that was ridiculous. He was probably feeling nostalgic because she was back in town. That had to be it. They were just two old friends simply hanging out, talking about the good old days.

But then why was she nervous?

CHAPTER THIRTEEN

At exactly eight o'clock, there was a knock on the front door of the cottage. Jolene opened it and there stood Bo Dean, on the welcome mat which had the words, *Welcome to the Sea* written on it. An odd choice of a welcome mat for a house by the lake.

Not knowing where they were going—not knowing if this was a date—she had fretted over what to wear. But she was relieved when Bo showed up dressed casually in a pair of distressed jeans and a grey long-sleeved shirt. Against Kendra's better judgement, Jolene had decided on a pair of dark jeans, a simple white tank top and a pair of flip flops.

"Hey," she said finally.

She was nervous. Why was she so nervous? This was not a date. This was just Bo.

"You look great." A big smile stretched across Bo's face showing off his pearly white teeth and it sent a hum in her depths instantly.

Okay, then why did this feel like a date?

"Uh, thanks." She bit her lower lip, skirting her attention

away from him so she'd no longer be tempted to allow her eyes to wander over him any longer.

"You ready to go?"

"Yep, just let me grab my purse."

"You won't need it," Bo said.

Jolene lifted her brows. "I won't?" She rested her hands on her hips and narrowed her eyes. "Just where are you taking me, Mr. Dean?"

"Can't tell you. But I can guarantee you won't be needing your purse." He smiled confidently.

The idea of not having her purse with her, gave her all kinds of anxiety. What if she needed money, or her I.D.? But she wanted to come across as being completely cool with this plan, so she eased her stiff shoulders purposefully.

"Okay, well, let me at least grab my phone."

"You may want to grab a sweater, too," he suggested.

"I'll be fine, my body temp runs hot." *Especially since Bo had arrived.*

Cristina called to them from the kitchen. "You two kids have fun. Don't do anything I wouldn't do."

Jolene shoved her phone into the back pocket of her jeans, waving at Cristina and Kendra and shoving Bo out the door.

She felt a bit guilty for leaving her friends. But the three of them had just spent most of the day together. Kendra and Cristina had decided to head over to Anders Bar and Grill for a drink while she went on this adventure with Bo. She cringed at the thought of them bumping into Owen, the creepy bartender.

When she climbed inside Bo's pick-up truck, the entire cab smelled of his cologne. It had the distinct scent of the ocean. She realized that quite possibly, he intended this to be a date. Or, maybe he was just as unsure as she was.

Bo's wheat blonde hair had been combed and gelled into what looked like his usual style. It made him look more distinguished than he had with his teenaged buzz-cut. His skin had a nice tan tone and hardly revealed any wrinkles where they should be at his age. The lake life suited him.

"So, are you at least gonna give me a hint?" she asked once Bo had backed out of the driveway.

"That would take half the fun out of it." He gave her a quick smirk before placing his attention back on the road. "C'mon, Ollie, you know I love to see you squirm."

Jolene rolled her eyes but inside, inside her nerves were going crazy, reacting to the sound of her nickname. This was how things always went between them when they were kids. Bo teasing her, flirting with her. He knew just how to push her buttons.

Even when she'd been a teenager, Bo knew how bad her anxiety was. But if he knew how much it had worsened, he wouldn't be wasting his time with her. Planning an adventure, picking her up, putting on cologne.

Over the last year, her anxieties had become so bad she'd started getting panic attacks. Her mother warned her of such things when she was just a kid and worried that she'd get ulcers. Though she hadn't given herself ulcers caused by all the worrying, not yet at least, she had acquired panic attacks instead. Jolene had heard of panic attacks, of course. But she hadn't experienced one herself until about six months ago.

At first, she wasn't sure what was happening to her. She'd been sitting at her desk in her office at home working, her body completely relaxed. Then suddenly her stomach did a flip flop, and she became instantly nauseous.

A whirling sensation began in her head along with quick breaths and an accelerated heartbeat. Her head felt fuzzy, and a slight pounding began. Then a raging heat coursed through her body, and she began to sweat. Her fingers shook as she struggled with the zipper on her sweatshirt she'd been wearing. It felt like she couldn't strip it off fast enough.

Then a suffocating feeling overcame her. Jolene began pulling at the collar of her shirt as if this would help air enter her throat and lungs more easily. Tears sprang to her eyes, and she thought, *this is it, I'm dying. Travis leaving didn't kill me, the symptoms, the medications haven't killed me, but this, this is going to kill me.*

And then, as fast as the episode came on, it dissipated just as quickly. It was there one minute, her caught up in the middle of it, and then, gone. Although the attack left her feeling drained.

When she still had a throbbing headache and felt more tired than normal three days later, she called Dr. Whalen her neurologist. She assumed it had been a side effect from the new medication he had recently prescribed her.

But after describing the episode to him in full detail, he told her without a doubt, she had suffered a panic attack. Jolene hung up the phone after talking to him feeling depleted. It was just one more thing to add to her long list of symptoms.

"How was your day with the girls?" Bo asked, bringing her out of her head.

He had his elbow bent, resting on the door with the window down. The evening air had already turned cool, and Jolene was grateful she'd worn jeans rather than a skirt or shorts. Yet her arms were bare in the tank top she'd chosen, and goosebumps covered them. She wrapped her arms around herself and hugged her body. When she didn't answer, Bo glanced in her direction.

"You cold?"

"A little," she lied.

"Sorry about that." Bo pushed the button for the power window, stopping it when there was only an inch remaining. "I guess I'm just used to the weather here by now. Been here long enough."

"The weather here is pretty similar to back home. Especially with the cooler mornings and evenings in the summer. We get that too." She unwrapped her arms from her body and folded her hands in her lap, taking notice of the white scars crisscrossing them.

"Then you must be cold because you're still a tiny thing," Bo said. "You sure you're doing okay?" He arched a brow at her.

Her throat thickened, defensiveness crawling up it. "I'm fine."

"You have a good doctor over there? One who's taking good care of you? Got you on the right meds?"

"Yes," she answered through gritted teeth. She was beginning to feel offended by all his questions, like she was the criminal being interrogated by the cop. "I have a wonderful doctor. He's the best in all of Central Oregon."

"Good. I'm glad to hear."

"I'm on some medications right now that seem to be fine so far. I'm on a pretty strict diet. And I do yoga and swim and I'm still running," Jolene explained.

"That's great. I was just stating the obvious. And I worry about you, that's all. Stop reading into my words like you always do."

"The diet and the exercise help to keep the symptoms at bay. I decided that I'm not going to let this disease take me down without a fight. I plan to beat the statistics. I spent three months in bed after my diagnosis and my separation. I was ready to give up. I was ready to give into the depression and the disease." Tears stung her eyes, and she bit the inside of her cheek. She did not want to get emotional; she did not want to cry.

"Jo, you don't have to—"

But she cut him off. "One day, my friend Joy came over to see me. I was in bed with the curtains shut and in the same clothes I'd been in for three days. Joy pulled open the curtains, drug me out of bed and put me in the shower fully clothed. She turned the cold water on, and I screamed at her while I stood in that freezing shower. I screamed until I couldn't scream anymore. And then I lost all energy and cried. Joy hugged me and cried right along with me. And you don't know Joy, she is a tough one. She doesn't cry, or hug. She sort of reminds me of Cristina. She doesn't take BS from anyone."

"Sounds like a good friend to have."

"She is." Jolene nodded. "I don't know what would've happened if she hadn't come and snapped me out of my depression."

He remained quiet next to her.

"Since Travis not only dumped me, but dumped the brewery in my lap and went back to being a realtor, Joy has been helping me. And she's the one keeping my kids right now since Travis had to take a last minute trip to Palm Springs."

Bo quirked a questioning brow at her.

She threw up a hand. "Please, don't ask. I'm fine. I enjoy brewing. In fact, I think I'm rather good at it too." A smile tugged at her lips and Bo's face relaxed.

She peered out the passenger window. The sky was turning a darker shade of blue as the night crept up on them. She'd forgotten how beautiful it was here. It reminded her a lot of home, of Central Oregon, but at the same time, it was different.

Here, there were all these large granite boulders surrounding the lake and the sides of the road along with tall sugar pines. At home, red lava rocks replaced the granite and juniper trees replaced the sugar pines. The air was clear but thick from the high elevation. It was harder to catch your breath up here. This thought concerned her. *Harder to catch your breath.* The fear of a panic attack loomed over her like a dark storm cloud.

"You know, between the diet and the exercise, I don't even have to take anti-depressants. The running, I think, is the secret. I didn't think it would be possible to continue to run after I was diagnosed. But my doctor told me to run as long as my body will allow it."

"That's great, I'm glad to hear it," Bo said. "Just try to take it easy. Especially this week, while you're here."

"Believe me, that's the plan."

"And speaking of good friends..." Bo's voice trailed off. He eased off the accelerator as he ventured down the twists and curves of the winding road.

"What about them?" Jolene asked, feeling those two pesky lines forming in between her brows.

"Did you talk to Cristina and Kendra yet?" He glanced in her direction for a beat.

She hesitated, twirling her earring. "No, not yet."

"You need to tell them, Ollie."

Zing. There it was again, an electricity swooping low in her belly. "I know, and I will."

"Just think about if the roles were reversed. You'd want them to tell you, wouldn't you?"

"Yes, of course." Jolene hated when Bo was right.

And he was always right. Nothing had changed there. Which made her think back to the night in the Sweet Shop when they were kids and he told her he didn't want to mess up their friendship by starting up a relationship.

"So today went well for you girls? You took the M.S. Dixie tour, didn't you?" Bo was obviously changing the subject.

She nodded. "Yeah, we did. It was fun. It seems less awkward between us. I worried it would be strange all week. I mean, it's been years since we've all been together." The reminder hit her again, that they weren't *all* together. Becca wasn't there. And it would never feel like old times.

"I think the three of us may even try to stay in better contact after this."

"That's great."

"It is, but," she hesitated, thinking back to the conversation with her friends from the night before. "I feel like all of the years apart have put a wedge between us."

"How so?"

"I feel like there's something going on with Cristina."

"Oh yeah, why's that?" Bo's vision drifted in her direction for a glimpse.

"I'm not exactly sure. I can't quite put my finger on it. But I think she's holding something back," she said.

"It's probably nothing."

"Well, I shared about my separation with Travis and Kendra shared something. But Cristina said nothing."

"That doesn't mean anything."

"No, maybe not," Jolene agreed. "But then Kendra made a comment to Cristina. Something like, we all have secrets. It made me think that she knows something I don't."

"It's true, ya know?"

"What's true?"

"That we all have secrets. Everyone does. That's why they're called secrets. If people went around sharing everything with everybody, there would be no such thing as secrets."

Bo reached a hand up to his hair then hesitated, as if remembering he couldn't run his fingers through the firm hair that had been stiffened with gel. He always used to rub his buzzed head whenever he got uncomfortable. She wouldn't mind running her fingers through his hair right about now.

"True," she agreed. "You seem to know a lot about this secret stuff. Just what are you hiding, Bo Dean?" she teased.

"Me? Secrets? Nah," he said with a slight shake of his head. "I'm an open book."

"Then would you please, tell me where we're going," Jolene pleaded, hands together, fingers interlaced.

"You'll know soon enough. We're almost there."

"Fine."

She pouted as she gazed out the front windshield. She tried paying attention to the landmarks on the road and the few street signs they passed, trying to guess where he might be taking her. But when she was a teenager, her and the girls didn't come to the south side of the lake very often. Typically, they'd stay on the north end. They'd pull out the family bikes from the Gibbs's shed and ride them to Ander's Bar and Grill for fries or the Tahoe City Sweet Shop for ice cream. The entire area had changed so much over the last seventeen years since she'd been there last, it was difficult to recognize where she was.

CHAPTER FOURTEEN

When the truck slowed, Bo took a left onto 15th street and then a right onto Venice Drive. Jolene recognized the streets. They were near the Tahoe Keys Marina. Did he own a boat? Was he taking her for a ride on it? Or taking her to eat at the Fresh Kitchen restaurant near the marina?

But he had told her to leave her purse back at the cottage. If they went to eat, she wouldn't be able to order a drink because she didn't have I.D. with her. And she couldn't pay for herself or even offer to pay. Because this wasn't supposed to be a date.

"You own a boat?" she asked.

Bo shook his head. His lack of response only generated more questions. If he didn't own a boat, maybe he borrowed one?

Bo pulled the truck into a parking spot at the marina. She was confused yet the excitement fluttered in her stomach. She wouldn't lie, the idea of someone taking the time to plan an adventure for *her*, was riveting.

"We're here," Bo said.

"What are we doing at the marina?"

"Just c'mon. It's nearly dark."

Jolene jumped out of the passenger side of the truck. Her nerves were on edge. And although she was excited, it caused anxiety to course through her, the fear of a panic attack etching. She felt for her phone in the back pocket of her jeans, relief setting in once she discovered its presence.

The sun was setting and as a result, the sky overhead was already turning from shades of blues and violets to shades of indigo and navy blue. The late evening air felt tepid on her bare skin and the water appeared calm in the Marina with the boats nestled in their homes for the night.

The two of them walked along the edge of the long docks in silence, Bo moving at a fast pace. He glanced over both shoulders before reaching out his hand to her as she trailed behind.

"C'mon," he urged.

She slipped her hand into his, no fingers interlaced. Yet somehow, this act of hand holding felt more intimate than when they held hands as children. A voltaic shock traveled from Bo's hand to hers, coursing through her entire body.

"Bo?" she called.

He turned to her; a finger pressed against his lips. "Shh."

"Bo?" she repeated in a whisper. "What are we doing?"

Glancing over his shoulder again, his eyes darted in all directions. He gripped her hand tighter. She felt the urgency in her need to be quiet.

"We have to hurry," Bo whispered. "And be quiet."

Jolene nodded.

A couple shuffled out of the Fresh Kitchen restaurant, noise following until the doors closed behind them. The man had his arm draped around the shoulder of the woman next to him as they both laughed.

"Officer Dean?" the man called.

Bo stopped them dead in their tracks. He dropped her hand, putting distance between them.

"Ricky." Bo acknowledged the man by reaching his hand out to him.

"Hey, man, how have you been?" Ricky asked.

"I'm doing just fine, thanks."

"Good to hear." Ricky gestured to the woman with him. "You know my girlfriend, Stacy."

"Right, hello, Stacy. How've you been?" Bo shook the woman's hand.

"Fine, thanks," the tall woman answered.

Jolene noticed the handshake between them lingered far longer than necessary. The woman's low-cut, red slinky dress hugged her perfect body. Red—Becca's color. Her long blonde curls flowed over her bare shoulders. The air was tense, but all she could focus on was the woman's dress as the memories flickered through her mind.

A red car, a red sweater, a red pool of blood.

"And who's this?" Ricky asked, gesturing to Jolene.

"Sorry." Bo placed his hand on the small of her back. "Uh, this is my friend, Jolene. She's visiting from Oregon."

"Well, Hello, Jolene." Ricky shook her hand, holding onto it for a beat too long while he waggled his eyebrows at her. "Well, aren't you a pretty sight." He gave a sly grin.

Her cheeks burned.

The woman, Stacy, put her hand out to Jolene. Their handshake was limp and quick. Stacy had to nearly bend down to shake her hand. Sometimes she hated being so short.

"What part of Oregon are you from, Jolene?" Ricky asked.

He had a tall build with a bit of a gut, maybe a beer belly judging by the stench of alcohol seeping from his pores.

"Central," she answered.

"Beautiful place. I've been over there to play golf with some coworkers. We played in Sunriver." His words came out some-what slurred.

"Sunriver is a wonderful place to play golf, very popular."

"Hey uh, Ricky?" Bo interrupted. "You aren't planning on driving tonight, are you?"

Ricky's previous happy expression and voice changed to annoyance. "No, Officer Dean. I'm not," he said using a mocking tone. "We're walking from here back to my place." Ricky swung his arm around Stacy's shoulder again and Jolene noticed the straining weight she bore as it hung like deadweight on her body.

"Would you like me to give you guys a ride home?" Bo offered.

"No thank you. It's a beautiful night, we want to walk." Ricky and Stacy locked eyes and then kissed passionately.

"Alright then, you two have a good night," Bo said.

Ricky unlocked his lips from Stacy's, before replying, "Will do. You two do the same. And hey, we should grab a beer sometime."

"Sure. Goodnight."

"Night," Stacy called over her shoulder as the two saun-tered off.

"Sorry about that," Bo said.

"About what?"

"Ricky is a realtor in town. Trouble seems to follow him. He's been involved with an incident or two with drugs in the casinos and nightclubs. And been picked up for drinking and driving on occasion. The other guys go easy on him, houses and land aren't cheap around here. Me? I have zero tolerance for that shit. Besides, I already have a house." Bo smirked.

"And Stacy?"

"What about her?"

"C'mon, I'm not stupid. I sensed the connection there. What's the story?"

Bo hung his head. "Stacy and I dated. It was a while back. I let it go on for longer than I should've. I knew early on she wasn't right for me. By the time I broke it off, she said she was in love with me."

"Harsh." Jolene breathed out.

"Yeah, I felt terrible. But we had nothing in common. And I mean, nothing. And no offense, she's not the brightest person. She really should've seen the breakup coming." Bo's eyes seemed to strain as he tried to spot the intoxicated couple, but they were no longer in sight. "It was a long time ago." He shrugged.

"Should you go after them?"

"No, they'll be fine. Ricky lives in Tahoe Keys. It's quite a walk but it should be good for them. Maybe they'll walk off some of the alcohol. Besides, this is a safe part of town."

She remembered that. If you lived in Tahoe Keys, you had money. The houses were fancy and spacious, and all sat right on the water with their own private dock for their boat. When she was a teenager, she didn't even know anyone who could afford to live in Tahoe Keys. Besides the Gibbs. But they wanted complete waterfront property, so they opted for a place in Tahoe City right on the beach.

"C'mon," Bo said. "Your adventure awaits."

Jolene had forgotten all about the adventure after running into Ricky and Stacy. The excitement had died down a bit and she found herself thinking about the cozy bed waiting for her back at the Gibbs's cottage. Sleep sounded tempting.

But Bo grabbed her hand, interrupting her daydream of sleep. They weaved past large, powered boats perched in their dry homes and past the closed marina office. Bo adjusted his hand and interlaced his fingers with hers. The same shock traveled through her veins again. And her cheeks went hot. She bit her lower lip and hoped her face was hidden by the indigo sky.

Bo Dean was holding her hand. If only seventeen-year-old Jolene could see her now.

He pulled her onto a dock. It was narrow and long. On both sides sat a multitude of boats nestled in for the night. There were sailboats, powered and fishing boats, and boats of all different sizes and colors. All of them featured names in different fonts. She read them as they passed. *Annabelle, First Edition, Cat Nap,* and *Lake Breeze.*

Bo stopped at a boat with the name, *My Fair Lady.* He jerked her hand, sending a jolt through her arm and her body was forced to move with his. He stepped over the side of the boat and put his hands around her waist to help her in.

"Bo," she whispered, "what are we doing?"

"If I remember correctly, you wanted to see the stars?" Bo said softly as he gestured up at the sky.

Her gaze flicked up and was met with a darkened sky speckled with tiny white stars. Slack-jawed, she gazed at them. Bo slipped his hand into hers again and pulled her through the boat and past the cockpit toward the stern.

He climbed onto the deck and yanked her up alongside him. He released her hand and laid down sideways on the flat deck, motioning for her to lie down next to him. Jolene hesitated while her thoughts battled. *Holy hell, what was she doing?* But this was Bo Dean, so, she gave in and laid down but put some distance between them.

Their breathing could be heard in the quiet stillness of the darkened night, heavy and quick. Her heart beat hard against her chest.

After nearly a minute of silence Bo said in a hushed tone, "You were right."

"Yeah? About what?" she whispered.

"You can't see stars like this in the city."

And all at once, the memory came flooding back to her mind like a dam had just opened-up. That night from so many years ago when she had urged him to skip the party and come here to look at the stars with her. That had been a defining moment in their relationship. Bo made the decision to remain friends as if he had drawn a line in the sand.

Until the night of the accident. When she'd thrown herself at him and instead of humiliating her and sending her away, he'd given her exactly what she'd needed.

Emotions coursed through her, causing her body to heat up. An uncomfortable sweat began, and the bare parts of her stuck to the deck of the boat. She wanted to say something, but her brain couldn't seem to conjure up the right words.

Because Bo was trying to recreate an experience they'd missed out on as teenagers.

The two of them laid there in silence again as she attempted to push away the attraction she felt for him, even while the desire burned through her. She gazed up at the sky. It had already turned from a navy-blue hue to black, causing the white lights to flicker more intensely against the backdrop of the darkness.

"So? What do ya think?" Bo asked finally, his growly voice cutting through the silence.

"What do I think?" She swiped her hand across the back of her neck.

"Well yeah. About the stars?"

"Oh, about the stars."

"What did you think I was talking about?"

"Oh, I don't know," Jolene bit her bottom lip, before stumbling over the next few words. "Maybe, what do I think about us sneaking onto someone's private property? Or, what do I think about you trying to recreate a moment we could have had twenty years ago?"

She felt Bo's intense eyes on her, but she kept her attention focused on the sky. Her body shivered and she couldn't be certain if it was from the cold or the nerves.

Bo cleared his throat. "That's fair." He tore his attention away from her and faced the sky again, studying the multitude of bright specks with her. "I've kicked myself nearly every day for the last twenty years for not bringing you out here that night."

Heat filled her face again. What was she supposed to do with that? His words threw her. She felt so unprepared for them.

"I doubt that's true," she managed to say.

"Well, it is." Bo's last words drifted. Then he said, "When I saw you Friday night, it was as if I had been woken up from a trance. Like I'd been living my life in a dream, not really living ya know? Until I saw you."

She hoped he didn't expect a response from her. Because she couldn't speak, her voice caught in her constricted throat. Her eyelashes fluttered and she worried she might cry. Hearing Bo's words made her head spin, and she was thankful she was laying down, otherwise she would've spun out of control.

"I guess I just figured, by bringing you out here tonight, that I owed it to you. And to myself. I remember hearing the disappointment in your voice that night. And I've been hearing it in my head ever since." Bo reached his hand up to his hair again and this time, he wrestled through the stiffness of hair product.

"Bo, you know you don't owe me anything," Jolene said, her voice hoarse. "That was a long time ago. Don't feel bad that you decided to just be friends. I loved having you as a friend."

"Yeah well, just because we were friends didn't mean we couldn't have been more. I was stupid."

"We were young. We all do stupid stuff when we're young." She elbowed him playfully in his side, lightening the mood. But he continued to lay still, staring up at the night sky.

"True, but I'm not young anymore. I can't keep making stupid mistakes."

Bo turned his head to face her. She could see him out of the corner of her eye, the lights from the marina reflecting on his chiseled face.

"You've walked back into my life and I don't intend on letting you go this time."

It took everything in her not to throw herself at him, because—hell, this was Bo Dean.

"Bo," Jolene whispered, "I'm still married."

"I know." He ran his hand over his lips. "I don't intend on letting you go without a fight. I should've fought for you all those years ago."

Her cheeks flushed and she hoped the lights from the marina didn't reflect the smile that pulled on her lips. But her smile faded quickly. The negative thoughts in her mind getting the best of her once more. *He only thinks he wants you, he's caught up in the moment. You're a boring people pleaser with no personality.*

"You don't even know me anymore, I've changed," she said flatly.

"I know you."

"No, you don't. It's been too long, there's been too much time and distance between us for you to really know me."

"Ollie," Bo whispered.

Her nickname lingered on his lips and caused every fiber in her body to stand on end and then unravel. He only had to utter that one word and she came completely undone.

Jolene's eyelashes fluttered again, matching the fluttering in her stomach. But it wasn't the typical nerves of anxiety she was used to feeling. It was a familiar feeling she hadn't experienced in a long time. And without a doubt, she recognized it as that feeling of first love. It started in the pit of her stomach and spread through every part of her insides creating an unforgiving ache.

Bo reached out his hand toward hers that she had resting at her side. He ran his thumb along the crease between her thumb and pointer finger and the light touch sent a shiver dancing up her spine. He hooked his pinky finger with hers and they stayed like that for several minutes, in silence, staring at the sky.

The bright white stars spanned across the backdrop of the inky sky and captivated her. She wished she could stay in this place and this moment forever, with Bo by her side. Maybe he did know her—the *real* her. And maybe he didn't see that boring woman she worried she'd become. Maybe he saw the girl she once was. And maybe, that girl was still in there somewhere.

The night had turned cool and there was a slight breeze blowing from the water. Bo propped himself up on his elbow and reached his hand across Jolene's body, his fingers caressing her arm. He moved his hand up to her shoulder and then her neck, cupping her head in his hand.

The breath in her throat caught and her head began to spin again. Feeling the ache in the pit of her stomach so present at that moment. And she wanted to forget about the rest of the world—forget about Travis, her illness, the brewery.

Bo leaned his head closer to hers and his breath heated her face. She worried he might kiss her but at the same time, she feared he wouldn't. He pressed his lips onto her forehead and held them there for a beat. Then, with his mouth hovering over her skin, he moved down the bridge of her nose until he reached the tip and kissed it. Each kiss lighter than the one before and bringing back memories of that night all those years ago.

Jolene's insides melted from his gentle touch like ice cream on hot asphalt. Bo's mouth guided downward and hovered above her lips and her body convulsed. The air between them burned and felt nearly unbearable. His lips brushed hers faintly, teasing them, leaving them wanting more. So much more. Her breath hitched as he made his way to her neck, planting blistering gentle kisses there.

Bo pulled away; his chest suspended above her. "You don't know how long I've waited to kiss you."

"Well, you haven't really kissed me yet," she said softly, smiling but already hating the distance between them. She needed his hot breath on her, his lips against her fiery skin.

"I know." Bo leaned back on his forearm, hanging his head.

"What is it? What's wrong?" She sat up, flustered and her body protesting at their separation. She leaned back on her elbows, her breathing quickened.

"I just don't want to screw this up. I feel like we've been given a second chance, and I don't want to make a mess of things again."

"I feel the same way. But to be honest, I shouldn't be kissing you anyway. This was a mistake." Jolene exhaled. She hung her head back and looked up at the sky again, her hair flowing down.

"Ollie—"

"Stop." She raised a palm at him. "Please," the word came out choked. She sat up straight.

"Ollie," Bo pleaded.

"Please, stop doing that."

"Stop doing what?" He reached for her hands.

"Stop calling me Ollie." But she regretted the words before they even came out of her mouth.

"But that's what I've always called you. It never seemed to bother you before." Bo moved to sit next to her, their legs hanging over the back of the boat, and their knees touching.

"I know, I know." She hugged her body, rubbing her bare arms. "But it's killing me." The words came out harsh and louder than sh"d anticipated.

"Wow, I'm sorry. I had no idea." He ran a hand over his hair.

"Look, I didn't mean that. It's just, it's just...I'm married. Still married."

"I know."

"I mean, it's not like I'm really married, but I am. We've been separated for a year, and it doesn't look like he has any intentions of working things out." She exhaled a bitter laugh. "But without the official papers, I guess I can't help but wonder. And when you call me Ollie, it just messes me up inside. It makes my head and my stomach feel crazy things. Not to mention, other parts," she mumbled, pressing her fingers to the sides of her face. "Things as a married woman, I'm not supposed to be feeling for someone else."

Bo gently tugged her hands from her face and gazed into her eyes. "Do you still love him?"

Jolene bit the inside of her cheek. She needed to catch her breath. The entire evening's emotions had snowballed, and she was breathing too fast. She flicked her attention away from his enticing green eyes and focused on her painted toenails, studying them while choosing her words carefully.

"I do."

"Ahh, you do huh?"

She finally looked at him. "How can I not? I've been with him since I was a kid. And he was there during everything with Jacob. I guess the loss of him brought the two of us even. And Bo, we have kids together. We're supposed to be a family."

"But if you're supposed to be a family, why aren't you? Where is he? Where is he when you need him most? This is bigger than when you lost Jacob, Jo. He left you as soon as you learned about your illness. And left you to take care of your kids without him." Bo's intense and gruff voice hummed across the top of the water.

"That's not fair. He helps with the kids. He's still a good father."

"Fine, I'm not here to argue with you on that. I don't even really know the guy. All I know is, if the woman I loved was going through what you're going through, I would move mountains to be with her, to take care of her, to protect her." Bo was on his feet now, standing in the boat, his movement causing it to rock.

Was Bo even talking about Travis anymore? Maybe he was talking about himself—*he* would move mountains to be with her? Her thoughts moved to his gentle, confident touch, and his soft kisses on her bare skin and it caused her mind to whirl. She spun her legs around so they were dangling inside the boat and she faced him.

"Just what are you saying, Bo?"

"You know exactly what I'm saying. I've already said it." He glanced at his feet as they shuffled back and forth causing the boat to continue to rock. "I won't let you go without a fight."

Tears pricked her eyes and her throat tightened. She shook her head and let out a strangled, "Bo." The confrontation was killing her. She just needed them to be okay again.

"Okay, so what? So what if you still love him. You have history and kids together. I get that. But we have a history together too." His sharp gaze pierced through her soul, and she knew he wasn't simply referring to their friendship. "You know we'd be great together. We've always known. This could be our second chance." Bo sat down next to her, pulling her hand into his lap.

"Bo," she repeated. "It's not that easy. Things are complicated. Not only with the kids and us living far apart. But have you forgotten about the dark ugly cloud that looms above me, this thing called Multiple Sclerosis?"

"Don't do that, Jo. Don't use that as an excuse. I want to be with you regardless of the MS. I know what I'm getting myself into." Bo raised her chin, forcing her to look at him.

Tears filled her eyes and threatened to spill. She urged them back, along with the negative voices that were consuming her thoughts. All the *what if's* and *what then's*.

"Ollie," Bo whispered.

Her body tingled in response to his voice, to her nickname. Tears slipped out of her eyes. The fear that overcame her earlier that she would never hear the nickname from his lips again, dissipated. And she could feel herself giving into him. All the years apart slipping away.

Bo cupped her face in his hands and swiped at her tears with his thumbs. "The biggest question is, do you love me?"

Jolene gripped Bo's bent forearms. She'd always loved him. Since she was twelve years old. Her eyes flicked back and forth as she scanned his. A reluctant smile formed on her lips.

Bo pressed his forehead against hers. "That's not an answer."

She knew it wasn't, but she wanted to stay like this, touching him and entangled with him for as long as possible.

"Hey!" a loud and rough voice hollered, slicing through the intimacy between them.

Bo and Jolene scrambled to their feet. A light coming from the dock moved toward them.

"Who's out there?" the man's voice called. "I know someone's there, I heard y'all talking."

Bo grabbed her hand and yanked her down to her knees in the boat. "Get down. And be quiet."

Jolene's heart slammed against her chest so hard she feared it might stop beating. Her breathing accelerated and the shrill anticipation someone might catch them caused her stomach to pinch. How had this evening taken such a horrible turn?

The man began to yell again. "This is private property. Y'all are trespassing on my boat!"

Bo moved on his hands and knees toward the cockpit. He motioned her to follow. She stayed close behind. He pointed underneath the steering wheel and then gestured at her. She slipped her body underneath as far as it would fit. There wasn't enough room next to her for Bo. He put his finger to his lips, making a *shh* sound.

He peered around the side of the cockpit. She pulled on his shirt and followed behind him disregarding his urge she should go back. They both watched the man move swiftly down the dock. It would only be a matter of seconds and he would be on the boat, and they would be caught.

And who cares? This was insane. Wasn't she a grown up? And yet here she was crawling around on her hands and knees.

"What the hell are you yelling at, Mr. Fennel?" a second man's voice called in a slurred tone. Jolene peeked her head up and spotted a man in a boat just two away from them. He stood, wearing only a pair of dark colored boxer briefs, and holding a wine glass. Her eyes were hazy, and she squinted to get a clearer view.

"I heard voices on my boat," the gruff voice declared.

"No you didn't," the man on the boat said. "You heard voices coming from *my* boat."

"Nah, wasn't you. I'm sure of it. I'm calling the cops and when they get here, they'll confirm my suspicions."

"Hey now, don't be calling the cops over here. Officer Dean

was already down here earlier this evening, and I don't need him coming back around, you hear me?" the man on the boat said.

Bo and Jolene shot a look at one another at the mention of his name. A tall thin woman dressed in only a man's button-down dress shirt stepped out from the cabin below the boat. Her long blonde hair cascaded down her back with some strands tucked inside the back of the shirt. Jolene recognized the woman, it was Stacy.

"I thought he said they were going back to his house?" she whispered.

Bo hunched a shoulder. "Guess he meant his houseboat."

"What's going on, Ricky?" Stacy held a glass of wine in one hand and placed her other hand on his bare back.

"This crazy old bastard thinks someone's out on his boat. I told him it was you and I talking. The sound carries out here on the water," Ricky said.

"Well, we weren't really doing much talking." Stacy shrugged, a sly smile playing on her lips. She glanced in the direction of the old man's boat, looked away, then looked back over once more for a beat too long, squinting her eyes. It was unclear if she'd seen them as she made no indication either way.

She caressed Ricky's back, taking a sip of wine from her glass before saying to the man, "Sir, we've been out here for like, a while, and I can assure you, we're the only ones out here. I apologize if we were too loud for you, I can get a little carried away sometimes." She leaned forward and put her hand next to her mouth as if she was going to tell the older man a secret. Lowering her voice, she said, "I've been known to be a loud lover."

The older man's body was only a silhouette from where

Jolene crouched, but she could see him shuffle his feet and rub the back of his neck.

"Now, if you don't mind, I've got like, a super early shift in the morning," Stacy said. Then she took a hold of Ricky's hand, tugging it. "Now, where were we?" She guided Ricky toward the cabin.

"Alright, Mr. Fennel, now go on back home and go back to bed."

The older man sighed and mumbled under his breath. He stood on the edge of the dock, watching Stacy and Ricky slip back down to the cabin below. Taking one last look around, he shined the flashlight at his boat and the two of them hunched lower. Then he took a few steps forward until he was in front of it. Leaning down, he pressed his lips to his palm then placed his palm onto the boat. "Don't you worry, I'll always protect you, my fair lady."

The man strolled away and as soon as he reached the other end of the dock, Bo and Jolene climbed out of their hiding place. She stood and stretched out her cramped legs. Then she let out a deep breath, pressing her hand to her chest.

"You alright?" Bo asked.

The rhythm of her beating heart had finally slowed. "Yeah, I'm okay. I thought for sure we were gonna get caught." Jolene exhaled a quiet laugh. Then she muffled her mouth with her hand.

"I can't imagine," Bo said. "I kept thinking, what would the chief say. I've never done anything like this before. At least not since I was a teenager. What a rush."

"Yeah for sure." She laughed again.

"That was kinda fun," Bo admitted.

"But I shouldn't be laughing. That poor man is going to think he was going crazy." She couldn't help herself, she let out another giggle.

Bo smiled. "On that note, I think we should call it a night."

"Agreed. I'm exhausted."

Bo climbed out of the boat and stepped onto the dock, reaching his hand out for Jolene. She slipped her hand into his, where it fit perfectly, and he lifted her onto the dock. The night was dark and only the dim light from the marina guided their steps.

Bo came to a stop abruptly and put out his arm to stop her.

"What is it?" she asked.

Bo put a finger to his lips.

"Who's there?" the gruff voice called again. "Ricky? That you?" Mr. Fennel moved in their direction.

Bo leaned over and whispered into Jolene's ear, "we're gonna have to make a run for it."

Her jaw dropped. Was he serious? Hiding out on the boat had been kinda fun and exciting. But hadn't this gone far enough? Shouldn't they just come clean with this poor guy? But before she could say these things aloud, Bo grabbed her hand and tugged. The two of them darted down the sidewalk and past the Fresh Kitchen restaurant.

The man called after them, "hey you, trespassers, go on, get out of here. Next time the cops will get you, if I don't get to you first!" he hollered. "Damn kids."

Jolene stumbled and a vivid image of her falling came to mind, but Bo caught her. He gripped her hand as they sprinted. And they didn't stop until they reached Bo's truck. Her breathing was hard and fast and she doubled over at her waist feeling the rush of adrenaline.

"You okay?" Bo asked.

She started laughing again. And this time she couldn't stop. Bo joined in with her, both trying to catch their breath.

"I'm fine," she managed to say in between laughs and waved a hand while her eyes watered.

"Damn kids," Bo mimicked the older man's words.

And they both laughed even harder as they climbed into the truck.

CHAPTER FIFTEEN

"How did I let you guys talk me into this?" Cristina panted.

She trailed several feet behind Jolene and Kendra on the lake shore, her feet sinking into the wet rocky sand as she dragged them along. She looked like she was running with ankle weights on. Jolene felt like a teenager again as she listened to Cristina whine.

"C'mon, Cris, you'll be thanking us later," Kendra cheered. She turned around and ran backward, encouraging Cristina to pick up the pace by clapping her hands together.

Jolene slowed her pace until Cristina caught up.

"Doubtful. I think I'll be hating you more later than I do right now," Cristina huffed.

"I'm not going to lie, you're going to be sore. But once the soreness wears off, you'll feel great." Kendra's positive attitude could be contagious at times but, this was clearly not one of those times.

"You wanna take a break?" Jolene asked.

"No," Kendra interrupted. "No break, she can do this."

Cristina rolled her eyes, wiping sweat off her forehead with the back of her hand. Jolene passed her a sympathetic look. The three women continued the three-mile lake shore route.

They'd just reached the halfway point and turned around when Cristina started complaining again.

"Screw it, I'm walking the rest of the way," she said in between shortened breaths.

"No, you can't give up," Kendra insisted.

But Cristina had already stopped. She rested her hands on her hips, trying to catch her breath. Jolene stopped and offered Cristina some water from her water bottle. Kendra ran in place alongside them, pumping her legs and clapping her hands repeatedly.

"You have to just keep pushing yourself. You can do it, c'mon."

"You're like the freaking energizer bunny on crack," Cristina said.

Jolene couldn't help but laugh. Cristina wasn't wrong.

Kendra continued to run in place but stopped the clapping. "Okay, okay," she resigned, laughing. "I know I can be a little intense at times—"

"A *little*?" Cristina arched her brows.

"Okay, a lot intense," Kendra admitted. "But you know I'm only intense about the things I'm passionate about. And you know that includes running."

"I know, but *you* know I've never been a big fan of running. I only agreed to this because you two agreed to a relaxing day at the lake today. Followed by a night of drinking."

"Yep, you're right. And that's just what we're gonna do," Jolene said.

"Cris, can you at least try to finish? I'll slow my pace, promise."

Cristina narrowed her eyes, giving Kendra a skeptical look.

"Honest, cross my heart." Kendra drew an imaginary X across her heart with her finger.

It was like they were kids again. These two used to constantly argue or give each other the silent treatment. Sometimes they'd go several days without speaking to one another, making it awkward between the four girls. They spent nearly every waking moment with one another. When Cristina and Kendra were fighting, it put a strain on the entire group—especially non-confrontational Jolene. If Becca was here, she'd tell them both to get over themselves, finish the damn run and then get their butts in the lake.

Cristina exhaled a deep sigh. "Fine."

Kendra jumped up and down in delight. "Yay! You don't know how happy this makes me."

"But promise me," Cristina said, pointing a finger in Kendra's face, "if I do this, if I actually finish this thing, you stop bugging me. And the rest of the day will be spent relaxing. Agreed?"

"Agreed."

The three women set off again on the three-mile course, this time at a slower pace than they had before—just as Kendra had promised.

"You got this, Cris. I'm so proud of you," Kendra cheered.

"Shut up, Kendra," Cristina said in broken speech through shortened breaths.

"Not much farther now," Jolene whispered.

"Thank, God."

She could second that notion. She welcomed the slower pace. After waking up with a pounding headache, she couldn't wait to get back to the cottage and take a couple pain pills. Maybe if she could get a nap in at the beach, she'd feel better by evening. The girls had plans to stay in and share a few drinks around the fire pit which sounded amazing.

Taking a break from Bo wasn't a bad idea. Things had grown too serious the night before.

Jolene must have been so deep in thought because next thing she knew, she was lying face down on the beach. Gritty sand coated her lips and pain shot through her body. The ache in her head had worsened.

"Oh my goodness, Jo! Are you alright?" Kendra bent down on her knees next to her.

"What happened?" Cristina asked, coming along her other side.

Together, the two women helped her back onto her feet. She wiped the sand off her lips with the back of her hand. When she looked down, she discovered sand on her knees as well. She tried brushing it off, but blood oozed out in between the corroded sand.

"Ouch," Jolene finally muttered.

"Are you okay?" Cristina asked.

"Yeah, I'm fine."

"You don't look fine," Kendra said. "You're bleeding."

"It's not that bad. I'm okay."

Once she was steady on her feet, she realized the pain wasn't too bad and her knees looked more pitiful than they felt. The worst part of all of this wasn't the gritty sand in her mouth or the bloody knees. She'd just fallen in front of her friends—friends who didn't know she had MS.

"What happened?" Cristina asked.

"I guess I wasn't paying attention and tripped."

"You clumsy ho," Cristina teased.

Jolene smiled, grateful for Cristina's comment. It made the embarrassment bearable. And distracted her from the reality of her condition, the disease, her life.

"C'mon, let's get you back to the cottage. You're going to

need some Band-Aids on those knees." Kendra linked her arm in Jolene's.

Cristina took her other arm. "That should look attractive at the beach today." And she grinned.

"Are you sure you'll still be up for going today?" Kendra asked, watching Jolene wince as she attempted the steps of the back deck of the cottage.

"Oh yeah, I'll be fine. I'm looking forward to relaxing with my girls,"she said.

"I'll check for a first aid kit in the bathroom," Cristina said once the three of them were inside the cottage.

Jolene followed Cristina into the bathroom closest to her room. Taking a washcloth from the basket on the counter, she ran it under the cold water from the faucet. She sat on the edge of the bathtub and proceeded to wash the blood from her knees. Cristina was right; her legs were in bad shape.

This tripping and falling happened more often and each time it did, she worried about the day she couldn't run anymore. Tears welled up in her eyes and not because of the pain. She let her hair hang down, framing her face to shield her eyes from Cristina.

"Jackpot." Cristina pulled a plastic bin out of a cupboard. "Let's see what our choices are. Hmm looks like Barbie or Frozen."

Cristina held two boxes of Band-Aids in the air, one with pink hearts and dolls with unrealistic bodies and the other featuring two girls and a talking snowman from a popular Disney movie. Jolene frowned at her choices. The last thing she wanted to do was go to the lake in her bathing suit sporting pink Barbie Band-Aids on her knees.

"Please tell me I have a third choice."

Cristina smirked as she reached into the bin and pulled out a box of tan bandages. Jolene exhaled a sigh of relief. Not that any color of Band-Aid would look good on her knees, but surely a solid color would draw less attention.

"Thank God," she said, taking back out the two boxes Cristina had first held up. She glanced back and forth at them, studying the pink and princess details.

Grabbing a dry towel off a rack on the wall, Cristina bent in front of Jolene with the first aid kit.

"Do you think Ms. Gibbs bought these for her grandsons? Barbie?" Jolene raised her eyebrows.

"Nah, she's probably had them since Lark was little." Cristina's diligent hands froze, and she stopped drying her knees, glancing up at her.

"Lark? That's Becca's daughter's name?"

Cristina nodded.

Learning the name of Becca's daughter after all these years, caused a pinching feeling in her stomach. Knowing her name made it feel real. Becca had a daughter. And she'd just lost her mother.

"Where is she? I mean, who's taking care of her?" But she wasn't sure she wanted to know anything about her.

"I'm not sure, Jo. Probably Becca's parents."

"I think I might want to meet her before I head home."

What was she saying? She went from not wanting to know anything about her to wanting to meet her?

"Oh, I don't know. Do you really think that's a good idea?"

"No," she blurted before exhaling a mirthless laugh. "Probably not. But I feel like I owe it to her. Or owe it to Becca."

"Think it over the next few days. If you still want to meet her before you leave, I'll contact Mr. Gibbs for you."

She nodded. Maybe after they spread Becca's ashes at the end of the week she wouldn't feel like she owed Becca anything.

Cristina pulled the first aid cream out of the bin. "Okay,

let's get you fixed up." She applied the cream to the pads of the Band-Aids before placing them carefully on each of Jolene's knees.

A memory came to her mind. When the four girls were around fifteen, they'd pulled out the bikes from the Gibbs's shed and rode to the Sweet Shop for ice cream. On their way back to the cottage, she hit a patch of loose gravel and her tire spun, causing her to skid and get tangled in the bike. Blood gushed out of her knees and Cristina had cleaned her up then too.

"There, that should do it." Cristina twisted the cap back on the tube of cream.

"Thanks." Jolene sniffed.

"You always did need me to take care of you," Cristina teased.

The reality of Cristina's words hit hard. Because, well, she was right. Cristina jumped to her feet and cleaned up the mess of the Band-Aid wrappers and placed the kit back in the cupboard.

"How have you been able to manage without me for all these years? I mean, you can't even run anymore without tripping over your own two feet."

Cristina's teasing words were true. She honestly didn't know how she'd managed to survive without their friendship all these years.

She forced out a laugh. "Well, thanks again. You always did look out for me and make sure I didn't end up making a complete fool of myself."

"Well yeah, I had to be seen with you." Cristina smiled. Then she gestured at the bruise on her shin. "Damn you're embarrassing. Guess now you got bloody knees to match that bruise on your shin. You always were clumsy."

Jolene tucked her chin to her chest. Her eyes glossed over

again as she stared at her mangled legs. The tears would make Cristina uncomfortable. She never knew how to handle them. She was too tough for tears. Too tough for a lot of things. Like put up with being abused by her ex-husband. She'd been so proud of Cristina for choosing the leave him, yet she'd never told her.

Cristina cleared her throat. "Ok, enough time spent playing nurse, let's get ready for the lake. We need to get there early or the lot could be full, and we'll have to try another day. And I don't know about you, but I'd like to sleep in at least a few days while we're here."

"Agreed." Even though Jolene couldn't sleep in if her life depended on it. "Give me ten minutes."

Jolene wiped at her eyes and exhaled. She didn't care if her knees throbbed, she needed to stop crying and put on her big girl panties. They were heading to Sand Harbor beach, known as the crown jewel of the Lake Tahoe beaches. With its reputation of having finer sand, giant boulders surrounding the lake, and pools of emerald water, it wasn't unusual for the parking lot to be full by 9:00 a.m.

After over an hour of driving from the cottage, they were relieved to not find the sign indicating the parking lot was full when they arrived at 9:15 a.m. They lugged all their beach gear to their chosen spot on the sand. Kendra laid out a large beach blanket and Jolene set up an umbrella to give them shade when the sun rose higher in the sky later in the day.

Cristina placed the small cooler directly under the umbrella. They had it filled with bottles of water, crackers and cheese, grapes and individually prepared salads they picked up from a grocery store on their way. Cristina had complained about all the healthy food, referring to it as "*Jolene and Kendra food.*"

Although Lake Tahoe was experiencing record high

temperatures for this time of the year, the water would still be freezing. But Jolene couldn't miss the opportunity to take pictures of the so-called *crown jewel beach*. She grabbed her phone from her bag and headed toward the shoreline, holding down on her straw fedora hat so it wouldn't blow off.

Turning around, facing her friends on the sand, she snapped a picture of them. Then she changed the option of the lens on her phone's camera to forward facing and snapped a picture of herself. She sent the picture in a text to Julia. And sent the same picture to Joy.

JOY

Damn! You're looking smoking hot babe!— kiss emoji

JOLENE

You're too good to me

JOY

It does this cold heart of mine good to see you relaxing

JOLENE

You keep telling yourself that but you and I both know you have a heart full of hot goo.

JOY

Guilty. Now if you tell anyone I'll have to kill you.

JOLENE

Fine. Give my kids a kiss for me.

JOY

Settle for a fist bump?

JOLENE

Fine

She laughed.

The bright blue sky reminded her of the beautiful skies

from home. She closed her eyes and inhaled a deep breath. The sound of the water as it formed waves, curling and then breaking on the sand at the shoreline, roared in her ears. And for just a moment, with her eyes closed, she let herself picture Becca here with them and her heart squeezed. No doubt Becca would be in that freezing water now. She'd be all the way under, swimming and loving every second of the exhilaration.

When her phone chimed and she peered down at the screen, her stomach fluttered at the sight of Bo's name on the screen. They hadn't spoken since the night before and she felt uneasy about how they'd left things.

BO

See you tonight?

Her thumbs hovered over her screen before responding.

JOLENE

I'd like that. But...

BO

But?

JOLENE

But promised Cris a beer drinking sesh.

BO

No boys allowed?

JOLENE

Probably not. But I'll check with the girls.

BO

Good.

Smiling like a silly schoolgirl, she walked down the shoreline, taking in the scenery around her. She could stare at this serene backdrop forever. The contrast between the granite boulders and emerald water with the azure sky above and the

Sierra Nevada mountains behind was breathtaking. She couldn't stop taking pictures at every angle possible. She'd need these memories after she was home, when her brain got too fuzzy to remember.

Jolene returned to her friends underneath the umbrella and applied sunblock. She found it a tedious task as she maneuvered around the bandages on her knees. Such a pain. She assumed there were bruises forming underneath the Band-Aids because her knees were throbbing. The fall gave her more aches and pains than normal, so she chased three Tylenol with her water.

"Okay, ladies." Kendra jumped to her feet. "Let's get a pic of the three of us."

The women had taken a similar picture once. But that had been before selfies on cellphones. Becca had extended the camera out with her long arm. After the picture had been developed, both Becca's face and red bikini were blurry from being closest to the lens. But all their smiling faces were impossible to miss. What had happened to that picture? Or to any of the pictures? The girls used to constantly take photos when they were together. The only one she'd seen since arriving at the cottage, was the picture framed on the wall by the entryway.

"C'mon, lazy bum. Get up." Kendra yanked Cristina's arm. "I just want one picture."

"Fine," Cristina grumbled. "But then you promised, no giving me crap the rest of the day."

"Promise." She put her palms up in surrender.

After Kendra took a few pictures, trying to get just the right one, the three women laid back down on the blanket. Kendra tapped away on her phone and Cristina hopped on hers as well —toggling back and forth between Facebook and Instagram.

The only social media account Jolene had was Instagram

and she'd only created it to follow her children. Several years ago, she had a Facebook account but had disabled it at the suggestion from the brewery's financial advisor. He advised that her family's personal information could backfire against the business. She only used Facebook when she updated the High Desert Brewery's business page and Carrie had been handling it for the past several months.

Her mind spiraled at the thought of Carrie. Had she lied to her? Was it possible? Carrie and Travis—in Palm Springs? Together?

THE WOMEN RETURNED to the cottage late in the afternoon. Jolene didn't notice her sunburn until she saw her naked reflection in the mirror. "Crap on a cracker," she said out loud, studying her reflection. Her shoulders and stomach seemed to have gotten the worst of it. There was a soft pink hue painted across her nose and cheeks.

When she glanced down, she saw her red legs. At least the sunburn helped hide the ugly bruise on her shin. But now she'd have two white squares where the bandages remained on her knees. Cristina was right; she *was* embarrassing.

After she showered, she threw her wet hair up in a messy bun, applied foundation to her face to help hide the sunburn and brushed on a coat of mascara. She was too tired to do anything more. She put on a pair of jean shorts and an over-sized sweatshirt. The temps would be cooler when they planned on hanging out around the fire pit, but pants might irritate her injured knees and now her sunburn.

The shower hadn't eased the aches in her body and neither had the nap she'd taken at the beach earlier. Peering down at herself and seeing the bandages and sunburn, she felt defeated.

But she'd made a promise to Cristina they would spend the evening together relaxing around the fire. And she was determined to make that happen. But she'd need a nap first.

She laid down on the soft comfy bed in the room she was calling her own for the week and brought her knees up, curling into a ball. Sleep came quick. But her mind did not rest.

CHAPTER SIXTEEN

When Jolene awoke from her nap, her knees still throbbed. But thankfully her body appeared to be on the mend. Relieved, she climbed off the bed, feeling ready for an evening with her friends.

The guilt had set in earlier in the day when Cristina complained about the healthy food choices in the cooler at the lake. It was all *Kendra and Jolene food*. She grumbled that she didn't get to choose anything she wanted to eat, and they weren't doing any of the things she wanted to do either. So, tonight was for Cristina.

"Perfect timing, lazy ass," Cristina said when Jolene strolled out of her bedroom. "Pizza's here." She carried two brown flat boxes in both hands above her head.

"Pizza?" she asked in the middle of a yawn. "It's dinner time already? How long did I sleep?" She placed her palms on the sides of her face and slid them down.

"Forever." Kendra grabbed three plates from the cupboard and placed them on the kitchen island countertop.

"What time is it?" she asked, her voice sounding hoarse.

"Seven," Kendra answered.

"Whoa, I slept for over three hours."

"And probably a few more at the lake today," Cristina reminded her. "What's gotten into you? I thought you didn't sleep much?"

I don't. I guess it's all finally catching up to me." She shrugged.

"How are you feeling? You know, since your fall this morning?" Kendra's gaze shifted toward Jolene's knees.

"My knees are a bit sore, but I'm okay." She lied. They throbbed and her whole body ached. "How are you feeling, Cris?" She tried to take the focus off herself, as usual.

"Like I got hit by a truck." Cristina exhaled a mirthless laugh. "Still don't know why I let you guys talk me into that run."

"But you finished, didn't you?" Kendra said pointedly.

Cristina puckered her face into a scowl.

Truthfully, they all had finished the run, and finished together. With Jolene injured, the other girls had to help her back to the cottage.

"Enough." Cristina held up her hand. "No more talking about it. You promised, Kendra, no exercise talk. I fully intend on stuffing my face with pizza and beer until I completely forget about my aching body, or I pass out. Whichever comes first." She smirked.

"Sounds good to me." Jolene inhaled the delicious scent of melted mozzarella and sundried tomatoes. "And this smells great, where'd you get it?"

"I ran over to Jiffy's Pizza. Gluten free for you two calorie counters, and greasy thick crust for me." Cristina placed three pieces of pizza overflowing with toppings onto her plate.

"Thanks, Cris, that was super sweet."

Cristina shrugged. "Don't sound so surprised. I can be

sweet once in a while. Besides, you did say you were providing the beer for tonight, right?" Cristina raised her brows at Jolene.

"Oh, right. I put it out in the fridge in the garage. Mind helping me?"

Cristina shrugged again and reluctantly left her plate of oozing mozzarella on the kitchen counter while she followed her out to the garage. She knew what the shrug meant—Cristina wondered why she couldn't grab all the beer herself. But it would be a lot of weight for her to carry. Joy had given her two cases of beer and the girls hadn't even broken into the stash yet.

Jolene pulled on the handle of the fridge and Cristina crouched down, peering inside. She glanced back at her with her eyes wide and her jaw hanging open.

"I've died and gone to heaven." Cristina's eyes crinkled as a wide smile drew across her face. The bothersome task of putting her pizza down to assist her with the beer seemed to have vanished.

"And you doubted me," she teased.

"Never again. I should have known you'd take your beer seriously, just as I do." Cristina grabbed one of the open boxes that held twenty-four cans of beer. She headed back into the cottage, carrying it in her forearms.

"It looks like there are two types of beer in that box," Jolene said, following behind Cristina with empty arms. "Then I think there's at least one or two different ones in the other box."

"Well this should be a good start," Cristina called over her shoulder. "Hey, Kendra? Check this out." She held out the box.

"Wow, guess I'll get to try some of the famous Travis McCabe beer," Kendra said. Then flashed a look at Jolene as if regretting the words she'd just spoken. She fumbled over her next ones. "I mean...uh, you know. You know me, I'm a wine girl, that's all. I'm not much of a beer drinker these days."

"That's the least he could do. That jackass owes Jo more than just free beer." Cristina pulled a beer out of the box, read the side of the can, and then cracked it open. Putting the cold can up to her lips, she tipped her head back and took a long swill of it. "Ahh. This is his original IPA. And I love it." She took another drink. "Best one I've ever tasted."

Jolene smiled, feeling delighted but at the same time—awkward and strange. Why did she take delight in Cristina's approval of the brewery's beer? This was Travis" concoction—his creation, his dream. She had nothing to do with the recipes. She simply brewed it.

"Not that I want to compliment him, but I'm sorry, I gotta hand it to the rat bastard, he makes a fine beer," Cristina said.

"Cristina," Kendra hissed.

"It's fine." Jolene removed two pieces of pizza from the box and placed them on her plate.

"You do still have a hand in the business, right?" Kendra asked, folding her long arms in front of her.

"What do you mean?" She asked before taking a bite of the pizza. The artichokes and mushrooms along with the sundried tomatoes complimented the pesto sauce perfectly.

"I mean, if something should happen between you two. Say, more permanent." Kendra narrowed her eyes.

The pizza caught midway in Jolene's throat and stayed there. She grabbed a beer out of the box, cracked it open and hoped it would dislodge the trapped pizza.

"Damn, Kendra, and you talk about me being blunt," Cristina said.

"What?"

"You caused Jo to choke on her pizza. Stop talking about all this depressing shit. We're supposed to be having fun."

"I didn't mean to. Honest. I'm so sorry." Kendra rubbed Jolene's back.

Both Kendra and Cristina were always trying to take care of her. And she was sick of it. When were they going to realize she didn't need them to take care of her, to watch out for her, to fight her battles? Sure, they were her friends and that's what friends did for one another. But to her, it always seemed like these two were going above and beyond the normal call of duty.

How would they treat her when they finally learned about the MS?

"It's okay. It's not like I haven't thought about it. I mean truthfully, I've probably thought about it a thousand times over the last year.

"But it doesn't mean you need to think about it today, or this week for that matter," Cristina said.

"I didn't mean to upset you. I'm just looking out for you." Kendra squeezed Jolene's shoulder.

"I know, I said it's fine. *I'm* fine," she tried to reassure her friend.

"Here," Cristina shoved a beer into Kendra's chest, "shut up and drink."

Kendra hesitated, then accepted the beer. She cracked it open and pulled a glass out of the cupboard. Jolene watched as Kendra poured the contents of the can into the glass. The liquid came out fast and created too much foam causing it to overflow and spill onto the counter.

"Oh crud." Kendra placed the glass down and hurried to retrieve some paper towels to clean up the spilled beer.

Okay, so Jolene felt a tad bit responsible. She knew Kendra would do that, she was always in a hurry and impatient. She should have showed her how to pour the beer into the glass so it wouldn't create all that unnecessary foam. But she didn't, instead she just stood there and watched.

Walking over to the cupboard, she selected a glass and picked up her beer from where it sat on the counter. "Alright,

Kendra, I'm going to teach you a technique for pouring beer into a glass so it gets the correct amount of head on top."

Kendra turned and looked at Jolene, her mouth gaped open. "I'm not even sure what you just said. What does *head* mean?"

"Oh, I can tell you what it means." Cristina gave a wicked grin.

Jolene rolled her eyes but couldn't help from smiling. "Not that kind. It's the foam on the top of the beer."

"It's like you're speaking a foreign language," Kendra said.

"Just watch." She opened the beer and held it in one hand while holding the glass in her other. Tilting the glass, she began pouring the beer slowly letting the liquid hit the side of the glass as it filled. When the can was empty, she presented the beer with the perfect amount of head on top.

"Whoa, I'm impressed," Cristina said.

"I have to agree with Cristina." Kendra placed her hands on her hips.

Feeling rather pleased with herself, Jolene smiled while her cheeks warmed. With the other women still watching her with interest, she closed her eyes and lifted the beer to her nose and inhaled. Taking a sip, she allowed the bubbling liquid to tickle the inside of her mouth. It tasted perfect.

"Should we head outside again to eat?" she asked.

"Sure, sounds good to me," Kendra replied. She had cleaned up her mess and poured the remaining contents of her beer into her glass just how Jolene had shown her.

"Let me grab another beer." Cristina reached for a second can of the IPA.

"You're already done with your first?" Kendra asked.

"Hey," Cristina pointed a finger in Kendra's direction, "You promised. No giving me a hard time. Beer and pizza, that's what you said, right?"

"Right. Sorry."

"You guys go on ahead, I'll put this beer in the fridge, so it stays cold."

She emptied the beer from the box, placing them one by one into the fridge, hiding a few of the Porter's in the crisper drawer in case Bo decided to stop by.

The conversation remained light and comical between the three women. They shared stories from each other's lives, about work and the kids. Some spouse stories, but she didn't mind. She still had a spouse—and as much as she hated to admit, she still loved him. But maybe not in the way she once had.

Jolene's phone chimed from where it sat on the table next to her plate.

BO

Boys allowed?

She'd completely forgotten to ask her friends if they would mind if Bo stopped by. The three of them were having such a great time and enjoying one another's company. The idea of interrupting it caused anxiety to bubble in her chest. But at the same time, a deepening craving to see Bo swooped low in her belly.

"Hey," Jolene began, "would you mind if Bo stopped by later?" She ran her fingertips over the sweltering skin on the back of her neck. "I mean, it's no big deal if you'd rather he didn't come."

"Don't be silly." Kendra swatted at the air. "Of course he's welcome to come over. That is, if you want him to."

"I do," she muttered.

"Does he have any hot coworkers? Ya know, any policeman buddies he can bring along?"

"Cristina!" Kendra shrieked.

"What? I'm a happily married woman, but that doesn't

mean I can't flirt, can't have fun, does it? Besides I'm only kidding." Cristina rolled her eyes as she pushed her chair away from the table and headed toward the French doors.

"Hey, Cris," Jolene called. "Would you mind grabbing me another beer? A Porter this time, please."

"Sure. What about you, Kendra?"

"Oh, why not? I'll take another one of these please." She held up her glass. "It's no wine, but this stuff isn't half bad."

Her phone chimed again.

BO

Well?

JOLENE

The rule has been lifted for you

BO

Good, be over after awhile

Her heart fluttered in her chest causing her to feel silly and young. She placed her phone back down on the table next to her empty plate. She'd eaten both pieces of the pizza in record time while nursing her first beer.

Cristina returned, arms overfilled with cold cans. She handed one to each of the women before sitting back down to join them.

The next text that came through was from her daughter.

JULIA

How are you feeling?

She hesitated before responding. It would be best not to tell her daughter about her fall that morning. It would only worry her and the last thing she needed was Julia convincing Joy to bring them here. And worse—Travis once he returned from his trip.

JOLENE

A little tired and fighting a headache but, I'll
be fine.

How are you and Cole?

JULIA

We're fine. Take care of yourself and don't
forget to have some fun.

She didn't want to nag but she'd sent a text to Cole every day she'd been there and hadn't heard back from him. She worried her son was still upset with her for not bringing him along to Tahoe City.

She tried again.

JOLENE

Haven't heard from Cole. Worried...

JULIA

He's ok. I'll bug him to text you. Love you

JOLENE

Thanks! Night Jules, love you!

Bo came sauntering around the back corner of the house then, making his way up the steps of the deck. He had a six pack of beer under his arm and a bag of pretzels under the other. Just the sight of him caused goosebumps to dance up her arms and a goofy smile to tug at her lips.

He was dressed in a sweatshirt and shorts along with a pair of worn Chuck Taylor's. His hair looked unkempt and lacking product. Jolene preferred his hair this way rather than styled. She bit her lip while she resisted the craving to run her fingers through it.

"Well, well, well," Cristina said, narrowing her eyes at Bo. "Look who's here."

He nodded. "Cristina."

Cristina smiled. "Well at least he comes bearing gifts. And the best kind of gifts at that." She gestured at the beer and pretzels in his arms.

"Always." He grinned, showing off a mischievous spark in his green eyes. "Hey, Kendra."

Kendra, tapping away at her phone and completely oblivious of his arrival, presented her trademark smile—wide and revealing no teeth. Then she drew her attention back to her phone.

"Hey, you," Bo said in a sweet gravelly tone. He gave her shoulder a soft squeeze.

The innocent touch of his large hand on her shoulder sent a jolt of electricity through her body, as if waking it up. But she was relieved he didn't try kissing her or pulling her into a hug, even though she craved it. It would be too awkward in front of her friends. Plus, then she'd have to explain things to them.

And how could she, when she didn't even know herself?

When Cristina had questioned her about their non-date the night before, she left out the intimate details. Cristina was disappointed but Jolene wanted to keep that part of the evening private. She was in fact, still married. Even if she had to remind herself of the small detail. Because, well, she didn't feel married.

"Hey," Jolene greeted him, glancing at the bottles. "What kind of beer is that? I don't recognize the name." She eyed the bag of pretzels. "And I hope those are gluten free pretzels."

"What? No, honey how was your day? It's all nag, nag, nag," Bo teased. He pulled out the empty chair next to hers and dropped into it.

She felt the blush heat in her cheeks.

He leaned in. "I'm only teasing, Jo."

"I know," she muttered, while staring at the label on the beer bottle in her hands.

"This beer was brewed right here." Bo pulled a bottle from the unmarked box.

This information piqued her curiosity. "Like as in, Tahoe City?"

"Yep. A buddy of mine brewed it. He's a home brewer, so nothing like your brewery. Not sure he's looking to do anything more than that. It's just a hobby right now. He brews some for local charity events and stuff. This is left-over from an Alzheimer's fundraiser last month."

"It always starts as a hobby," Jolene mumbled and she tried to not wonder what her life might look like if Travis's brewing had only remained as a hobby.

She opened the beer, pouring it into her empty glass and held it under her nose to inhale the scent before taking a sip. The typical hoppy scent of an IPA lingered while the apricot undertone was subtle.

"Not bad." She licked her lips. "Did you bring enough to share with everyone?"

"Sure, help yourselves, ladies," Bo said.

"Huh? Oh, thanks but I think I'll just stick to this one," Kendra said, looking up from her phone and holding her glass in the air before taking a drink.

"Cris?" Bo held up a bottle, waggling his brows.

"Oh, what the hell? I'm game. Hand one over."

Bo handed it to Cristina. She nodded to him. The two of them seemed to have a relationship that was comfortable. How often did they see one another over the years? Jolene had never really given it much thought. About her leaving and everyone else staying, remaining friends and life moving on without her.

"Ollie, what happened to your knees?" Bo stared at her legs in utter horror.

"I'm fine. I fell during our run this morning. The big ugly bandages make it look worse than it really is."

"You fell? Did you hurt anything else?" Bo did a quick scan of her body with an intense gaze.

"No. I said, I'm fine." Her tone was firm, and she looked at him intently.

Bo picked up on her not-so-subtle hints and didn't push the conversation further. His eyes met hers and for a moment she could see the worry in them. He broke their eye contact and placed a hand on her thigh.

Bo's touch sent a warm tingling sensation to travel from her leg and into the rest of her body. It felt amazing—*really* amazing. But as much as she wanted him to keep his hand there, she wished he would move it as well. Her friends would most definitely give her a hard time about it later and she wasn't prepared to explain their relationship to them.

"She didn't tell you?" Cristina asked.

Bo shook his head.

"Yeah, she took a gnarly fall. She's still our clumsy girl." Cristina smiled.

Jolene winced. She wasn't clumsy. She was, well, she had feet that sometimes didn't work properly.

"Did she tell you what happened on her run yesterday?" Kendra asked.

Bo shook his head again, looking at Jolene with intensity.

"Well, it seems our girl here has herself a stalker," Cristina teased.

"What do you mean?" Bo barked out.

"It's nothing." She waved him off.

"That creepy bartender over at Anders Bar and Grill."

"What about him?" Bo asked through gritted teeth.

"Cristina, I said it was nothing."

"That wasn't nothing. The dude grabbed her arm, pretty hard she said."

Bo had a fire in his eyes Jolene had never seen before. "Why didn't you tell me?"

"It was just a misunderstanding. No big deal." She shot Cristina a look, raising her eyebrows at her.

Which she responded with palms up and mouthed, "What?"

"What happened?" Bo asked.

"He asked me out. For a drink. A cup of coffee."

Bo stabbed his fingers through his hair, leaning back in his chair.

"I said it was no big deal," Jolene continued. She gave his arm a light pat. "I said no, of course. And then, he went on his way."

Bo exhaled. "Good. But you need to stay away from him. Owen is not a decent guy. Please promise me, you'll tell me if he ever comes around here again."

She nodded, taking his words of warning to heart. But she didn't need them—the guy creeped her out enough without his warning.

"Kendra," Cristina said, changing the subject. "Are you ever going to get off that phone?"

Kendra looked up. She glanced around as if she'd forgotten where she was or who she was with.

Everyone stared back at her.

"Sorry." Her gaze flickered back down. "Let me just text Quinn and then I'll put my phone away, promise."

"You already made me a promise you would drink beer and have fun tonight. It doesn't look like you're doing either. You're only on your second one and you're nursing it at that. Jo and I are well into our third."

"I'm sorry," Kendra repeated. "Just one more sec." She held

up a finger, tapping away at her phone vigorously before finally resting it on the table. "Okay, I'm all yours."

Was Cristina right, Jolene was already on her third beer? She gazed at her half empty glass—not good, she needed to slow down. Or better yet; just quit altogether.

"Hey, I have some of our brewery's Porters in the fridge. Let me grab you one." She slid to the edge of her chair.

"I got it. Bo placed a hand on her shoulder and jumped to his feet.

"Wow, Jo, you better keep him around," Cristina teased.

Heat crawled up her neck and pooled into her cheeks. She hoped Bo hadn't heard Cristina's comment on his way inside. But she was sure he had because she caught a glimpse of his side profile. The lines fanned out near his eye and the corner of his mouth curved up.

She placed her face in her palms.

"Hey, remember when none of us could drive yet and we'd take the bikes out of the shed and ride them into town?" Cristina asked.

Jolene winced, hoping Cristina wouldn't bring up the time she crashed, and needed her injuries cleaned up then as well.

"How could I forget? I gained ten pounds my sophomore year from all the fries we ate at Ander's." Kendra took a sip of her beer.

"Totally worth it," Cristina countered.

"Agreed. Ander's fries are still the best." Jolene raised her glass before taking a sip.

"Mmm fries. I could go for some fries right about now," Cristina mumbled.

"Hey, remember that one party we all went to up at Incline Village?" Kendra asked.

Jolene tipped her beer can at her. "Was that the party

Becca said she'd be the designated driver for and then got completely wasted?"

"Yep, that's the one. She got caught up playing that drinking game with those rich kids."

"That's right." Jolene nodded, the memory clearing in her mind, and she exhaled a mirthless laugh. "She never did back down from a challenge."

"Nope, she did not. She was a fighter that's for sure." Cristina picked up her beer and took a drink.

Bo came out of the cottage holding four beers in his arms. He set three of them down in the middle of the table and opened the fourth one for himself. He sat down next to Jolene again and took a long drink of his beer.

"Unfortunately, that night it backfired on her," Kendra said. "She was supposed to be our designated driver so all of us had been drinking. Then since she got totally smashed, we had to call Jacob to come all the way to Incline Village to pick us up."

"He was so mad too." Jolene shook her head.

"I remember that. He gave Becca the silent treatment all the way back to the cottage," Cristina said.

"He was mad because we woke him up and he had to go to work in a few hours. And I think he was a little mad Becca got that drunk when he wasn't with her." Jolene's throat went dry, talking about Becca and Jacob felt too real and raw, causing emotion to spike in her.

"What about the night we went to that tailgate party in Truckee?" Kendra said.

"I almost forgot that." Cristina smiled, leaning back in her chair.

"Hey, I think I was at that one," Bo said.

"Right." Jolene nodded, the memory coming back to her.

"You had just broken up with...who at that time? Ashley?" She smirked at him.

"Good memory." He gave her a wink. "And you were dating some jerk presumably."

"Yes, as a matter of a fact I was. He spent the entire evening at the local pizza joint watching whatever game was on T.V. at the time. I was super mad at him and I think I had too much to drink that night."

"And that was the only night I *did* drink," Bo said.

"Oh, that's right. We were all shocked to see you drinking. You never did when we were in high school." Cristina shoved his shoulder. "Always the goody-goody," she teased.

"You two danced together that night, didn't you?" Kendra pointed at Jolene and Bo with her glass.

The two of them looked at one another. Bo's lips curved into a smile, and she felt her cheeks blush. His green eyes appeared a shade darker than normal in the night and her body hummed, causing her to look away and brush her fingertips against the flushed skin of her neck.

"We did. I made a complete ass of myself that night, I'm pretty sure," Bo said, still staring at her.

"You did. And it was hilarious." Cristina laughed. "You were all over Jo. Freaking her out by the bonfire," Cristina said, referring to the popular dance of the 90's.

Bo hung his head in embarrassment, rubbing a hand at the back of his neck. "Don't remind me," he muttered.

Cristina laughed again and the other two girls joined in. "Who knew you had been hiding all those moves?" she teased.

"If I remember correctly, Jolene seemed pretty into it," Kendra said.

"Oh yeah?" Bo turned and glanced at her again, one eyebrow raised.

Her skin prickled under his powerful gaze. "Yes, and if you remember correctly, I was pretty drunk."

"Yeah well, we all were," Cristina said. "Including Becca. She was a mess that night."

The reminder of Becca, or the mention of her name again caused silence between the four friends. They each sipped on their drinks and looked out into the darkness of the night. The soft light from the moon and stars danced on the surface of the lake. Jolene pulled her knees up to her chest, wrapping her arms around them.

"You cold?" Bo rubbed her thigh. "Want me to grab some blankets from inside?"

"No, I'm fine."

"We were supposed to sit around the fire tonight," Cristina reminded them.

"Right. Guess we didn't get that far," Jolene said.

"I can go down and start the fire," Bo offered.

"It's a little late now." Cristina's obvious disappointment hit Jolene in the center of her chest. "It's only Monday, we have a few more days here. We could plan on doing it another night."

"Are you sure?" Jolene asked.

Cristina waved her off. "It's fine."

"Well how about I grab a couple blankets?" Bo pushed to stand.

"I can get them." Jolene hurried to her feet but couldn't catch her balance fast enough and she stumbled, bracing herself with the table.

"You're such a lightweight. I think you've had enough to drink," Cristina teased.

"Sit, relax, I'll get the blankets," Bo insisted, placing a firm hand on her shoulder once again.

"I'll help you," Cristina offered, following Bo inside the cottage.

An odd feeling snaked through Jolene. Jealousy maybe? But why would she be jealous? Bo and Cristina were old friends, just as they all were. But maybe they'd remained close all these years and she had no idea because she hadn't been around.

Maybe if she could've gotten over the hurt of losing Jacob here, she would've come back sooner. But still, after all these years, she felt Jacob's presence everywhere—down by the fire pit, out on the dock, in the kayaks. They used to have kayak races across the short width of the lake. Becca and Jacob against her and Travis. Of course, Jacob and Becca would always win, Jacob used his math skills to factor in the wind direction and pressure and Becca would use her perseverance.

A few minutes later, Bo and Cristina returned with a couple of blankets, and handed them out to each of them. Jolene gladly accepted. Her legs were covered in goosebumps. She laid the afghan on her lap, glad to hide her mangled legs as well.

"Better?" Bo asked.

"Yes, thank you." She pushed her bangs out of her face.

"Looks like you got some color today."

She glanced down at herself. "I did. I put on sunscreen, and we even had an umbrella, but I still managed to get a little sunburnt. I guess we were there quite a while."

"I got sunburnt and had sunscreen on too. How this one didn't is beyond me." Cristina gestured at Kendra.

"It's called SPF 100," Kendra said. "We aren't getting any younger, ya know? Sun causes wrinkles. You guys look great though, you don't need to worry about wrinkles. But in my business, everyone worries about them."

"You look great too, Kendra. You don't need to worry about all that."

"Thanks, Jo. I shouldn't after what I spend on face lotions and creams Botox."

"That's such a waste of money." Cristina slumped in her chair. "Why do we kill ourselves trying to fight the clock? I say we just sit back and let the aging happen. Who the hell cares what we look like. If people don't like it, screw them, they don't have to look."

"I'm with Cris, we shouldn't care so much about our appearance, we should just enjoy life." Jolene peeled at the label on her beer bottle.

"That's easy for you two to say. Your husbands aren't cheating on you, with younger, less wrinkled women."

Ouch. Jolene took the words like a blow to her stomach. She picked up her beer and took a drink, nearly choking it down. But she needed to do something to distract her so she didn't do something ridiculous—like, oh I don't know, cry or something.

"Oh my goodness, Jo, I'm so sorry," Kendra said.

"It's fine," she muttered.

"No, it's not. Seriously, I'm sorry. I should be more sensitive to your situation."

"Kendra, it's fine," Jolene repeated. "Besides, it's not like Travis cheated on me. At least not that I know of." And she didn't think she wanted to know.

The four voices went silent. Bo cleared his throat and Cristina chugged her beer—loudly.

"Well, on that note, I think I'm going to call it a night. I'm really tired." Kendra pushed her chair away from the table and stood. She placed a hand on Jolene's shoulder. "You get some rest, you want those knees in top notch shape to run in the morning." She smiled, flashing her brown eyes at her and causing warmth to expand in her chest. "Night everyone."

Once Kendra was gone, it was still quiet between the old

friends. Cristina glanced back and forth between Bo and Jolene and then stood. "Okay. Me too. I'm gonna head to bed."

"Please don't," she pleaded.

"I'm actually freaking tired from the torture you guys put me through this morning. Thought the alcohol would help but unfortunately, it can't revive a dead body." She exhaled a mirthless laugh. "Night you two, don't stay up too late." She winked at them and sauntered into the cottage.

"Night," Jolene called.

Another cool breeze passed, and she pulled the blanket tighter on her body. Now that the two of them were alone, part of her wanted to pick up where they left off the night before.

"I'm guessing you still haven't told them?" Bo asked, interrupting her thoughts.

She bit her lower lip. "Not yet."

"It's going to get harder the longer you wait."

"I know." And she did know. But knowing didn't make it any easier. "I meant to tell them. I was going to tell them tonight. But things turned awkward, and it just didn't feel like the right time."

"Probably not the best idea I came." Bo took a drink of his beer.

"It's not that. It's fine you came. Everyone loves you."

"I don't know about that."

"You didn't just hang out with me in school, you hung out with them too. And Becca."

"Yeah, I guess." Bo shifted in his seat. "Want me to get you another beer?"

"Nah. This is three, so I better not. I've already gone over my limit."

"Right, your two-beer limit." Bo smiled as he slipped off her sandals and set her legs on his lap, adjusting the blanket over both of them. "How are you really feeling? Since the fall this morning, I mean."

"I'm okay. Just tired. I fell asleep at the lake for a while and then after we got back, and I showered I slept for a few more hours."

"Probably the fall, and everything else," Bo said.

"I guess."

"You sure your knees are okay? Those are some big Band-Aids."

"Stop, I know. They're so ugly." She placed her face in her palms, embarrassed. But at least she was keeping him entertained, no boring woman here.

"No, but seriously, how are your knees?"

"They're fine. I got quite a few cuts on them. But I'm most worried about them bruising. The one on my shin is bad enough. Cristina made fun of me for being clumsy. She's right, I am clumsy. Look at these ugly legs." Jolene pulled off the blanket, showing off her bare legs.

"You are not clumsy," Bo said. "I mean, I guess you are, but it's not like it's your fault. And your legs are not ugly. As a matter of fact, I've always thought you had rather nice legs."

Her face went hot. And despite the cool air, the rest of her body heated with desire. She tried to not smile at the compliment. But it had been so long since she'd received one—a genuine one—she'd forgotten what it felt like.

And this wasn't any man, this was Bo Dean.

"You've always had a nice smile too." Bo reached his hands underneath the blanket and rubbed her feet, massaging them with an unbelievably gentle touch for how large the man's hands were. He worked his way up to her calves, caressing them. It sent a twinge through her, and she shrieked.

"Stop, that tickles." She laughed.

"Sorry, I'm not trying."

Bo moved his hands up to her thighs, being sure to skip over her knees. His strong hands kneaded her sore muscles and sent all kinds of feelings to course through her body. When he moved his hands under her thigh, she let out a yelp again and squirmed. He laughed and then caressed her thighs with a lighter touch. But she wriggled and couldn't stop giggling.

"Stop," she said in between spurts of laughter.

"Okay, sorry. I wasn't trying to tickle you. I was hoping you'd feel better if I massaged your muscles."

"They do that to me in physical therapy and I have the hardest time staying still. I'm so ticklish." Jolene pushed his hands away.

Bo pulled his chair next to hers and reached for her hands, pulling her close to him. Their faces were only inches apart now. A rush of heat shot through her. And this was it, he was going to finally kiss her.

He leaned forward, drawing closer to her and he pressed his lips to her bare neck and then behind her ear. Her body answered to his touch with a swoop low in her belly. She was ready, longing for him to kiss her. It had been so long since she last kissed Bo Dean, she'd forgotten what it felt like. But she hadn't forgotten the intensity of it.

Unexpectedly, Bo pulled back and embraced her in a tight hug. It was nice and all but c'mon, he'd gotten her all worked up and for what? *A hug?* He said he wanted to date her, he said she was beautiful. He said he'd waited so long to kiss her, and yet he still hadn't. Her mind spun while her body craved him all at the same time.

"Bo?" she whispered. "Are you gonna kiss me or what?"

Bo exhaled a quiet laugh in her ear. "Soon."

She pulled back; brows raised. "What do you mean, soon?"

"Not tonight. It's not right."

"Not right? Why?" She frowned.

"Because, we've been drinking. More importantly, *you've* been drinking. I don't want our first kiss remembered that way. I don't want our first *anything* to be remembered that way. I want you to be completely sober when you kiss me, that way I know you'll mean it."

Jolene placed a palm on his cheek and studied his face. The boyish charm was still there but now in a man's face. His chiseled chin and facial stubble present, reflecting a long day. She liked this man he'd become—she respected him, she trusted him.

"You know I was? Completely sober." Her eyes danced between his.

"Right, I know."

Pressing a kiss to his jaw, she released his face and adjusted her body so she could rest her head on his shoulder. They were obviously still forgetting that night—pretending nothing had happened between them all those years ago. She leaned against his chest, resting her head in the crook of his neck. Bo pulled the blanket over them both and wrapped his arms tight around her body.

"As long as you know," she whispered.

CHAPTER SEVENTEEN

W eights on her chest, weights on her arms and feet. No, scratch that—sandbags attached to her arms and feet. An anchor lassoed around her torso, pulling her down. This feeling was recognizable.

It had been a long time since Jolene felt it. Six months, maybe seven. She couldn't be sure. But without a doubt; it hadn't been long enough.

Opening her eyes took effort. Once they were open, pain shot through them straight through her head. The light in the room was too bright and it hurt, causing her to jolt her head and body. She cleared her throat, but it felt like sandpaper.

Attempting to open her eyes again, she tried to take it slow this time. It took work, a great effort of work. She squinted at the nightstand next to her, hoping to find water there. But nope, nothing.

Closing her eyes, she tried to focus on sitting up. If she could get the energy to pull herself up, maybe she could get water. Or she could call out to her friends, but she wasn't sure her voice worked. With the pain in her throat, she didn't think she could even speak.

In an attempt to pull her heavy body to a sitting position, she felt an enormous amount of fatigue. Her eyes fluttered open and then shut, then open and shut once more before closing for good. Her body surrendered to the weight of the sandbags and the anchor that pulled her down into sleep again.

———

JOLENE'S BODY began to shake. Was she dreaming? Was she awake and trembling uncontrollably? She heard a voice. A familiar voice. Travis maybe?

"Jo? Jo, are you okay?"

She could sense the worry in the man's voice. It wasn't Travis. She hadn't heard that tone of worry and concern in his voice for a long time.

"Ollie?"

It was Bo. He was here, with her. She needed to open her eyes. She needed to see him. She longed to see his sparkling green eyes, his chiseled chin, and that smile with all those pearly white teeth.

"Bo," she said, her voice quiet and scratchy. She didn't even recognize the voice. Was that really *her* voice? "Bo?"

"Ollie, what's wrong? Are you okay? Do you need me to take you to the hospital?"

"No, no," she answered quickly. "Water. Just water, please?" She found her voice, recognized it, but it still sounded strange.

"Sure thing." Bo was up and gone in the blink of an eye. Or had she fallen asleep again? She couldn't be sure.

"Here." Bo held out a glass of water.

Jolene forced her eyes to open again, and she stared at the water. "I don't think I can even sit up."

Tears welled in her eyes. How had they come so easily when everything else seemed to take so much effort?

"Let me help you," Bo offered. He placed the glass of water on the nightstand and then put his hands under her arms, helping her to a sitting position.

He propped her up with the extra pillows. A few tears from each eye slipped out and she didn't have the energy to lift her hands to wipe them away. As if Bo read her mind, he swiped at them with his thumbs. He picked up the water glass and held it to her lips. Tilting it slightly, she drank a sip. The cool liquid trickled down her throat easing the dry sandpaper feeling.

"What's going on? You're scaring me." Bo pushed her loose strands of hair out of her face. "The girls didn't even tell me you were still in bed."

A thought flashed in her mind—she must look like a mess. She'd pulled up her wet hair into a messy bun after her shower the afternoon before and she'd gone to bed with it like that. She was also still wearing the same sweatshirt and denim shorts. How embarrassing, going to sleep in the same clothes was becoming a habit on this trip and it was so unlike her.

"I think I'm okay now." But she couldn't even lift her head. She kept it pressed against the headboard. She was just so tired.

"You don't look okay."

"Gee, thanks," she said, her words dripping in sarcasm.

"Is this a flare up or something?"

She swallowed. "I think so."

"What's gonna happen?"

"I don't know."

"What do you feel like?"

Like death, like she'd been hit by a train, like an anvil was sitting on her body. But instead, she said, "I feel really tired and completely out of energy."

"What can I do for you?" Bo asked.

"The water was enough. Thank you. There really isn't much you can do."

"Jo, I can't leave you like this. You gotta tell the girls. Someone has to take care of you."

Jolene pinched her eyes closed. It hurt too much, so she opened them. "I know."

"Are you sure you don't need to go to the hospital or something?" Bo rubbed her thigh.

"Only if it doesn't subside after twenty-four hours. Give me until tomorrow, then check on me okay."

"I'll come straight over after work tonight."

"Wait. You're supposed to be at work now. What are you doing here?" she asked, noticing his sheriff's uniform for the first time.

Bo's gaze danced around, not making eye contact any longer. He shifted on the edge of the bed.

Her stomach pinched, then twisted with a heightened sense of worry. "Bo? What is it?"

He cleared his throat. "Let me go get the girls."

"Wait, Bo," she called. But he'd already left the room.

Cristina and Kendra appeared at the open doorway, quiet and with sympathy smeared on their faces. Jolene had never seen them this way. But then she remembered, she *had* seen them this way.

When her brother died.

Jacob had been like an extra limb of Jolene's. They'd spent so much time together, even before he started dating Becca. She'd taken the loss of him tremendously hard. Her friends had felt useless in consoling her. And she hadn't let them. Instead, she'd needed space. Cristina, giving her too much space that their friendship had been severed almost completely. And Kendra, who had stuck it out. She'd been the one to stay in constant connection with Jolene.

"What's going on?" she asked.

But as her two friends moved closer toward her, she pinpointed the look on their faces. *They knew.* Bo had told them. She shot him a glare. He glanced down and shuffled his feet.

"Girls, I'm fine. It's not a huge deal, really. Please don't treat me any differently. I'm the same as I've always been. I can do all the same things I've always done. Just don't give me those looks of pity, please," she pleaded.

"Jo." Kendra sat on the bed next to her, reaching for her hand.

"Don't Kendra, don't feel sorry for me. I'm really okay." Jolene tried to pull her hand away but had to give up, she didn't have the strength.

"We love you, Jo and we're here for you, always," Kendra said softly.

"Yep, for sure." Cristina sat on Jolene's other side.

"I appreciate that. And it's really all you can do for me."

"And if you don't have enough strength left to do it yourself, I'll kick Travis's ass." Cristina punched a fist into her hand.

"Okay, guys, stop. You can't blame Travis for this. He had his reasons. He just couldn't deal with the MS anymore, and at least he was honest," she said.

"Wait." Kendra's brows pinched together. "What? MS?" Kendra's eyes searched Jolene's.

"What are you talking about?" Cristina stood, first glancing at Jolene, then back at Bo who was quiet while he leaned his back against the wall.

"Wait, what were you guys talking about?" she asked.

"We're referring to why Bo is here," Kendra said.

What *was* Bo doing there? It was a workday; he should be at work.

"What the hell, Jolene?" Cristina shouted.

"Alright, that's enough," Bo raised his voice at Cristina.

"You have MS? As in Multiple Sclerosis?"

The walls seemed smaller now, the ceiling lower and the room hotter. Everything began to draw in closer to her Confusion swirled around in her brain. The pain in her head and eyes and the weight on her body. It was all too much. Tears formed in her eyes again and spilled as she nodded.

"Oh my," Kendra said, a hand covering her mouth.

"This is BS Just when were you planning on telling us?" Cristina asked.

"I said, that's enough," Bo barked, moving in front of Cristina. "Jo needs support, not accusations. If you can't do that, then I suggest you leave."

Cristina pushed around him. "How long have you known?"

"About a year," Jolene mumbled.

"Holy crap, Jo." She pinched the bridge of her nose.

Bo took Cristina by the arm and pulled her into the hallway. Kendra shook her head and squeezed Jolene's hand.

"Why didn't you tell us?" Kendra asked.

"I don't know. I guess because I didn't want you guys to feel sorry for me. I didn't want to see that look of pity, the one you're giving me right now."

"I don't mean to." Kendra glanced down.

"I know, no one does. This kind of news has that effect on people."

"I just don't understand." Kendra shook her head. "How did this even happen? Are they sure? You've seen a specialist, got a second opinion, a third?"

"Yes, I have a great doctor. And they're sure. I'm sure. I've had symptoms for years. I had an MRI and a spinal tap last year that confirmed the diagnosis," Jolene explained.

"I just wish you would've told us." Kendra's voice sounded small.

"It's not like you girls could have done anything."

"I know, but we could've been there for you."

"How? You're all the way in L.A. and Cristina is in Reno. The three of us haven't really been all that close these last several years." Tears threatened again.

"I know," Kendra admitted. "But we need to change that. I want to be here for you. I want us to be close again."

"I want that too."

Kendra patted her hand. Cristina stood in the doorway listening before slowly entering the room again. When she reached Jolene's side, she hesitated before sitting down on the edge of the bed.

"Look, it's not like I'm angry with you," Cristina began, "it's just, this is big news. It's a shock to us. You've had an entire year to process it and we're just finding out. And I have no right to be angry. I guess I'm just mad at this thing...this sickness."

"Me too," she said.

Bo cleared his throat. The women on Jolene's sides both sat up straight and an uneasy feeling crept up in her. Kendra gave Bo a look but she couldn't place it.

"What's going on? You said something about the reason why Bo is here. If it wasn't because of the flare up, then why are you here?" she directed the question at Bo who couldn't meet her eyes.

Shuffling his feet back and forth, he clutched a manila envelope in his hands. This was the first time she'd seen Bo in his fireman uniform. She couldn't help but notice how attractive he looked. The short-sleeved button-down shirt appeared a size too small for his large biceps and filled out chest. His hair had that styled look, stiff with hair products. He looked grown up with the gun on his hip, and completely irresistible. If she had the energy, she'd yank him into the bed with her.

"This is the absolute worst timing," Bo began. "When this arrived on the Police Chief's desk and I got word of it, I wanted to be the one to deliver it. Although," he paused, rubbing at the back of his neck, "I'm regretting it now...seeing the shape you're in."

"What are you talking about? Bo, you're not making any sense." She pushed her fingertips to her eyes. The light was hurting them again. She didn't have enough energy to sit up any longer and she had the urge to give into the comfort of the bed and just sleep.

"Jo," Bo's voice drifted in her ears. "You okay?"

Jolene's eyes fluttered open. She wished he would just hurry up with whatever he was trying to tell her so she could go back to sleep. Didn't he realize that the only way she was going to get over this, was to rest?

"I'm okay. What is it?"

Bo held out the envelope and placed it on her lap. Her vision traveled to it. But her brain couldn't register what she was supposed to do. Pick it up? Open it? But she didn't want to. She wished all three of them would just leave her alone and let her rest.

Why was this so important now, that Bo would need to leave work? Why would she need to see what was in the envelope—an envelope that was delivered to the Sheriff's department and concerned her? The confusion was too much.

"Do you want us to open it?" Kendra asked.

She nodded.

Kendra opened the envelope slowly and pulled out a stack of papers, holding them in Jolene's line of vision. The three of them stared at her as her gaze moved across the page, reading the words. Tears burned her eyes.

Suddenly she wished she wasn't here, in this bed, at the cottage, in Tahoe City. She wished she hadn't even come on this stupid trip in the first place. Jolene closed her eyes. She opened her mouth to speak but it took a moment for the words to come.

"Please go."

"We can't leave you, Jo," Kendra said.

"I want to be alone," she growled through clenched teeth.

"We're not going anywhere," Cristina said. "Unless it's to make the eight-hour drive to Oregon to kick Travis's ass. This guy has some nerve. Serving you divorce papers while you're here? He couldn't even be a man and do it himself. He's lucky there's eight hours between us." Cristina was up on her feet, pacing the floor in the bedroom.

"Cris, not now," Kendra whispered. "Is that the real reason he left? Because of the MS? Because of your diagnosis?" she asked.

Jolene closed and opened her eyes in intervals now. She didn't know when they were open or closed anymore and she didn't have the energy to care. The voices that filled the air of the room sounded distant and she could feel consciousness slipping away from her. All of it too much to bear—the flare up, the revealed secret, the divorce papers.

"Jolene?" Cristina asked.

"Let's leave her alone," Bo suggested.

"How long have you known?" Cristina asked Bo.

"Since Friday night. I noticed some things and guessed. I happened to guess right."

"How did we not notice?"

"My aunt has MS, so I suppose it was easier for me to recognize."

"So, did she tell you? Is that the real reason that piece of crap left her?" Cristina asked.

"Yes," Bo said.

She watched the three of them. The sympathy and pity on their faces. Or was she mistaking it for worry and concern? She couldn't be certain.

Bo bent down next to her. "I'll be back as soon as I'm off work tonight." He kissed her on the forehead.

"We'll take care of her," Kendra assured Bo.

"We're not going anywhere," Cristina said.

Kendra pat Jolene's hand and whispered to her, "Never give up the fight."

CHAPTER EIGHTEEN

An entire day gone, missed, wasted. An entire day irretrievable because of the flare up. But Jolene did thank her lucky stars it had only stolen one day from her. If she had ended up having to go to the hospital, she could've been stuck there for days, being pumped with drugs and fluid through an I.V. She'd heard stories of this in her MS support group.

When she appeared somewhat more energized later in the afternoon, Cristina and Kendra talked her into moving out onto the couch. They propped her up with throw pillows and brought her blankets. They offered her food and drinks. Her friends were treating her better than she could've imagined. It was sweet but at the same time, awkward. She didn't like to need them—to be taken care of. She'd gotten through the loss of Jacob without them, and she wanted to get through this without them as well.

Bo came over after work just as he'd promised. But Jolene wasn't the best company. She dozed in and out the entire evening. He fixed her tea and tried doing most of the talking. She liked hearing him talk. Telling stories from work and reminding her of the pranks they played on one another when they were kids.

At one point, she awoke on the couch to find Bo asleep on the other end. He had his head rested on a throw pillow, knees curled up and feet in front of her. Her body felt cramped from having little to no room trying to share the couch with a man who was 6' 3". But she hated to wake him. The poor guy had worked all day and then came straight over after.

Jolene awoke again, this time to a gentle touch on her face. She found Bo knelt in front of her, pushing her hair out of her face. She probably looked horrible. She needed a shower, badly. And yet, this sweet and attractive man didn't seem to mind.

"Hey, Bo." Her words didn't come out as scratchy as the morning before, but still, it didn't sound quite like her normal voice.

"Sorry I fell asleep here."

"No, I'm sorry. I've taken up so much of your time."

"Don't be sorry, Jo. If I didn't want to be here, I wouldn't be. Don't do that." Bo shook his head.

"Don't do what?"

"Don't be sorry for everything. Don't act like you're not important enough for people to make time for."

She nodded. This would not be an argument she'd win. He was right. She was always doing that. And she absolutely hated when he was right.

"You never complained before either," Jolene said somberly.

"You don't complain when someone is important to you." He tucked a loose strand of her hair behind her ear. "You give them all the time they need. And give them *what* they need."

She bit the inside of her cheek. He was making it obvious he was referencing a particular moment—the night of the accident. After she'd lost Jacob, and when she'd gone to the Dean cabin. She had left her parents and Travis and she'd run to Bo. She'd run to his comforting eyes and arms.

THEN

Standing outside of the Dean cabin, Jolene holds pebbles in her bandaged hands. Each one makes a ping sound when they hit Bo's window. It takes most of the handful of pebbles before his light turns on. When his window opens and he hangs his head out, she nearly loses it.

"Ollie," he breathes out his nickname for her.

And her insides shatter, breaking completely then. The tears fall again without any sign of stopping, streaming down her cheeks like rivers. Jolene collapses to her knees and lets her sorrow devour her.

Bo is at her side in what feels like only two heartbeats. He wraps his long arms around her, holding her close to his chest and all the while, whispering and shushing in her ear. "Oh, Ollie...I'm so sorry...I've got you...shh, Ollie."

"Where were you?" Jolene screams into his chest, her words coming out broken through her sobs. "Do you know I lost my brother today?"

"I know, I was there."

"I needed you."

"Jolene." He rubs her arms. "I was there. At the hospital. I thought you were okay. I mean, Travis was there."

"But I still needed *you*," she says, even though she knows how irrational and unfair she sounds.

She's dating Travis and Bo is dating Jessica. She doesn't have the right to demand his support. But in this moment, she doesn't care. She needs him to take her mind off all the loss and heartache.

"I'm sorry." Bo rubs a hand over the stubble of his shaved head.

"I need you," she says.

And before she has thought it through, he wraps his arms around her, pulling her in close and tight. The agony eases, but only slightly. She inhales his familiar beach scent and releases more fits of sobs into his chest.

Bo swipes his thumbs under her eyes, but it's pointless, the tears don't stop. Jolene stares into his green eyes and catches the longing there, at the same time she feels it too. He brushes a kiss on her cheek, then another on her forehead. He presses a trail of kisses down her nose.

When his lips hover over hers, she doesn't hesitate, the craving for him is too strong. She grips his shirt and pulls him toward her and their lips crash together in a lustful, needy way. His are soft and moist, just as she's always imagined they would be. She tastes them, hungrily. But as Bo's lips move against hers, the fleeting thought enters her mind, *she shouldn't be kissing Bo, she's with Travis.*

But as soon as Bo slips his tongue in her mouth, her own responds with fervor and all prior thoughts and misgivings disappear. Jolene's crying hasn't stopped—hot tears run down her face, landing onto Bo's as they kiss. It only seems to intensify her craving for him, the desire to be close to him burns. His hands are in her hair and the butterflies flutter in the depths of her belly. She caresses his face with her hands wrapped in the white bandages and it feels awkward, causing her to finally pull away from him.

Bo gasps. "I'm sorry," he says, breath ragged. "I shouldn't have...*we* shouldn't have..."

"Bo, I don't want to be alone tonight," she whispers.

He stares at her for a beat, but there's no hesitation evident on his face. Pulling her into him, Bo says, "You don't have to be. You know I'm always here for you."

He picks her up, carries her into the cabin and lays her down on the leather sofa. She peers up at the tall wooden beams meeting at a point in the middle of the ceiling. The scent of old wood and apples swims in the air. She imagines one of Stella Dean's famous apple pies cooling on the counter.

The familiarity of the Dean cabin rushes through her. But rather than comforting her, all it does is make her grief worse and all she wants is to forget about everything. She grips Bo's shirt and pulls him down on top of her.

"Are your parents here?"

"No, they're at home. It was supposed to be just me at the cabin this weekend. You know, for all the graduation parties." He pauses, catching himself. "Sorry."

The bitter reality hits Jolene like a car smashing into the wall in a NASCAR race. She chokes on new sobs as they rush in, each a new wave of grief. Bo holds her close, nuzzles her neck and kisses her forehead. Before long, they're kissing, and their body parts are in a tangled mess.

NOW

There hadn't been any words she could say for Bo's slip up when he'd mentioned graduation or parties. It hadn't been as if he was being insincere. Graduation parties had been on the agenda for the weekend for all of them. But because of the acci-

dent, all that changed. And Jolene would never forget her graduation night. Because it would be remembered as the night she
lost her brother, at the fault of her best friend.

Bo had held her for hours while she cried and mourned the
loss of Jacob. They made love that night—the first time for both
of them. And then they'd fallen asleep in one another's arms.

That night had been the only other time the two of them
had fallen asleep together—until last night. So many years had
passed, she'd tried to forget all about that night. Not because it
hadn't meant something to her but because she had never told
Travis. She'd never told anyone.

All along she had thought it was Travis that she always ran
to when really, it had been Bo all along. It was funny how your
mind created memories the way it wanted to.

Bo cleared his throat. "I gotta go. I need to go home and get
ready for work. I'll text you later to see how you're doing. If
you're feeling up to it, maybe I can come by, and we can watch
a movie or something?"

"I'd like that." She smiled.

Bo leaned over and kissed her on the forehead. She was
beginning to think this would be as far as the kissing between
them would go. Maybe they were only meant to be friends.
They'd seen one another nearly every day since she arrived in
town and there'd been no kissing yet. But she definitely felt
passion and chemistry each time she was with him.

She admired Bo before he slipped out the front door of the
cottage. The time on the clock on the stove read 4:52. Kendra
would be heading out for her run soon. Unfortunately, she
wouldn't be joining her today.

It may be early, but Jolene was wide awake. She sat up,
stretched, and climbed off the couch. She padded across the
wood floor in her bare feet and into the kitchen. How had
she gone an entire day without caffeine? She pulled the out

the coffee and inhaled the grounds, taking in the glorious scent.

Glancing down at herself, she blew out a sigh of relief. Thankfully Kendra had talked her into changing clothes at some point the day before. The last thing she wanted was to have Bo see her in the same clothes for two days—shower or no shower. Kendra had picked out a pair of pajamas from Jolene's suitcase. A navy-blue V-neck shirt and navy-blue and white striped cotton shorts. At some point, she'd taken her hair out of the messy bun, leaving it flowing out around her shoulders in unruly waves.

"Jo, you're up," Kendra said as she entered the kitchen.

"Morning."

"I'm so glad to see you up and around. How are you feeling?" Kendra gave her a side hug, wrapping her arms around her shoulders.

"I'm actually feeling okay." Jolene pulled a mug from the cupboard.

"You really gave us a scare."

"I know. I'm sorry," she said, then instantly remembered what Bo had said that morning. *She wasn't an imposition to everyone, and she apologized way too much.* "I should have told you sooner. At the very least, at the beginning of this trip."

"Well, I'm glad we know now." Kendra smiled, then hopped onto a stool and laced her running shoes. "I hope you don't mind me sneaking off to get in a quick run. Do you need anything before I go?" Kendra combed through her bangs with her fingers.

"No, I'm fine. You've been so great. Thanks for taking care of me. Now, go, enjoy your run. And hey, maybe you could do an extra three miles for me while you're at it."

Kendra pouted. "I wish you could join me."

"Me too. Hopefully I'll be up for it tomorrow." She crossed her fingers.

Kendra waved before slipping out the back door of the cottage. Jolene went to the window, watching her friend as she moved swiftly down the steps and onto the rocky sand. Longing stirred in her belly. She wanted to be out there, feeling the rush of the wind on her face and the uneven sand beneath her feet. Running kept her from being depressed. The longing in her belly turned into frustration, moving through her body with an unruly force.

Backing away from the window, she returned to the kitchen. She couldn't let herself go down that route. The frustration would turn to anger and the anger to self-pity. And self-pity was the worst feeling of all.

The coffee pot beeped, signaling the brewing process had completed. She poured herself a cup, wishing it was triple its size. She needed more caffeine today, justifying it since she'd missed out on having any the day before.

Regardless of the lost day and missed opportunities with her friends and Bo, she only had one concern on her mind weighing her down. *Travis wanted a divorce.* After almost fourteen months of holding onto hope he'd come around, he'd miss her, he still loved her, had vanished. All her dreams of being a whole and complete family again had shattered. And of all days to hear the news, on a flare day. To be honest, she was angry. Not even sad, just angry.

She had shed some tears the day before. After she woke up and stayed awake long enough for her mind to wrap around the reality of the situation. The finality of it. She was devastated to receive the divorce papers. But mostly she was furious of the way he'd chosen to serve them. He'd sent them to the sheriff department for one of the deputies to deliver to her at the cottage. *Coward.* And how humiliating. She didn't know which was worse—if an unknown deputy had delivered them or having Bo bring them over.

Jolene grabbed her black fleece jacket, slipped her feet into a pair of sandals, and took her coffee with her out the back doors of the cottage. She inhaled, allowing the crisp, fresh air to enter her lungs. If she couldn't run, she at least wanted to be outside, catching the sunrise and breathing the morning lake air.

As she descended the steps of the deck, her feet moved slow and a bit unsteady and she held onto the wood railing for support. Once she reached the sand, she didn't think twice, she kicked off her sandals. And when her feet touched the sand, a cold rush shot through her.

It took her much longer than normal to reach the dock. Her toes drug across the uneven sand. The wooden dock was cold but not in the same way as the sand. At least it was sturdy. She walked to the end of the dock, placed her coffee cup on it and sat down, leaving her feet dangling off the side.

Two people at the neighboring dock untied a canoe and got in. They waved to her as they began to paddle far out into the lake. In no time, the two people were paddling in uniform and the green canoe was merely a speck on the blue horizon.

The Gibbs had kayaks and canoes on the rack next to the cottage. She'd love to take them out again just like they used to when they were kids. Why hadn't they done that yet? But then she remembered, she had missed an entire day, maybe her friends had done it without her.

Jolene finished her coffee and made her way back to the cottage. When she reached the fire pit, she spotted Kendra on the deck. She ascended the steps and was winded by the time she reached the top.

"Hey, you okay?" Kendra reached underneath her elbow.

"Yeah, I'm fine," she said in between labored breaths.

Kendra pulled out a chair for her. "Here, sit down."

"Thanks." She eased herself into it.

"So, when you fell the other day," Kendra paused as she sat down. "Was it because of the MS?"

"Yes."

"I can't believe you let Cristina go on and on about how clumsy you are."

"What was I supposed to do? Just blurt out, I have Multiple Sclerosis? It's kind of a buzz kill, believe me."

"Yes. That's exactly what you should've done."

She gave her friend an incredulous look.

"Well, you still should've at least told us. We could've been more sensitive to you and what you're going through." Kendra took a sip of a thick, green concoction. "We feel just terrible."

"And that's what I didn't want. I didn't want you guys feeling sorry for me. I hate that part of all of this." She slumped further in the chair and peered down into her empty coffee mug.

"But we are sorry. We're sorry you have to deal with this."

"It's not something I have to 'deal with'," Jolene said, using air quotes. "This is something I have to live with. This is a way of life for me. This isn't a broken leg that's going to heal or a virus I'm going to get over once it runs its course, this is a permanent diagnosis. I'm forever going to have to eat a strict diet, limit my exercise, take medications, and expect a flare up to happen at any moment." Her voice had risen without intention, and her hands were shaking, and she felt like chucking the coffee mug. She hadn't meant to raise her voice at Kendra. She just wished she didn't have to explain this to her.

"I'm sorry, Jo." Kendra's eyes filled with tears.

Great, and now she'd upset Kendra. She couldn't remember the last time she'd seen her friend cry before this trip. Kendra was strong and always had everything together.

She was a no-nonsense lady. She had a schedule and stuck to it. Regardless of how busy she was at work; she was a wonderful mom to her son Quinn. She could pack a complete nutritious lunch for him, apply flawless makeup, and carry on a phone meeting with a potential client, all at the same time.

"No, I'm sorry. I didn't mean to go off on you." She pinched the bridge of her nose. "This isn't your fault. This is something I have to live with, it's not your burden to carry."

"But we want to help you. And it's not sympathy. Friends should tell each other things and be there for one another. Help each other out when they need it. We've been crappy friends to you."

"It's really not your problem to take on. I don't want you to feel bad for not being there for me. I'm the one who chose not to tell you. And I actually have a good support system. I have Joy and a few other ladies from book club that live near me. They help with the kids when I'm flaring. And I attend an MS support group. Not to mention my doctor, he's amazing. The best in all of Central Oregon."

"That's great, I'm so glad to hear that."

"But I'd love for us to be closer. You don't know how much I've missed you and our friendship. Especially now with not only the MS, but with Travis," Jolene said.

"I want that too." Kendra reached out and patted her hand. "I know I'm busy and it seems like I don't have time for you, but I will make time. If you tell me, you need me, I will make myself available to you. I mean it, Jo."

"Thank you."

"So." Kendra pulled her hand away, leaning back in the chair. "What are you going to do? Are you going to sign the papers?"

"What else can I do?" Her shoulders tightened.

"Well, at least promise me you won't sign them until you've

read through them all. And maybe you should get a lawyer," Kendra suggested.

"I can promise you I'll read them. But I don't think I want to go through the hassle of hiring a lawyer. I just don't have the energy for a fight."

"Read them first. Then make the decision about hiring a lawyer, okay."

She nodded.

The back door opened, and Cristina appeared, her long dark hair with burgundy streaks down and messy. She was dressed in a grey matching sleep set of shorts and a tank top. In one hand, a cup of coffee and in the other, a sweatshirt.

"Morning, Cris," Jolene said.

"Yeah, morning," Cristina grunted. "Surprised to see you up and so chipper."

"Guess I couldn't sleep anymore."

"And I thought I slept a lot." Cristina winked at Jolene. "Want me to refill your coffee?"

"That would be great, thank you."

When Cristina returned, she handed Jolene a full cup of steaming hot coffee and she joined the other women around the table.

"How you feeling?" Cristina asked.

"I'm okay. I'm up at least. I made coffee and even walked down to the dock."

"Yeah, but she was completely out of breath when she returned." Kendra raised her brows, her face smeared with concern. "You shouldn't have done that. Don't you need to take it easy? Are you even supposed to continue running?"

"My doctor said I can keep running for as long as my body will let me. It's therapeutic for me."

"I think you're crazy. You have an excuse to get out of exercising and you're not taking advantage of it?" Cristina let out a mirthless laugh.

"I have to keep moving. It makes me feel better and will prolong my mobility. I'm prepared to use a walker or scooter, but I don't want to earlier than I have to."

"I'm a bit ashamed to admit, I don't know much about Multiple Sclerosis," Kendra said, stirring her green smoothie with the straw.

"I guess neither do I. All I know is it's not good. But I'm going to learn. That way I won't feel so helpless the next time you need me," Cristina said.

"Me too."

"That's really sweet, ladies. Thanks." Jolene sipped her coffee.

Cristina cleared her throat. "Jo, you might want to check your phone." She pulled Jolene's phone out of her own sweatshirt pocket and slid it across the table.

"Oh, thanks. I completely forgot." When she picked up her phone, it revealed two voicemails and eleven text messages. Yikes, that was a lot of texts.

Anxiety stirred in the pit of her stomach as she scrolled through the texts. There were six from Julia, one from her mom, two from Joy, one from Travis and one from her son Cole.

COLE

Worried about you mom...love you

The words sent a warm tingle through her body and her eyes went glassy, tears threatening. She scrolled to the text from Travis and debated deleting it before even reading it. The guy had some nerve, texting her. But she supposed she didn't have to respond. She didn't owe him anything.

But he was the father of her children and nothing would

change that. And part of her would always love him in some way. But her days spent pining after him were over.

TRAVIS

Hope you're resting. Don't push yourself.
Thinking of you.

He's thinking of me? Yeah, right. The text caused a multitude of feelings to course through her—sadness, anger, resentment, worry, love, confusion. It was unfair that Travis had this power over her. She wanted to scream or cry or punch something.

Jolene could text him and question his relationship with Carrie, but what good would it do? He'd already filed for a divorce. It didn't matter if he had cheated on her with Carrie or if the two had started up a relationship after they were separated. None of it mattered anymore. Their marriage was over.

"You okay?" Kendra asked.

"I'm fine." She set her phone on the table, pushing it away from her, pushing Travis away from her.

"Texts from Travis?" Cristina questioned.

She nodded.

"Tell that rat bastard you don't need him anymore. You're doing just fine on your own. You're better than fine. A chick Brewmaster?" She shook her head. "You're a badass."

"I don't know about that. But I am pretty proud of myself for learning the ropes and taking it over. And I really love it."

"That's a relief," Kendra mumbled.

The women were silent for a moment, the sound of a seagull flying overhead and the lake water lapping on the shore was quiet in the distance.

"You know what I feel like doing today? Swimming. Doesn't that sound amazing?"

"Do you think that's a good idea? Won't that use too much energy?" Cristina asked.

"Yeah, Jo, I really think you should relax today," Kendra said.

"If Becca were here, she'd tell me to get over myself and get my butt in the lake. She'd say, *swimming is good for the soul.* And don't you think I need something good for the soul today?" She raised her brows, staring at her friends defiantly.

Cristina and Kendra exchanged a look.

"Fine. If you want to swim, then swimming it is," Kendra said, smiling and shaking her head slowly.

CHAPTER NINETEEN

The sun beamed down on the three women as they swam in the cold water that flowed from the melting snow of the mountains and filled the lake. Regardless of the icy water, it refreshed Jolene and renewed her aching muscles.

It felt like heaven.

She floated on her back, passing Cristina and Kendra who were treading water to keep warm. "Let's jump off the dock, like we used to do."

"Are you sure you're up for that?" Kendra asked.

"Stop asking me. If I suggest something, then I'm up for it."

"Okay, yeah let's do it."

"C'mon, sluts, last one on the dock makes dinner," Cristina called over her shoulder as she swam toward the ladder that hung off the side of the dock.

Jolene had the advantage over the other women, she'd been swimming regularly at the public pool for the past year. The win was in the bag. She swam fast, kicking her legs and letting her hands dive through the water. If only Becca could see her now, and see how far she'd come.

Climbing up the ladder and reaching the top of the dock, she pumped her fists over her head and cheered. She'd arrived first. Next came Cristina and then Kendra.

"I think you cheated, you were closer to the dock." Kendra laughed. "But I don't mind making dinner."

The three of them stood on the end of the dock, beads of water dripping from their wet bodies and hitting the warm dock. Jolene glanced down, the surface of the water was only about a foot and a half away. It rippled and lapped underneath the bottom of the dock. Standing in the middle of her two friends, she reached both of her hands out, grabbing onto theirs.

Cristina rolled her eyes.

"Ready?" Jolene glanced at Kendra and then back at Cristina. "Let's count, like we used to."

"Oh for the love, is this freaking necessary?" Cristina complained.

After receiving the death stare from both Kendra and Jolene, she reluctantly began counting them off. The other two women joined her. "Five, four, three, two, one."

They leapt off the edge of the dock with a combined squeal. The wind hit her wet body sending a chill through it and a feeling of exhilaration.

When she entered the icy cold water, it hit hard, like stepping out of her warm home and into a negative three-degree winter day in Central Oregon. It woke up her body and her mind. She felt like a teenager again—alive and carefree. Like a future full of new opportunities awaited her.

There was a new sense of clarity Jolene hadn't experienced in a long time. Often the symptoms of her disease left her confused and her mind foggy. But at that moment, her thoughts were clear. She needed to let go of the hurt she felt being at this place—the place she'd lost Jacob all those years ago. Just because she lost him here, didn't mean she had to be sad here.

Jacob wouldn't want that. He'd want her to remember all the positive and fun memories this place held.

"That felt amazing," she said.

"It really did," Kendra agreed.

"It's freaking freezing!" Cristina exhaled on a jittery breath.

Jolene swam to the ladder again, pulling herself up onto the dock. She needed to do this one last thing, in honor of Jacob— cannon balls off the dock. Backing up, she took off in a sprint, her bare feet padding against the wooden dock. Then she leapt off the edge, tucking her knees in and holding onto them with her hands in the air. When she plunged into the water, it splashed out all around her.

The girls were still shrieking when she came up for air. She laughed as she treaded water. "I have missed this so much. I've missed the lake. And the cottage. And this entire town. I've pushed it away for so long and I just can't do it anymore. I love it here."

"Me too. I've always loved it here." Kendra weaved her hands in and out of the water.

"I've been up here quite a bit over the years and brought my girls. We always have a great time. But nothing like when we all used to come here together. I think it was our friendship that made this place so special. We were really lucky to have each other. And to have such a great place to enjoy and make memories," Cristina said through chattering teeth.

"I've decided to finally bring my kids here. I'm going to try to bring them in August. No more excuses," Jolene announced.

"That's great." Kendra treaded water next to her.

"And now I won't have to try to convince Travis how important it is to take a vacation with his family."

Their family vacation to Hawaii came to her mind. She had planned the trip twice before they'd actually gone. Both times

Travis had backed out last minute giving some inadequate excuse regarding the brewery.

It had been their dream to take the kids to Hawaii since they had honeymooned there. They wanted them to experience hiking the Koko Crater Railway trail and show them the view of Honolulu and Hanauma Bay at sunrise. To jump off the rocks of La'ie Point and into the warm, crystal blue waters. To discover the deliciousness of chocolate cream pie from Ted's Bakery.

"I'm all for this miraculous breakthrough, Jo, but I'm freezing as hell. Let's head back. Plus, I believe Kendra may need to do some grocery shopping before she makes dinner." Cristina smirked before she began swimming back to shore.

The other two women swam behind her, matching stroke for stroke with one another.

THEN

The hike down the trail is two miles long but the terrain is mild. Jolene and her friends have made the familiar trek so many times over the course of the last few weeks, they could do it while sleepwalking. They pass the time by rating the lead singers in their favorite bands by best voice and who would be the best kisser. After a unanimous vote, Billie Joe Armstrong of Green Day takes the number one spot as best voice while Mike Shinoda of Linkin Park wins as best kisser.

Rarely do they talk about what they'll do with the money after they find it. They gave that up after the first week of searching for the stash. She figures this is in part due to the hope dissipating they'll find it and another part due to them having no idea how much money is even there. Or if there's any money at all.

Maybe it's a rumor, or an urban legend. Someone stashing a substantial amount of money feels very cliché, very 80's movie-esque—like The Goonies. But this is no movie.

At any rate, on the days the girls meet up at the Gibbs's cottage and grab the bikes, parking them at the Sweet Shop and making the two-mile hike to the coordinates entered into the GPS are Jolene's favorite. The four of them have something bigger than a friendship bonding them together now.

"Almost there," Becca calls over her shoulder as she leads them single file on the trail.

"Good. Because when we're done, a burger at Ander's is calling my name." Jolene watches her feet move over the terrain of compacted dirt and pine needles.

"Yessss," Cristina says. "My mouth is already watering."

They round a corner in the trail, a mound of granite boulders piled high to the left of them. The same mound they've passed every time. But today, Becca stops, and Jolene nearly slams into the back of her.

"What's up?" She steps on the heel of Becca's shoe.

"I think we need to check the boulders again." Holding up the GPS, Becca glances back and forth from the screen to the giant rock formation.

"Ugghhh," Kendra groans. "Becks, we've checked around them a hundred times. It's not there."

"But look." The girls crowd around the GPS as Becca holds it out. "According to the coordinates, the geocache should be in this location. And unless it's buried underneath our feet on this trail, it's gotta be somewhere around the boulders."

"It's not, okay?" Cristina rips the GPS from Becca's grip. "Can we just look somewhere new, please? How about that tree? If someone gives me a boost, I could climb it. The stash could be up high."

"Wait. Shh. Just wait a second." Jolene presses her fingers to her temples, her eyes searching the ground, then glancing back at the rocks, her mind spins over Becca's words. "Becca? You still have that portable shovel in your backpack?"

"Uh...yeah, I think so. Why?" Slipping the pack off her back, Becca sets it on the ground and crouches in front of it.

"You can't be serious? Not you too?" Cristina whines.

Kendra leans her back against one of the boulders. "You think it's buried in the trail?"

"Not exactly," Jolene mutters.

She surveys the boulders, walking around them while her brain deciphers just how she's going to get underneath them. She hops up onto the lowest boulder and crawls to look over the edge.

"What are you doing?" Kendra asks.

"I think it could be underneath the boulders. Buried."

"Seriously?" Cristina asks, disbelief in her tone.

"If I can slip in between those two, there's a big enough gap that someone could've dug in the ground and hid it there." Jolene reaches her hand out. "Becks, hand me the shovel."

Kendra yanks on the back of Jolene's shirt. "Don't, Jo. It's too dangerous."

"I have to try. We've looked everywhere else."

"Only if you think you can do it, otherwise, Kendra's right. It's not worth it."

Cristina hops up on the boulder next to Jolene and peers down. "Jo's the only one small enough to fit down there."

Jolene makes eye contact with Becca. "I can do it."

Becca nods.

Scooting across the boulder on her backside, she sucks in a breath and slides in between the two granite boulders that are closest together. Her feet land on the ground below with a thud and she exhales. She takes the shovel and bangs the tip of it into the ground until she hears a *clank* sound. Turning her body sideways, she crouches and finds the shovel has hit a smaller rock. She leans the shovel against one of the boulders and wraps her hands around the small rock and pulls. It only budges slightly.

"What is it?" Cristina calls down to her from a top the boulder behind her.

Becca and Kendra crowd in next to her.

"Maybe nothing. But let me check something."

"Be careful," Kendra hollers.

"Okay, mom," Jolene snickers.

She tries the rock again, this time using more strength than before. The rock shifts an inch or so. It isn't big enough to weigh that much, so why can't she lift it? And then her mind reels back, snagging on Becca's words—*unless it's buried.*

She straightens and reaches for the shovel again, wrenching it into the ground and stomping on the edge. When she puts pressure on the shovel, it lifts the rock. She kicks the shovel further into the ground and when she raises it, the rock elevates even more so. She bends and pulls on the rock, giving it a hefty yank. This time, along with the rock comes about a four-inch round, white PVC pipe, that's been buried in the ground. The rock is attached somehow to the cap of the pipe.

The girls suspending above her let out a combined gasp. Jolene holds the pipe in her hands, spinning and gazing up at them.

"Holy crap, we found it." Cristina clamps a hand over her mouth.

Becca smiles. "*Jolene* found it."

"Oh. My. Gosh." She starts to laugh. She doesn't even

know what's inside, but she doesn't care. After all these weeks, they'd actually found it. The mystery stash.

Becca pumps both fists over her head and screams. "Woohoo!"

Kendra hugs Cristina and Becca. And Jolene can't stop laughing. Cristina cups her hands around her mouth and exhales loud catcalls causing them to ricochet off the boulders and trees. And suddenly they're all joining in.

NOW

Dinner hit the spot perfectly. Kendra outdid herself. She made shrimp with brown rice and sautéed vegetables. Jolene had to be careful what she ate. No gluten, very little dairy and no red meat. So it was difficult to trust someone to cook for her.

Her phone chimed.

> **BO**
>
> Off work, heading your way.

"Lover boy coming over?" Cristina's voice purred.

"He is, I hope that's okay." She didn't even bother correcting the nickname.

Cristina shrugged. "Fine with me. I definitely don't mind the view."

"What Cristina meant to say is, it's totally fine with us. We love having Bo around and we just want you to be happy. And it seems like he makes you happy," Kendra said.

"But what's the deal with you guys?" Cristina rinsed their empty plates while Kendra loaded them into the dishwasher.

"Same as what I told you yesterday when you asked, and the day before."

"Okay, but seriously. You've seen him every day since you got here." She turned the water off and eyed Jolene.

"And he's always had a thing for you, everyone knows it." Kendra dried her hands on a towel.

"I don't know." She felt her cheeks blush as she spun her hoop earring with her finger. "I do really enjoy spending time with him."

She poured herself a glass of the wine Kendra had opened during dinner. She originally declined a glass but now she wanted something to help calm her nerves. Bo said he was on his way over and on top of that, the girls were questioning their relationship. She didn't know how to answer because she didn't know herself.

She poured a glass of wine for Kendra and Cristina too, and the three of them sat on the sofa in the living room. They dressed casually for the cooler evening spent relaxing inside the cottage. Kendra and Cristina wore yoga pants and oversized sweatshirts.

Jolene dressed in a pair of jeans and an aqua blue thin sweater, the color bringing out the blue in her eyes. She looked like a mess when Bo saw her that morning.

"So, you guys sleep together yet?" Cristina blurted.

She choked on her wine. "Cristina! We haven't even kissed."

"Seriously?" Cristina raised her thick brows.

"We don't want to rush things." She studied the wine in her glass.

"Rush things? You take things any slower, you're gonna be a nun."

"And we don't want to mess up our friendship," Jolene said, ignoring Cristina's last comment. "Besides, still married, remember?" She waggled her fingers in the air, revealing her wedding ring.

"Ha! That ring doesn't count now that he's served you with divorce papers."

"Maybe it's a good thing you two were friends first. You have that to build on. You've known each other forever, you probably know everything there is to know about each other," Kendra said.

"Yeah, but it's been a long time since you have really talked, you probably don't know *everything*." Cristina fiddled with the stitching on the throw pillow she had hugged to her chest.

"What about you? When you and Phillip finally started dating after working together for all those years, did you feel it helped your relationship? You know, because you had a friendship first and knew each other so well?" Jolene asked.

"Sure, it helped." Cristina shrugged. "But you can't know everything. And sometimes you don't want to know everything. It's not always pleasant."

That was true, maybe knowing everything could be boring. What would be left to talk about if they knew one another so well? Having a twenty-year gap in their relationship would definitely give them things to talk about.

A knock sounded on the door. Cristina stood to answer it. Jolene thought about her life with Travis, the family they'd created, her health. She had so much baggage. Not to mention all the miles that separated her and Bo.

Cristina entered the living room with Bo trailing behind. She lifted her hands gesturing to him as if she were Vanna White on Wheel of Fortune. "I present to you, your booty call."

She gasped and her face grew hot. Making eye contact with Bo seemed impossible now, although she couldn't help herself. She glanced at him, and his face was also red. It reminded her of when he was a boy and blushed over everything. The poor guy got embarrassed so easily. But she had found it to be adorable and still did. It was nice having this simple reminder of a way she knew him.

"On that note." Kendra got up and tugged on Cristina's arm. "We'll be leaving now. C'mon, Cris."

Bo shoved his hands inside his jean pockets as he shuffled his feet back and forth. The sleeves of his black Henley shirt were pushed up and the top two of the three buttons were undone. Her face grew warmer as her vision drifted to the open buttons of his shirt, revealing just a bit of his tan chest.

"Please, Bo," Cristina called over her shoulder. "Promise me you'll give her some action, she really needs to get laid."

"Oh. My..." Jolene's words trailed as she buried her face in her palms.

"Well, that wasn't awkward at all." Bo chuckled, moving into the living room, and sitting down beside her on the sofa.

"I'd apologize for her, but you know Cristina."

"Sure do. She hasn't changed at all. You'd think her being a mother and a teacher that it would have helped, but apparently not." Bo smiled.

"Yeah, but then, it wouldn't be Cristina."

He nodded.

You couldn't fix what wasn't broken and she wouldn't want Cristina to be any other way. Her familiarity was comforting. And besides, change made Jolene anxious.

Her brother Jacob had always taken her sensitivities into consideration. He liked to try to prepare her before the bad news hit. Like when the family cat, Sammy, had died after being hit by a car. Jacob had been the one to play interference when she returned home from school and almost saw the county truck parked out front. He'd let her down easy and even made the county workers wait for Jolene to say goodbye before taking the cat's mangled body away.

But he wasn't here now to prepare her for all the change—

the MS diagnosis, Travis leaving her, learning how to run the brewery without him, the possibility of a new relationship with Bo. It had been hard to live her adult years without him looking out for her like he'd always done.

"So, how you feeling today?" Bo turned his body toward her, resting his ankle over his knee.

"I'm okay. I rested quite a bit. Then the girls and I went for a swim."

"You sure that was a good idea? You felt up to swimming?"

"I did. And it felt incredible."

"That's great. It's good to see you with some energy." He rested his arm on the back of the sofa, then placed his hand on her shoulder, giving it a firm squeeze. "You really gave me a scare yesterday."

Jolene dipped her chin. She folded her hands, setting them in her lap and studying them, taking notice of the white criss-cross scars. If he chose to be with her, to have a relationship with her, a life with her, there would be more days like yesterday. There would be far worse days than yesterday.

"I know," she said.

"I hated seeing you like that. I felt so helpless. As a policeman, my job is to help people and yesterday, with you...I don't know, I just felt so useless." He rubbed her shoulder before grazing her neck.

The heat from his hand on her bare skin warmed her entire body. She gazed into Bo's green eyes and at that moment, there was the same comfort she felt when she'd entered the cold lake water earlier in the day. Something, maybe fate, maybe God, had brought them together. The timing of all life's events for them both seemed to bring them together for this perfect moment.

Jolene gave up waiting for Bo to make the first move. Reaching out for his other hand, she interlaced her fingers with his. He tilted his head in question. But there was no doubt, she was sure. She hadn't been surer about anything in her life.

Bringing her body in closer to his, he moved his hand to the back of her neck and caressed it. Then he pulled her into his chest, and she released a moan. Wrapping her arm around his back, she tethered her fingers through his hair. She'd longed to do it ever since she saw him that first night at the bar.

Bo exhaled a deep sigh. "Ollie," he whispered, taking her face in his palms, and lowering his lips to hers.

Jolene sucked in a breath, inhaling his intoxicating ocean scent. He smelled like citrus and bergamot with a hint of tobacco. When he pressed his lips against hers, a tingle traveled through her body and her limbs went numb. In that moment, she tossed all her insecurities and questions of will-they-or-won't-they-work-out right out the window.

The kiss started soft and slow before growing more passionate and earnest. His tongue parted her lips and when it reached hers, she responded.

Slipping her hand inside the open buttons of his shirt, she grazed her fingers over his smooth chest. Bo let out a soft moan against her mouth as he moved his hand down her neck, and the sound caused the air to get caught in her throat.

She felt alive, her body awakening to each sensation. She gave into the passion and willed him in her mind to never, ever let her go.

CHAPTER TWENTY

E ven well into the afternoon the following day, her night
with Bo left her feeling weightless. She walked around as
light as a feather, like she was air breezing throughout the day.
Nothing could ruin her mood and bring her down from the
cloud she'd been riding on since the night before.

On the corner of the island in the kitchen sat the stack of
the signed divorce papers. After the swim with Cristina and
Kendra the day before, she felt at peace about the divorce. This
is what Travis wanted, so what was the point trying to hold on
any longer? Signing the papers left her hopeful about her
future.

Jolene had found a picnic basket in the garage and packed
it. She filled it with cheese slices, crackers, and cold pasta salad,
strawberries, and brownies. A tune played in her head, and she
hummed *You Were Always on My Mind* by Willie Nelson
without realizing.

Kendra had gone into South Lake Tahoe to do some work
and Cristina had left in a rush early that morning, saying there
was a family crisis at home that couldn't be ignored. She had

the cottage to herself and besides the sound of her humming, it was quiet.

She wanted to surprise Bo by driving over to his cabin off Dean Lane with a picnic style dinner in tow. After his help and affection during her flare up, it would be a way for her to say thank you. Her heart was full of appreciation and, well, love. There was no sense trying to fight it.

She loved him.

She'd always loved him. Even when they were teenagers and Becca used to tease her and Bo after they'd finish a day of fishing. Becca would say, "Is it true, do blondes, like, really have more fun?" Although Jolene didn't know how much truth there was to the blonde thing, she did know that they always had fun when they were together.

THE DEAN FAMILY cabin sat on a dead-end gravel road only a few feet away from the lake. It was the only house off the short road. Bo's parents had the cabin built for them before they had children. They were older than Jolene's parents and then waited a few years after getting married before having children. They had only used the cabin as a vacation home as they'd always resided in Reno. Having Bo live in the cabin year-round felt strange.

When she pulled up to the cabin, Bo's blue Chevy pick-up truck was in the driveway. Her skin tingled in anticipation. Pulling her SUV off the road, she parked in front of the cabin. Gathering her purse and the picnic basket from the passenger side, she headed up the flagstone walk.

It was obvious Bo had been busy updating things, like the worn boards on the wrap around porch and the broken flag-stones on the walk. But most remained the same. Seeing the familiar log cabin caused the memories to flood back to her mind.

Jolene had loved coming to the Dean cabin. Almost as much as the Gibbs's cottage. But here, at Bo's family cabin, she was free to be her true self. She didn't have to worry about how her hair looked and she didn't have to put on makeup. Her brother's old Sacramento King's baseball hat, worn jeans with holes and a fresh face was her trademark look here.

Bo's parents, Bart and Stella were the sweetest people. They invited her over constantly and treated her like a daughter. She recalled a morning from when they were teenagers, Bo had picked her up from the Gibbs's cottage and brought her back to his cabin with him to fish. The best place to catch rainbow trout was right off the edge of their property.

Jolene had convinced Bo to dive into his mom's apple pie that was intended for that night's dessert. Stella had been so pissed. It was hilarious. Her cheeks warmed and a smile tugged at the corner of her lips.

So many memories. Some she'd forgotten about. Like having to take her baseball hat off when Bart Dean said Grace before they could eat.

As she headed up the steps, she placed her trembling hand on the wood railing while her heart beat wildly. She wasn't sure if the nerves were because she was back at the Dean cabin or if it was because of what had happened between her and Bo the night before.

Standing on the welcome mat, she pushed her unruly bangs out of her face. She glanced down, giving herself the once over. Luckily, her knees had healed enough to take the bulky bandages off. But they'd left ugly scabs and light purplish bruises. She dressed in a pair of jeans, a button-down shirt with the buttons undone and a pair of wedge sandals.

With the picnic basket hanging off one arm, she exhaled a

deep breath and knocked on the front door. Her heart thumped louder with each second she stood there waiting. It felt like an eternity before the door opened. And when it did, a young striking blonde woman stood before her.

What the hell? She was taken aback. The air in her throat constricted and she had to fight to breathe. With her legs threatening to give out on her, she had to use all her strength to stay upright.

"Hi...I, uh...I, um..." Jolene stumbled over her words.

The woman looked young—*really* young. She was tall and lanky with long, straight blonde hair. She had a delicate face, a turned-up nose sprinkled with light freckles. But what Jolene noticed most of all, was her sparkling green eyes. They were glasslike and breathtaking. And familiar. She'd seen this woman's face before but couldn't recall where.

Her first instinct was to ditch the picnic basket and run back to her car. But her feet wouldn't move. It was as if she had sandbags attached to them weighing her down.

"Are you looking for my dad?" the beautiful blonde asked.

Dad? Did she mean, Bart Dean? But Bo was an only child. Bart and Stella didn't have any other children. And she was much too young. The thoughts in her brain swished around and she felt lightheaded. Blackness filled the edges of her eyes.

"Uh, Dad," the blonde called over her shoulder. "There's someone here."

"Well, who is it?" a husky voice came from inside the cabin.

But not just any husky voice...Bo's husky voice.

Dad? What? Jolene's knees went weak, and then, blackness.

WHEN JOLENE CAME TO, her eyes fluttered open and took in her surroundings. Darkly stained wood came to a peak at the vaulted ceiling above her. She was laying on a sofa, a soft pillow propped behind her head. She knew exactly where she was. But didn't know why was she there?

Then it hit her—hard. The memory of the beautiful blonde. *Um, are you looking for my dad?* She shot up to a sitting position. Her head pounded. She rubbed her temples and pinched her eyes shut. When she opened them again, two images appeared and hovered over her.

"Hey there, beautiful," Bo said. "You okay?"

"D-did...did I faint?" she stuttered.

"You did."

"Did I...did I fall?" she muttered.

"You did not. Thanks to Lark here." Bo placed his hand on the blonde girl's back. "She caught you before you hit the floor. Good thing too, you wouldn't want a nasty bump on your head. Although, I suppose you could add it to your collection of other injuries." He chuckled under his breath.

Was he trying to make jokes? Because he had some serious explaining to do. This was big. Huge. His attempt at making light of the situation by joking caused her skin to burn.

"Lark?" she questioned.

But now that she got a better look at her, she knew exactly who this blonde girl was. Especially after learning her name. This was Lark, Becca's daughter Lark. And she was here, at the Dean cabin...calling Bo, *Dad*. It all came to her fast and hard. Her head began to spin.

"Yes." Bo patted Lark's back. "This is Lark, my daughter. Lark, this is Jolene McCabe."

"Jolene? As in, Jolene Oliver?" Lark asked, her voice soft.

She nodded, confused. She glanced at Bo, then back at Lark.

"I've heard a lot about you." Lark smiled and when she did, her eyes crinkled in a familiar way, just as Becca's had when she smiled.

Jolene thought about the picture of Becca and Lark on the mantle in the Gibbs's cottage. She recognized her upturned nose just like Becca's. But Lark's eyes were green, unlike Becca's whose were a chocolate brown, and instead she had Bo's sparkling green eyes.

"Well," she snapped, as she swung her legs over the edge of the couch. "I wish I could say the same about you." She stood, stumbled, and then caught her footing before snatching her purse off the coffee table and stomping toward the front door.

"Jo, wait." Bo called to her.

She whipped around, looking at him before glancing at Lark, who stood there fidgeting with the hem of her shirt and a grieved expression on her face. This wasn't how she wanted things to go when she met Lark—*if* she ever met Lark. There were things she planned on saying to her. Things about her mother. But this new information that had just unfolded, this secret, it hit her like a frying pan to the face. Her stomach pinched in that familiar way.

"It was nice to meet you, Lark. And I really am sorry about your mom. She was a good friend..." her voice trailed off.

Was Becca a good friend? Would a good friend have a child with her friend's crush and then never tell her? She couldn't finish her sentence. She was too overcome with anger and sadness all balled into one. Turning back around, she rushed out of the cabin and hurried down the front steps.

"Wait, Jo. C'mon, would you just wait a minute?" Bo called, chasing after her.

"There's nothing to say. Just leave me alone." She fumbled in her purse searching for her car keys, tears already streaming down her face.

Anger, deceit, confusion, all the kinds of emotions someone could possibly feel, she felt at that moment. She'd been such an idiot.

"No, I'm not going to leave you alone. Now, would you just let me explain?"

"You're an *open book, no secrets*," she spit out, "that's what you told me wasn't it?" Jolene found her key and jabbed it at him. "You lied to me."

She turned and pressed the unlock button before opening the door of her SUV. Bo reached out and pushed the door shut before she could get in. She whipped around to face him, attempting to put on a brave face.

"Just wait a minute, please. I'm sorry, okay? I wanted to tell you about Lark, I really did. I just," he paused, stabbing his fingers through his hair. "I guess I just wanted to wait for the right time."

"Wait for the right time? Like when? After I had fallen in love with you?" her voice cracked. "Well, it's too late for that," she bit out.

Bo seemed taken aback for a moment. Like he'd forgotten what they were even arguing about. His expression softened and he moved closer to her.

"Don't touch me." Jolene put up her palms.

"Ollie," Bo whispered. "C'mon, don't do this."

"Don't do what?"

"Don't push me away."

"You know what, Bo?" Standing in front of him, she looked him in the eye. "I'm not pushing *you* away. You've pushed *me* away." She opened her car door and stepped in.

Bo held onto it, refusing to let her go. "That's not fair," he said.

"You're right, it's not. None of this is fair," she agreed, hating all of it, the arguing, and the confrontation.

"Would you please come back inside and talk to me."

"Yeah right. Like I'd just go back in there. I told you to leave me alone, and I meant it." With those words, Jolene couldn't make eye contact with him any longer. She stared forward out the windshield. Then she whispered through an exhaled breath, "please, just let me go."

Bo bent down. "I can't, I won't. I've waited twenty years for you. I'll give you some space, but I won't let you go."

"Please," she whispered.

With that, Bo stepped back. Without looking at him, she closed the door, and pulled away, gravel spewing from her tires.

JOLENE DROVE IN A FURY, heading back in the direction of the cottage. The tears flowed with little effort, one after another, rolling down her cheeks. Stupid. How could she have been so stupid? To trust him. She was too trusting. What had she been thinking?

She would return to the cottage, pack her things, and leave tonight. The thought of spreading Becca's ashes made her furious. How could she give Becca a proper memorial if she was this upset with her? But she was more than upset, she felt betrayed—by two of her best friends.

And thinking of friends, had Kendra and Cristina known about Lark? About Becca and Bo having a child together? Jolene had a sinking feeling, they did. And now she felt betrayed by her two other best friends.

Anger stirred in her belly. She couldn't head to the cottage. Facing Cristina and Kendra right now seemed impossible. They were supposed to be her friends and they hadn't told her. All of them had kept this secret from her for years. For how many years? How old was Lark? Fifteen, sixteen, seventeen?

Taking a turn off Manson Blvd, she headed to Commons Beach. She couldn't go back to the cottage now. She would go later, once she knew Cristina and Kendra were asleep. Then she'd pack her things and leave in the night. Because really, she didn't owe Becca anything, as far as she was concerned, they were even now.

The parking lot had a few open spaces, beachcombers still squeezing out what was left of the daylight hours before dusk arrived, and the beach closed for the day. Pulling her SUV into a space, she parked and stepped out. She followed an unmarked narrow trail surrounded by trees and shrubs.

Jolene's feet wobbled in her wedge sandals on the sandy path. She bent over and unhooked them, slipping her feet out. Then she slung the sandals over her fingers while she made her way down the trail.

Once she reached the beach, the air felt cool on her skin. She walked in her bare feet, the rocky sand sinking in between her toes. Her tears had stopped, finally. Just the idea of shedding anymore tears for Bo made the anger bubble to the surface once again. She wouldn't cry for Becca anymore either.

She was done.

The waves lapped over the sand at the shoreline with intense force. She moved closer to the edge of the water. It would be freezing but she had an urge to get her feet wet. To feel the iciness of the June lake water. And then, if she stood in it long enough, the numbness. Because she didn't want to feel anything at all.

Jolene stepped into the water, letting it flow over the tops of her feet. It sent a shiver up her spine followed by a shock of pain. But she didn't care. First, the pain from the cold would come and then the welcomed numbness would follow.

Taking another step forward, the next wave rushed over her feet and reached her ankles, soaking the bottoms of her pant legs. She inhaled a sharp breath, but stood her ground, letting the cold water work its magic.

The sun sat low in the sky and the cool evening air blew through her thin shirt. She shivered again. It was as if her bones and nerves were being frozen. It hurt like hell.

Closing her eyes tight and balling up her fists, she shouted out loud. The sound surprised her. But it was gratifying. She cried out again, this time louder and in a deeper tone.

"Ahhhh!"

At first, they were shouts of anger. But after a few more hollers, they were shouts of defeat. She felt defeated. Life had won and she had lost. And isn't that just like life. It makes you think you are doing great, handling everything it throws at you like a champ. Then, *wham!* Trouble hits and you're left treading water, trying not to drown.

The numbness finally took effect. At last, she didn't feel pain. She inhaled a deep breath, holding it for a beat before exhaling. Like inhaling the new and exhaling the old. Letting go of all she once knew. She let go of the life she once lived, she let go of Travis and of trying to control her disease. Her focus needed to be on herself and being a good mom to her children. She couldn't waste any more energy on Bo and certainly not Becca and the child they created.

Glancing down, Jolene watched as the water moved over and in between her feet. The sparkling stone on her finger caught her attention. She slipped off her wedding ring and twirled it around her finger a few times. Then she reached her arm back and pitched it forward with force, hurling the ring out into the water.

She exhaled, experiencing the release and absolution, letting peace wash over her. And unexpectantly, a laugh bubbled up in her. Because look at her, she'd become a cliché.

CHAPTER TWENTY-ONE

When Jolene climbed inside her SUV, her feet were corroded with sand. She did her best to clean them, then decided to drive barefoot. But to where? It was too early for Kendra and Cristina to be sleeping and if she went back to the cottage now, they would try to stop her from leaving.

The sound of incoming texts chimed inside her purse. She ignored them. She didn't care who was trying to get ahold of her. It was probably Bo, trying to explain himself, Cristina or Kendra wondering where she was, or maybe Julia or Cole.

With that last thought, she had a twinge of mom guilt. She almost caved and looked at her phone. She didn't want to miss anything from her children. But she needed to be selfish now. Tonight, she'd spend the evening by herself.

Tomorrow she would be mom again.

Heading down Manson Blvd, Jolene's stomach growled. She'd been so distracted by everything with Bo and left in such a hurry she'd forgotten the picnic basket at the Dean cabin, and she was just now realizing how hungry she was. It was too early to head back to the cottage anyway so stopping somewhere to eat it would kill some time.

When she spotted the Anders Bar and Grill sign, she pulled into the parking lot without hesitation. Not wanting to take the risk of running into Bo, she parked around the back of the restaurant in case he happened to see her car if he drove by.

She fished around in the back seat for a beach towel to try to rid her feet of the sand once more. She couldn't very well walk into a restaurant with dirty feet even if it was as laidback as Anders. After finding one she was pretty sure she'd used at the lake a few weeks ago, she swung open the door of the SUV and hung her legs out. The chilly breeze of the night hit her face with a shock, sending a shiver through her body. In the amount of time it had taken her to drive from the beach to here, the temperature had dropped substantially.

After clearing most of the sand from her feet, Jolene strapped on the wedged sandals. She stood and her ankle wobbled. She grabbed a hold of the top of the door frame of the SUV. The last thing she needed was to fall and skin up her knees again. And no doubt it would be worse hitting asphalt. The sandals were terribly uncomfortable and impossible to walk in.

As she gazed longingly through the darkened parking lot at Anders entrance, she suddenly wished she hadn't parked so far away. Besides it being a long walk, it was dark—eerily dark. The sound of mosquitos buzzing filled the air and Jolene tried swatting them away. Then she heard a noise near the dumpster to her left. She whipped her head in the direction of the sound but there was nothing. She was just being silly.

She inhaled a deep breath before releasing it and shut the door of the SUV and started the long trek across the parking lot. The sound of footsteps to her right caused her feet to halt and she spun around abruptly. There was a man and woman walking hand in hand through the parking lot. She exhaled a sigh of relief while they climbed into an older Chevy Camaro and sped off.

Exhaling, she picked up her pace again but then remembered she hadn't locked her SUV. She turned to face the car, her hand fumbling around in her purse until they located her keys. Footsteps sounded again—presumably another happy couple heading to their vehicle. But when a dark shadow crossed the corner of her eye, she whipped around and inhaled a sharp breath.

In an instant, all she could see was darkness. Then, with a blunt force she was pushed backwards until she slammed into the side of her SUV. Pain shot up her spine. The dark image moved fast. It forced her to spin around so her chest and forehead were pressed up against the cool metal.

Jolene let out a shriek. A forceful hand gripped the back of her head, fingers intertwining through her hair tightly. Until he yanked and her throat constricted.

"Please," she croaked, her hands reaching up and grasping her neck as she tried to fight the force pulling her head back.

"Shh." It sounded like a man's voice.

Through wet eyes, she gazed at the dark sky speckled with bright stars. She thought about the last time she'd looked up at the stars in the night's sky. She willed herself to imagine being back there, with Bo.

"Please," she begged again.

"Now you want to be polite?" he said with a grunt, before slamming her head against her SUV and she yelped.

Pain burned in her forehead. Survival instincts kicked in and she brought up her elbow and jabbed it backward in one swift motion—hitting the man in his gut.

He let out a bark and released her. She scrambled to grip the SUV's door handle, but the man was too quick. He pushed her chest against the car again and pressed the weight of his body into her, grabbing her wrists in one of his hands and holding them above her head. He pulled out a knife, releasing the blade in a quick motion. He ran the back side of the blade down the side of her face.

Jolene released quiet sobs. "Why...why are you doing this?" she whimpered. "What do you want?"

"You," the man growled.

"Please, please stop!" she pleaded.

As she wriggled her wrists, she glanced up at them with the large hands that gripped them like a clamp. Through cloudy eyes, something familiar came into her vision. On the man's forearm was a tattoo. A black widow tattoo. Her stomach did a flip flop.

Creepy dude.

"Owen?" she whispered.

All movement on his part ceased, although he didn't ease up his tight grip around her wrists.

"Owen, please. Don't do this."

"All I wanted was a few minutes of your time, one date, but no, you couldn't even give me that," he sneered.

"Okay, fine," she relented. "Let's go inside and have that drink."

"Too late." He huffed a mirthless breath into her face. "All you lake women are the same. You're a tease."

She swallowed the hard lump in her throat. "I'm sorry."

"I don't want your apology," he sneered, his hot breath licking her neck. "I'm gonna teach you a lesson just like I did with the last one."

Her head spun. "Wh-what one?"

"Your little friend from the cottage by the lake."

Jolene's heart slammed, hard against her chest.

Owen's dark eyes danced over hers as realization set in. A

sickening smirk drew on his lips. "You didn't really think she drowned all on her own, did you?"

Her stomach lurched. "Wh-what did you do?"

"Technically, I didn't do anything. I was with her that night, watching from the shoreline," he explained, as he breathed sweltering, pungent air onto her face, and she trembled against him. "I could've saved her. She even cried out for me. It was pathetic." He chuckled to himself.

Nausea hit her in waves. She shook her head. "No. Why?"

Owen ignored her, and yanked open the back door of her car and pushed her inside, forcing her onto the seat. "Why don't we go for a little ride."

But before he could close the door, a dark figure drew both of their attention to it. And without warning, Owen was being hauled backward. The sound of a voice she recognized boomed and then her vision finally cleared.

It was Bo.

The two men were instantly in a tangled mess. She stayed in the car out of the way while Bo clutched Owen's shirt collar and threw him against the side of the car. Bo recoiled his arm and hurled an upper cut, meeting his fist with Owen's jaw with a loud *crack*. The strong punch caused Owen's head to ricochet against the car.

When Bo recoiled his arm again to go in for another punch, Owen protected his face with his arm, preparing to block the next blow. Bo's arm froze midair before he lowered it, clenching and then releasing his fist several times. He let him go, giving him a forceful shove into the car one more time before taking a step backward.

A crowd of bystanders outside of the restaurant stood watching, some with phones out.

"You're not worth it," Bo said.

"I didn't do anything. We were just talking?" Owen

screamed, adjusting his jaw in his hand. "I'll have your badge for this." He spat out a mixture of blood and saliva onto the asphalt.

"Your word against mine." Bo glared. "You picked the wrong gal to mess with this time."

"I'll get a lawyer and I'll sue," Owen threatened back.

"Good luck."

"I think you cracked my jaw." More spitting of blood.

Bo ignored him. "Be lucky I didn't shoot you," he warned, placing his hand on the holster at his side and glancing at Jolene.

In one swift motion, Owen swung out his arm, catching the blade of his knife on Bo's side. Immediately blood seeped through his shirt at his side. Sirens blazed through the night air, causing a moment of distraction. Bo reached for Owen's wrist, banging his arm against the car until he dropped the knife.

He raised his hands. "Okay, okay."

Bo kicked the knife out of Owen's reach. He took hold of his wrists in one hand and turned his body before pushing him up against the car. He pressed Owen's wrists tight behind his back—Bo's hands taking on the form of handcuffs.

He turned his attention on Jolene. "Hey, you okay?"

She nodded, unable to find her voice.

A police car zoomed into the parking lot, the red and blue flashes of light bouncing off the inky night sky like a boomerang. An ambulance followed behind, both vehicles blocking Jolene's SUV like a barricade.

Bo handed Owen over to two police officers who put him in handcuffs and threw him into the back of the police car. A young man in a uniform jumped out of the ambulance and hurried onto the scene. He approached Jolene who had finally stepped out of the car. He bent in front of her while she trembled, hugging her body.

"Ma'am, my name is Connor. I'm an EMT. Are you injured?" his voice was gentle yet commanding. He looked young, no more than his mid-twenties.

"Ma'am," he tried again. "Are you hurt?"

"I...I," she stammered, trying to find her voice and the right words. "I'm okay."

Bo rushed to her, slightly shoving the EMT aside, and brushed the pad of his thumb over the gash on her forehead. "You're bleeding."

"I'm fine." She pushed her bangs out of her face, a few strands sticky with blood.

"Sir," the EMT said sternly. "This woman may need medical assistance, I'm gonna have to ask you to step back."

"I know, I'm the one who found her. I'm the one who witnessed the attack. Connor, it's me, Officer Dean." He turned, allowing the EMT time to recognize him. "Just give me a minute with her."

The EMT nodded, holding his hands up in surrender and taking a few steps. "Sure thing. One minute."

She shook violently. Bo reached for her, but she wrenched herself away from him.

"Don't touch me!" she shouted.

"Ollie," he whispered, reaching a hand up to her head with a gentle touch, he grazed the gash on her forehead.

He squeezed her shoulders and then ran his hands down her arms, not once breaking eye contact with her. She couldn't believe he'd come to find her. She tried not to imagine what might have happened if he hadn't. Fresh tears spilled again, as the relief flooded her.

When she finally didn't recoil from his touch, he pulled her into him. She wrapped her arms around him, digging her fingers into his back.

"It was him, it was Owen," she said through sobs before

lifting her head. "He was with Becca that night. He could've saved her, but he watched her drown."

His forehead wrinkled. "Wait. What? Are you sure?"

She nodded. "He told me."

"Officer Dean," the EMT said, his patience running thin. "We really need to check you both out."

"Okay, okay." Bo pulled away and lifted her chin with his finger and thumb. "Ollie, they need to check you out. You're bleeding."

Jolene searched Bo's green eyes for the comfort she could always find in them. But they were glossy and clouded over and she didn't know if she trusted these eyes anymore. She nodded reluctantly.

The EMT reached out to her and took her under the elbow. "Ma'am, besides your forehead, are you aware of any other injuries? Does anything else hurt?"

Jolene wanted to say, *yes everywhere hurts*, but that wasn't the answer he was looking for. "Uh...the back of my head. And my ribs."

"Let's get you into the ambulance and we'll check you out further." He escorted her the few feet toward the ambulance where the back doors were open.

"Hey, uh...Connor?" a paramedic called to the EMT.

Connor glanced up, Jolene's elbow still in his hand. The paramedic stood at Bo's side, lifting his shirt. She wrenched her arm from the EMT's grasp and rushed toward Bo.

"Officer Dean, you're bleeding. When did you get injured?" the paramedic asked.

"I'm fine." Bo brushed the paramedic's hands away.

"You're not fine," the man responded. He called to the EMT. "Looks like a knife injury." Then directing his attention to Bo again. "What happened?"

"I said I'm fine, please just take care of the woman." Bo

pressed his hand to his side and more blood gushed out. "I'm, I'm...fine." Then he collapsed to his knees.

Jolene dropped next to him, wincing from the pain in her ribs. "Bo!" She grabbed his hand, squeezing it in between hers.

The paramedic kneeled in front of Bo and tore his shirt open. Blood oozed and the paramedic reached for supplies from his medic bag. He placed layers of gauze on the wound, applying pressure with his hand.

"We need to get him to the hospital. He's losing quite a bit of blood."

"Bo, oh my goodness, Bo. This is all my fault. I'm so sorry." She swiped at her wet cheeks with the back of her hand.

Dark red blood soaked through Bo's torn shirt and seeped in between the paramedic's fingers. It carried a distinct metallic and sweet copper scent. It infiltrated Jolene's nose and her stomach churned. The familiar scent was too much. She trembled and then turned and threw up.

"Okay, ma'am, we need to get him into the ambulance and to the hospital. And I don't think it would be a bad idea for you to get checked out either. You wanna ride in the back with him?" the EMT asked.

Next thing she knew, the two uniformed men had strapped Bo onto a stretcher and had wheeled him into the ambulance. Strips of gauze and tape wrapped his wound to hold pressure. She took her place next to him and held his hand.

"I'm right here, Bo," Jolene whispered.

He reached a hand to the bandage on her forehead, wincing. "You okay?" he said on an exhaled breath.

"I'm fine. Let's just worry about you for once, okay?"

Bo smiled at her and gave her hand a squeeze before his eyes fluttered shut.

CHAPTER TWENTY-TWO

After the ambulance reached the hospital, the EMT and paramedic wheeled Bo into the ER on the stretcher. Jolene was escorted into an examining room by a nurse and given a pink gown to change into. Painted white walls with beige curtains separated small rooms. The ceilings were covered in white panels and the floor was a polished beige sheet of vinyl. The ugly strip of brown rubber trim ran all the way around the length and width of the room. It carried the typical hospital smell—bleach trying to cover up the scent of illness and death.

Jolene waited alone in the room, perched on the edge of the examining table. The sheet of paper crinkled underneath her bottom every time she tried to re-situate on the table. It hurt to sit. Her ribs ached and she found it difficult to breathe. She cinched the pale pink hospital gown around her tighter. But she didn't care about her injuries. She needed to know if Bo was okay.

A male ER nurse, clipboard in hand, came in and read over her chart. He had dark eyes and hair, and a friendly smile.

"Hi, my name is Billy and I'm one of the ER nurses on duty tonight."

She tried giving him a smile.

He performed all of the necessary vitals, pulse, temperature, breathing, pupils and blood pressure. While he cleaned the gash on her forehead, he asked, "Mrs. McCabe, can you describe your pain to me?" He applied a bandage to her forehead. "Is it sharp, dull, constant or does it come and go?"

"I don't know." She bit her lip. "I guess it's constant and throbbing. Like how a headache feels."

"Where exactly does it hurt?" He bent, giving her a better look at him. At such close proximity now, she could see his eyes were more hazel than brown. His eyes suited him, matching his gentle voice.

"Um...well my head." *Duh, that was obvious.* She supposed she didn't have to tell him that.

He smiled. "Right, and anywhere else?"

"My back," Jolene hesitated. She looked up at him through wet eyelashes. "And my chest, my ribs I suppose."

"On a scale of one to ten, how much does it hurt?"

"I don't know, maybe a four or five." She balled the thin gown in her fists.

The nurse quirked an eyebrow at her, one corner of his mouth curving up. "You know, you don't need to be tough right now. That's what I'm here for. I want to help you, but I can't do that if you're not being honest with me." His eyes looked at her with intensity.

"Fine," she muttered. "Probably more like a seven or eight."

"Now we're getting somewhere." He smiled at her. "Let's get you a chest x-ray. Your breathing is a bit thready so we'll check for broken ribs or collapsed lungs." He jotted something onto the paper attached to the clipboard. "Is there anything I should know about your medical history? Such as, any prescriptions you're taking, if you have any medical conditions, any past surgeries."

"Well, where should I start? It's quite a long list, we might be here all night," Jolene chuckled mirthlessly, then winced from the pain at her side. "I recently started taking Avonex. Then I take Zanaflex for muscle stiffness and Symmetrel for fatigue. Of course, if I can't sleep, I take Ambien and then I take a probiotic and about a million vitamins."

He wrote as she spoke, then glanced up. "MS?"

She nodded. "Correct."

"Okay, let's get you that x-ray. If your lungs are clear, you'll be free to go with instructions to follow up with your primary care doctor." He held onto her elbow, assisting her to her feet.

A sharp pain like an electric shock poked into her side and she winced, bringing her arms in across her chest.

"Even if your x-ray checks out, you're going to need to take it easy for a few days. My guess is you've got a couple bruised and fractured ribs. Icing it should help. But don't be surprised if your ribs are sore for several weeks. Maybe even months." He leaned back on the counter crossing his ankles and folding his arms. "Listen, I'm serious. Take it easy, you hear me?" He looked pointedly at her.

She nodded. "I hear you."

"Good. Now, let's go get that x-ray."

After her x-ray, she dressed back into her clothing and was then directed into a room with a curtain drawn closed. She carefully pulled it back and found Bo, sitting up on an examining table, his legs dangling off the side. He had fresh bandages covering his wound and more dressing wrapped around his entire middle.

He lifted his head, smiling when he met her gaze. She folded her lips in between her teeth and entered the room cautiously, taking a seat next to him on the table.

"Ollie," he breathed out. "I'm so glad you're okay. I was so worried." He ran his thumb over the bandage on her forehead before grazing his fingers down to her cheek, and finally cupping her face.

Jolene put her hand over his and held it there for a moment before bringing it down into her lap. She could still see the worry in his eyes.

"You were worried about me? I was worried about *you*. There was so much blood and I...I didn't know how bad it was."

"That was nothing. A couple stitches and I'm as good as new. Been through worse."

"Really? Worse than that?" She bit the inside of her cheek.

"Jo, I'm a cop. Or did you forget?"

She shook her head. She hadn't forgotten. But she supposed she hadn't thought about how dangerous his job was. "Kendra and Cristina are on their way to pick me up. Do you need a ride?"

Bo cleared his throat. "Lark is coming to get me. Thanks though." He glanced down at his feet like they were suddenly the most interesting thing to look at in the room.

And there it was. Like a blow to her chest—the reminder of how this whirlwind of a night began. He had a daughter—with Becca. She slowly released Bo's hand and returned her own to her lap.

"Look, Jo—"

"How did you know how to find me?" Jolene interrupted.

"I didn't. I drove to the cottage and when you weren't there, Kendra said maybe you'd be Ander's. But when I drove by there, I didn't see you there either. I was wracking my brain trying to think where you might have gone. I checked the lake too. Then I backtracked all the same places."

She twisted her fingers in her lap, studying the crisscrossed scars. "But I told you to leave me alone," her voice came out sounding strained.

"How could I leave you alone? Ollie, I can't even begin to imagine..." Bo's voice trailed, his eyes glistening.

She couldn't imagine what might have happened if he hadn't come. She was grateful to him, but it didn't change anything between them. Pushing herself off the examining table, pain shot through her middle and she felt instantly nauseous.

She inhaled a deep breath. "I should go wait out front. Thank you, Bo, for being there tonight."

He reached out and grabbed a hold of one of her hands. "If you really want to thank me, let me help you."

"That doesn't make much sense. You want me to thank you for already helping me, by letting you help me more?"

Bo let out a nervous chuckle. "I suppose I do."

She tugged her hand free from his grip. "I don't need your help, Bo. I have been taking care of myself for over a year now. And believe it or not, I've learned that I don't need a man to take care of me."

"I never said you needed a man to take care of you. But I'd like to, if you will just let me."

He looked sincere. "But you don't want to."

"You're wrong, I do."

"No, you don't. Listen to me," Jolene pleaded, her eyes filling with tears. "Because I don't think you understand. Mornings like the other day, when I couldn't even get out of bed, and nights like the other night when I stumbled and hit my leg on the barstool and days like the other day when I tripped and hurt my knees while running, those days are going to happen all the time. Not just occasionally. All the time, for the rest of my life. Some days I can't remember things and some nights I'm restless and can't sleep. I get headaches that put me out of commission for countless hours and blurry vision that keeps me from being able to brew beer. And this is just the beginning. I'm only going to get worse."

"I know that, I know all of those things," Bo said.

"But I'm okay with all of that. I have to be. Because this is my life—my body. But you get a choice. Don't you get that?"

"Ollie, I get it. I do. And I am choosing you."

Hot tears spilled, rolling down her cheeks. Bo wiped them away as she tried to recover from the zing of lightning that ran through her at the sound of her nickname from his lips.

"You don't always have to be strong. You need to let someone else do that for you once in a while. And I want to be that someone." He had both hands on her arms, caressing them as he spoke, more gently now. "You're always acting like you're not worth anyone's time or efforts, or like you don't deserve to be happy. You are worthy of happiness, don't you get that?"

Jolene shook her head, unable to believe his words. Because she couldn't. He was right once again, she didn't think she deserved happiness or love or anything else positive this world could possibly offer her. Because look where it had gotten her.

And suddenly his words were too much, the air in the room too stuffy and her mind too cloudy. "It's just too much, this is all too much. Look, I appreciate what you did for me tonight, I really do. You have no idea. But...whatever we thought might happen between us, it's just not going to happen." She pulled away from him.

"Don't say that. You're not thinking straight. Get some rest and we'll talk tomorrow."

"I have to go," she managed to choke out the words, taking a few steps backward.

"You're not just pushing me away because of your illness. This is because of Lark, isn't it?" Bo asked with a bitter tone.

"I don't even know her, Bo. You made sure of that, didn't you?" her words cut through the air.

"I wanted to explain but you didn't even give me a chance."

"There is nothing to explain, not anymore." Jolene shrugged. "We're friends, friends don't have to tell each other everything." She sniffed. "Look, I gotta go. Just promise me Owen will not go unpunished for Becca."

"You have my word."

She nodded and then took a few more steps backward before turning around.

"I didn't love her you know," Bo called.

She froze without turning back around, his words feeling like an arrow shot straight through her heart. "You had a baby with her."

"But I never loved her." Bo got up off the table, meeting her by her side. "Never."

Jolene dropped her head and held up a hand. "Don't. Not tonight. I can't do this tonight."

"Then when?"

"I don't know," she said through an exhaled sigh. "I don't know if I'll ever be ready to have this conversation."

Bo stepped toward her, reaching for her, with his eyes, his words, his hands. "Ollie, please."

She searched for the comfort in his green eyes, but she couldn't find it there. Sadness washed over her at the realization. She placed her palm onto his firm chest and forced a weak smile, opening her mouth to speak.

"Dad?" a frantic voice called.

They both turned. Lark came rushing into the room, her eyes searching and full of terror. She was taken aback when she saw Jolene, there with her dad.

Jolene took a few steps away from him. Lark was momentarily frozen as she stared at her. Maybe she was unsure how to act around this woman she'd heard stories about all her life and had finally now met.

"Hey, sweetie," Bo greeted his daughter.

Released from her trance, Lark rushed into her dad's open arm, being careful not to squeeze him. "Dad, oh dad, I was so scared."

"I'm fine, I'm fine. You know me, I'm like a cat, nine lives and all." Bo smirked.

Lark rolled her eyes. "Yeah well, I think you're about out of lives."

Jolene glanced back and forth between Bo and Lark, taking in the view of the closeness of their relationship. Lark made eye contact with Jolene, and she attempted to smile but it was awkward, and she felt terribly out of place.

Finding it difficult to catch her breath, she needed to get out of there. She turned abruptly to leave, and when she did, she almost ran directly into Kendra.

"Oh my goodness, Jolene! You scared us half to death," Kendra said.

Behind her, followed Cristina who appeared distraught.

"What the hell happened?" Cristina said, then took in the sight of Jolene with Bo and Lark behind her. "Oh, damn," panic sounded in her voice. Her gaze searched back and forth between them all before resting on Jolene.

"Oh damn is right," Jolene muttered.

Then she stomped past both Kendra and Cristina, flinging back the curtain and slamming her palms against the door and pushing it open. The sounds of her friends' voices calling behind her drifted away the further she went. When the automatic glass doors sensed her, they slid open before she stepped out.

"Jo, please stop?" Kendra called.

Jolene spun around to find both Kendra and Cristina. Just

the sight of them caused her heart to split. They both knew this huge secret and had kept it from her—for years.

"How could you guys not tell me?" Her skin prickled with anger.

"I'm sorry, Jo. I wanted to, I really did," Kendra said, sliding a look in Cristina's direction.

"I told her not to," Cristina admitted.

Jolene looked at her, her eyes burning with intensity. "Why? Why would you do that?"

"Because, it wasn't our place."

"It wasn't your place?"

"This was Bo's secret to tell, not ours," Cristina said.

"Oh yeah? And how long have you known?" Jolene shoved her fists onto her hips.

Cristina hesitated, glancing down at her shuffling feet.

She narrowed her eyes. "How long?"

"Forever okay? The whole time." Cristina lifted her hands from her sides. "Is that what you want to hear? Because it's the truth. And I knew you wouldn't be able to handle it."

Tears ran down Jolene's face and she crossed her arms, hugging her body. The exhaustion of the day's events came bearing down on her. Defeat sat like a weight on her shoulders, threatening to crush her.

And Cristina was right, she couldn't handle it.

CHAPTER TWENTY-THREE

L uckily the gash on Jolene's forehead where it had met the side of her SUV didn't look so bad the next day. In the shower that morning, she'd taken the bandage off and cleaned the cut. Once it was dry again, she put a small Band-Aid over it.

Staring at her reflection in the bathroom mirror made her even more sad and anxious. Ugh, she looked like a mess and today would be a big day—a long and stressful day. As if spreading Becca's ashes wasn't going to be hard enough, now she had this tension between Kendra and Cristina and herself. All because they'd kept the secret about Lark from her.

She didn't know any more than that because she had vetoed the conversation the night before—demanded the other women drop it. They'd apologized profusely, but she couldn't deal with it. Especially not after the night she'd had followed by the traumatic morning. She'd spent a few hours at the police station answering questions and leaving a statement. Jolene wouldn't let Owen off the hook for what he'd done to Becca.

And now, she had an emotional and hard day ahead of her.

A day she'd planned on skipping out on. At least until the incident in the Ander's Bar and Grill parking lot.

After she'd left the station that morning, Bo had sent her a text asking if she was okay. Then he asked if they could talk, in person. As much as she didn't want to, for the obvious reasons, she had agreed. She needed to let him have this final conversation, to say his piece, to have closure. And if she was being honest, she needed it as well.

JOLENE FIDGETED with the hem of her navy-blue dress while she walked toward Bo who stood at the end of the dock. He turned to look at her as she approached, then returned his gaze toward the lake after she reached his side. The picnic basket she'd forgotten the day before in her haste, sat on the dock in between them.

The late morning sun glittered across the surface of the lake, making it feel like a perfect day to be spent out on the water. But the raw reality hit her—it would not be a perfect day. This would be the hardest day since arriving in Tahoe City. Today, her, Kendra and Cristina would take the canoe out into the middle of the lake and say goodbye to Becca. An ache formed and sat in the pit of her stomach like indigestion. She wanted to force it out, to throw up the ache.

An image of Becca came to her mind. Her chocolate brown hair pulled into a high ponytail and standing on the dock in her red bikini. Her toes curled around the edge of the wood, hands overlapping each other and held high above her head. Bending her knees and springing off the dock, streamlining gracefully into the lake water. Becca had been a skilled diver and swimmer.

A wave of nausea hit her at the memory of last night and Owen's confession.

I could've saved her.

"Jo," Bo called, interrupting her thoughts.

The sound of his voice startled her. As if she'd forgotten he was even there. Irritation mixed in with the ache in her stomach. She was annoyed he stole the image away from her mind and then angry that every image, every memory of Becca would be tainted. It was Bo's fault for this. How was she supposed to honor her friend and spread her ashes in the lake when she was angry with her?

"How are you feeling today?"

"You already asked me that. By text, remember?" She crossed her arms.

He glanced down at his shuffling feet. Then he ran a hand down his unshaven face.

"What about you? How are you feeling?" she asked.

"I've been better."

"I bet."

"But I'll manage."

Jolene nodded. She knew him well enough to know he was in pain. He hadn't even taken the time to shave today. This was the first time all week she'd seen him unkempt. She couldn't help but find him completely irresistible like this, a few day-old beard and messy hair, vulnerable.

"Look, I know you're busy today," Bo began. "But I figured this may be my last chance."

"Bo, please." She pressed her fingers to her eyes.

"I figure you owe it to me to at least listen."

"I owe it to you?" she snapped.

"Yeah. You said it yourself, we're friends, right? Friends listen to each other."

"Fine." Jolene kept her vision forward, focusing on the moving water.

"I never meant to hurt you," Bo began again. "And neither did Becca."

With the mention of Becca's name, her eyes glossed over, threatening tears. She silently cursed herself, because she wasn't going to shed any more tears over this.

"It's not like we planned it. I mean, you know. We didn't plan Lark. Don't get me wrong, I love her. She's the best thing to ever happened to me. She made me grow up. She made me a better man." Bo turned his body toward her. But she stood with her arms crossed, facing the lake.

"You don't owe me an explanation for loving your daughter, Bo," she muttered.

"Let me finish. I don't think you even realize how hard it was for me when you and Travis got engaged."

Jolene turned and looked at him, her brows furrowing in confusion.

"I was a mess. You remember that I wasn't much for drinking then. Well, I started drinking, all the time. I guess I was trying to drink away the disappointment of knowing that the two of us weren't going to end up together," Bo paused, dropping his head and sighing. "The night of your wedding a bunch of us went out. Everyone from your wedding party. We went to some dive bar in South Lake Tahoe."

She nodded, remembering hearing about her wedding party going out together while her and Travis headed to the airport in Reno for their honeymoon in Hawaii. Cristina and Kendra went and got wasted and sang karaoke.

"I drank a lot that night. Kendra and Cristina can vouch for that, I'm sure. Although they were pretty drunk as well. Anyway, you remember I'm not much of a dancer either. Well, Becca was there—"

"Wait, what?" Jolene spoke, her voice coming out hoarse. "Becca was there? But why? She wasn't in our wedding party. I didn't even invite her to the wedding."

"I know. I think someone let her know we were all there. Or she just showed up. I don't really remember." Bo raked a hand through his hair and let out another sigh. "We were both really drunk, and well, it just sort of happened."

"It just sort of happened?" Jolene repeated Bo's words, needing to hear them from her own lips.

"Lark was born the following April. And Becca and I never slept together again. It wasn't even an option, you know, us being a couple. She knew I was in love with someone else. And she was never into me. Never. And once Lark came, she put all her love and energy into her. When I encouraged her to date, she said she didn't have enough love or time to give after giving it all to Lark." He shuffled his feet. "But honestly, all she ever wanted was for you to be proud of her. She wanted you to see how good of a mom she was."

Unable to restrain the tears any longer, her eyes filled and they spilled, rolling down her made-up cheeks. All this information clouded her brain. It was too much to process. As much as she didn't want to hear about Bo and Becca being together, she never knew about Becca as a mother. She'd missed out on so many years of her life. That, stolen away from her too. Cristina had said the same thing about Becca, she had been a great mom to Lark. Jolene wished she could've seen it herself.

"As much as I wish I didn't have to hurt you by this, I can't wish that it didn't happen. Because like I said, having Lark was the best thing to happen to me." He shoved his hands into the pockets of his shorts. "I stopped drinking. Well, besides the occasional social beer here and there, and I went to police academy. She made me grow up. And I never could've imagined you would enter my life again."

"I appreciate you telling me, I really do. But it doesn't change anything between us." Her stomach pinched and she swallowed past the lump in her throat. "I'm sorry."

"I'm sorry too. I'm sorry I didn't tell you sooner." He took her hands into his.

"I love you, Bo. I'll always love you." She flicked her gaze up to his, searching his eyes. "So much has happened in your life and in my life the last twenty years. I think we should focus on the good memories and the close friendship we had. We can't go back. We can't undo things, and neither of us want to. You have Lark, I have Julia and Cole. And I think...I think it's best for everyone if we part ways now."

Bo shook his head. "I can't. I told you that I won't let you go again."

"Stop, please." Jolene tried to tug her hands away, but he gripped them tighter.

"There's a reason the two of us have been brought back together. We've been given a second chance. How can you not see that?"

"You lied to me," her voice broke.

"I didn't lie, I omitted information."

"Important information," she spit out. "You had to have known I'd be upset, you having a child with Becca. You know all I've been through with her."

"Why do you think I didn't jump at the opportunity to tell you right away?"

"Right away? We spent nearly every day together the past week. You made me believe it was possible we might actually have a future together. And yet, you didn't trust me enough to tell me about the most important thing, the most important person in your life?" At last she successfully pulled her hands away and backed up.

"Please don't leave again with things like this," Bo pleaded, hurt shining in his eyes.

"You're the one who's making this harder."

"Because I don't agree. The universe or God or something larger than us has given us a second chance."

Tears continued to spill out of her eyes, and she swiped them away with her fingers. Her chest felt constricted from the crying, making her ribs ache even more. She shook her head, trying to shake away Bo, this conversation, the pain—all of it too much.

"So what if you've been through a lot or I've been through a lot. So what if we've taken a few different turns along the way. We've been brought back together now."

"Just stop," Jolene said, shaking off his touch. She pressed her fingers to her eyes again. Then wiped her wet cheeks. "I'm done. I'm done having this conversation. If you can't accept just being friends," she hesitated. "Then, I suppose this is it for us. This is where we say goodbye."

"Ollie," Bo choked out the word and his eyes watered. "Don't do this, please. Don't push me away."

Jolene picked up the picnic basket from the dock and stepped further away from him. "Goodbye, Bo. And good luck...with everything." She took one last look at him before turning around and walking toward the cottage.

"I won't say goodbye."

Jolene did not stop or turn back around at the sound of Bo's words.

CHAPTER TWENTY-FOUR

A tall cylinder tube featuring a painted lake scene with tan colored sand and blue water, confronted Jolene. It rested on the kitchen island in the cottage. The three women sat on the stools surrounding the island, staring at it. Mr. Gibbs delivered the tube holding Becca's ashes to the cottage earlier in the afternoon.

The choice of this style of cremation urn was fitting. It suited Becca and her love of the lake, the cottage, and swimming. The tube was made of biodegradable materials which would be perfect for spreading Becca's ashes in the lake.

Knots formed in Jolene's stomach at the mere thought of Becca's remains being inside the cylinder tube. How had Mr. Gibbs been able to hand it over to them so easily? Why hadn't he wanted to spread Becca's ashes? Or Ms. Gibbs? Or, even Lark? What did Lark think about not being a part of this tribute to her mother? Thinking of Lark caused her thoughts to move to Bo and settle there.

"I think the red peonies are a beautiful touch," Cristina

said, picking up a red blossomed flower and bringing it to her nose.

Jolene cleared her throat. "I agree."

"Thanks, girls." Kendra picked up a flower and a pair of scissors, snipping off the stem. "They were Becca's favorite."

Jolene took the flower blossom from Kendra and placed it on a damp towel that covered the countertop. "She sure had a thing for red, didn't she?"

Cristina exhaled a laugh. "A thing? That's an understatement. She was obsessed."

"Almost everything she wore was red," Kendra pointed out.

Studying the spread of red flowers strewn out on the countertop, Jolene's mind flashed through images of Becca. Her favorite red bikini. Her red prom dress. Then her fuzzy red sweater she loved to bring out every winter.

"Remember how much her mom hated it too?" Cristina asked. "Becca was such a bad ass."

"Ms. Gibbs hated everything Becca did." Jolene placed two more flowers onto the damp towel.

"But she sure looked beautiful in red, didn't she?" Kendra asked, her voice quiet as she snipped the stem off another flower.

"She did," Jolene agreed, taking the cut flower from Kendra.

Kendra had bought two dozen red peonies to place in the lake when they spread Becca's ashes. This way the women could keep track of the ashes and watch them drift in the water. They would make a nice tribute to the ceremony.

One of the hardest things after last night had been telling the girls about Owen's confession. Cristina wanted to kill him herself. Kendra got on the phone with her lawyer. But Jolene had learned that morning at the police station that Owen was already being charged with attempted assault and aggravated battery assault against a police officer.

"I still can't believe that slimeball," Cristina huffed. "Leaving Becca out there, alone. And then to attack you. They better keep him locked up for life."

"Well, if I have any say in the matter, he will be," Kendra said.

"I just don't want to even think about him anymore." Jolene shuddered.

"Good. He doesn't deserve our time. So, are we gonna start drinking before or after this thing?" Cristina asked, brows raised and her face serious.

Kendra placed the cut flowers into the picnic basket Bo had returned. "Probably not the best idea to drink before heading out on the water."

"As tempting as it sounds to have some liquid courage before doing this, I have to agree with Kendra," Jolene said, her mind already thinking about Becca.

"Fine." Cristina sighed dramatically. "Then let's get the show on the road, shall we?"

"I've got the flowers ready." Kendra slipped the handles of the basket over her arm.

"I suppose I'll grab the, uh, I don't really know what to call it. The ashes? Becca? Oh hell, this sucks." Cristina hesitated then picked up the cylinder tube.

The three women headed out the back door of the cottage, down the steps and onto the rocky sand. They made their way over to the wooden stand that housed two kayaks and one canoe. Cristina and Kendra each took one end of the canoe and lifted it off the stand.

"Dang this thing is heavy." Cristina set the canoe down, it made a thud as it hit the sand.

"I'm sorry I'm not much help," Jolene apologized.

"It's fine, don't worry about it. Cristina's just being a wimp. It's not that heavy, right, Cris?" Kendra looked at her pointedly.

Cristina rolled her eyes. "Right, whatever you say. Let's just get this thing in the water."

"I'll go to the shed and get the oars," She offered.

"Are you sure? You shouldn't be lifting or carrying anything," Kendra said.

"It's fine." Jolene waved before making her way to the shed.

By the time she returned with the oars, Cristina and Kendra already had the canoe in the water. Kendra stepped in first, taking a seat on the small wooden bench in the back. Cristina got in and reached out for Jolene's elbow and hand to assist her into the canoe. She hesitated at first, not wanting help. Because, yeah, she was stubborn and just because they were doing this didn't mean everything between them was fine. Stepping into the canoe was a strain and her ribs felt as if they were being ripped away from her rib cage. The pain made her queasy and she was thankful that she didn't drink any alcohol before getting in the canoe.

Once Jolene was sitting on the small bench in the middle, Cristina took her place at the front and her and Kendra began to paddle. They went at a slow pace, rotating the oars from side to side of the canoe. They were in search of the perfect spot on the lake to say goodbye to their friend.

After passing a few kayaks and paddle boards, Cristina lifted the oar out of the water, laying it across her lap. Kendra did as well. Jolene looked around before peering over the side of the canoe. The water was peaceful and clear, like glass. She could see granite rocks resting at the bottom. The landscape ahead featured soaring green sugar pines and canyons.

"This is perfect," Jolene whispered, her chest expanding with emotion.

Cristina smiled over her shoulder at the other two women. "I thought so too. Although, I'm not sure I'm ready to do this."

"Me neither," Kendra admitted.

"I'm thinking I could've really used that drink." Cristina turned around on the bench, facing them.

"Is anyone else wishing that Mr. or Ms. Gibbs would've done this instead of us?" Jolene asked.

"Me," Cristina mumbled.

"Me too. But Becca wanted us," Kendra said.

"But why?" the question slipped from Jolene's mouth without intention. But now that it was out, she realized she meant it. "I'm serious. If I had just five minutes with her, I would ask her, why?"

"Really? If you had five minutes with her, that's what you would ask her?" Cristina snorted a laugh. "How about, how could you sleep with the guy I crushed on for like, six years? How could you have a baby with him and then never tell me?"

"Cristina," Kendra hissed.

"What?" Cristina shrugged.

"No, she's right. I would. I would totally ask her how she could possibly sleep with my best friend. The person who knew me best. The one guy I thought was right for me but the timing was never right. And then she had his baby. How could she not tell me? And how could she move on so quickly after losing Jacob?" Heat flashed across her cheeks and her throat burned.

"Okay, c'mon, girls," Kendra interrupted, saying it like a warning.

"What? What's the problem? Can't handle being real? C'mon, your turn. What would you ask Becca if you had five minutes with her?" Cristina asked.

"I'm not doing this. *We're* not doing this," Kendra raised her voice.

"Why not? What are you afraid of?"

"This is not why we're here. This is completely disrespectful. You're ruining the ceremony. You're ruining everything," Kendra bit out. "I knew this would happen."

"And there it is." Cristina stiffened. "It's not Becca you need five minutes to speak your mind with. It's me."

The air in the boat suddenly felt stuffy and humid and Jolene glanced back and forth between her friends. "Okay, okay, Kendra is right. This is about Becca. Let's all just remember why we're here."

"No, I wanna know. Tell me, Kendra," Cristina demanded.

Kendra pursed her lips.

"C'mon, don't hold anything back. I think we need to get it all out in the open before we can even think about paying tribute to Becca." Cristina waved her arms around causing the canoe to rock from side to side in the water and Jolene's queasiness worsened.

"Fine. Just remember, you asked for this?" Kendra narrowed her eyes into slits. "You knew I had a thing for Jamie Driscoll, and you went out with him anyway," she spat.

"Ha," Cristina huffed. "Are you freaking kidding me? That's why you're mad? It's been like twenty years, get over it already."

"Hey, you asked." Kendra pointed a finger at her. "And you know what? It wasn't the fact that you went out with Jamie or slept with him for that matter. It was the fact you never even apologized for it."

"Okay, okay, I'm sorry," Cristina said with an exasperated tone. "There, you happy now?"

"No, I'm not happy. You should've apologized twenty years ago. And actually meant it."

Cristina rolled her eyes. Jolene's stomach twisted from

anxiety because once again, she was caught in the middle of their arguing—literally.

"You're not so perfect, Kendra, you know that?" Cristina said, an accusing look in her eyes. "You are so judgmental."

"What are you talking about?"

"You know exactly what I'm talking about." Cristina narrowed her eyes. "Remember when I told you I was leaving Mason?"

Kendra pressed her lips together.

Jolene glanced over her shoulder at Kendra and then back at Cristina. "Wait, what are you talking about? I've never heard this story."

"That's because you and I weren't really speaking then," Cristina explained before continuing. "When I told Kendra I was leaving Mason, she gave me so much crap. Telling me how I needed to sacrifice my children's happiness over mine and to suck it up."

"I don't think I said it like that. Besides, you didn't tell me he was abusing you."

Cristina deadpanned. "Should that even matter?"

"No, you're right. I'm sorry." Kendra glanced away.

"When we were kids and Becca's parents were always fighting, weren't you the one who said cheating was grounds for divorce? Well, I didn't guilt you into staying with Devin—to put your children's happiness over your own. I told you to kick that prick's butt to the curb."

"You're right—okay?" Kendra's face went stony. "You're right about it all. I'm not perfect. I never said I was perfect. My marriage is falling apart, I'm a mediocre mother, and I think it's obvious after this week, that I'm a terrible friend. I put you down, Cristina. I'm sorry."

"You did, you ho." She snorted a laugh. "But the thing is, we all feel inadequate at times. As moms, as wives, as friends.

But that's why we have each other. So we can be real and honest. And forgive each other."

The two women shared a smile across the canoe.

"And Jo," Kendra paused, shaking her head. "I'm sorry, I should've told you about Lark."

Jolene blinked. This was the last thing she expected, having Kendra list out all her flaws, and apologize.

"I let you get all wrapped up in your feelings with Bo and then it blew up in your face. I'm so sorry that I contributed to you getting hurt. I just thought, well that it wasn't my place. I really thought Bo would've told you, first thing. I mean, he adores Lark."

"You're right, it wasn't your secret to tell. It was Bo's."

"But you need to know, he never loved Becca," Cristina interrupted. "He's only ever loved one woman, and that woman is you. Hell, you know I would've jumped on that when I was single, but he's only had eyes for you." Cristina tried to laugh.

"I appreciate you telling me." Jolene glanced at each of them. "Both of you."

"And Kendra," Cristina began, "you're right. I—"

Kendra held up her hand, interrupting Cristina. "Enough. You apologized, and I should've apologized too. I'm sorry for guilt tripping you, of always making the wrong choices. You've been through a lot, and I know the tough decisions you've had to make are for your kids. And I respect you for that."

"Uh...before you start respecting me, you ought to know. I'm not a great mom, hell I'm probably not even a very good one." Cristina exhaled a deep sigh before continuing. "That being said, you know yesterday when I had that family emergency? My daughter, Montana, is currently at an inpatient eating disorder facility. Yesterday she had a bad day. I had to give consent for a feeding tube."

Jolene gasped. "Oh, Cris. I'm so sorry."

"We're just taking it a day at a time. And we're hopeful she'll get through this and still have a bright future ahead of her. But it won't be easy. Her doctor told us to expect more setbacks like yesterday. It's still early." Cristina looked at Kendra. "See, I told you I'm not a great mom."

"C'mon, Cristina, that is something completely out of your control. You can't accept responsibility for that. You're being way too hard on yourself. I've been way too hard on you." Kendra combed her straight bangs with her fingers. "And before you go giving me the mom of the year award, you should know, Quinn got kicked off the basketball team for smoking weed."

Cristina's eyes widened. "No way, seriously?"

"Seriously." Kendra sighed. "I had to bribe the principal with a visit to the magazine."

"So, he's back on the team?"

"Yes, he's back on the team."

Cristina busted up laughing.

"Well, ladies, I had to bribe my son with the newest iPhone just to get him to *join* the basketball team," Jolene exhaled a mirthless laugh.

"I guess it's safe to say, that none of us are getting the mom of the year award."

"No we are not." Kendra's shoulders relaxed and she smiled. "I really am sorry though, Cristina."

"And I'm sorry about Jamie Driscoll. For real this time, that was a shady thing for a friend to do. I don't know what I was thinking."

"You were young, he was hot, you weren't thinking. I'm just being dumb. And you're right, it was such a long time ago."

"Okay, we're good now, right?" Cristina asked. "This all got way too real and serious."

"Unfortunately, it's not over yet." Jolene picked up the urn and held it out to Cristina.

"Damn," Cristina muttered, taking the urn.

"I'm really glad we got all that taken care of first. You know, before spreading Becca's ashes," Kendra said.

"Me too." Cristina held the urn, turning it in her hands and admiring the lake scene painted on it. "How about I start then Kendra, then Jo. And Jo can toss the urn in at the end."

Jolene nodded. "Sounds good." She'd agree to just about anything to get this thing over with. Shifting on the small hard bench of the canoe, she winced from the pain. Her stomach twisted like a tornado burrowing its way into the ground. She wished she was anywhere but here. What would she say to pay tribute to Becca? How would she say goodbye to someone when so many loose ends still existed?

Opening the urn, Cristina peered inside. She exhaled a deep sigh before slipping her hand inside. She grimaced and released a muffled noise under her breath.

"What's wrong?" Jolene asked.

"This is worse than I thought. I think I might hurl." Cristina closed her eyes and took a deep breath before opening them again. "Okay, I'm fine." She pulled her hand out of the urn and dust from the ashes slipped through her fingers and flittered down into the boat. Shaking her head a few times, her eyes glistened.

After clearing her throat, she began. "Becca, you were the fiercest chick I ever met. Life threw you some curve balls and you just kept swinging, you never let it get you down. You were a freaking amazing mom and I will strive to be as good at it as you were for the rest of my life. May you rest now knowing that even after you left, you still brought us three together. You were and always will be the glue that holds this dysfunctional group together." Cristina stretched her hand over the edge of the boat and opened her fist, releasing the ash above the surface of the water.

The three women watched as the ash danced in the wind before settling on the water. Then Jolene handed Cristina half a dozen peonies. Cristina cast them, one by one into the lake amongst the ash floating near the canoe.

"That was beautiful," Kendra whispered, smiling at Cristina and wiping at her wet cheeks.

Cristina passed the urn to Jolene who then passed it to Kendra. She reached inside and shrieked, pulling it back out in one quick motion.

"What's wrong?" Jolene asked.

"I...I...can't do this," Kendra stammered. "I didn't know...I didn't know it would feel like this."

"Feel like what?" she asked again, her heart beginning to beat wildly and out of control.

"You can do it, Kendra, it's okay," Cristina coaxed.

"No, no I can't. It's awful. I thought it would be soft. But it's coarse. I just...can't." Kendra shoved the urn in Jolene's direction.

"It's okay, but at least still say something. And then toss the flowers in," she suggested.

The tears were coming in a constant flow from Kendra's eyes making Jolene's eyes thick with grief. It was rare to witness Kendra breaking down this way.

Kendra nodded, picking up two red peonies. "Becca, there's so much I wish I could've said to you." She sniffed. "But now, there's no time for that. And probably none of it matters anyway. I have always loved you and respected you for your courage and bravery. I'm thankful for our friendship and I will always hold you in my heart. Wherever you are now my friend, may we see each other again someday." She tossed the two peonies into the lake and then reached into the basket, pulling out a few more flowers and tossing them out onto the water. The red peonies gathered, floating next to the canoe.

Jolene cleared her throat. "Okay, I suppose it's my turn." She clutched the urn in her hands, studying the blue and brown paint strokes. "I've been stressing over what I was going to say and now that the time is finally here, I'm still stressing." She exhaled a laugh in between her tears. "In all honesty, Becca, you and I had the tightest bond of anyone in the history of time. We let things get in the way of that bond at times. Even now, after you're gone, things are still trying to get in the way. But I will always love you. And most importantly, I need to say this out loud, I forgive you, Becca. And I hope you forgive me for letting a wedge get in between us and losing all those years. So, my friend, may you carry on in peace knowing you have been forgiven."

When she reached her hand inside the urn to grab a handful of ashes, her stomach flip flopped. Kendra was right— the ash didn't feel fine and soft as she suspected. Some was coarse and there were bigger rough pieces mixed in. Jolene's stomach burned and threatened to force bile up her throat. She squeezed her eyes tight.

Breathe, just breathe.

Opening her eyes, she extended her fist over the lake and spread her fingers apart, releasing the ash. She watched as the cinders sauntered down and skimmed the surface of the water. Then she dropped six red peonies into the water that surrounded the ash as if they were protecting the embers.

Protecting Becca.

Securing the lid back on the cremation urn, Jolene tossed it over the side of the canoe. It landed behind the trail of peonies floating on the lake's surface. Then the three women cast the remaining peonies into the water, surrounding the urn.

Jolene extended both arms, reaching for Kendra and Cristina's hands. They accepted and before the urn sank, she whispered, "Never give up the fight."

"Here, here," Kendra and Cristina spoke softly in unison.

The three of them watched the ceremony of the ash and flowers in silence, hand in hand. The peonies enclosed the ash, funneling the relics through the water, causing Becca's remains to intertwine with the lake. A promise she would be a part of it forever.

BY SIX O'CLOCK, the women had already engorged themselves on pizza and wine. And then they began cracking open the beer from High Desert Brewery that Joy had sent along with Jolene. Saying goodbye to Becca and spreading her ashes over the waters of Lake Tahoe had been arduous. But they'd done it together.

The fire burned hot and radiant, creating a glow reflecting off each of the women's faces. They were huddled around the fire pit, roasting s'mores, drinking, talking, and sharing memories of their time spent together.

Jolene tried not looking at her phone. She'd expected to receive numerous texts from Bo. But he hadn't sent any, not even one. This irritated her more than if he had actually texted her. It was as if he was already forgetting her, and she wasn't even gone yet. Every time Kendra glanced at her phone, it stirred the craving inside Jolene to look at her own.

"I've come to a decision." Kendra put her beer can to her lips and tipped it back, taking a long swill before continuing. "When I get home, I'm going to have a talk with Devin."

"Oh yeah?" Jolene raised her brows.

"I'm going to remain hopeful that he will want to change. That he will want to go to counseling and want to work on our marriage. I mean, I do still love him." She stared at the blaze of the fire, Jolene followed her gaze, getting lost for a moment by the constant flame and spark. "But...if he doesn't want to, then I suppose there isn't anything else I can do about it," Kendra said, still mesmerized by the fire.

"Wow, big decision." Cristina pushed a marshmallow onto the end of a roasting stick. "You sure about this?"

Kendra nodded her head methodically. "I don't really feel I have a choice anymore. Not after hearing about how strong Becca was. And after seeing how brave Jolene has been with everything she's been dealt, and Cristina, you're the strongest one in our group, always have been. I can't just continue to let Devin walk all over me and use me just so neither of us have to put up with negative publicity. It's not fair to Quinn. And quite honestly, it's not fair to me."

"Good for you," Jolene said.

"And Jolene, you give me hope. I'm sorry for saying it, but this thing with you and Bo—"

She interrupted, "there is no 'thing' between me and Bo." She attempted air quotes with her fingers despite holding a beer in one hand.

"Regardless what you say, you guys do have a thing. You two have a bond. I've never really seen something quite like it. I know you talk about how you and Becca had a bond, and don't get me wrong, I know you did. But the bond between you and Bo is different, it's bigger. You two have been friends since you were twelve years old. Not many people become friends at twelve and then stay friends. And now, look at you two. You've been brought back together, at what may look like the wrong time, but to me, it feels like perfect timing. Your bond is inspiring." Kendra shrugged. "All I'm saying is, it gives me hope. If things don't work out with Devin and I, I'm hopeful there is someone else out there for me. Someone that will love me, for me, all flaws included."

"Ha," Cristina said, the marshmallow on her roasting stick hovering over the flame. "What flaws? We all know you don't have any flaws. You're damn near perfect."

"Stop, I do too. You never had to live with me." Kendra smiled.

"Thank God." Cristina rolled her eyes playfully and smirked.

"I hear what you're saying, about being friends a long time and all. But that's just it, we're friends. I can forgive him for lying to me and stay friends with him. But that's it. There's just too much, it would never work out for us to be anything more." Jolene wrapped a blanket around her shoulders. "Besides, my home is in Oregon. His home is here. I'm not sure why I even gave us a second thought. We were doomed from the start."

"Please don't give up on you two. You never know what could happen in the future," Kendra said.

"I'm afraid too much has happened in the past for us to *have* a future." She took a sip of her beer before gesturing the can in Cristina's direction. "What about you, Cris? You going home a changed woman? It seems Kendra and I have seen the light, how about you? You doing anything different?"

"For starters, I need to get my daughter healthy. There's so much delicious food she's missing out on." She sandwiched the toasted marshmallow and chocolate in between two graham cracker squares. "Like s'mores." She raised the finished dessert in the air. "No, but seriously. I think the three of us are good for each other. We make each other better. And I've been thinking, we should try to meet here again. Maybe next summer."

"That sounds fun, but I can't promise I'll be able to get away," Kendra said.

"I think that's a great idea," Jolene agreed. "C'mon, Kendra, it's a year away. I'm sure you can plan ahead to sneak away for a few days."

"Yeah, we don't even have to come for a week," Cristina said. "C'mon, you big slut, you know you wanna? You wouldn't be able to handle it if you knew me and Jo were here without you." She waggled her dark brows.

"Fine. But we'll have to plan it soon. I will need at least a year's notice."

"Give me a break, you act like you're some kind of a rock star on tour or something, God forbid you plan to hang out with the little people," Cristina teased.

"Oh stop, you know it's not like that. But the magazine's only been in print for one year. There's no way of knowing what will be happening with it in another year."

"I'm sure it will be ten times more successful than it already is," Jolene said.

"Thanks. And you're right, Cristina, we're good for each other. We're each other's cheerleaders. Always have been, always will be." Kendra raised a beer in the air before taking a sip.

"I think Becca would want that," Jolene said.

"What do you mean?" Cristina asked.

"I think she'd want us to meet here again next summer..." Jolene's words trailed, realization setting in. You've got to be kidding. How did they not see it before now? She shook her head, a smile stretching across her face.

"What?" Kendra gave her a skeptical look.

"She's got that freaky look in her eye," Cristina said. "What's wrong?"

"Nothing. Nothing's wrong." Jolene pulled another beer from the cooler. "This week we've focused so much on how strong and brave Becca was but none of us remembered how smart she was."

"Yeah, she was smart. And bossy. So what?" Cristina finished off the s'more, licking her finger.

"What are you talking about?" Kendra asked.

"This was her whole reason for asking us to come here, together, to spread her ashes. Don't you guys see it now?" Jolene stood to her feet. "I don't think it had anything to do with spreading her ashes. This was her final attempt at bringing the four of us back together. She hoped we would fulfill the pact we made all those years ago because she felt responsible she'd ruined it." She raised her beer up to the sky. "Touché, Becca. You succeeded. We're gonna keep up the pact after all. We're coming back next summer."

"Holy hell, you're right," Cristina said.

"Dang, how did we not figure this out sooner?" Kendra asked.

"Because, we've all been caught up in our own lives. Even though we've been here, we haven't really been here. We haven't been present." Jolene sat back down and pressed her hand to her forehead. "We've been so focused on all the details of today, I guess we didn't have a chance to realize the true meaning of Becca's request. I was confused this whole time, wondering why she chose us. I just can't believe it wasn't obvious before."

"She's good," Kendra said, stretching out the last word.

"Like I said, she's a bad ass." Cristina smirked.

CHAPTER TWENTY-FIVE

After Cristina and Kendra had their luggage loaded in the back of Cristina's 4Runner, they hugged Jolene tightly.

"I can't believe how much I'm going to miss you ladies," Jolene said.

"I wish we could stay longer, but my flight leaves in two hours." Kendra glanced at the time reflected on her phone. "If we don't leave now, I risk not getting checked in on time and I can't miss my flight. I promised Quinn I'd be there tonight for his basketball game. It's the last one of the season. He's in the starting five."

"That's amazing. You must be so proud."

Kendra pulled Jolene in for one last hug before climbing into the passenger side of the vehicle.

"So, we'll talk soon?" Jolene asked.

"Yeah, I'll contact Ms. Gibbs and see if there's a week available for us to use the cottage next summer. Then I'll let you know." Cristina opened the driver's side door and got in. "You drive safely. And get some rest. You'll need it, I want you prepared before facing that bastard husband of yours," Cristina called before shutting the door.

She smiled, shaking her head. There would be no way she could change Cristina's mind regarding how she felt about Travis. And yet, Jolene welcomed it. Knowing Cristina had her back once again made her feel valued. She'd missed it. She'd missed her.

The windows came down and the women waved and shouted goodbye. Jolene stood next to the driveway, waving back as the 4Runner sped off down the road. Her heart gave a tug, she was really going to miss them. She exhaled a deep sigh before heading back into the cottage to retrieve her belongings.

Inside, the dishwasher hummed while she closed the curtains in the kitchen and family room. She pulled the white linen across the French doors and paused, taking one last look at the dock stretching out across the lake. She wouldn't be leaving the memories here any longer. This time, she would leave this place and bring all the memories with her. Holding onto each one as a treasure to cherish forever.

After she loaded her luggage in the back of her Tahoe, she locked the front door of the cottage behind her. Then she went around to the garage where the lock box sat mounted on the wall. She placed the key inside and then climbed into her SUV.

There would be two stops she'd make before heading home. This entire week spent in Tahoe City she hadn't made it to Buffy's Book Cafe. Since the first day of her arrival in town, she'd wanted to go there. But the week had gone entirely too fast. But before she went there, she drove to the Sweet Shop, parked her car out front and abandoned it while she made the two-mile hike down the trail with the old coordinates entered into her phone.

The geocache was easier to find this time around. At some point, over the last eighteen years, the stash had been moved to a more accessible location. More accurate to the coordinates provided than when Jolene and her friends had searched for it. Stuffed underneath the inside of a carved-out granite rock was a small white PVC pipe. She brushed her hand against the dusty, worn plastic as tears pricked in the corner of her eyes.

Twisting the cap off, she found a small snow globe with a tiny Empire State Building inside covered in snow. Jolene took it out with careful fingers, giving it a slight shake and watching the faux snow fall. A smile tugged at her lips. She stuffed it into her pocket.

Becca would always be a part of Lake Tahoe. From her memories and imprint left on every piece of the city, to her ashes in the lake. But Jolene wanted to be sure she'd always be a part of this geocache. It had been something the girls had bonded over one last time before their friendship was severed.

She pulled the small, old ratty log and nubby pencil out of the pipe. Using her finger, she dragged it over the page, stopping when she came to the most recent entry. A couple on their honeymoon from New York City who had left the day before. Now the snow globe made sense.

Jolene penciled in the log the following words: "Becca Gibbs was here. Never give up the fight." After she dated it, she flipped to the first page to find their entry, swiping at a fallen tear.

We did it! After four weeks we found the stash. 5 vintage $100 black poker chips from the Sahara Tahoe Casino. Great geocache! —The Tahoe City Girls

Jolene closed the book and shoved it and the pencil back inside the pipe. From her pocket, she pulled out a red swim cap. She folded it and set it carefully into the pipe before returning the cap and hiding it back into the carved rock. She turned the heavy rock over, pushing it back in place so it gathered with more granite boulders in varying sizes. It felt like the end of a book. The end of an era. She was fairly certain The Tahoe City Girls geocaching days were over.

STEPPING inside Buffy's Book Cafe, Jolene was instantly greeted by the smell of old books. The scent carried a mixture of staleness and dust. Her nerves stood in attention, and she wanted to bottle up the scent to smell it whenever she wanted.

Moving further into the cafe, her nose caught a hint of cinnamon and coffee. On a small white antique table, a spread of snickerdoodles arranged in a circular design sat next to a large silver coffee pot. There were stacks of white paper cups, stirring sticks, sugar packets and a silver cream pot.

As much as the snickerdoodles tempted her, Jolene walked past, ignoring their teasing. Her attention was drawn to the ginormous bookcases that lined the walls and were overstocked with books. There were three wooden tables with mismatched wooden chairs tucked in around them, a floral sofa and two soft pink oversized chairs congregated towards the back. A long stainless-steel counter with six matching bar height stools ran down the front wall just behind the glass windows of the front of the cafe.

Jolene's gaze danced around from the many stacks of books arranged all throughout the room. She couldn't be certain if the placing of the stacks was intentional or not. However, her OCD screamed at the lack of uniformity. Her pulse picked up speed and the beat of her heart grew louder. The long-sleeved shirt she wore felt suffocating. She pulled at the collar and pushed up her sleeves.

While she tried to calm her anxieties, inhaling deep breaths, a woman with a loud, happy voice approached her.

"Hello, welcome to Buffy's Book Cafe, I'm Buffy," a tall woman greeted, pressing both hands to her chest.

"Hi, thank you," Jolene said.

"Is this your first time into the cafe?"

She nodded.

"I'm so happy you made your way in here. This cafe is my baby, and by baby, I mean it's a dream—a dream come true. And I want to show it off to everyone." The woman's eyes were round with excitement and her smile gleamed. She talked fast, only taking a breath on occasion to wait for a response from Jolene.

"Did you drift in here by accident? You look a bit lost—are you okay, sweetie? Are you a book lover?"

"I...I am," Jolene managed.

"You're a book lover? Oh yay!" Buffy shrieked and clasped her hands together in front of her. "You just made my day. I'm so happy to meet you. Again, I'm Buffy and if it isn't obvious yet, I own the place. Please look around and help yourself to coffee and a snickerdoodle. I baked them myself, fresh this morning. Don't you just love snickerdoodles? Don't they smell divine?" Buffy inhaled dramatically while closing her eyes.

"They do smell wonderful. But I'm gluten intolerant. That's really nice of you to offer those things to your customers."

"Oh sad." Buffy stuck out her full lips in a pout. "I'll have to remember to offer a gluten free treat from now on. In fact, I'm going to make a note of it right now." Buffy pulled the pencil out of her hair that was holding a bun in place on top of her head, letting her brown locks cascade over her shoulders. She had a cute look, making her appear younger than she probably was. "Please excuse me, but feel free to have some coffee and take a look around. And don't hesitate to ask me any questions. But if you're looking for a particular book and you're in a hurry, no promises I'll find it in time." She gestured a hand at the stacks of books lined in front of the counter where the cash register sat. "I'm having a hard time getting all of my books organized." She giggled and then sauntered away.

Hesitating at first, but then deciding on some coffee, Jolene fixed herself a cup. Then she began perusing the bookcases overflowing with beautiful hardbacks, letting her fingers trail over the bindings. The selection was astonishing. There was a first edition of *Interview with the Vampire* by Anne Rice, a signed first edition of *The Notebook* by Nicholas Sparks and a 60th anniversary edition of *Catcher in the Rye* by J.D. Salinger. A tingling sensation coursed through her, and her mouth began to water. She wanted to stay all day and look through Buffy's books.

And help her organize them.

Placing her cup of coffee on an empty table, Jolene began with a stack of books that interested her. Even though she already owned two other copies of *Catcher in the Rye*, she didn't own this edition. She felt a thrill of excitement zing through her as she placed the book on the small stack. Another one caught her eye, a newer copy of *Emma* by Jane Austen. She picked it up and thumbed through it, examining the pages and the overall condition.

The bell above the door chimed causing her attention to break away from *Emma*. Instantly she recognized the customer who entered the cafe. It was Lark. Jolene grimaced and at first instinct, she wanted to run. But she wasn't running anymore, nope—not from people or problems or circumstances.

From across the room, Lark and Jolene made eye contact. Lark offered a slight smile.

"Good morning, sweetie," Buffy's voice called from somewhere in the cafe.

"Morning, Buffy," Lark greeted.

Jolene watched Lark out of the corner of her eye. She fixed a cup of coffee while holding a snickerdoodle in between her teeth. The soft cookie broke off in her mouth and Lark caught it in her hand. Then she shoved the cookie back in between her teeth while she finished emptying sugar packets into her coffee.

Jolene spotted Lark coming toward her. Choosing not to run was going to be harder than she thought. She tucked her chin and her breathing quickened once again, that pinching feeling in her belly returning.

"Hey," Lark said, her voice sounded small and her face unreadable.

She stood near the table where Jolene's stack of books sat. The look in her green eyes was intense, making it difficult for her to glance away. She forced a smile and a greeting. "Hello."

"Can we sit for a minute?" Lark asked.

She hesitated. Heat coursed through her body and words got caught in her dry throat. But she agreed with a nod and took a seat. Lark slung a bag off her shoulder, placing it on the empty seat next to her before sitting down.

Studying Lark, Jolene put the paper cup to her lips and took a sip of coffee. Without meaning to, she took notice of Lark's features—divvying them out one by one. Lark had Bo's eye color, however the round shape was Becca's. She had Becca's round face, but Bo's chiseled chin just softer, more feminine. And she had Becca's height and Bo's blonde hair. Also, without intending to, she admitted to herself that Becca and Bo had created a beautiful child. Lark was striking.

"I'm glad I caught up to you," Lark began, her voice soft but obviously holding something back.

Raising a brow, she was still unable to find words as they sat somewhere caught in between her head and her throat.

Lark's eyes shifted around the space inside the book café. "I try to come here every Saturday when I stay with my dad. I've been helping Buffy organize the books. As you can see, I still have a lot of work to do." She smiled. The familiarity of it reminding Jolene of Becca and causing the pinch in her stomach to twist.

"She does have quite a lot of books crammed in here. Her selection is impressive," Jolene managed to say.

"It is, isn't it? Sometimes I get distracted from organizing and start reading the books when I'm supposed to be putting them away." She exhaled a laugh before turning her tone serious. "I think my nana or maybe Cristina told my dad you might be stopping here today before going home." Lark paused, looking at her as if waiting for a response.

Jolene offered her nothing but a confused expression.

"Okay, so anyway." Lark reached into the bag sitting on the chair next to her. She pulled out eight thin books and set them on the table in between them.

Jolene glanced down at them, now even more confused. The books ranged in color and in size. Some appeared more worn than the others. The book on top of the stack was black and had gold writing across the cover featuring a famous May Angelou quote.

"These are for you." Lark pushed the stack of books toward her.

She frowned. "What do you mean? What are these?"

"These are, *were*," Lark corrected herself, her hands still grasping the journals, "my mom's journals. And she wanted you to have them."

Jolene shook her head slowly, confusion spiraling through her while her mind tried to play catch up. This didn't make any sense. Why would Becca want Jolene to have her old journals? She bit the inside of her cheek and placed her hand on the book sitting on top of the stack, brushing her fingers over the cover. Her fingers grazed the indents of the gold lettering.

"I...I don't understand."

"Mom specifically said these were to go to you." Lark's eyes shimmered with tears.

"But...why? Why would she want me to have these?" Jolene's eyes burned and her throat yearned for air.

Lark hunched a shoulder. "I don't really get it either. But all I know is this is one of the things she wanted me to do. While you were here, spreading her ashes, I was supposed to give you her journals." Her voice had grown louder, her softer tone now carrying an edge to it. "Look, just take them. I promised my mom." She pushed them even further in Jolene's direction, then sat back and wiped at a tear on her cheek.

A nod, then Jolene's own eyes glassed over. Seeing this girl, who wasn't much older than Julia and who had just lost her mother nearly broke her in half. She cleared her throat. "Okay. I'm not really sure what I'm supposed to do with them. But I'll take them."

"Read them." Lark shrugged again. "Then maybe you could tell me about them," her voice softer again, some of her earlier defiance receding.

"I can do that."

"Mom read me some. Of course, she skipped over all the good stuff." Lark smiled. "She didn't want me to know all of the wild things she did. But she read me some of the stuff she wrote about your friendship with her." She looked at her with green eyes full of intensity. "Your friendship was the real deal, wasn't it?"

"It was." Jolene wiped at a tear that had slipped out of her eye. "Your mom was something."

"She was," Lark agreed, stirring her coffee with the wooden stir stick, and making the cream swirl.

Jolene picked up the book on top of the stack, setting it on the table, before picking up the next book in the stack.

This one had a brown leather cover and binding. It had the word *Journal* imprinted on the cover. The next two were identical in color and size, a pinkish rose color with gold lined pages.

As Jolene made her way through the stack, she came to the one on the bottom. This one was white with all different colored hearts outlined in black. She opened it up and thumbed to the first page.

September 4
Dear Diary,

Today was the first day of 9th grade. It would've totally sucked but I met a few cool girls. One girl's name is Jolene. Old school name but everyone calls her Jo so I guess that's cool. I hope we'll become good enough friends to share clothes. Because her clothes are pretty cute. Oh, and I saw a bunch of hotties heading to the field in their football uniforms after school! Hoping to hit up the first football game next Friday with Jo and her friends. Night, sleep tight, never give up the fight!

Closing the journal, Jolene brushed away the tears on her face. She cleared her throat. "I've never forgotten her mantra. *Never give up the fight.*"

"She signed every entry that way. And that is what she used to say to me every night when she tucked me in. *Night, sleep tight, never give up the fight.*" Tears swam in Lark's eyes.

"That's sweet," Jolene offered. "But Lark, I'm still confused as to why your mom would want me to have these."

Lark hunched her shoulders in a shrug before releasing them. "I don't know why. She didn't explain it to me. I was actually hoping that you could do that."

Shaking her head, she couldn't offer an explanation. "I'm sorry, I don't know."

"Maybe she just wanted the two of us to meet."

"Maybe." Jolene's heart swelled and she felt herself smile. "And I'm glad we did."

Lark returned the smile, this time appearing less forced which eased the tension in her shoulders slightly.

"Maybe after you read the journals, you'll figure out why she wanted you to have them. And if you do, will you let me know?"

"If I do, then yes. I will definitely let you know."

"Thanks." Lark picked up her coffee and took a sip. "I wanted to tell you, for whatever it's worth. I'm really sorry about what happened with your brother Jacob."

"Thank you. Me too." She set the journal covered in hearts back on the stack with the others.

"And I know my dad told you my mom never met anyone else because she devoted all of her time and love to me. But that's not really true."

Jolene raised a brow.

"I don't think she ever got over Jacob. And losing him. She didn't read those things to me from her journal, but she talked to me about Jacob. I think she wished he was my dad. Not that my dad's a bad guy or anything but then she would've had something to hold onto when Jacob was gone." Lark's expression held years of pain.

"That makes sense," Jolene whispered.

"Well, I better let you get going and I need to get to work. These books aren't going to organize themselves," Lark said with a smile and stood.

Jolene stood too, moving toward Lark, and reaching out her hand. "Thank you for coming to find me. And for bringing the journals."

Glancing down at her outstretched hand, Lark dismissed it and went in for a hug, surprising her at first. But while the two embraced, she felt a connection to Lark, and she wanted to cling to her longer.

Lark pulled back, swiping at a tear with her finger. "I'm sorry."

"Oh please, don't be sorry," Jolene insisted. "It's okay."

"I just feel like I've known you for years. My mom talked about you so much growing up. My dad too."

"Your dad too, huh?" She couldn't help herself. As much as she didn't want to put Lark in the middle of her and Bo's relationship, she was curious.

Lark nodded. "It was hard for me to decide who you were closer with, my mom or my dad."

"And what was your conclusion?"

"I decided you were equally close with them. They both love you."

"Well, I loved them both too." Then Jolene scolded herself for using past tense, how inconsiderate she sounded. "*Love. I love* them both."

Lark raised a brow, eyeing her. "Do you? You know, still love my dad?"

The question was blunt. And Jolene battled in her mind how to answer. Of course she still loved Bo, but it didn't matter. She looked down at the table where her hand pressed as a brace for her body.

"Sometimes love isn't enough. Sometimes there are things that happen in this world that we have no control over, and we just need to accept them and adapt the best way we can."

Lark opened her mouth to speak but then shut it again, biting her lip instead. She nodded, picking up her empty bag off the chair. Then she gave Jolene a pained smile. "I'm glad I finally got to meet you."

"I'm glad too. You take care. And take care of your dad, will you."

Nodding one last time, Lark took off, walking toward the back of the café. But she turned and said, "Hey, Jolene? Sometimes love is all we got." Then she joined Buffy who was kneeling in front of a stack of books.

The journals sat next to the stack of books Jolene had set aside earlier. She leaned her weight against the table, sorting through the stack. She decided on *Emma* and *Catcher in the Rye*. As much as she wanted the other two, she couldn't spend that much money on books right now. A divorce resided in her future.

Taking the stack of journals and the two books she planned on purchasing, she headed to the cash register. Buffy spotted her and met her on the other side of the counter.

"Oooo, splendid choice," Buffy said, picking up the copy of *Emma*. "I absolutely love this book. Isn't Jane Austen the greatest author of all time?"

"She really is."

Buffy rang up the charges for the books and placed them in a tote. Jolene paid before placing the journals into the tote with her purchased books.

Buffy eyed her.

"Lark gave these to me, they're her books."

Buffy smiled and nodded. "Ahh, you must be the friend of her mother's."

Jolene was taken aback. "Yes, I was."

"Those were her mother's journals." Buffy gestured at the tote with her chin.

"Yes, they were." Her head spun with confusion.

"Lark told me about the journals. And you. I think it's pretty amazing you coming here and doing what you did."

Buffy handed Jolene her receipt. "You're going to do something wonderful with those journals, I just know it."

"Thanks."

"You take care, sweetie. And good luck. I look forward to reading it." Buffy smiled and sauntered to the back of the café, joining Lark.

"Wait," Jolene called after her. "Read what?"

But Buffy didn't hear her. Jolene picked the up the tote and walked toward the door. She glanced over her shoulder, taking one last look at Lark—half of one best friend and half of the other.

CHAPTER TWENTY-SIX

The sun wasnt quite high enough to generate sweltering heat, thankfully. Which made it the perfect time of day to take a walk through the neighborhood. Since summer began, Jolene and Joy, along with the other ladies from book club had been meeting every Friday morning. They walked the same route Jolene ran, the one that went through the neighborhood of Shady Pines and down Main Street and looped back around.

After saying their goodbyes, Jolene admired the recent paint job on the porch as she made her way into the house. Even though the divorce was final, Travis kept his word by maintaining the exterior of her home. It was the place his children called home after all. And didn't he at least owe it to her now that he'd admitted he was officially dating Carrie Underwood's doppelganger? She may be a forgiving person, but she was no idiot. In the best interest of the business, she'd replaced Carrie with a new brewery manager. Someone who was more than qualified for the job—Joy.

"Hey, you two," Jolene greeted her children as she made her way to the refrigerator for a bottle of water. They were sitting on the barstools up at the kitchen counter. One in front of a laptop and the other holding their phone. "It's a beautiful day, who wants to join me in the garden?"

"Hey, Mom." Julia glanced up from the laptop and smiled. "Sorry, no time for gardening. I'm looking at your pictures from when you were in Lake Tahoe. The Gibbs's cottage looks amazing. And so does that beach you went to. What was it called again?"

"Sand Harbor." Jolene twisted the cap off the bottle of water. "What about you?" she asked, pointing the bottle in the direction of her son.

"Sorry, no can do. I'm doing the same. Looking up all the excursions we can go on while we're in Lake Tahoe." He was scrolling on his phone, checking out the lake, hiking trails, and the Heavenly Resort.

"Okay, okay, fine." Jolene exhaled a laugh before taking a swig of water. "Just don't pick out all the expensive things to do, alright? We're on a budget." She tousled Cole's hair and then walked out of the kitchen. Picking up her gloves and gardening mat, she headed out the back door, stepping onto the concrete patio.

Glancing around her garden, she didn't know where to begin. Her mind got lost, thinking about Lake Tahoe. In just over a week, she would be taking Cole and Julia to Tahoe City, finally. Just the three of them. Ms. Gibbs was thrilled about the news of their visit and offered the cottage to them without hesitation.

Cole and Julia were shocked when Jolene told them about their trip. Cole's eyes went round with excitement, like a little kid on Christmas morning. She hadn't realized just how much going to Tahoe City had meant to him. It meant a lot to her as well. She couldn't wait to take her kids to the Sweet Shop and to the best beaches around the lake where they could do cannon balls off the docks. This trip would be the perfect end to summer vacation before school started again.

Jolene had her reservations about returning to Tahoe City, because how could she not? The way she and Bo left things ate away at her daily. But she didn't see how they could have done things differently.

And besides, she hadn't even heard from him since she returned home. Not even a single text. It was just as well. It made it easier this way. They'd both gotten the closure they needed. But it didn't take away the ache in her heart, the craving for him, the desire. The longing was enough to keep her up most nights.

Ever since she returned home from her week spent in Tahoe City, she'd kept herself busy. She awoke early, spending every morning in her office, reading and writing before she headed to the brewery. It took her almost three weeks to read through all eight journals and make an outline of the manuscript she'd began. It would be a book about childhood friendships, possibly a nonfiction—a memoir.

Reading Becca's journals took her on a roller coaster ride. At times, they were emotional and sad. And other times, they were funny and exciting.

The most difficult entry to read was the one from the day Lark was born. Before that entry, there had been almost a full year of nothing.

April 22
Dear Diary,

Today I became a mom. It all feels surreal. But when I look at her, I feel peace. Peace I haven't felt in years. And when I hold her, I feel whole. Also something I haven't felt in so long. Not since before I lost Jacob. It's as if Lark is a

*gift from him. As weird as that sounds. I was worried once
she came along that all I would do was resent her. Because
she would be just another reminder of what I lost. And a
reminder of betrayal. When I found out I was expecting
Lark I felt ashamed. I didn't know how I could forgive
myself for betraying Jolene, again. But now that Lark is
here, all of that has been washed away. From this day
forward, I promise to be the best mom to Lark and always
put her needs above my own. I believe she is my little angel
sent from Jacob, a chance for a fresh start, a chance to make
things right. When Jolene sees how selfless I've been, I
know she will understand. Because once you're best friends
with someone, you know them better than you know yourself. No matter how much time has gone by. I'll prove it to
you, Lark. One day, you'll meet Jolene, and she will just
love you. As much as your dad and I do. Night, sleep tight,
never give up the fight!*

The sound of birds chirping brought Jolene back. She knelt
on the mat and slipped her gloves on, marveling at her garden.
Joy did a fantastic job tidying up the flower beds and keeping
the weeds out of her vegetables. She even planted the baby
sprouts Jolene started indoors due to the late frost in Central
Oregon. Things were coming along nicely, especially her
zucchini plants which tended to be difficult to grow here.

After about an hour, the bright sun, now higher in the sky
radiated powerful heat down on her. She had on Jacob's old
Sacramento Kings baseball hat to help keep the sun off her face.
Sweat trickled down her back and she took this as a sign to quit
for the day. She couldn't over-do it and risk being cooped up
indoors all weekend. Joy and Tim had assured her they would
cover the duties at the brewery so she and the kids could go
hiking.

Rising to her feet, she brushed the dirt off her knees. As she did, she thought about Tahoe City and the ugly bandages Cristina had put on her knees that day. It felt like so long ago. She swiped her forehead with the back of her wrist before tugging one of the gloves off.

"I always was a sucker for you in that hat," a man's voice cut through the afternoon air, startling her.

Jolene peered through sunbeams and squinted, her eyes surely playing tricks on her. Because when they focused and sent the message to her brain, telling her it was Bo standing there, she couldn't believe it. Bo Dean was *here*.

"What are you doing here?" her words unintentionally came out accusatory.

"My favorite memory of you is that time I picked you up and brought you to the cabin and we fished for hours," Bo began, taking a few steps in her direction. "You of course, were wearing that exact hat. I shouldn't be surprised you still have it after all these years." He shook his head. "And remember we ate my mom's apple pie that was supposed to be for dessert after that night's dinner? Man, she was pissed." He chuckled. "You, in that hat, faded tight jeans, scarfing down apple pie. Do you know how hard it was for me not to just grab you and kiss you?"

She was standing about eight yards from Bo and took off her other glove. She tried to play it cool. "So, why didn't you?"

"Because I was an idiot. I think we've established that by now." He took a few more steps in her direction, not taking his eyes off her.

"What are you doing here, Bo?" she repeated, her feet planted on the ground. It took all her strength not to run toward him and fling herself into his arms.

"You seriously have to ask me that? Isn't it obvious? I told you I wouldn't lose you again. You're stuck with me." He stopped, lifting his arms out and then shrugging. His loose hair blew in the afternoon breeze.

"Bo," Jolene mumbled, lowering her chin to her chest where her heart pounded uncontrollably.

"I drove eight hours to say this to you, the least you can do is listen, you stubborn woman." He took a few more strides, slowly as if afraid he might scare her off if he advanced too quickly. "You were the first girl I played ball with, you were the first girl I danced with, and you were the first girl to have my heart. And," he paused. "I want you to be my last. I want you to be my last everything."

He took a few more steps in her direction, closing the distance between them with each step. "Ollie, you're the one I've been waiting for. I want to clean up your knees after you trip and fall, I want to stay on the couch with you when you can't get up, I want to bring you pain pills when you have a headache. I want to be by your side to encourage or comfort you or just stay quiet when I need to be. And I want you to tell me when I'm being an idiot and when I'm wrong."

Only a few feet remained between them, Jolene still hadn't moved an inch. It was taking all her strength now.

"Ollie, I believe in you. I believe in us. I know we're going to have to work at this, we're probably going to have to work damn hard, but I'm all in. One hundred percent." He reached her finally, pushing his chest against hers, his breathing quick.

"You're such an idiot." Jolene gazed up at him through wet eyes.

Bo pushed her hat off her head, letting it fall to the ground. Then gathered her hair in his hands before cupping her face. "This isn't one of those times you can tell me I'm an idiot or wrong," he whispered. With the pad of his thumb, he brushed a tear off her cheek.

"Shh, just shut up." She put a finger to his lips. "You're my best friend, Bo Dean. I love you. I've always loved you. And... I'm all in too. I want you to be *my* last everything."

Bo's lips curved into a wide smile, and he pulled her face into his, sliding his lips over hers. When their lips crashed against one another's, she felt the passion and the urgency she had each time they kissed before. It felt perfect and confusing all in one.

But most of all—it felt right.

When they finally broke apart, both breathless, Bo directed Jolene's attention to the side of the house. Standing in the back yard, next to the concrete patio was Lark, holding a basketball. Next to her was Cole and Julia. All three of them smiled conspiratorially.

She tilted her head and narrowed her eyes. "What's going on?"

"I have a confession." He rubbed at the back of his neck. "Our kids have been texting the last few weeks."

Her brows shot up. "What? What do you mean? My kids and Lark?"

"Yep, turns out they kinda love us. And want us to be happy. Imagine that?" He grinned.

Jolene's heart swelled and overflowed with joy at the image of their kids, of what possibilities it meant for their life and their future.

"How long can you guys stay?" she asked, their bodies still clinging to one another.

"However long it takes."

"What takes?"

"To figure things out, all the details." He bent down, craning his neck to the side, brushing his lips against hers again. "I'm a police officer, I'm sure I can get hired anywhere." He shrugged. "But if I stay here, no promises that I'm gonna start wearing flannels." He winked, taking her hands in his.

She laughed, giving him a playful push in the chest. She didn't need flannels. She didn't *want* flannels. She just wanted him—his beach scent and his heart of loving and giving to others.

Bo backed up slowly, pulling her with him and giving her a head nod to come with him, before he dropped her hands and took off in a sprint toward the kids.

Bo snatched the basketball from Lark.

"Hey!" she protested before laughing.

He gave his daughter a mischievous smile, before running around the side of the house. Jolene, Lark, Cole, and Julia following close behind him. They found Bo in the driveway underneath the basketball hoop.

Bo pointed at Jolene, then back at himself—challenging their three children against the two of them. She smiled at him, the familiarity comforting. Because yeah, the two of them had made a perfect team back in the day. Between Bo and Jacob, they'd taught her well.

She ran under the hoop, motioning she was open to take the shot. He passed it to her, and she went in for the perfect lay-up. The ball slipped effortlessly through the net making a swish sound.

"Nothing but net," Bo and Jolene said in unison.

A NOTE FROM THE AUTHOR

Dear reader,

MS has a special place in my heart. A few years ago I was faced with this possible diagnosis, (which is what prompted me to write this story). It was scary and eye-opening and writing this book was therapeutic. While my MS symptoms are currently in remission, I still live with the possibility of this being a reality for me. Studies show that this illness is linked to endometriosis. MS is becoming more widespread by younger people. Because of medical advancements and technology, people are able to receive a diagnosis sooner, giving them a longer, fulfilling life.

My heart aches for those who have lost loved ones to this debilitating disease. I long for the day when doctors, scientists, and technology can cure MS so no one has to live with its effects.

Thank you to those of you who gave personal insight to the research of this disease for this book. And thank you, reader, for possibly opening yourself up to a new issue.

Love,
Starla

ACKNOWLEDGMENTS

First, thank you, Jesus for giving me a dream and the abilities and the resources to write and publish this book.

To my husband, Jeremy. Thank you for supporting me in the big and small ways on this author journey. It's not me alone but because of you as to why I'm able to pursue this author life.

To my kids, Jensen, Jaidyn, and Jace, thank you for supporting me and encouraging me.

A shoutout to Jen Chen Tran who took a chance on me and this book and offered me representation. Thank you for championing this book and helping me make it shine. It wouldn't be what it is without you.

To my hype girl, Bethany Dodson, thank you for always encouraging me to go after my dreams. And for not letting me quit when I think I can't keep doing this author life.

To my ride-or-die beta reader, Lissa Ruck. Thank you for reading everything I write. Thanks for sharing my books on social media. I'm so grateful for you!

Thank you to my mom for encouraging me to keep going and reminding me to get sleep too. Thanks to my dad for raising me to dream big. To my in-laws, thank you for buying all my books and checking in on my journey. Thanks to my siblings, and extended family, for the support, love, prayers, and encouragement!

Thank you to my beta readers and CP's who encouraged, and gave valuable insight: Shellie Short, Bethany Dodson, Lissa

Ruck, Jodi Becker, Diane Rubatino, Janine McCoy, and Savannah Hendricks.

To the members of Starla's Squad, and my ARC team, a huge thank you for your time and willingness to give this book a chance and for the early reviews. Thank you to my online support system, the friends, connections, bookstagrammers, and authors—I am forever grateful for you. Thank you to everyone who pre-ordered, and thank you in advance to those of you who leave a review. Thank you for not only believing in this book but believing in me as well.

And also thank you to my childhood friends for our treasured friendships and helping to inspire this book.

ABOUT THE AUTHOR

 Starla DeKruyf is a romance author of sweet stories with a dash of spice that always end in happily ever afters. She writes books that play like movies in your head about characters you wish you could hang out with. Follow her on her socials so you can have fun and be awkward together! When Starla isn't writing, she's probably drinking coffee and spending time with her husband, kids, and her rescue pup.

ALSO BY STARLA DEKRUYF

Pineridge series—book 1:

Eight Days of Christmas

Pineridge series—book 2:

We Fell in Love in October

Pineridge series—book 3:

A Little Bit Yours

Juniper Ridge series—book 1:

A Pumpkin Patch and A Fling

A Standalone Romantic Comedy:

The Heart Rehab Experiment